FATES DEFIED

CALL OF THE NORNS
BOOK 3

AIMEE VANCE

REVEL BOOKS

Revel Books
Paperback ISBN: 979-8-9882650-1-6
Ebook ISBN: 979-8-9882650-5-4

Cover Art and Illustrations
Copyright © 2025 Aimee Vance

Editing and Proofreading by
Brittany Corley

www.aimeevancebooks.com

*For anyone who stared the difficult things
right in the face and did it anyway.*

*And this one is also for me.
I did it.*

Important Character Key

deceased before the beginning of Fates Defied
~~banished~~

The Norns

Urd
Verandi
Skuld

The Promised

Shelbie Smith

The Eriksson Clan

Erik Gormsson and Frida
    Gunnar Eriksson and Signe
      Viveka - adopted
      Revna
      Ulf
      Erik
    Tove Eriksdottir and ~~Raud Uthredsson~~
    Magnus Eriksson and Astrid
      Birgitta - adopted
      Bo - adopted

Njall Gormsson and *Tora*
    Domari Njallson

Björn and Yrsa, and family
    Kara - adopted
    Yvar - adopted

Kare and Thyra
    Arne
    Bodil

Thorsten and family

The Dragons

Hadriel
Nidhoggr

The Dogs

Thor, Shelbie's dog from the future
Freki

The Hilviggson Clan

Draugr "The Demon" Hilviggson and Hilda
    Signe

Vermund Oathbreaker
    Viveka

Raud Uthredsson

The Birgersson Clan

Asmund Birgersson & Family

Hamund Otkilsson & Family

The Valkyries

Hilda
Signe

The Varangian Guard

Domari Njallson - *Akolouthos*
Grim - *Komes*

PROLOGUE

Wind whipped through Hilda's dark hair as she sprinted through the forest, moonlight streaking between the trees. Her breaths clouded the autumn air, the breeze biting at her cheeks with each step into the darkness. The beating war drums in the distance mirrored her heartbeat, a steady and deadly *bum bum bum.*

Despite her speed, her passage was silent, only the soft bristling of the trees swaying in the wind. She'd traveled these woods before, knew the way even in the dead of the night.

A war horn bellowed in the distance, more faintly this time, and her forehead burned in answer. She clenched her jaw against the pain, the raven mark of the Valkyrie hidden just beneath the skin alight with magic, calling her to battle the way it always did.

But tonight, there would be no turning around and fighting the growing hoard at her back. Not now.

As much as the blood of the Valkyries called her to battle, nothing could detract from the mountain in front of her. The dark snow-tipped peak loomed in the distance, rising high above the trees and into the night sky. It was a foreboding sight, especially with the bright lights flashing green, then blue, then purple, then the brightest pink above her.

In a different place and time, Hilda would have paused to admire her home's majesty, breathing in the pine and sensing the magic in the earth. But everything was tarnished now. The memory of when she'd last climbed this mountain mixed with the pain that led her here today.

The war horns faded as she climbed, the silence almost as ominous as the peak before her. No matter if Hilda had outrun them, she wasn't naïve. Draugr would never stop hunting her. She'd left him with the ultimate betrayal, and the Demon was never denied.

She moved faster; the mountain calling her home, the way it did for all Valkyries. As she passed the timberline, the forest gave way to sheer rock faces. The challenging journey tested the mettle of those who dared to reach the gates of Asgard, keeping the unworthy at bay.

Her fingers raked against nearby trees as she propelled herself up the foothills of the mountain, bark stinging against her frozen skin. As she leaned into the incline, she saw glimpses of what her life could have been. A baby girl wrapped in her arms as she sang her child to sleep. Kissed her brow. Taught her to fight. Watched her grow into a young woman, as fierce and deadly as all the Valkyries before her. But it wasn't meant to be; that Fate unwritten in the Tapestry of time.

Bitterness clouded her mind enough to send her off balance. Her feet slipped, and she fell to the ground, knee crashing against the rocks as she gripped the tree roots around her to keep from sliding backward. She gasped, desperate for something to hold on to as blood streamed down her leg. The power of the gods flowed through her, casting a blinding light out into the night as it healed the physical wounds, but her heart was beyond repair.

A single tear slid down her cheek. She dropped her chin, fingers shaking, and curled in on herself and let a silent scream rip from her throat.

Fate was a cruel thing, choosing Hilda for this Thread. Destining her to know the love of a mother and child for mere hours before having to say goodbye, leaving her newborn daughter to the most daunting task.

She hadn't understood the runes that led her to Draugr's door two years ago. Didn't understand why *she* needed to seduce the cruelest Viking in decades, carry his baby, and leave her infant in his bloodied hands.

Ragnarok rides at your child's heels, the Norns had spoken, and who was she to deny Fate?

Ever the loyal Valkyrie, determined to prove her worth to the gods, Hilda had done what they said.

Two years passed, and the consequences of her chosen path were no easier to bear. Her pulse pounded in her ears, hands shaking in rage over the lot she'd drawn, wishing for anything but the Fate in front of her.

It wasn't supposed to be like this. It *shouldn't* be like this.

A wolf howled in the distance, piercing the otherwise quiet night, and she breathed deep, grasping for calm. Her power ebbed, the light extinguishing as the last of the scrapes on her hands and legs closed. The only evidence of her struggle was the tears in her skirts.

Gritting her teeth, she pushed to her feet and dropped the heavy furs from her shoulders, leaving any sign of her life before this behind. She slid the golden bracelets from her arms and ripped the jade brooch from her dark blue dress, tossing them aside. Her fingers raked through the braids encircling her crown and the curls hanging down her back, yanking on the strands as she braided them back into a more severe style fit for battle. The dirt covering her face moved, magic humming in her veins as it merged into black wings over each brow, long lines extending down her nose.

Here, at the foot of the god's realm, she wasn't a warlord's wife. She wasn't a sister, a friend, a mother. She was a Valkyrie.

Her eyes flashed the brightest green as she tied off her braids and ripped a slit in her dress, giving herself more room to move. Goosebumps raised across her legs as the fabric flapped in the wind when she righted herself, but she was beyond feeling. No matter the path that led her here, she knew what had to be done.

Chin held high, she emerged from the tree line and stared up at the mountain, finding the first handhold. She'd climbed it once before to claim her place as one of Odin's chosen Valkyries — she could do it again.

Her fingers dug into the stone, cold and unforgiving as

she eased into a rhythm with each step she rose into the sky. The lights dancing in and out of the clouds brightened with every passing second, flashing a rainbow of color above, but the beauty of it was lost on her. With a singular focus, she climbed, muscles burning with the movement.

The wind howled around her, sending her dress and braids flying in a cyclone as it threatened to tear her off the cliff and to her death below. But the gods didn't choose Valkyries at random — Hilda had gone to Hel and back since the day she stepped foot in Draugr's village.

She was a Valkyrie, chosen by Odin to fight alongside the Vikings in battle.

An invincible warrior.

Brutal and bloodthirsty.

Death incarnate.

And now, a mother willing to do whatever it took to protect her child.

Against all odds, that mattered most to Hilda. Righteous anger fueled her every move as she grappled her way to the plateau high in the sky. Her fingers curved over the edge, gripping the icy stone, but she didn't let go. *Couldn't* let go.

Her heart raced as she hefted her body onto the ledge, then sprawled on the stone, sweat dripping from her brow despite the cold.

Silence descended like a blanket thrown over the world below, leaving an eerie emptiness in its wake. Gone was the biting wind, the sound of the trees rustling below, the smell of the frigid mountain air. Even the clouds parted, leaving only the glittering stars above, twinkling between the rainbow of gaseous lights.

One by one, the colors separated, energy flowing around her as they reached down toward her like a hand descended from the heavens. She lifted her arm, fingers splayed wide as she twirled her hand in the sky, letting the ribbons dance in and out of her grip. Each caress was like a drop of water, quenching her thirst for vengeance, washing away the anger, easing her thundering pulse.

As a chilling and deadly peace settled over her, she closed her fist around the lights, pulling the power toward her. Light, as green as her eyes, shone through her closed fingers as she pushed it into her chest. Her back arched on a gasp, chest heaving as a fire lit in her. The magic of the realms merged with her own Valkyrie powers, an explosion of light cast over the still scene from every inch of her exposed skin.

Her lips turned up in a smirk as she pushed to her feet, inspecting her body glowing with the power of the gods. Pale green light streamed out of her, rising until the colors shifted and joined into a rainbow starting several feet from the ledge, ascending into the sky above.

With a deep inhale, Hilda took a running start, skirts flaring around her as she leaped off the ledge, refusing to look down at the drop several hundred feet below. Her arms circled, pushing her momentum toward the rainbow bridge. Momentary panic clawed at her, hoping the gods wouldn't deny her entry as she floated through space, but gave way when her feet slammed down on solid ground.

The impact sent her to a knee, her hands reaching out to catch her balance. She grinned wide, a soft chuckle escaping when she lifted her head, taking in the glittering gold towers of Asgard rising high above her.

Gone was the night sky, the twinkling stars, the foreboding mountain. Instead, she stared at the brightest sun, the human realm of Midgard below her long gone.

She straightened, warmth surrounding her as her torn and tattered dress transformed into battle leathers. Magic coated every inch of her skin as she took on the true form of a Valkyrie. Her fingers rose, tracing over the raven on her brow, knowing it stood out as black as the darkest night against her pale skin. It was the last sight many saw in battle before meeting their final death, an omen that Odin had come to collect his due.

But this wasn't battle; here, in the realm of the gods, she was far from invincible at the mercy of the gods she was meant to blindly obey.

Her grin disappeared as bile rose in her throat. She swallowed down her fear, knowing there was no turning back.

With swift steps, she raced across the rainbow bridge, entering Asgard. Armed guards stood in front of the gilded doors, as still as statues decked out in golden armor, battle spears held in one hand an axe in the other.

"Valkyrie." A guard held out a hand to stop her as she hurried toward them.

She skidded to a halt when her Valkyrie mark burned, even the guards able to access the power of the gods to command her. At the last minute, she remembered to duck her head in respect.

Though Hilda was strong, the might of the gods dwarfed her own power.

"Reporting," she said, glad her voice didn't betray the rising unease thrumming in her veins. There was no reason to be here — Odin could see everything she did in Midgard. But she couldn't erase the image of the baby she'd left behind.

The guard opened his mouth right as a tall, copper-haired male rounded the corner, a hammer hanging in his grip. His red beard was trimmed close to his face and skimmed the edges of his chiseled jaw. Everything about him radiated power, even the belt around his waist cinched tight over his tunic.

Hilda sucked in a breath, blinking at the sight of the deity in front of her.

"Problem, Valkyrie?" Thor's voice rumbled like thunder. His wary glance shot from the guard to Hilda and back, and she bowed, heart racing. Thor was the god of the common people, but also a fearsome warlord, not known for his patience.

She shook her head, bowing deeper in his presence. "Reporting for Odin," she repeated.

Her eyes raised, inspecting the hammer in Thor's hand, the scrollwork etched into the silver, worn with use, glinting in the light. *Mjölnir*, the most legendary weapon of the gods, crafted by the dwarves, able to change the Fates.

"Rise." Thor's head tilted as he stared at her. His attention was like a vice, making it difficult to breathe, but she did as instructed.

With a brief nod, he strode past the two guards and

pushed open the doors leading into the great hall beyond. Fourteen gilded thrones formed a semi-circle, all filled except the one Thor walked toward at the front.

Hilda's chest tightened as she stepped into the room, her breath catching at the grandeur before her. Like the Viking halls in Midgard, pillars dotted the edges of the room, a golden shield hanging from each one. The ceilings were painted with colors as bright as the bridge outside, depicting a continuous and dynamic war.

Above her, Viking history unfolded. Women marked by the Valkyries with the black raven between their brow, just like her, scattered among the scenes. But none were as bloody as Ragnarok, the battle predicted for their future.

She moved into the center of the room, dropping to one knee. She bowed her head, and all chatter ceased. Her heart stuttered at the attention of the Æsir gods, the feeling as crippling as taking a physical blow to the chest.

"Valkyrie." Odin's voice rang in her mind, the word a quiet whisper against her racing pulse. *"Why are you here?"*

Mind-speak alone told Hilda she shouldn't have come, but this wasn't about her.

"The job is done." Her words echoed off the round chamber as she dared to lift her head. "I gave birth to the next Valkyrie. She shares the blood of the Demon, the Viking foretold to bring Ragnarok to your gates. The Norns have called her to this Fate, tying her to her father's doom and the god's salvation."

Odin rose from his chair and crossed the room to her, his golden spear tapping with each step and plain robes swishing against the floor. His long grey beard brushed against the fabric, hair skimming his shoulders moving in a phantom wind. Two black wolves paced at his side, their heads reaching mid-waist against the towering god, eye-level with her. They alone were enough to have Hilda's mouth run dry.

"Excellent." Odin stopped in front of her. Head tilted to the side, his one remaining eye studied her, seeing far more than he should.

Heartache.

Pain.

Doubt.

"She won't be enough to stop him," Hilda blurted out before she lost her nerve, hands trembling. She squeezed her eyes shut for a second, picturing the battles raging above, only this time her child led the charge. "My daughter is doomed to an impossible Fate. This is all for naught. The Tree will fall. You underestimate Draugr. She isn't enough."

Silence gripped the hall, shattered by a cacophony of whispers as the gods, scandalized by Hilda's blasphemous words, leaned across their gilded thrones to talk among themselves.

Odin slammed his spear against the floor, magic rushing from the tiles up the wooden shaft, illuminating runes carved into the weapon. Like a wave crashing over the shore, the room descended into silence once more. An invisible force slammed her shoulders down, pressing her chest into the floor as she genuflected to the gods.

Her body shook, not with terror but anger here in the presence of the gods who sat on their pretty thrones and didn't interfere. No matter what happened next, what was done was done. She couldn't take the words back. She *wouldn't*, even if it meant her death.

As a Valkyrie, she was an extension of Odin, a follower and executor of his will, with no purpose beyond his own. But the moment her baby's gaze met hers, her unfaltering loyalty to the gods snapped.

With a shaky breath, she lifted her face and stared at the dark-haired god to Odin's left, a sly smile tilting Loki's lips. Uneasiness swept through her, and she flicked her eyes to Odin's right, meeting Thor's questioning gaze once more.

He was who she'd come for.

The god of the people, the protector of Midgard.

The only one who might care what she had to say.

"We cannot change the Fates." Odin dismissed her, just as Hilda knew he would, turning back to his throne. "The Norns wove this story long before our time. They will continue to weave our Fates until this story is done. If your daughter is not enough, we will protect Asgard, just as we always have."

"But what of the Vikings in Midgard?" she asked, the bright green eyes of her infant seared into her memory. Her hands fisted against the tile floors, attempting to keep her anger at bay. "Who will shield them from the destruction Draugr brings?"

Odin spun, his hardened gaze burning her as sure as a fire. "You are out of line, Valkyrie," he growled, and she ducked her head once more. "Leave now, before I strip you of your powers and ban you from entering Valhalla."

Her chin tremored, a mixture of defeat and fury holding her in place a moment longer. Breathing through her nose, she straightened and held her chin high. With a quick nod, she turned and left.

As she passed through the gates back to the rainbow bridge, a clap of thunder pulled her to a stop, and she glanced over her shoulder.

Thor towered above her, her eyes meeting his mid-chest. "What's your name?"

"Hilda," she answered, breath shaking with her last sliver of hope.

He nodded, then lifted his hand to the buckle at his waist, unhooking it from his broad hips. The moment the belt released from his body, it shrunk in his hands to a smaller size, perfect for her thin frame. Without waiting for her approval, Thor moved forward, laced his arms around her torso, and secured it.

Megingjord settled on her hips, magic warming her and settling into her skin, then disappeared as if it had never been there. She stared at her waist, then looked up at Thor, not daring to believe her eyes.

In his outstretched hands laid his hammer, *Mjölnir* glistening in the rainbow lights cascading around them. "Take it."

Hilda's hand shook as she lifted the weapon, her fear mixed with disbelief that he would give her this gift.

"*Megingjord* gives you the strength to carry it across realms, but not enough to use the power within," Thor said. "Your daughter is not alone in this fight to the end. The dragons are rising again. A warrior of my choosing will come when the time is right, one strong enough to wield *Mjölnir*. Until then, guard it with your life."

Hilda nodded, her hands closing around the supple leather grip, the weapon weightless. No magic emanated from the hammer itself, but she could sense the dormant power laying within.

"Go." Thor touched her chin and lifted her face, wiping away the angry tear that slid free. "Find the warrior. You can't change the Fates, but paired with the dragons, whoever is strong enough to wield *Mjölnir* is your last hope to defy them."

With that, he turned and strode back across the bridge toward the golden gates of Asgard. She looked down at the weapon, Thor's words ringing in her head.

Find the warrior.

Her jaw clenched, fearing the future, the Hel her daughter would go through between now and then. Fingers tightening around the hammer, Hilda sprinted back across the rainbow bridge.

This was her chance to defy Fate, and she wouldn't waste it.

1

DOMARI

Viking Era, Present Day

Thunder rumbled in the distance, far-off lightning glowing in the early evening sky as Domari crept through the melting snow. His leather boots sank as he slowed. The icy wind from a spring storm blew in from the ocean they'd been heading toward for days.

With every passing sunset, hope dwindled among the Eriksson clan that traveled at his back, worry for the women and children who had gone ahead pushing them faster. Knowing Draugr the Demon's men hunted their loved ones as they trekked to Torvik, Asmund's village on the sea, sent a ripple of urgency through the entire clan.

No one had complained about the relentless pace Domari had set, nor the damp weather this spring brought.

Restless energy coursed through him, like a crackling fire under his skin, desperate to break free. His grasp tightened on his axe's leather grip. He spun it in his palm as he looked into the valley below him, like so many they'd passed over the last week.

The rocky terrain was dotted with pines and birch, steep and uneven as it descended into a gorge below. A small clearing showed to their right, more than likely a bog, but it caught his attention.

Something here was different.

Instinct had him pause, hiding under the cover of the trees as he watched the storm in the distance, looking for the source of his unease. Holding up a hand, he stalled the rest of his group at his back. They quieted, just like he knew they would. Everyone here a fighter to some extent, aware of the danger they rode toward.

Freki, the black pup who'd followed them from the Eriksson's village, padded to his side, nose raised into the air. Domari's dark brow rose, staring down at the dog who frequently chased his own tail.

"You feel it too, boy?" Domari reached down to scratch the dog's head. Undeterred by his touch, Freki's nose twitched as if caught on something.

Domari stared back out at the woods, wind ruffling the fur draped over one shoulder as he tied his dark hair up into a knot. His eyes scanned the horizon, coming back to the bog and searching for what had caught the dog's attention. Fresh pine mixed with the smell of petrichor, the scent clean as the late spring storm rolled toward them. Thunder rumbled again, followed several seconds later by a bolt of lightning, illuminating the sky just enough to see smoke rising above the treetops.

A deep hum rattled through Domari's chest. He

dropped to his heels, grabbing both sides of Freki's face and scratching behind his ears. "Well done, pup."

The dog's tongue lolled out to the side, his face lighting up in a smile as Domari touched his forehead to the dog's, then stood.

With a flick of his finger, Magnus approached, the usual light in his eyes replaced with a steely focus. He didn't look like the mischievous young cousin, but a fearsome Viking covered in tattoos and face paint, ready for battle. Björn, his uncle's most trusted soldier, joined them as Domari pointed to the tops of the tree line.

"Smoke," Magnus said, a deep v forming between his brows.

"Draugr's men?" Björn's arms crossed over his barrel chest. His large belly and grey beard were deceptive, hiding the power and might of one of the best warriors Domari knew. Björn's gaze swept the area into the valley below them, likely looking for any sign of a traveling party.

But if this was part of Draugr's army, this wasn't an ordinary traveling party. They were hunters. Warriors. *Vikings*. They didn't leave tracks to be found, weren't prey to be picked apart.

Magnus slid the sword from the sheath at his hip, jaw clenched tight, then turned to look behind him at the rest of their clan waiting for their lead.

A low chuff had Domari following his gaze. Shelbie picked her way forwards, her large black dog matching her weary stride. Yrsa had dressed her in a long emerald gown, not quite tall enough for her frame, skimming the tops of the hiking boots she'd worn when they'd traveled through time. She'd braided her blonde curls back from her face, but strands rose from her head in a halo, a reminder of everything good she was. Her dress flowed around her as she walked, the cloak over her shoulders cinched with the Eriksson's wolf brooch marking her as one of them. Her beauty was distracting, as was the pendant at her neck casting a pale glow over her freckled face and clear blue eyes.

"Is it them?" She fingered the gold chain around her neck.

He hummed. After spending months together, the sight of her shouldn't affect him the way it did, stealing the breath from his lungs. Reaching a hand around her nape, he pulled her into his chest, trying to qualm the restless energy crackling under his skin.

"Maybe," he answered. Shelbie's arms encircled his waist, the heat of her searing even through his leather armor over his tunic. "We won't know until we approach."

"So, what's the plan?" She tipped her chin up toward him, searching his face for answers, but he hardened his jaw, looking back over the treetops.

Shelbie hadn't seen him fight against Draugr's forces in his attempt to save Gunnar and Signe, and he hoped he could protect her from this for a little longer. While he knew Shelbie loved him, chose this life, and was meant to be here at his side, she had no idea who he was.

Not just a hunter. A warrior. A Viking.

A *monster*.

Draugr had taken everything he held most dear. No hope, no salvation, no pity could be found in his soul. There was only vengeance.

"Is Hadriel near?" Domari forced his focus on her instead of the need to destroy anyone who hurt his family. His hands tangled in her hair as he touched his forehead on hers.

She shook her head then stared up at the darkening sky, but the black dragon was nowhere to be seen. "He knows it's more important to watch out for the children. I don't think he's coming."

"Good." He dropped a kiss to Shelbie's brow, then let her go, stepping past her to rejoin Magnus and Björn. "Stay here with Björn and Yrsa. I'll be back for you once it's safe."

Her breath caught, but she gave him a brief nod. The stone around her neck glowed brighter as she grabbed Yrsa's outstretched hand, the two women thrumming with power. Even though Yrsa's dragon was long gone from this earth, the strength of the Promised still radiated from her, although far less intense than from Shelbie.

Tearing his focus back into the forest ahead, Domari waved the rest of his clan to the sides, the same battle-hardened mask he'd worn for a decade settling over his shoulders. Like the black paint smeared on his face, his soul was darkened with each life he took, each breath he stole.

But this was different.

In the Varangian Guard, he had fought for a king and country not his own. This… this was his *family*. There were no lengths he wouldn't go to protect them. To save them. To end any who threatened them.

He dipped into the killing calm as lightning streaked across the sky, thunder rumbling louder now. On soft feet, he ducked low beneath the trees, creeping toward the rising smoke and whoever sat beside it.

With quick glances to his left and right, Domari watched his clan approach as if they'd done this a thousand times before. While they were far from the Guard, the hired swords renowned around the world, the Erikssons were Vikings, through and through.

The sound of wings was the only sign of their passage, birds fleeing at the oncoming storm. Cupping his hand over his mouth, Domari let out a croak, identical to the ravens flying overhead. His clan stopped, waiting for his signal as he peered through the trees into the camp several dozen paces ahead.

Firelight danced off the faces of battle-hardened men and one woman closest to the fire. Her hands shook as she passed out rations to the fifteen Vikings scattered throughout the small area. Domari held his breath, looking for any sign of recognition that these were the demons who had taken everything from him.

Several lean-tos were set up around the clearing, readying for the oncoming storm, but there were no signs of other women or children.

He debated turning back and leaving what was probably a hunting party alone, not needing to draw attention to his clan. Movement to his right caught his attention, Magnus hiding in the trees, pointing—

The woman cried out. Domari's gaze snapped to her. The largest man dragged her across the ground and into his lap. Her jerky movements knocked aside a shield at the man's feet, leaving it face-up. Another flash of lightning, and

Domari saw the white dragon, the symbol of Draugr's army, and grinned.

The woman fought against her captor's hold, and Domari let out a second croak.

Arrows flew from all sides of the camp, followed by pained cries. The Erikssons circled and moved positions around the clearing, just like he'd instructed them over the last few days, making themselves an invisible target. Lightning flashed through the sky in time with the thunderclap that sent the trees shaking, guiding his way as he rushed forward on silent feet, axe held high.

With a burst of speed, Domari ran through the tree line, an axe in each hand. He flew through the campground and came down swinging. Magnus crashed down beside him, taking up the spot at his back as they rained down blows, one after the next.

A low buzz took over Domari's mind, blocking out the sounds of death around him. He screamed and released all the anger deep under his skin. Blood sprayed with each strike, each blow sending men to their knees. One for Gunnar, one for Signe, one for each of the children these men had left orphaned and alone.

If the white dragon painted on the shields they carried wasn't confirmation enough, the speed at which these men fought back, gathering themselves into pairs like Domari would have done, told him these weren't hunters. They were the men he sought, the Demon's force that had been trailing everyone he loved.

Bitter, savage energy flowed through his veins as he took one life after the next, never thinking through his actions.

After all, this was what Domari did best. Like a weapon wielded by an angry god, he cut through enemies, working his way toward the cowering woman and the man standing over her.

A deep laugh boomed through the clearing as he ripped his axe free of a fallen Viking. "They said the *Akolouthos* rode with the Erikssons, but I didn't believe it." The man spat to his side, then grinned, flipping his sword in his hand and stepping toward Domari. "Your people are weak. No one from the little farming clan would be enough of a warrior to rise to the head of the Guard. Must have fucked your way to the top, hm?"

Domari's chin dropped, his fingers tightening on the leather grip of his axe. Thunder clapped in the sky above. "Let her go."

"Her?" The Viking frowned, then sent a kick to where the woman crawled across the ground, cowering. She screamed as his foot connected, pulling her hands down over her side. No matter, she kept moving, clawing her way toward the forest as the sounds of death filtered in behind Domari. "She's useless, just like your women and children I've been promised."

Rage licked like a fire at Domari's skin, his pulse hammering in his ears, but he didn't move, waiting out his prey.

Lightning slammed down in the clearing, a tree engulfed in flames as it tipped. The deafening crack was enough to have the Viking charge, closing the space between them. He screamed and raised his sword to strike, grey teeth bared.

Domari blinked, a cyclone of energy and heat from the

nearby flames licking across his skin as time seemed to slow. His body hummed with energy, like the fire was lit from within, desperate to break free.

Warrior, a deep voice said inside his head, rumbling like the thunder overhead. *Rise.*

With a clap of thunder, his axes lifted as his opponent's sword descended, blocking the blow. As if snapped from his reverie, Domari screamed. Veins bulged on his neck, and he shoved his hands to the side, throwing the Viking back several feet with his momentum. He stalked forward, his opponent stumbling, surprise written all over his face. Rage slammed down over his features as he righted himself, raising his sword once more.

But Domari was done with this game. In a burst of energy, he pivoted, body twisting to the side.

His foot connected with the Viking's face, blood exploding from his mouth as his head ripped to the side. Domari's body followed the spinning motion, an axe sinking into the man's neck and another in his side before his opponent could even recover from the blow.

Wide eyes greeted Domari as his body dropped to the ground, his final breath stuttering free.

"Well, that was quick," Magnus said next to him, hands on his hips.

Breaths heaved through Domari's chest as the sights and sounds of battle returned to him.

Freezing rain fell, the fire sizzling as Arne and Bodil tossed snow over the fallen tree to put out the smoke.

A dozen bodies lay dead or dying, all but the woman huddled on the edge of the forest. Domari turned toward her, sheathing his weapons and holding his hands to the side. Bodil across the clearing, covered in blood, was enough of a reminder that even Viking women were to be feared, but that voice that drove Domari into battle was silent, the violent energy in his veins gone.

"I mean no harm." Domari dropped the rest of his weapons on the ground as he approached.

She scurried back, hand gripping her side, and stared up at him. Her body trembled, but she bared her teeth, ready to fight. A Viking, through and through.

"Our women," Magnus said, his tone gentle as he approached. "Have you seen them? Draugr sent his men to follow my children."

Her eyes flicked to the woods behind Domari, then back to them, some of the fight leaving her.

Thunder rumbled low in the sky, but not loud enough to hide the sound of footfalls scrambling through the underbrush peeking through the melting snow. A blur of motion dodged between trees, a messenger leaving the camp.

Magnus spun and sprinted through the woods. He pulled a bow from his back. The big man shouldn't have been able to move with such speed but driven by the same inner fire to protect what was his, he flew. Domari had no doubts the messenger sent to alert Draugr of the attack wouldn't survive the night.

"He'll kill you," the woman said, and Domari turned back to her. "Ragnarok is coming. The Demon is going to kill us all."

A raven croaked in the sky above, flying through the freezing rain, and circled above where Shelbie stood on the hillside above, cloak billowing to her side. The dogs stood to either side of her, black and ominous as the bird overhead. Her pendant glowed green, a steady light in the storm, promising a future Domari had never dared let himself dream of.

A future worth fighting for.

"Not if I kill him first."

2

DOMARI

Domari dipped his whetstone into the ice-cold river, flowing faster as the riding party came closer to the sea. He spread his fingers beneath the surface, the water passing through them, and the dirt from their journey washed away.

Freki and Thor lapped at the water on either side of him, the black dogs dark against the rising sun. Their likeness was striking—a wolf-like build, long fur, and a curled tail. Freki was still a pup, not yet fully grown. He radiated life and energy, diving into the river, running through the shallows, and chasing a raven away from a nearby tree. Shelbie's dog, Thor, on the other hand, had a coldness about him, as if he understood his job was to protect.

The same coldness Domari saw in his own reflection, rippling in the current beneath him.

Scooping the water up over his arms, he scrubbed at the signs of travel and battle he'd never be rid of no matter how many times he washed himself. His skin was red from the cold, making the black lines of the tattoos on his forearms stand out that much starker in contrast. Ten bands, one for each year he'd fought to erase the worst of his deeds from his conscience by fighting for the Varangian Guard. It wasn't as glamorous or honorable as he'd pictured, but then again, killing never was.

"There you are," Shelbie said, rocks crunching beneath her boots as she approached from the nearby camp they'd set up to ride out the storm last night. "I should have known Thor was with you."

Shaking the last of the water off his hands, Domari stood. He turned to smile at Shelbie as her dog crossed the rocky shore to stand between her legs, watching her back. Reaching forward, Domari tugged on her cloak until she wrapped her arms around him, resting her cheek on his chest.

"He was meant to join us." Domari planted a kiss on the top of Shelbie's head. "That dog is as much a warrior as I am."

As if in answer, Thor let out a huff, then growled low in his throat until Freki glanced their way. With a yip, the young pup bounded out of the water, shaking it from his fur, and took up his position between Domari's legs, mirroring Thor.

Shelbie chuckled, and the sound soothed something broken deep inside Domari. He slid his hands up Shelbie's back until he cupped her jaw, tilting her face up to his. "Good morning, *haski*."

"Hi." She smiled up at him, blue eyes sparkling like the river behind him. He traced his fingers through the fur at her collar, then through the curls at the nape of her neck, too short to be caught by her long braids. "You were gone when I woke up."

"Getting the horses ready." Domari laid a gentle kiss on her lips. "We ride again at dawn."

She nodded, looking over the remains of the campground they'd hastily set up after last night's skirmish. Yrsa stood near the fire, handing out rations to everyone as they prepared for another day of travel. Magnus and Björn worked side-by-side, organizing riding parties, ensuring everyone had a hunter with them who knew the terrain well. Smoke swirled, obscuring the world in a hazy glow, a chilling echo of the fires in the Eriksson village they'd fled.

No matter that everyone chatted calmly while they broke camp, Domari couldn't bring himself to participate. Not with the rescued woman, beaten and battered, sitting at the edge of their camp, avoiding them all. She served as a cautionary tale, reminding them of the disastrous consequences if they failed to thwart Draugr and his forces.

Shelbie squeezed his sides, drawing his attention back down to her, and he placed another kiss on her lips. "Tonight, right?" she asked, a hitch in her voice. "One more day until we reach Asmund's village by the sea, and find our people?"

He nodded, resting his forehead on hers, sensing the weariness in her. Although Shelbie looked the part of the Viking sorceress, he saw the way she limped, hand on her back after a week of hard travel. "My horse is saddled and ready for you. Let Mjölnir carry you today, saving your energy for whatever lies ahead in Torvik."

Her nose scrunched as she pulled away from him, the closest Shelbie came to showing how anxious she was. "I'm going to try to contact Hadriel again." She lifted her hand to the onyx pendant around her neck, now dull and lifeless with her Promised dragon so far ahead of them. "Maybe he'll answer this time, now that we're closer. I just want to know they arrived and are safe."

Unease sat heavily in Domari's chest over Hadriel's absence, wanting that same reassurance that their women and children had made it safely to Torvik. But he'd seen how quickly using her powers drained Shelbie, and it was a risk he couldn't take. He brushed a thumb across her jaw, pulling her attention back to him. "Wait. Tonight, we find them. The dragon and our clan."

Her freckled face turned up toward his, their noses brushing for only a moment. "Tonight."

"Don't shut me out, Domari," she whispered into his chest, her fingers digging into his back. The words mirrored his own sentiments the last few months when she'd been hiding the visions her Promised powers had given her. "We'll face whatever is coming together, stronger because of it. Don't shut me out."

He squeezed her tighter. When had they switched roles?

Domari couldn't find the words to reassure her, but he hoped she understood the depth of his love. Unlike his time in the Varangian Guard, he now had something to fight for, and that changed everything.

"It seems like yesterday that you found me," Shelbie

murmured as she stared at the rocky beach on the river's edge. "When I saw your boats, that's when I realized something was wrong. Vikings and time travel weren't just fictional. They were real, and I was right in the middle of it all."

He hummed in agreement, remembering the day vividly. The memory of last night's battle, and the one before, faded in his mind, replaced by the image of a woman, bloodstained and crumpled on the shore. She'd opened her eyes, the clearest blue shining up at him, and immediately, his world had changed, much to his annoyance.

"Forget how to talk?" Shelbie poked his ribs, mischief dancing in her eyes. He caught her hand, and her skirts ruffled in the breeze. "I know you know how."

Domari chuckled, pulling her in to kiss her one last time before he pushed her toward his horse, helping her mount.

With a sharp whistle, the clan began to move, lumbering forward as they'd done for days. The storm had melted the last of the snow, trickling water dripping over the rocky terrain. Bogs formed in the wooded areas, hoarding the snowmelt for the creatures residing within the forests. Pops of yellow, purple, and white peeked between the green grass, wildflowers blooming overnight. Everything was new and fresh, promising life if they made it through whatever came next.

Domari's eyes scanned their party as they descended a steep hill, one of many they'd face before they arrived at the coast later today. The woman they'd rescued last night had yet to talk to anyone but Yrsa, but that was a problem for another day. With a hand resting on Shelbie's leg, he walked by her side.

Unable to keep quiet for long, she finally spoke. "Tell me something."

"Like what?" He rubbed his thumb across her thigh, unsure if the touches were for him or her. Either way, he couldn't help himself.

She shrugged, lips pursed in thought. "Are the Norns gods? How does that work?"

Domari's hands stilled, thinking of the three sisters who wove the Fates of all Vikings. He had seen them twice: once in Constantinople the night he left the Guard, and again in the village, the night they announced Shelbie had time traveled and needed to return home. "They're not gods, no. They exist outside the deities tied to *Yggdrasil*. The Tree, as you know it."

"So, gods *adjacent*. Before all of this, I hadn't heard of them — just Odin, Thor, and Loki. And only them from Marvel movies, which is a reference you won't get and there's no point in explaining."

Domari opened his mouth to answer, but Magnus cut him off, throwing an arm over Domari's shoulders as he stuck his head between him and the horse. "Don't ask him to tell you stories unless you're trying to fall asleep. That's all Domari's good for."

Shelbie laughed, the sound as light as air, and it effortlessly lifted Domari's spirits. He shrugged out of his younger cousin's hold, dropping his hand from Shelbie's side in the process.

"Well, then let's hear it, storyteller."

Magnus cleared his throat, matching his strides to the horse and adopting a dramatic, theatrical tone. "In the beginning, there was fire and ice. Where they met here in our lands, the first giant was formed, Ymir. Following him was Buri, who then had a son, Bor. Together, Bor and Bestla had three sons, Odin, Vili, and Ve. Together, the three eventually turned on Ymir."

"This sounds like a very narrow family tree," Shelbie commented. "Maybe more of a bush."

Magnus shushed her, placing a tattooed finger over her mouth. She smiled behind his finger, and Domari shook his head at the pair, but already his mood lifted, soaking in the warmth the two radiated.

"Ymir's body was broken, forming the earth. His blood filled the seas, his bones formed the mountains, his hair sprouted forests, his skull framed the sky, and his brain the clouds."

"Well, that's disgusting." Shelbie frowned, and Magnus shot her a serious look for interrupting his tale. "No wonder the Vikings are remembered as bloodthirsty killers. Do you tell children this story? Do they ever sleep again?"

"Are you done?" Magnus threw his hands in the air. "Perhaps I *should* let Domari explain it. His story would be over now. That man has no stamina."

Shelbie cackled, head thrown back, and Domari rubbed at his chest, wondering how he'd gotten so lucky as to win her love. She was sunlight, the brightest dawn after the longest day, a promise of a future he'd never imagined. If only he could protect her long enough to earn it.

"See?" Magnus said, eyes cast over his shoulder as he watched Domari with raised brows. "He didn't even bother to argue."

"No point in arguing," Domari said, his voice a low rumble. "Besides, Shelbie has never complained about my stamina."

Her freckled cheeks pinked, eyes full of a fire he loved as she openly admired him, and he smirked. Traveling with the clan, they hadn't had much time alone. But the feeling of her skin against his was unforgettable.

"*Anyway,*" Magnus said, drawing Shelbie's attention back to him. "The world formed. Odin and his brothers formed the realms, including the human realm where we are now, Midgard."

"And Asgard is the realm of the gods, right?" Shelbie asked, and Magnus whistled in approval.

"Look at you, knowing things."

She bowed her head, the necklace around her neck swinging forward with the small motion. "Thank you, Chris Hemsworth."

"Is he a wise man in your time?"

A wide smile overtook her face. "Sure. We'll stick with that."

Magnus continued his story, telling her of the other seven realms, all nine thought to exist within *Yggdrasil* itself. He outlined the creation of the first humans, and the *Æsir* and *Vanir* gods, highlighting the importance of Odin, Thor, Loki, Freya, Frey — the key players, according to him. She followed his story, asking questions, and Domari saw the understanding light up on her face, amazed by her ease in adapting to new things.

"What about Valkyries?" she asked, and Domari's breath caught in his throat.

Magnus hummed, shooting a hesitant look Domari's way before he went on. "Valkyries are god-like women chosen by Odin. The bringers of death, the turners of battle tides, the keepers of Valhalla, and the eyes of Odin. No one truly understands their powers, so rare among us. But to fight alongside a Valkyrie in battle is to ensure victory. They cannot lose."

Her bright blue eyes shifted between Magnus and Domari. "Do you think they're real?"

"I'd like to believe they are." Magnus shrugged, his voice wistful as his lips turned down in an uncharacteristic frown. "That they'll come to our aid."

Domari studied his feet as he walked, lost in his memories.

Signe's piercing scream echoed in his mind, her green eyes glowing as she swung his sword, her soul lit on fire. He knew that kind of singular focus but fighting alongside her had been unreal. Unnatural. He'd always been a gifted warrior, referred to jokingly as a god among men by his fellow Guard, but even he couldn't compare against the brutality Signe had dealt.

If what he'd seen was true, she'd stolen the air right from the men's lungs, dealing a killing blow *without* a weapon.

Draugr hadn't come to reclaim his long-lost daughter.

Draugr had come for a Valkyrie.

How a Valkyrie had found her way to the peaceful

Erikssons was beyond Domari's comprehension, but none-theless, she had. He couldn't imagine that Gunnar recog-nized what Signe was, but Draugr certainly knew.

That had to be why he came, why he risked his men for such a small farming town hardly worth looting. But telling Magnus and Shelbie that they'd had a Valkyrie among them, and now she was with the enemy, would do nothing to boost morale. The opposite — it ensured their loss.

Shelbie's laugh, high and full of joy as she shoved at Magnus's arm, pulled him back to the present. Domari watched as the two bantered, but he'd lost track of their conversation.

Her pendant glowed a soft green, stealing his focus. There was no hiding that Shelbie was the last of the Promised, Fated to change the world. And men like Draugr would stop at nothing to possess those kinds of weapons. That was what Signe and Shelbie were to him — weapons to be wielded to bring the end of the world.

Ragnarok.

A rebirth for the fading warlord.

Even if Draugr failed, the bloodbath it promised made any who fought fit for the halls of Valhalla, enough to moti-vate the most vicious of men.

The clouds darkened overhead for a moment, and without looking up, he knew it was Hadriel passing over, watching their steady progress. Shelbie tilted her head up to the sky and closed her eyes, the pendant glowing against her skin.

No matter how desperately Domari wanted to load

everyone he loved onto a ship and carry them far away to safety, he couldn't.

He refused to give up hope that Gunnar was still alive, that Signe could find a way to return to them. But even more than that, Shelbie's Fate was tied to this coming battle, and nothing could make him leave her side. Not even knowing a Valkyrie would ride against him, and he had no chance to beat her.

3

SHELBIE

"**O**din's beard," I muttered. Pain radiating up my spine, and I bent forward in the saddle, searching for relief. "I thought I was in better shape than this."

Domari's hand slid across my low back, rubbing down the center. His fingers dug into the muscle as I hugged Mjölnir's thick neck, my eyes closing. The comforting touch would've been better if I wasn't still riding and could lay down, but I wasn't about to look a gift horse in the mouth. Pun intended.

Despite spending the last several months living on a horse ranch in the foothills of the Rocky Mountains, nothing had prepared me for a week's worth of walking and riding across the rocky terrain toward the coast.

To think, last year I thought this sounded *fun*.

"Not to worry." Magnus jogged up to my side with a smile. "I'll make a Viking of you yet."

My back muscles screamed as I sat upright, trying to rid

myself of the tension. With a flick of my hand, I flipped my blue fur-lined cloak away, exposing the green dress tied tight with a leather belt etched with runes. "Have I not dressed the part?"

Magnus raised a blond brow and glanced down at my hiking boots that were very much *not* Viking. Tugging on my cloak, I hid my modern boots, then rolled my eyes at Domari's younger cousin. "Shut it."

"I said nothing."

I waved a hand in front of his face. "You said *lots* with that Dwayne Johnson eyebrow of yours."

"Would I like this Dwayne Johnson? Is he a fighting man?"

An unattractive snort escaped me, my shoulders shaking with laughter. "Actually, you'd love him. Huge guy, covered in tattoos, and yes, he does fight."

Magnus nodded. "A Viking then."

"Not in the least."

Domari's hand dropped from my back to my thigh, squeezing gently. I looked over at him, but his focus was far in front of us, watching the horizon.

"You can go up ahead." I patted his hand. He turned to look up at me, dark eyes searching my face, so I smiled and nodded. "I'm good. I promise."

"No visions?"

I shook my head, pulling my hand from his to the pendant around my neck. The onyx stone was warm to the touch, but didn't hum with the power it would once my dragon and I were reunited. From what little I understood, it was always this way for the Promised, our powers stronger together.

For better or worse, I hadn't had a vision of the past or future on our journey, the magic that had crippled me in the modern world ebbing. My fingers trailed over the gold chain, the metal cool to the touch, no hint of the power of the dragons and gods I was supposed to wield. With a sigh, I dropped them back to the reins trying to let go of my worry over how truly powerless I was, no matter that I wore a magic pendant.

Domari leaned in and kissed my hand before moving through the crowd of travelers, taking his place at the front. Björn, Kare, and Thorsten joined him, their heads together just as they'd been last fall when I first met the trio of hunters. Then, they'd been wary of me, but in good spirits.

Now, I couldn't say the same. There was no laughter, no smiling, no storytelling, aside from Magnus. Like that first journey together, he left and rejoined me throughout the day, bringing berries and playing with the dogs in turn. My friend had been talkative on the days we'd traveled together, but I saw it for what it was: a distraction, for him and for me.

"Domari's been quiet," I said when Magnus rejoined me next. He bit into a strip of dried meat that looked like the jerky my dad made growing up in Colorado. My stomach rumbled, and Magnus handed me what was left of his meat.

I took it, even though I didn't particularly want it. The things I would have done for a taco were obscene. Luckily, I was surprised by the smoky taste mixed with garlic and onion. "That's not bad."

Magnus scoffed. "Of course, it's not. I made it." He pulled several more strips from a satchel around his waist, handing one to each of the dogs at my side before biting into one for himself. "And when isn't Domari quiet? That's normal. I'd be concerned if he was starting conversations. *That* would be cause for alarm."

I chuckled, but it sounded false even to my own ears. "He didn't come to bed last night after you came back from the skirmish."

His lips smacked together as he finished the last of his jerky, then he wiped his hands on his pants. "Domari has always been that way, the broody bastard. He's worried, like we all are. About you, about Gunnar, about what we'll find in Torvik. Give him space. He'll come back." Magnus clapped his hands together, turning to walk sideways beside my horse, grinning ear to ear once more. "Want to hear the story of when Thor wore a dress to trick the giants into giving his hammer back?"

Without waiting for confirmation, Magnus launched into the tale, his arms waving around as we walked. Several other villagers chimed in to add to the story, and I laughed when I was supposed to, listening even though my eyes never left Domari.

Space, I could give him, even if I hated it. I wanted to throw myself into his chest, wrap my arms around him, and beg him to tell me every one of his worries. But Domari wasn't that way, and I knew that.

He was quiet. He was steady. He was as loyal as they came. And gods, he was *handsome.*

Like last fall, his hair was shaved short on the sides, longer on the top where he often wore it tied in a topknot off his neck. His tunic fit perfectly across his broad back, emphasizing all the muscles I knew hid underneath. At almost six feet, I was used to being eye-to-eye with most men, but Domari towered over me. He made me feel small and feminine in a way I was not accustomed to, and I loved it.

But more so than even our physical connection, Domari's quiet resolve was the perfect match for my wild and off-the-rails personality. I stumbled through life, not knowing what the hell I was doing. He reined in my chaos, loving me through the storm. No matter what lay ahead in our future, I was glad Fate had brought us together.

As if feeling my attention, Domari looked over his shoulder. His gaze raked over me, then met my eye, checking on me how he so often did. My lips tipped up in a small smile, not wanting to add my anxiety to his long list of concerns.

We traversed through another valley, the scenery beginning to change as we neared Torvik. The snow had melted the closer we got to the coast, leaving behind green grasses and a cacophony of wildflowers that reminded me of Colorado's spring. Nothing here was the same as the Eriksson's land, sprawling in the wooded valley between the mountains. Instead, the salty brine air of the ocean overshadowed the fresh scent of the forest, marking just how far we'd come.

We crested another hill, and a horn bellowed in the distance, loud and unsettling. On the second blow, Magnus's body went rigid, his eyes snapping to the horizon. Squinting against the bright afternoon sun, I followed his gaze to where the rough terrain gave way to farmland and a fortress beyond.

Domari didn't stop, leading the Erikssons down the final descent. Villagers stood scattered around the land, stopping to watch our approach. Eerie silence took over our traveling party, not wanting to startle anyone or appear threatening when our destination was so close. The only sounds were the gentle footfalls and whinnies of our horses, the flags above the fortress walls snapping in the wind, and the gulls on the beaches beyond.

Swaying in the saddle and staring at Torvik's massive walls, I ran my fingers through Mjölnir's thick black-and-white mane for comfort.

Vertically stacked logs angled inwards supported a parapet at least twenty feet above the ground. Everything was rounded, circling the cliffs to the north and the sea beyond. I chewed my cheek, unease rippling through me as I saw the archers on the wooden ramparts, monitoring us as clearly as the farmers in the field. While the Erikssons village had provided plenty of blatant reminders I'd landed in the medieval era, the sight of the defensive stronghold in front of us left no doubt.

An imminent reality I had been doing my best to avoid.

The horse's coarse hair raked over my palm with each mindless pass I made over his neck, glancing out over the fields to take in the neat rows of crops villagers tended and planted. A woman stood with a child between her legs, hand raised over her eyes as she watched us pass, a woven basket on her hip. A man stilled his horse, what looked like some sort of wheeled plow turning over fresh earth in the spring sun. No one approached, but the hardened looks on their faces screamed *Viking*.

Magnus lifted a hand as we passed, waving in the woman's direction, and she hugged her child tighter to her chest. It was understandable, seeing as he was a hulking imposition covered in tattoos, but so was the man pulling the plow next to her.

Friendly or not, Magnus was terrifying to look at. He didn't touch any of his weapons, but his fingers splayed open, close to the dagger sheathed on his belt, just as wary as the villagers we passed.

"Should we be worried?" I asked him, my voice low. My pendant warmed against my chest, the black stone shining with a green glow from within as a shadow passed in the clouds above. Hadriel was here somewhere but stayed out of sight. Not the worst idea since a giant dragon flying with us didn't scream *peace*.

Magnus hummed noncommittally. "Asmund was an ally of my father's, and they're expecting us. Domari and the other traders have been to Torvik before. From what I know, they're a peaceful clan, focused more on trading. But never underestimate a Viking. We all learn a hundred ways to kill a man by our third winter."

I scrunched my nose, trying not to let worry take root. "I should put your shitty words of inspiration on a corporate poster. Maybe over a picture of a kitten."

"At least make it a bear or a wolf, or something terrifying." Mischief lit his eyes as he reached a hand down to pet Thor walking at his side. "They may be traders, but they're just as cutthroat as the rest of us. This is the last outpost before most trading voyages make way to Constantinople. The Birgerssons are the wealthiest clan on the coast. You don't get rich by being generous, Shelbie. Greed drives everything here."

His steps quickened as we neared, my horse following his lead. Astrid, Magnus's pregnant wife, was beyond those walls, as were the children they'd taken in, his mother, and the rest of their village.

"Hold," Domari called from up ahead.

Our procession stopped. Everyone shifted from foot to foot, uneasiness wafting through the group as we waited a hundred yards from the gates.

With a look over his shoulder, Domari waved me forward. Björn, Yrsa, and the other Erikssons parted, making room for me to walk through the center of our party. I nudged my heels into Mjölnir's sides, and the horse answered, clopping his way to the front of the line.

The distance was short, not long enough to steady my racing heart. The enormity of everything ahead of us sat like a crushing weight on my chest and grew heavier with each step. I gripped the reins in my right hand, my fingernails digging into the leather and my eyes darting to the side.

Not only did our people stare at me, but *everyone* here was. My pendant glowed brighter, casting a green glow against my chest with the growing power that meant Hadriel hid just above the clouds in case I needed him.

I'm here, my dragon rasped in my head, that same smoky presence I'd been without for the past few days. *I'm always here, my Promised.*

I let out a choked breath, realizing how different things were compared to only a few months ago when I was alone on the coast of Sweden. The sky darkened, and I glanced at the clouds, searching him out.

How had I come to depend on him, on these people so quickly? My life had been so solitary, Thor the only one dependent on me.

Now, they *all* depended on me.

I shifted uncomfortably, offering a small smile as I fiddled with the stone around my neck, trying to think of anything other than the crushing pressure I felt. These people were counting on me, on this legendary power of the Promised, to protect them. But how could I offer protection when I was completely clueless about how to do any of this? Hell, I didn't even know what kind of powers I was supposed to have aside from Seeing visions the Norns gave me and accidentally healing people after battle.

You are not alone, Hadriel answered my unspoken thoughts, the way only he could.

A chuff had me looking down, spying my dog right at Mjölnir's side. Like the dragon concealed in the clouds, Thor never left my side, nor did Magnus only steps away. Domari's chocolate eyes were on me, radiating the steady comfort they always did.

Despite my anxiety about what was to come, I held my

head high as I rode the rest of the distance to him. Between the brooding expression on Magnus's face, my pendant now glowing bright green against my shadowy cloak, and the two black dogs who walked on either side of me, we were an imposing sight.

Domari's dark gaze swept over me as he grabbed Mjölnir's reins when I neared, holding the horse in place to his right as we approached the gates. Magnus stood to my other side; the briny breeze thick with tension.

Guards stood atop the wall above the now closed gate. Archers pointed their weapons at us, but neither of my men flinched, so I hooked my fingers in the saddle leather, hiding my trembling hands.

"Greetings," Domari called, his deep voice ringing out. He raised his free hand, showing he held nothing. Mjölnir tossed his mane, stomping a hoof as he moved against Domari's hold on his reins. "We are the Eriksson clan, here to rejoin with our women and children and prepare for battle alongside Asmund. We bear no arms against your people. Should any harm come to you from our hands, may Thor strike us down."

None of the soldiers facing us moved, and I held my breath, unsure of what to expect. History hadn't painted Vikings in a kind light, and I was out of my depth to understand the mechanics behind a political alliance like this. With how closely knit the Erikssons were, I knew they wouldn't have entrusted their women and children to just anyone. But I'd also never stood in front of a medieval fortress with arrows pointed at me.

A large man appeared atop the wall, his dark hair and

beard hanging down below his collarbone. Like Domari, he wore a black tunic over brown pants, cinched at the waist with a heavy leather belt, a sword swinging at his side. Even from a distance, it was easy to see that he was a warrior, his hulking frame telling me he knew how to wield the weapon he carried.

Domari kept his hand in the air, tilting his chin up. "Asmund Birgersson, friend of Gunnar Eriksson," he called, "I am Domari Njallson, returned *Akolouthos* and captain of the Varangian Guard, and cousin to the Erikssons. I've come for my people."

Asmund opened his mouth right as the gate below him creaked, pushed open enough for a tiny body to slip through. A child, with braids matching Domari's golden-brown hair, sprinted past the guards, headed for Domari. My breath caught when the girl threw herself into him, wrapping her arms around his legs. Domari dropped his hands from the air, gripping the back of her head as he clung to her. My heart raced as I looked back up at Asmund, unsure how he would react to this new development. But he only shook his head with a small smile.

Domari must have seen the change too because he dropped onto his heels, his face level with the little girl as he held her by the shoulders. "How many times have you been told to stay with your family, Revna?"

"*You're* my family," Gunnar's daughter shot back, her eyes mere slits in her face. Soft laughter filtered in from both behind us and the parapet above, and I couldn't help but join them.

Domari grinned, brushing the hair that had escaped her

braids off her forehead. He kissed her brow, holding her to his chest before letting her go.

"I knew you'd come." Her little lip turned up in a smirk I'd seen on Domari hundreds of times. She scanned the crowd, her gaze sliding over me to Magnus and the other familiar clansmen before landing on Domari again. "Mama and Papa?"

My heart hurt for Domari as he held Revna's face, thumb rubbing across her jaw. "They're not with us, but I'm going to bring them back."

Revna nodded, her brow furrowing before a wash of calm swept over her. My cheeks burned, a tear dripping down my cheek as the young girl acted as tough as her mother.

Just thinking of Signe had my heart squeezing, remembering the sight of her fighting to free Gunnar. Even flying in on Hadriel's back hadn't been enough to spare them from Draugr's reach, and their absence was a gaping hole in everyone's hearts.

"It seems Revna has given you a far warmer welcome than I'd planned," Asmund said from where he now stood between the open gates. Several guards stood behind him, not touching their weapons, but the threat was clear. They were *friendly*, not friends.

Domari straightened, his hand sliding to Revna's, and my knee bounced in the stirrups.

With a shake of his head, Asmund clapped, then held his hands aloft. "Come! Rejoin your people. Tonight, we feast in honor of Frey. Let us celebrate those who are still with us, and a hope for the future."

Relief swept through me as Domari nodded, holding his free hand outstretched to me. I took it, sliding off Mjölnir's back and handing his reins to Thorsten. Together we walked toward the gates swinging open in front of us.

"Stay with me." Domari kissed my temple, holding me to his side. "Keep your pendant out, unless I say otherwise. I don't like the way they're staring at you."

I mumbled an assent, feeling the warmth of the stone on my chest.

A riot of noise met us once we passed the gates, families scurrying to greet each other. Magnus rushed by me, racing to Astrid and pulling her into his arms. His fingers laced through her long platinum blonde hair. She let out a choked sob, her pregnant belly shaking with the tears streaming down her face. A small boy perched on her hip and a girl about Revna's age held her leg, peering out from behind Astrid's skirts. Magnus squished the toddler between them and kissed his wife.

"*Astin min,*" he said over and over between kisses, hugging her and the little boy she carried on her hip. "I missed you so much." When he pulled back, tears shone in his eyes. Astrid smiled up at him, cupping his cheek until Magnus reached for the little boy she carried, plucking him from Astrid's hold.

"And you too, Bo. Did you grow already, my big, strong boy?" He lifted Bo's arm, inspecting his muscles, and I chuckled. Magnus had talked nonstop about the orphan children he and Astrid had taken in, but I'd yet to meet them.

Bo tucked his head into Magnus's shoulder, a content

smile on his cherub face. Copper curls peeked out from behind Astrid's skirts, little fingers gripping the fabric. A little girl stared up at Magnus until he squatted down, Bo on his lap.

"Did you think I forgot you, my Birgitta?" Magnus grinned. I squeezed Domari's hand tighter, unable to look away. While she didn't rush into his hold as Bo had, her tentative smile grew until Magnus scooped her up in his arms, too.

The sight reminded me so much of my brother and how he often carried his young daughters. My shoulders slumped, feeling the loss of everything I'd given up to be here. But one look around the street, at the families hugging each other as they walked down the dirt roads of Torvik, arm in arm, was enough of a reminder that I'd done the right thing.

This is where you belong, Hadriel said, and I knew it. I couldn't leave these people when they needed me most, no matter how terrified I was of everything to come.

Domari scooped Revna up and settled her on his shoulders, her delighted shriek pulling me from my somber thoughts.

"Can you see my dragon from all the way up there?" I asked, offering her a smile. If a five-year-old could shove her worries aside and carry on, then so could I.

She craned her neck to the sky, putting a hand over her eyes as she searched the clouds, then shook her head. "Not today, but I saw him when we traveled. Black and gold, just like Uncle Magnus's stories."

I nodded, my smile becoming more genuine. "That's right. He's pretty, isn't he?"

She grinned as an annoyed grumble rolled through my mental connection to Hadriel.

"Shelbie." Revna gripped Domari's hair like a saddle horn, tugging his topknot left and right. "I remember you."

"I remember you, too, Revna. The bravest little girl I've ever met."

Her shoulders straightened with the compliment, like I hoped they would. "Domari missed you after you left," she said as we followed Astrid and Magnus into town. "Mama said that was why he was so sad. That he had to go find you."

My cheeks warmed from her simplistic summary of everything Domari and I had gone through the past few months. Missing him felt like an understatement; too small of a word to describe how lost I'd been once I'd returned to my time.

I glanced out over the town while I tried to gather my thoughts for a response. Log buildings with thatched roofs lined both sides of the street, much smaller than the Eriksson's longhouses had been. Carvings of animals adorned some doors, others had antlers, but painted runes covered everything, mimicking the Eriksson's pre-battle body paint.

Merchants posed outside booths with wares ranging from pottery to fish, jewelry to pelts, clothing to weapons. One even had barrels of spices and herbs, the scents of dill and parsley mixing with more exotic saffron and peppers. Warmth radiated from a blacksmith's stall, weapons hanging on racks facing the street as a short man slammed a hammer down on an anvil in a steady pattern.

Voices rang out loud over the crowd, calling for attention from the passing party, pausing only when their eyes caught on us. The scents and sounds of the seaside market were almost overwhelming in their intensity after days of traveling over barren and rocky land. Everything was cleaner and more organized than I'd anticipated, but that seemed to be the way of all things Viking.

Here, everything was simpler. The roles were clear — protect your family and clan at all costs. The challenge was *survival*; storm, famine, or Viking invasion. Gone were my worries about societal expectations of a 30-something unmarried, childless dog-lady. There were no performance reviews, no mindless jobs to pay the bills, no lonely nights spent imagining a different life for myself.

There was only life or death.

As startling a realization as that was, this world, this time, felt right to me in a way I'd never experienced before. I was needed. I was wanted. I was loved.

And wasn't that all I'd ever wanted?

Squeezing Domari's arm, I leaned my head on his shoulder, savoring the comforting pine and musk scent he always had. "I missed him too. I missed all of you."

"She's back now, though. We both are." Domari's gaze swung over the gathered crowd, tugging on Revna's pant leg. "Where are your brothers and Frida?"

"Erik was napping" — Revna scrunched her nose at the mention of her baby brother — "and Ulf was with Yvar on the beach earlier. I left them when I heard the bell."

Astrid turned in our direction, frowning at Revna. "How many times have we told you not to leave the others? You cannot charge into battle by yourself. Slipping through the gates like that was dangerous, girl, and you know it."

Revna's smile dropped, her fierce expression every bit a tribute to her fiery mother, and I bit back my smile at the stare down. Astrid, to her credit, gave back every bit of the attitude the five-year-old dished out. I was surprised sweet Astrid had that mettle in her, but maybe all Viking women did.

Domari reached up and tugged on Revna's hand until her steely gaze swung down to the top of his head and away from Astrid. "She's right." He looked up at her, arching a brow. "Your mama and papa would have told you the same, and you know it."

Revna pulled her hand out of Domari's and crossed her arms, staring off into the crowd from her perch.

"That child." Asmund laughed as he clapped a hand on Domari's shoulder and squeezed. He shook his head, but a smile played on his lips as he walked at our side. "Even if she didn't have Signe's face, I'd know she was hers anywhere."

I chuckled, thinking back over the time I'd spent with their family last fall, remembering how fiery the little girl was even then.

"Thank you for watching out for my people," Domari said, his arm outstretched. Asmund returned the gesture, each of them gripping the other's arm just below the elbow.

Asmund bowed his head in respect. "It has been my pleasure. I know the Erikssons would have done the same."

Domari dropped his hand, and Asmund swung toward me, his eyes pausing on the pendant around my neck. "And who might you be?"

"Mine." Yrsa stepped to my side, her palm sliding into mine, grey-streaked hair flowing down her back. Our dresses swished with each step across the packed dirt paths, the cool breeze blowing in from the ocean. I had seen little of her after we'd left camp yesterday, but she and Björn had stayed with the woman they'd rescued from Draugr's men who'd left as soon as we reached the city walls. "Asmund, meet Shelbie Björnsdóttir. Domari's heart sworn. The last of the Promised, tied to Hadriel."

I blinked in surprise at her words. Yrsa laid claim to me three times over — hers, Domari's, and Hadriel's. I squeezed her hand in silent thanks, hoping she understood just how much it meant to me in the face of whatever we found here.

Asmund nodded, his gaze swinging between Yrsa and Domari, then to the sky overhead, but Hadriel remained absent.

"I've heard of you from your people, Shelbie Björnsdóttir," he said, his tone holding a hint of laughter I wasn't sure how to interpret. "Of the Norns speaking of your arrival, and passage through the realms. Even a black dragon watching over your children's passage, they attest to you. Tales of the fearsome Hadriel torching through the snow to hurry their passage, leaving food for them when he could... I hardly know what to believe. Only the tales of children and weary travelers, yes?"

His laugh boomed, and several of his men on the

surrounding streets chuckled with him. Yrsa's grip tightened on mine, and my spine snapped straight at his reaction. The Erikssons had all welcomed me with open arms, believing in the power of the Promised, but they'd seen me with Hadriel. They'd heard the Norns at the Winter Nights festival. They'd seen the power I could wield, if I could figure out how to do it again.

"Do not doubt her." Domari's voice dropped to a low growl, his hand outstretched. He placed himself between me and Asmund. "Do not doubt the power the gods have gifted her. Do not doubt everything that is coming our way, Asmund. You will be on the losing end of this story if you make an enemy of me."

Asmund's laughter died, any sign of his earlier pleasantries gone. A chill raced down my spine, and I glanced around the street. So many eyes focused on us. Hands rested on weapons, ready for a battle as Domari and Asmund stared each other down.

My Promised, Hadriel's voice rasped in my head before he let out a bloodcurdling screech. Birds scattered from the nearby trees, and screams ripped through the streets as people ducked for cover, searching the skies for the source of the sound that was so unmistakably *other*.

A warm rush of power spread from my head to my toes, a phantom wind lifting my cloak and hair from my nape as energy thrummed under my skin. The stone at my neck glowed the brightest green, casting a blinding light over the crowd. Shocked gasps came from those closest to me, and I fought the desire to shove the pendant beneath my dress, hiding everything that made me different.

Apparently, Hadriel didn't feel the same. If Asmund needed confirmation of who I was — *what* I was — then Hadriel was going to give it to him, whether I wanted that attention or not.

Asmund stepped back, shielding his eyes as he looked at the sky, then back at my pendant. A mixture of apprehension and fear washed across his face before he steeled his expression, settling into a look of indifference.

Not sure you're sending the right message there, bud, I sent to Hadriel as he screeched again.

Any who doubt you, doubt me. Fury poured through our mental connection; his voice thick with anger. *Trust no one.*

Great, I answered, reaching for Domari's hand as I fought the urge to flee from every watchful eye. His fingers laced through mine in a steady grip while villagers whispered to each other, their focus flicking from the sky to me and back. *Just what I needed to hear.*

"Come!" Asmund held his hands out, urging us into the village beyond, but the open welcome his words held before was now clouded with hesitancy.

Yrsa squeezed my hand one more time before she dropped it, heading back to where Björn remained with the rest of their family. A smile peeked out behind the grey beard hanging down to the older man's belly, and he offered me a brief nod of encouragement.

Domari didn't let go of me as he moved to the front of the group, leading his people into the village beyond.

Thor and Freki paced at my side, the former bored and ready for a nap, the latter's tongue hanging out the side of his mouth as his tail wagged. I ran my fingers through

Thor's coat, scratching behind his ears and forcing a smile at the villagers we passed.

Their eyes tracked our movements, a mixture of curiosity and fear I felt deep in my bones.

"You sure we're safe here?" I whispered to Domari.

He grunted a non-answer, and Hadriel mirrored his sentiments.

Trust no one.

4

SHELBIE

The closer we got to the sea, rows of small huts lined the streets with thatched roofs all alike in shape and size. The waves crashed against the shore in a steady beat. The wind was harsher here, seeping through my layers. Domari's hand never left mine as his head swiveled, a deep-set frown painted on his face.

"Up here," Astrid said, a hand on her belly as she pointed to the left. I shivered, huddling closer to Domari. "They've put us in this row of huts. It will be crowded, but warm."

He grunted, so I smiled for us, tugging on his arm. "This is great."

The door of the closest hut swung open. Frida walked forward with a baby on her hip and Revna's twin, Ulf, at her heels. Domari's aunt's eyes lit with delight. She threw an arm in the air with a cry. Magnus set Bo down then rushed into her hold, lifting her and the baby off the ground.

"Put me down." She laughed, swatting at Magnus's shoulder. He dropped his mother back to her feet, fixed her greying hair he'd mussed, then took little Erik from her hold to kiss him.

Frida scanned the rest of the Erikssons that moved around us. "Where is your brother? And Signe?"

My breath caught in my throat. Magnus held Erik tighter, a beat of silence passing. With each second, loaded and full of pain, Frida's smile fell.

"They're together." Domari cleared his throat, turning to look back over the hills we'd traversed to get here. "With Draugr."

Frida clutched at her dress over her heart, blinking rapidly as tears shimmered on the rims of her eyes. She ran a hand over Ulf's hair, as blond as his father. He hugged her leg, hair wild as he looked up at Revna, still sitting on Domari's shoulders.

"He's going to bring them back." Revna squirmed in Domari's grip. He dropped my hand to hang on to her, and I gripped my pendant. For as many visions as I'd had, why couldn't I learn to direct them, to see something useful? Like a looking glass, peeking in on our friends to ensure their safety.

My fingers tightened over the stone as overwhelming grief gripped me for all Signe had left behind to save her husband. These children had lost their mother and father in one fell swoop, and I was devastated and furious in turns.

Erik was tiny in Magnus's arms, his blond hair shining almost red in the setting sunlight. His head bobbed as he turned to look at us, piercing blue eyes just like Gunnar's in his little face.

"Hi baby." I ran my hand across his fuzzy hair, savoring the soft touch. He grinned a little gummy smile, and I couldn't help but match it. Already, he looked so much like Gunnar it was startling.

Tears gathered in my eyes, but I sniffed them back. This family had lost so much. Had gone through such hardship. I couldn't be the one to break.

Domari pulled Revna from his shoulders, setting her on the ground. In an instant, she was gone, running through the streets toward the beach with Ulf and Freki chasing her. Thor, of course, stayed right at my side with a *harrumph*.

"They've been excited for tonight, even before you arrived," Frida said, hands brushing over her skirts. Her smile didn't match her eyes, turned down and full of grief, but she waved us forward. "What a blessed day for the *Blot*. The gods are surely with us."

Magnus handed baby Erik to me unceremoniously, then picked Bo back up. I jerked back, staring down at the little boy.

Domari wrapped a hand around my waist. "Frida, you remember Shelbie."

"Of course, I do." She waved a hand through the air, dismissing him. "We've been waiting for you to arrive. Yrsa never lost hope you'd return. I shall give thanks to Frey for bringing you back."

Erik shifted in my arms, and I adjusted my hold on the baby, making sure I had a hand behind his back. "You're a wiggly little guy, aren't you?"

"Ready to move, that one." Frida chuckled, then grabbed the fabric of her skirts in one hand and ushered us down the street.

The sun had dipped behind the fortress walls as we approached the shore, torches hanging next to doorways lighting our way. Waves, gulls, and drums beat a steady tune, music drifting through the air painting a merry tune of celebration.

My boots sank into the white, glistening sand as I took in the sight. What had to be close to a hundred people gathered around several bonfires, dancing and singing as they tossed offerings into the flames. Stars twinkled overhead, filling every available space in the dark sky as the moon glowed golden, its rays highlighting the rippling waves on the sea.

I clutched at my cloak, pulling it tighter around my shoulders to fend off the biting wind, but no one here seemed bothered by it. Women walked by, placing greenery crowns on the heads of the women and children they passed. Astrid took one for herself, then put one on each of the children before turning to me, hands outstretched with one more.

"The *Blot* is a sacrifice to the gods, honoring them as spring comes," Domari explained, his breath caressing my neck as he leaned in close. His hand rubbed across my low back, and I silently thanked him for the explanation.

My eyes blew wide, looking around at my friends, then the fires. "Sacrifice?"

Magnus waggled his brows, firelight dancing in his eyes. "Ready for your first kill, Shelbie?"

My steps faltered, and I gripped Erik to my chest. Domari's hand shot out, catching my elbow to keep me from falling. Magnus tossed his head back in a laugh.

"Relax." Domari chuckled with his cousin. "The Birgerssons are as civilized as Vikings come. No one is getting sacrificed tonight."

Revna came racing toward us, eyes alight as she pointed behind her toward a large fire near the docks. "They just slaughtered a pig! He was *huge!* Stabbed him right in the belly as they caught the blood in a bowl" — she gesticulated wildly, arms flailing as she scowled, recreating the unnecessary visual — "then threw him in the fire. I even got a rune." She pointed at her forehead with pride, where a pinkish liquid was painted in a rune of protection on her brow.

I frowned, turning my head away as bile rose in my throat. "Oh, gods. Tell me that's not blood. Now I'm realizing you said it's called the *Blot*. You're literally saying blood, aren't you?"

Astrid's hip bumped mine, soft laughter coming from her as she placed the crown on my head. "Stay with me. We'll avoid the blessings together. No one would dare challenge a pregnant woman as we honor Frey."

Domari kissed my temple, his chest shaking in laughter. "You don't have to do anything you don't want to."

"No blood, thanks." I gagged, clutching Erik to my chest. He squirmed in my hold, mouth open as he wriggled across my chest. Frida held her hands out for him, and I passed the baby back.

"Go. Enjoy. Tonight, we celebrate your return." She patted Domari's arm and whatever joy he'd held on to at my reaction disappeared, that same heaviness settling back on his shoulders. "Tomorrow is a new day."

"I need ale," Magnus said, slapping his hard stomach. "And food if I'm to have enough stamina to appreciate Astrid properly and do Frey justice tonight. Come, wife."

Astrid blushed, and I wrinkled my nose, looking up at Domari. "Did he just talk about banging his wife in front of his mom?"

"My son never learned to hold his tongue," Frida said with a shake of her head. "Especially not tonight."

Domari held his hand out for mine, and I took it, letting him lead me through the crowds. "Keep your pendant hidden under your cloak, for now."

I stared at his broad shoulders, noticing the tension he carried there, and wariness set in. Scanning the crowds, I looked for any signs of Asmund or the warriors he'd walked with, but he'd left us when we found Frida.

"Tell me about the *Blot*." I moved closer to Domari's side so we could talk over the chanting and drums. Thor walked at my heels; his resting bitch face out in full force as the gargantuan dog kept everyone else at bay. "Why did Frida say, especially tonight? What's special here?"

He accepted drinking horns from a woman handing them out, passing me one then taking a large sip. I took a much smaller one, pleasantly surprised to find it was honeyed mead and not ale. With a tip of his head, Domari pointed toward the three largest fires on either side of the wide dock extending out into the sea. A pig roasted over the one closest to us, the smoke holding a savory note as it combined with the salty sea air. Two men stood on either end of the spit roast, turning it at intervals, leading a lively chant as Asmund and two women stood by his side, handing out meat to passersby.

"They honor Frey with the boar." Domari put his arm over my shoulder, holding me to his chest as Asmund's gaze settled on us from a distance. "The god of peace, prosperity, and good harvest. Asmund provides the meal for the entire clan tonight as a show of his great wealth and ability to lead his people."

"Are you worried about him?" I asked, the hair rising on my arms the longer Asmund stared in our direction. He chatted with those around him, but that steely gaze never strayed.

"Not tonight." Domari kissed the side of my head, then turned us to the next fire. "Tonight is for show. It's a power play, a reminder of how prosperous the Birgerssons are under his rule, and a reminder to those who wish to take his place."

I leaned into his hold, not sure I understood the political machinations of the time, but trusted Domari implicitly.

The next fire was different. Here, the townsfolk held hands, circling the flames and singing a happy tune as they tossed food items into the fire. Most had the same, red-tinged marks as Revna painted on their foreheads showcasing different runes. Firelight glinted off the gold jewelry both men and women wore, as if they'd put on everything they owned. "Offerings to Frey. We feed him, so he feeds us."

Domari twisted toward the largest fire on our right, crackling as it licked high into the cloudy night sky. Since there was no way the boar on the first fire had just been killed like Revna said, I refused to look at why this fire was different. His hands slid to my waist, holding me in front of him as he urged us closer to the flames. Here, the atmosphere felt charged.

A woman stood closest to the fire, scantily clad despite the chill breeze. A single strip of thin gold fabric covered her breasts, with two strips hanging from her waist to cover her front and back. Her torso and arms were covered in runes, and dark paint covered her brow, dripping down over her eyes and onto her cheeks. Long blonde hair hung down over her shoulders, tied in dozens of braids that made her look both fearsome and undeniably gorgeous.

Unlike the other bonfires, no one here sang but her, the steady beat of a drum driving her hips from side to side, her arms moving in a graceful dance with each throaty note she sang. Her eyes were closed, chin tilted toward the dark clouds above as a wordless tune floated through the air like a current.

I stared raptly, unable to look away from the mysterious woman, firelight dancing across her dewy skin as she neared the fire. Her arms moved fluidly in a pattern, over and over, as the smoke moved in the direction she guided it.

"She's drawing runes," I whispered, my eyes watching the steady movement of her hands.

Domari's chin rested on my head, his hands circling my

waist. "She's calling for Frey to join us. To bless our gathering. To answer our pleas."

"Does that work?" I asked him, my voice as low as I could manage.

"Some believe it does. She's asking for calm seas and good weather for their crops, hoping for a sign they will answer our call. Magic is everywhere in these lands, the ties to the gods strong despite the changing times."

As if she were listening, the woman's hands arched high into the sky, then pushed out toward the sea, spreading her fingers wide, her musical tone hitting a crescendo.

I stared out at the sea, waves crashing over the rocky cliffs and lapping against the dock, wondering if magic was as simple as that.

Ask, Hadriel's voice echoed in my head, the onyx stone heating against my skin as I thought through what I'd even ask the gods for. If I even believed in such a thing.

Anxiety warred in me, worry for everything that was to come nearly dragging me out to sea like the rising tide. More than anything, I wanted a sign that we'd make it to the other side of this. That my friends were okay and alive. Something to guide my way.

The woman's voice rose, growing louder as she lifted her hands toward the sky, then pushed upwards. I followed the movement and gasped as the clouds overhead disappeared, gone as if they'd never been.

In their stead was a shimmering night sky full of stars. They twinkled in the dark fabric of the night. A cry rose out over the crowd, people cheering and clapping each other on the back.

"They answer us!" they shouted, knocking together their ale horns as the celebratory air rose to a new height.

I blinked, trying to understand what had just happened, searching the skies for any hint of Hadriel.

"They answer *you*," a woman said, and I dropped my chin back down to look at the crowd. The woman near the fire pointed at me, her pale blue, almost white, eyes now open, settled on me. "You are the gods' chosen. The one they've been waiting for. The one who will see us to our very end."

Domari's hands tightened around my waist, holding my back to his front protectively. My breaths came rapidly as the stares of everyone around us settled on me. The need to run slammed so hard against my rib cage, I blinked against the smoke, looking for anyone I recognized in the crowd.

Magnus stood to the side with Astrid and the children, but seemed to see my pleading stare the moment my gaze found him.

"To Frey!" he boomed, holding his ale high, and some of the crowd turned toward him in answer. "May he make both our crops and women bountiful!"

Domari's beard scraped across my nape, the feeling holding me in the here and now.

"To Thor!" he yelled again, ale splashing over the sides as more people turned away from me. "May the god of the people lead us into battle!"

Louder cheers rose this time, everyone but the woman turning away from me. Her steady gaze never left me, the fire crackling in the wind casting a glow around her.

"To Odin!" Magnus boomed, loving the attention. "May he prepare the halls of Valhalla for those most worthy!"

A chill ran down my spine, the longer she stared at me, the onyx stone at my throat almost unbearably warm.

"And to Freya," she said, her voice carrying over the noise of the crowd like she'd whispered it in my ear. "For the goddess of war rides with us, and the dragon answers her call."

5

SIGNE

A low hum buzzed in her ears, the ringing drowning out the sound of everything around her. Even her eyes refused to focus, held captive by the headache that had plagued her for days. Her body felt heavy, disconnected and adrift from her mind. Moving of its own volition.

The constant pressure felt like a hand holding her under water for too long. Everything was just out of reach, just above the surface she couldn't break through.

"Signe," a deep male voice said behind her.

Turning toward the voice, she tried to blink away the fog that wouldn't clear and staggered. A hand clutched just above her elbow, holding her upright. The tight, almost painful grip on her arm told her he was speaking to her. Even the name he spoke seemed wrong. The voice she recognized. It pulled at some deep-seated memory, but she couldn't pull free of the riptide holding her down and away from her memories.

Here, in this void in her mind, she knew nothing. Felt nothing. Was nothing.

"Fight it, Signe," the voice said again, hand gripping tighter.

She tilted her head back, breathing deep. Smoke wafted through the air, the scent of burning oil, ale, and blood reaching her before her vision cleared.

With a gasp, she broke the surface in her mind, blinking against the brightness around her. Her head swung to the side, taking in their location. They were in a hall, the bottom floor where she stood empty save for men lingering around the edges, drinking ale from horns as they pointed in her direction. Wooden beams supported the walkway above, open to the room below. Torches hung on both floors, casting a glow on the dark, timber-lined walls.

She knew this place but couldn't remember *why* she knew.

Sound returned next, muted but enough for her to hear the laughter of the many men here, then the booming voice above her on the second floor. She squinted against the smoky haze of the room as a large man with reddish-blond hair like her own held an ale high in the air.

"Demons!" he called.

Signe fought back against the shiver that ran down her spine at the grating sound of his voice. Her mind raced, trying to connect dots to shed awareness on where she was, or why she was here, but nothing came.

The men in the room called in answer, ale splashing out of their raised horns, but Signe couldn't look away from him.

She *knew* him.

Raising a hand, she rubbed at her temple, trying to clear away the never ending fog that held her captive in her own body.

"... successful," he said, and Signe looked up at the man, realizing he'd been speaking to the crowd the whole time.

"Signe," the man at her back's voice whispered again, more urgent as he shook her.

Signe ripped her arm free of his grip, spinning on him as she bared her teeth in a savage snarl. She was feral, an animal in human skin, all sense of humanity lost as the tide pulled at her feet, trying to pull her back into the depths of her mind.

Some part of her knew he should be afraid of her, no matter how lost to the haze she was. But he showed no fear, didn't back away, didn't reach for the sword hanging from his belt, nor the spear sheathed on his back.

Emerald eyes met hers framed in a face that showed his age, grey streaking his dark hair at the temples. He was easily twice her size, but something about him made Signe realize he posed no threat to her.

"Fight it, Signe," he said, his chin rising as he tilted his head toward the balcony above them. "Fight through it."

She snapped her teeth, raging against the confusion holding her down. Something tugged at the back of her mind with urgency, and the crowd around her exploded in cheers. She turned away from the green-eyed man as frustration warred in her, looking back at the men all staring at her.

Her hands clenched at her sides, teeth grinding together

as she searched for *something*, some clue as to what was going on. Everyone around her shifted on their feet, the tension in the room rising until it felt the same as the buzzing in her mind.

Across the hall, a giant of a man shouted and punched the air, then ducked under the platforms that made up the viewing deck above. His thick black hair and beard draped down over his bare chest. Everything about him screamed *warrior*, right down to the leather pants and boots, a wide brown belt cinching the waist, like most of the men in the room. Two smaller axes hung from sheaths on the belt, but the corded muscles rippling through the man's chest and arms were enough to tell Signe that this man was a weapon in his own right.

The men on the viewing deck above grew louder as he stopped in the center of the room, sword hanging loosely in his grip. Signe straightened, the buzzing in her head fading when his dark eyes trained on her. He snarled, baring his brown, rotted teeth.

Signe's body hummed in acknowledgment of the threat he posed, her hands opening and closing on air as if she held a weapon she could wield against him.

"Oathbreaker," the man above called, his eyes trained in her direction. Her brow furrowed, the moniker sounding familiar. She looked over her shoulder at the green-eyed man behind her, who nodded.

"Fight it, Signe," the green-eyed man said again, his voice barely above a whisper meant only for her. With a shove between her shoulder blades, he pushed her toward the giant and into the center of the room.

Someone else might have retreated in fear, done anything to escape the imminent danger. But Signe wasn't just *someone*.

Her muscles clenched and she lowered her stance on instinct alone, stepping toward the man. The giant dragged the tip of his sword in the dirt floor, leaving a circle that encompassed most of the empty space, his eyes never leaving her face.

"A Valkyrie." He spat at her feet, his face twisted in disgust as he closed the circle and turned to face her. "Odin would never choose a woman as weak as you. I'll send you to Valhalla myself, where you'll perish every night as you will at my sword."

Her mind snagged on the word *Valkyrie*, but the man in front of her was too much a threat to allow her to concentrate on it.

With a shout, he rushed toward her, sword extended as if to run her through. Signe's body jerked, flying away from his reach as her hands stretched to the side. Adrenaline coursed through her body, and she moved in a circle around him. With each beat of her heart, the fog that had held her under receded, leaving her feeling clear-headed and singly focused.

Here, in battle, she knew exactly who she was.

Signe.

Victory, her father had named her.

Wild and untamed, from her first breath.

Signe dropped to a crouch, one hand on the dirt beneath her. She snarled in return, copper braid whipping against her face as she twisted her head to the side.

"Just because you can move quickly doesn't make you a Valkyrie. You're nothing but a whore, not worth your father's name," he growled.

The words meant nothing to her. Nothing mattered but the way her body buzzed, a storm raging beneath her skin threatening to break free.

Her free hand lifted, fingertips burning as she pointed at Vermund, her memory recalling the green-eyed man's name.

The giant moved toward her again, but now it was as if he moved in slow motion. His lumbered gait was slow and uneven as he lifted his sword to strike.

Signe breathed deep; her body posed to react again as he charged. She rolled to the side, easily dodging the blade that came down where she'd just been, which only frustrated the giant more.

He shouted as he swung again, and again, each attack more uncontrolled than the last. She could feel the eyes of everyone the room, the voices rising in volume as excitement built. It was a show they wanted, to see her unleashed.

Her body moved swiftly out of his reach, taunting him with each miss. A heady rush filled her as she smiled up at the man, feeling more alive than she had in days.

"Is that all you've got?" she called, her voice loud enough for the men leaning over the rails above them to hear.

They laughed, and the giant raged, veins popping out on his neck. He threw the sword to the side and pulled the axes from his belt, one in each hand. He moved toward her, blades swinging toward her in a wide arc.

A laugh bubbled free from her, and she flipped through the air, soaring out of his reach and behind his back.

He spun, dirt flying from his boots grinding into the floor beneath.

The burning in Signe's hand turned to an outright flame, searing her from within as she rose from the crouch she'd landed in. Shoving her shaking hand away from her, a scream erupted from her mouth, sounding foreign to her own ears.

Instantly, the spear she'd seen on Vermund's back flew directly into her outstretched hand. She spun, whipping the weapon through the air in a whirl as she moved toward the giant, momentarily stunned by what she'd just done.

The heckling from above stuttered, and Signe smirked, adjusting her grip on the wooden shaft. Vermund's arms were crossed over his broad chest, his expression devoid of the shock Signe found on everyone else around her. Everyone except the man who'd spoken earlier. He leaned over the railing above, his grin showing smug satisfaction.

The roar at her side drew Signe's attention back down. Quickly, she held the spear up across her chest, blocking the axes swinging down. The giant loomed over her, putrid breath blowing in her face as she set both hands on the shaft, shoving hard against the man towering over her. A blast of strength shot through her body, jarring the giant as he was pushed back. His dark eyes expanded in shock, and Signe tilted her head back on a laugh that silenced the crowd around her.

"A Valkyrie, you say?" She stood to her full height. She spun the spear in one hand lazily, then rested the butt of the weapon on the dirt floor. "Does that mean I get to decide your Fate?"

The giant charged forward again, axes swinging with more accuracy this time, but Signe batted them to the side with the spear, moving the weapon as if it were an extension of her own body. He flew back, as if hit with a battering ram instead of a wooden spear, his back cracking against a wooden support beam. The floor above them shook, and any lingering chatter in the hall came to a screeching halt.

"A Viking of your stature and brutality seems an easy fit for Valhalla, upon first inspection." She spun the spear again, twirling it in her fingers before passing it to the other hand in a seamless motion. The sarcasm in her voice was a taunt as clear as if she'd waved her hand in a *come-hither* motion.

Like she knew he would, the giant moved, grabbing his axes from where they'd landed in the dirt.

He moved, the axe in his left hand swinging too close to her face, but Signe arched back, then snapped upright in time to slap away the attack from her right with the spear again. The giant retreated, breathing hard as he regained his composure.

"Bravery you have in spades, knowingly entering combat against a Valkyrie. Odin will honor that trait." She tossed the spear into the air just above her hand as she looked around the room at the men watching her closely. She knew these halls, knew these men, knew this place. "But honor, you lack."

As a challenge, she turned her back on the giant. The

moment he charged toward her, she snapped her empty hand into the air, fingers curled into an empty half-circle.

A choked sound escaped him as she turned to watch him reach for his neck, dropping the axes at his side. They clattered to the dirt floor six paces from her, and the giant fell to his knees, eyes bugging out while he gasped for air that wouldn't come.

Signe tightened her hand. The giant clawed at his neck uselessly, unable to escape the magic pouring from her.

She stepped forward, smiling down on the dying man, not stopping to consider *how* she'd brought him to his knees. The power flowing from her felt good, *right,* serving the justice of the gods.

"A coward, that's what you are. A rapist. A murderer. A slaver. A *demon,* Nasi Orestsson. May you rot in the darkest pit in Nilfheim, never to see the glowing halls of Valhalla."

She closed her fist, and Nasi gasped his final breath, body tipping forward as he fell at her feet.

The hall was silent around her, only the flickering flames of the torches moving. A single clap rang through the room, and Signe's gaze swung to the man on the second floor.

Draugr Hilvigsson.

The Demon.

Her father.

"Well done, my daughter." He grinned, clapping again as he surveyed his men and their stunned reactions.

Signe took in the mixture of awe and fear of those around her until her gaze landed on Vermund Oathbreaker. Her uncle stood with his posture relaxed, arms crossed over his chest as he leaned against one of the support beams. His green eyes bored through her, leaving her feeling exposed in a way she didn't fully understand.

Movement at the back of the room drew her attention, and two men shuffled out, carrying a man between them. The captive's golden hair moved in the night air, head tipped forward as he struggled to walk. Something deep inside her stirred, memories pushed through the anger clouding her mind.

Before she could move to follow, Vermund pushed off the wall, striding toward her. She didn't have time to react. He tugged her arms behind her back, shackling them in cold iron. The metal clipped into place, pulling at her muscles with the added weight. The pinch of pain was enough to have her drawing in a breath, but more than the pain, she felt the fire in her hands dissipate.

As quickly as the magic that thrummed under her skin had arrived, it was gone, leaving her a mere mortal once more.

Her eyes blew wide, then shuttered to a glare as she studied her uncle, but Vermund showed no sign of the harsh but supportive uncle he'd once been to her. Everything had changed, and yet, everything was the same.

"Our day has come!" Draugr bellowed over the gathered crowd, ale held high, and the men answered his call. "We've returned my daughter to her rightful place, here at my side. Nasi's broken body serves as our witness to the power of the Valkyries thrumming in her veins, a sign of the gods' favor."

He swung his arm wide, gesturing at the giant at Signe's feet, but her eyes never left the balcony above. As Draugr moved, she noticed the man standing behind and to the right of her father, his dark eyes trained on her. Tattooed symbols covered his head, painting him in black ink as dark as the rock hanging around his neck. She held his gaze, anger rising in her as she studied Raud, the man who'd betrayed her family and dealt a killing blow to her husband.

Her fists clenched, itching for the magic she'd used to end Nasi's life moments before, but none came.

"Don't even try it," Vermund said at her back, his low whisper lost to the sounds of the room cheering in answer to her father's words. "You're powerless here, unless he unleashes you. If you fight against him, break his rules, it won't be *you* who will pay the price."

Her eyes snapped to her uncle over her shoulder, studying him as if she could pluck the unsaid words from his mouth.

Gunnar was here.

And he was still alive.

SIGNE

"Drink."

A horn touched Signe's lips and liquid poured into her mouth, tearing her gaze from the hall the man had been dragged down. She spluttered but drank deep as Vermund tipped it up, forcing the ale on her.

Her eyes narrowed and she reached for the magic in her veins she'd wielded moments before, but the burning under her skin was gone, washed away as fog crept back in. Ale dripped down her chin, soaking into her green tunic, but the cool liquid did nothing to tamp down her frustration.

Ripping her head to the side, Signe closed her mouth, then spat the liquid back in her uncle's face. Ale dripped from his beard, but he didn't react, not even as the room erupted in laughter at his expense. Her chest heaved as she clung to her memories before they faded — worry for Gunnar, heartbreak for her children she'd left behind, confusion as to how she'd gotten here, hatred for how helpless she felt.

Vermund wiped the ale from his face, shaking his head and working his jaw. Men around them spoke, but the voices bled together into an incoherent wave of sound as she studied the man she'd idolized. Once, those green eyes had gazed at her with kindness, helping her when she'd needed saving from her father's wrath, but any softness had long since left her uncle.

She should have known he couldn't be trusted, just as vile and poisonous as her father. Vikings earned their names, and *Oathbreaker* was a title Vermund wore with pride. No matter how he'd cared for her as a child, he'd turned on her, just like everyone else in her life.

Everyone, except Gunnar. Her loyal, steadfast husband. The love of her life.

Her chest ached, and she wished for the mind-numbing fog to come back, to take away this pain, this guilt threatening to swallow her whole.

"I'll kill you," she whispered.

The room spun around her, the buzzing starting up once more, and she shut her eyes. Her chin dropped, and she blinked rapidly, whatever they'd laced her drink with making her groggy again already.

Signe tugged her arm out of her uncle's grip, staggering to the side as the last of the adrenaline ebbed from her system, giving way to the mind-numbing nothingness she was becoming familiar with, day after day.

"He'll make it worse if you fight back," her uncle said, mouth hovering over her ear. He grabbed her arm and tugged her toward the door.

Signe stumbled, the ground churning under her feet like a stormy sea, tugging her down.

"Unhand me," she demanded, but the words slurred, sounding far-off as he pulled her from the hall and into the cool night air.

A deep chuckle sounded from her right, and Signe whirled on the guard stationed at the door, nearly losing her footing. He looked familiar, but already her memories faded, lost to the creeping fog.

"Never thought I'd see the day a Valkyrie walked among us." The guard shook his head. "And, to think, she was here all along."

"The gods smile upon Draugr's might." Vermund's fingers tightened on Signe's arm as he jerked her into the night air and away from the hall.

Signe sagged, the strength to fight back against him leaving with each step away from battle. Tipping her face up to the night sky, she gaped at the stars, twinkling just out of reach. The same stars she'd gazed upon her whole life, trapped in this world of never ending sorrow, all the while wishing for more.

She'd known it once, stolen a sliver of happiness never meant for her, but that was gone. With a deep breath, she gave in to the tide pulling her down, succumbing to that same state of nothingness.

Everything was a blur as Vermund dragged her through the night, and into a longhouse not far from the hall. Her eyes glazed, the space feeling familiar in the worst way, but her memories were out of reach. Maybe that was for the better.

Vermund pushed her forward and she tripped, landing on her knees as her head sagged. Yanking her up, he pulled a chain from the wall, securing it to the shackles around her wrists.

Signe slid to the side, her palms finding a thick, soft fur beneath her, and she sank onto it, curling into herself and gripping the fur.

Her uncle crouched in front of her, gripping her chin as his green eyes focused intently. He spoke, but as before, her senses were lost to her as if she was underwater. Drowning.

He shook his head, then dropped her chin, walking back out of the longhouse and into the night, as free as she was trapped.

She closed her eyes, breathing deep, trying to find the strength to battle again, but there was nothing left.

"Sleep," a voice cut through the buzzing, as clear as ever.

She opened her eyes, peering into the darkness, searching for the source. Shadows swallowed the longhouse, the only light coming from the moon outside the open door and the hearth burning at the center of the room, twenty paces away.

Blinking, Signe tried to clear the haze, but it was too much to fight against.

"Sleep," the voice said again.

She let her body burrow into the fur, listening to the command as she focused on the darkness. Something rattled, but she couldn't look away from the spot on the other side of the room, directly across from her.

The moon shone through the door, cutting a slice of

pale light through the space, and a man leaned into it, showing the outline of a gaunt face, sunken with pain and sickness, but alive.

His lips tipped up into the barest hint of a smile, one she didn't deserve. Tears gathered in her eyes, dripping down her cheek as they slid to the fur. With a deep breath, she closed her eyes.

"I'm with you, *elskin min*. I'm with you, always."

SHELBIE

"Quiet!" Asmund's voice boomed over the apprehensive crowd gathered on the rocky outskirts of Torvik. He raised his hands above his head, wind pulling his tunic sleeves as he stood on a rock above his clan. The initial celebratory air that had followed the *Blot* was gone, replaced with fear-wrought tension in every wayward glance our way.

Everyone was afraid of the future, but none more so than me.

Cliffs rose high into the sky at his back then leveled out to the clearing we'd gathered in before plunging into the sea below. Dark clouds lingered over the water, moving closer with the promise of a storm later, but the weather held for the moment.

"They bring war to our gates!" a man called from the crowd. The mass of voices chimed in to agree with him, as chaotic as the churning sea beneath us.

Three days had passed since we'd arrived in Torvik,

settling into the homes and tents allotted to the Eriksson clan on the north side of town. My plain, brown clothes and braided hair blended in with the crowd, but the stone pendant on a gold chain hanging around my neck ensured I never would. Paired with the whispered stories of my strange tale and my modern mannerisms, I was distinctly *other.* Even with my pendant covered, curious and downright hateful looks found me, whispers passing as easily as the wind whipping off the ocean.

As much as I wanted to let Domari shield me from the many eyes in the crowd, I held my chin high, hiding the worst of my nerves.

"We have no fight with the Demon," another shouted closer to me. The man turned his back on Asmund, holding his hands up to his fellow clansmen. Reddish-brown hair skimmed the tops of his shoulders, touching the cerulean cloak pinned atop his tunic. Gold clasps held it in place, rings glinting on his fingers adding to the signs of his prosperity. "He'll come to destroy our homes, our farms, our trade. We will pay the price of his vengeance, reaping no rewards for this unnecessary kindness. This battle is between Draugr and the Erikssons. Banish these parasites from our city. Remove the sickness before it kills us all."

"Hamund Otkilsson," Domari whispered, bending low enough for me to hear the disgust laced in his tone. His arm laced around my torso, hand resting lightly on my hip. "The wealthiest trader in Torvik, aside from Asmund himself. Gunnar has hated him for years."

"Can't imagine why." I leaned back into him, savoring the comfort he provided.

Hamund spewed hatred toward our clan with every word leaving his mouth, and my shoulders drew tight. As much as I wanted him to shut up, the *Thing* was surprisingly democratic, allowing for anyone to say their piece.

"Years ago, they traveled together to Novgarod, separating before Hamund continued on to Miklagard — the open markets in Constantinople." Domari's hand flexed on my hip, fingers digging into the fabric. "Hamund was a terrible hunter, barely able to keep himself alive, let alone gather enough furs to sell on the market. Yet he brought home more wealth than any other. Most of the traveling party he left with didn't return home, aside from his own men."

I frowned. "So Hamund killed the other traders and stole their wares?"

Domari grunted, not taking his eyes off the man.

"Send them on their way." Hamund spun back toward Asmund. "And send word to Draugr that we pose no threat."

Domari sighed, the sound as full of frustration as I'd ever heard. He moved toward the front of the crowd.

I don't like this, I sent out to Hadriel, glancing out over the water in search of my dragon. Curly strands of my hair escaped my braids, pasting against my forehead as the chill wind whipped through the crowd off the rising sea. Even in late spring, the air had a bite to it, and I tucked my hands inside my sleeves, thankful for the warm weave of the fabric. There was no sign of the black beast dotting the horizon, but the stone around my neck warmed, telling me he was near.

"The Erikssons and Torvik have a long history." Domari's voice rang out over the crowd as he took his place in the front, just below Asmund. His dark tunic rustled in the wind, covering his upper arms and chest, but leaving his forearms bare save the ten bands inked into his skin. "Erik and Asmund traded together for years, joining our clans in successful trade missions to Miklagard. Gunnar and I stopped here last summer to ensure our alliance was secure, even without knowing what lay ahead. We are stronger together, the way we've always been. If the call for help was reversed, you know my people would be here, ready to fight at your side."

Grunts of agreement rang out, mostly from the familiar faces of the Eriksson clan at my back, but others scattered through the crowd mirrored the sound. Asmund nodded as well, and I breathed a shallow sigh of relief. Even if Hamund was the loudest voice, not *everyone* here hated us.

"Draugr invaded our homes, stole our chieftain and his wife, threatened our children, and brought war upon us, without provocation. If you need further evidence of his vile wrath, look to the faces of the children among my clan. Almost all are not our own, but orphans left after he raided their homes and senselessly killed their parents for no reason other than he *could*. Even if the Erikssons weren't here, you're not safe from his reach, his poison, his greed. Draugr's thirst for more won't be satisfied until he pulls Ragnarok down upon us all."

Worried whispers answered Domari, and my fingers rose to my throat, running across the warm chain. Magnus's hand dropped to his axe, his posture stiffening, and moved to block the view of the children behind him, ringed with adults. Gone was the wide grin he usually wore, his intensity making him as fearsome as the Vikings of lore. It didn't hurt that he towered over everyone around him either, the scowl on his face enough to make everyone take a step back.

"And we're to trust a deserter? You left your clan for the Guard without a word, then the Guard to return home," Hamund jeered, encouraging the crowd with wide arms to ridicule Domari too, and Domari stiffened. "You have no honor, Domari Njallsson."

Even without knowing the rumors about Hamund, I instantly hated the man. I ground my teeth together, wishing I understood my powers better and could strike him down from here with a thought.

Need a snack? I called out to Hadriel, and a rumbled chuckle answered in my head.

Domari opened his mouth to speak, but a deep roll of thunder shook the earth, setting everyone on edge as the wind picked up.

"The warrior speaks true," a woman's voice rang out, the cliffs amplifying her voice, and my eyes snapped to her. She stood on the rocks closest to the shore, lightning crackling in the sky beyond. Robes the deepest blue draped over her shoulders and head, hiding her face from the crowd, but the dark braid peeking from beneath the fabric was etched into my memory.

Images flashed through my mind, memories and dreams merging into snippets as I saw her in a seaside village much more modern than this one, pushing me to take a rune bracelet that had set this journey in motion.

On the platform during Winter Nights as she'd announced to the Erikksons that my presence in their time had altered the Tapestry of Fate and sent me back to the future in hopes of repairing it.

At the loom, weaving the Fates of the world as she studied the missing threads — *mine.*

Standing on the rocky beach beside her hut as she bestowed the pendant around my throat to Yrsa, marking her as a Promised.

Verandi.

One of the three Norns; not a god, but not *not* a god. Here, yet again, to mess with my life.

Verandi reached for the edges of her hood, fingers glowing with magic as she let the fabric tip back enough to show the greying hair at her temples. My heart thundered as I searched the clearing for her two sisters, Urd and Skuld. Past, Present, and Future, the three Norns were the weavers of Fate, and I'd quickly come to dread their presence. Every time they showed up, my life was irrevocably changed.

Waves crashed against the cliffs behind her, sending a spray of water over the crowd, as if the sea were just as concerned with her sudden presence. Part of me wanted to take a running leap, plunging into the watery depths below to escape her piercing gaze, but I braced myself as the stone at my neck heated against my skin. Even the wind died down, no one daring to speak as she looked over the crowd.

"Ragnarok is coming, whether you choose to fight or not." Her words sent a chill down my spine. Thunder rumbled again in the distance, and I fought to steady my breathing, my lungs constricting as panic loomed on the edges of my mind. "Fate has called forth the last of the Promised, and Shelbie answered our call. Your only chance to survive what's coming, to stop Ragnarok from ending the world as you know it, is to side with her, to support her, to offer aid in her time of need."

Verandi held out her hand, the billowing sleeves of her robe dancing in the wind as she pointed at me.

The stone at my neck heated to an almost unbearable burn as everyone around me stepped away, leaving me in a clearing by myself for all to look upon. Bile rose in my throat, the expectation in the eyes around me feeling like a crushing weight.

Breathe in, breathe out.

What was I supposed to do? Parade wave? Give a speech? Just the thought of opening my mouth was enough to make the bile inch higher, my heart racing in my chest.

Breathe in, breathe out.

Panicking, I searched for Domari, watching as he pushed through the frozen crowd to get to me, but he was too far. I was too alone.

Breathe in, breathe out.

My eyes locked with his, trapped behind a wall of people.

A screech rent the air, sending loose rocks tumbling down the cliff toward the crowd. Everyone moved to get out of the way as black wings rose above the cliff, Hadriel hovering over the peak at my back.

You are not alone, he answered in my head, and my cheeks heated at the anxious tears threatening to spill over.

Every eye shot to the dragon, black wings spread wide as

he blocked out the sun, beating steadily in the coming storm. He screeched again, the sound terrifying in its might, then blew a plume of fire high into the sky away from the crowd.

If anyone here hadn't seen Hadriel before, they had now. He was inescapable, his immense size as terrifying as the heat washing down on us. With every flap of his wings, wind rushed over us, swirling with the stormy breeze in a cacophony of imminent danger. Families huddled together as screams rose, people rushing to hide from his imposing sight.

The onyx stone glowed, casting a greenish light from within as Hadriel hovered above me. Everyone but the Erikssons pushed away from me, their focus flicking back and forth between the dragon above me and the pendant around my neck.

Easy, killer. I willed my heart to steady as I smiled up at him, glad for his presence as a mixture of terror and awe took over the faces left in the crowd.

Even on that first day I'd seen him, the fear that should have been there in the face of such a vicious creature just… wasn't. No matter how I questioned if I could do everything these people seemed to think I could do, if I could be what the Norns needed me to be, I knew my tie to this dragon was real.

My Promised, he echoed the thought in my head, *you're right where you need to be.*

Domari finally made it to my side, pulling my hand into his. I squeezed back, knowing Hadriel was right.

This *was* where I was meant to be.

The dragon lifted into the sky, away from the cliffs and toward the sea beyond and into the coming storm. Lightning flashed around him as he wove effortlessly between the clouds over the water, showing off until we lost sight of him.

Domari squeezed my hand again, and I pulled my eyes away from the sky to the man at my side.

"She's gone," he said.

I turned to look over the crowd, searching for Verandi. My brow furrowed in confusion. Sure enough, she was gone, disappearing as quickly as she'd arrived. "Super."

My shoulders sagged as Domari pulled me into his arms, holding me tight. My hands circled his waist and I tilted my face to the side, soaking in his warmth but still taking everything in. Between his steady presence and Hadriel's reassurance, I knew I wasn't alone in this. But the burden still seemed mine, and it was a weight I didn't know how to carry.

Asmund hopped down from his perch, walking toward us as the gathered crowd dispersed. He clapped Domari on the shoulder, then smiled when I pulled my face away from Domari's chest, already missing his warmth.

"They'll come around." Asmund gave a quick nod of reassurance, but it did nothing to quell the memories of the angry faces in the crowd. "No one in my clan is stupid enough to ignore the Norns, let alone instigate a fight against a dragon, and yours made sure to make his presence known."

Domari pulled an arm away from me long enough to grip Asmund's. "Your support in our time of need won't be forgotten."

Asmund dropped his hand, a small smile playing across his weathered face. "Don't make me regret it."

Domari stiffened, but nodded, and Asmund strode through the crowd back to the heart of Torvik. With a deep breath, Domari pulled my hand into his, tugging me toward Magnus and the rest of the Erikssons, then led us back into town.

I returned Astrid and Frida's tentative smiles as fat raindrops fell from the sky, the storm quickly approaching. Thunder rumbled, and I moved to let the women pass with the children, urging them onward and toward shelter before the worst of the storm hit.

Revna and Ulf ran by, followed by the children I'd seen with Magnus and Astrid, then two older girls, Kára and Viveka, whom I didn't know as well. A sword as long as her leg swung at Kára's side, hanging from a belt over her tunic and pants, unlike the other girls in town. Her brown hair was braided in rows against her scalp, as severe as the girl's serious expression. I hadn't spoken to her yet, but from what Magnus said, she wasn't very talkative even on her best days.

"I need to check on the horses before the storm." Domari kissed my temple. "Go home with the others, and I'll be there soon."

I nodded, watching him go though I wanted to sprint after him, feeling desperate for his grounding presence.

"I owe your dragon my life," Viveka said from my right. I turned, noticing the girl was waiting for me to catch up. The steady rain plastered her dark hair to her forehead, but it was her eyes that caught my attention — the same emerald green as Signe's.

Pain and sorrow lived there, hidden behind that Eriksson strength. I wanted to find that strength, wear it like armor the way these women did. She stared at me, the attention almost eerie in its intensity.

"I'm glad he was able to help."

"We wouldn't have survived without him." She turned her bright eyes to the storm clouds Hadriel had disappeared into. "I couldn't have kept the children alive on my own."

I smiled, opening my mind to the connection between Hadriel and I so he could feel her gratitude. Her gaze swung back to me, tears rimming the edges before she blinked them away. "You have to save her, Shelbie. You can't leave Signe with Draugr. He'll break her spirit, leaving nothing behind but the shell of who she once was. Whoever you thought you knew will be gone."

My heart ached for the pain in the girl's gaze and the thought of my friend, but I was at a loss as to how I could do anything to bring her back.

Despite what the Norns and Hadriel said, there was nothing special about me. I was just a 31-year-old hot mess who'd accidentally traveled back in time, thrown into a world beyond my wildest dreams, woefully inadequate to wield the magic Fate had dumped on me.

I nodded mechanically, unable to find the words to reassure her, then pointed in front of us to urge her toward home.

DOMARI

Wiping his wet hair off his forehead, Domari walked down the muddy streets towards the hut he and Shelbie shared with his family. Spring storms had plagued them for days since the *Thing*, and he could tell everyone was tired of staying inside. Luckily, the rain was finally letting up, so he pulled open the door to prop open, and laughter carried through the air.

Revna ran across the small room with a shriek, a bright smile on her face as Viveka darted after her, Ulf trailing behind. His little niece dove between his legs and out the door into the fading rain beyond, her laugh trailing after her. Viveka skidded to a halt, cautious as she stared up at Domari, but nodded politely and scooted by, following Revna outside. Ulf paused at the door, glancing between where his sister had darted out into the last of the storm and his grandmother kneading dough near the hearth.

Domari pushed the door open for him to follow. "Clean

up before you come back inside. If you get mud on the furs, you'll clean them yourselves."

Ulf grinned, then rushed out into the last of the storm, laughing as he splashed in the puddles dotting the streets.

Seeing the children happy after everything they'd been through was a balm to his soul, as was the sight of Shelbie standing at the back of the hut, Erik on her hip. She bounced and rocked as she talked to the baby, blowing raspberries until he smiled in return.

He walked closer to the hearth, unable to take his eyes off Shelbie. It was surreal to see her back here, in his world, and looking so natural.

"How is she adjusting?" Frida stilled her hands and nodded her head in Shelbie's direction.

Domari hummed. "I haven't had much of a chance to speak to her lately. But, knowing Shelbie, she'll put on a brave face and rise to the challenge." Breaking his focus, he bent and kissed his aunt on the forehead. Her hair was greyer than he remembered, the lines in her face deeper set than before, but she'd been through a lot in the last few months. "How are *you?*"

She waved him off, then shoved her hands into the bread again before flipping it. "Fine. Focused. Doing everything I can for those here still in my care."

He nodded, hearing the unspoken words. Signe and Gunnar *weren't* here, nor was her beloved husband, Erik's namesake, who'd passed last autumn. "Don't lose faith."

Frida bumped Domari with her hip. "Go. Get Shelbie out of here. You've both been thrust into a role neither of you signed up for, but I am so grateful you've stepped up."

She waved a flour-covered hand in the air. "Make sure she knows how much she's loved so this is all worth it."

Scratching at his beard, Domari debated where they could sneak off to for a moment alone. Even if Shelbie didn't need it, *he* did. He hadn't been this surrounded by people needing him since he left the Guard, and even then, it had been men who were used to being self-sufficient and followed orders.

Eventually, his life here would be full of battle plans, but so far, his job had been more people-focused: finding housing for everyone, distributing food and livestock appropriately, figuring out day-to-day responsibilities for his clan in Torvik, and keeping an eye on children who were suddenly his responsibility. In the few days he'd taken over Gunnar's job, he'd found a new deep-seated appreciation for the man.

Shoving off the table, Domari closed the space between the hearth and Shelbie, scooping Erik out of her hands. She looked up, blue eyes wide as Domari leaned down and kissed her. "Come with me."

Frida held her hands out for the baby, sliding him into the wrap on her chest as she returned to the hearth, then waved them off.

Not waiting for any argument, Domari grabbed the soap from beside the fresh water pale, then pulled Shelbie toward the door.

"Where are we going?" She slid her fingers between his.

Grabbing a torch from the wall, he lit it, then stepped through the door. The storm had passed, but the day was still plenty grey. He pulled her hand up to his mouth, kissing her knuckles, but didn't answer. She'd see soon enough.

Skirting the crowded streets, Domari led them to the water's edge, walking along the rocky outcrop. Dozens of boats were moored in the water and along the docks, bobbing in the choppy sea still churning after the storm. Waves splashed high on the rocks around them, but he stepped lightly, never letting go of Shelbie's hand.

It had been years since he'd spent more than a day in Torvik, but the landscape hadn't changed. Trusting his memory, he led them across the slippery rocks and away from the sounds of the bustling streets behind them. Together, they worked their way down the shore until reaching the narrow mouth of a cave. Holding the torch high above his head, he tugged Shelbie inside.

"What's this?" Shelbie's shoulders bunched as she stepped sideways through the narrow opening.

"Trust me." Domari squeezed her hand, his lips tipping up as he moved deeper into the cave.

"Explain to me how a man of your size found whatever it is that's back here." Her teasing voice echoed faintly as the rocks closed in around them. "Why would you even try exploring in here?"

Domari chuckled, listening to the faint sounds of trickling water ahead. "You underestimate my sense of adventure, Shelbie."

"I can think of lots of adventures that would be preferable to being crushed by ten tons of rocks, or stuck sideways in a cave until my heart explodes from claustrophobia. Cliff jumping. Riding a wild stallion bareback. Eating food in the back of my parents' refrigerator with an unreadable expiration date. All equally likely to kill you as this."

He squeezed her hand and shoved his shoulders through the last of the cave, pushing into a large cavern. Shelbie slipped free, her chest bumping into his back as he held the torch high. She gasped, dropped his hand, and looked up at the rock walls rising high above them, stalactites hanging from the domed roof overhead. The torchlight bounced off the water pooling below, dark and still.

"It's beautiful," she whispered, mouth hanging slightly ajar as she looked around the cavern.

Domari smiled, then tugged her hand to move around the outside of the pool to a wider rock to their left. Her gaze drifted down, following him as he stopped on the water's edge. He propped the torch in a crevice between the rocks, then slid his hands to the belt around his waist, loosening the buckle before letting it drop to the ground.

Shelbie's eyes snapped up, gaping at Domari as he pulled his tunic over his head, then bent to undo his boots, removing them as well.

"What are you doing? You can't possibly be planning to go in there." She pointed incredulously between Domari's naked body and the water beyond.

He grabbed the soap from his pocket and dropped his pants, looking over his shoulder long enough to see the heat in her eyes. She stared unabashedly, her gaze roaming over his abdomen and down, drawing a deep chuckle from his chest.

With a flick of his hand, he tossed the soap bar into the air, then stepped into the water and left it on the ledge of the pool. It was cold, but warmer than the ocean beyond these walls. Stones beneath the water formed a natural shallow end, rising to just above his hips. Beyond that, it dropped off to depths Domari couldn't touch.

"You coming in?" He sank into the water, then dunked below the surface, letting the water wash away the remnants of the days' labor. Here, beneath the surface, everything was dark, silent save for the sound of the water lapping gently on the rocks. Lost to all senses, his mind filled in the blanks, showing him his worst days, but he refused to give in to the dark memories. Not now, not when he had Shelbie waiting above for him.

With a shove, he broke the surface, gasping for air. Light from the torch flickered in the dark cavern, but Shelbie stood on the edge of the pool, a deep-set frown marring her face.

Domari pushed his hair back from his eyes as he tread water. "Not going to join me?"

"Just making sure you didn't accidentally awaken some creature that's been alone in these waters for a century, desperate for a snack."

He laughed, the deep rumble bouncing on the rocks above. "This isn't the first time I've swam here. The water is mostly fresh, not as salty as the sea beyond. It's the closest I can find to a hot spring for you."

"I've read way too many versions of this exact scenario" — Shelbie waved a hand in the air — "with some lizard-dragon thing rising from the deep. I'm not getting in there."

"Last I checked, you weren't afraid of dragons."

"*My* dragon, sure. Other dragons, I'm absolutely afraid of them."

"Nothing lives in these waters."

Shelbie scoffed. "Sure. That's what they all say."

He grinned, sliding his hands across the surface as he waited her out. "Don't trust me to keep you safe?"

"I don't trust *myself* to swim faster than you when the creature arrives, that's what I don't trust." Her eyes raked over the surface, looking for anything that might lurk beneath as she pursed her lips.

"Don't you want to be clean? I know how obsessed you are with bathing. I thought you'd dive in ahead of me, sick of quick dips in the frigid river or bathing out of a bucket."

"You have no idea how badly I want to be clean." She wrinkled her nose and her shoulders dropped, her body relaxing from the tense state she'd been in for days. Her pendant had slipped out from under her dress, and it shone softly the way it always did, the faint green light more obvious in the dark cavern. "This is incredibly stupid. If I get in there, I can never again critique the woman who goes to check on the weird sound in the basement at the beginning of every horror movie. And it's so freakin' dark you wouldn't see the giant mouth coming for you until you were literally swallowed."

"So, make it less dark."

Her head snapped up, eyes meeting his. "What? How?"

Domari swam closer, perching on the shallow ledge, then nodded at her pendant. "It glows. I've seen you do it before, so do it now. Light this cavern up. Let those beasties in the deep know exactly who dares to swim in their waters.

Scare them so bad they wouldn't dare nibble on your toes, no matter how hungry they are. The last Promised would make a meal they'd soon regret."

She didn't laugh the way he'd hoped. Her hand rose, fingers toying with the stone around her neck, and Domari waited. As far as he knew, she hadn't attempted to intentionally use her magic yet. The last thing anyone needed was to scare her off, but time was something they weren't guaranteed.

"I don't know how." She sighed, her hand dropping away from her neck.

Dropping to the rocks, Shelbie pulled off her boots and dipped just her toes in the water, sliding them back and forth, but didn't meet his eyes. "How am I supposed to do any of this, Domari? Everyone expects me to be this ace in the hole, the main line of defense between your people and an absolutely horrific Viking warlord even Signe is afraid of. Explain to me how that's a good strategy when I've ridden on Hadriel's back *once,* and probably can't even lift your sword, let alone wield it."

Domari moved forward, tugging on the bottom of her foot until her body slid closer to the water. She let out a soft *eep* but didn't resist when he moved closer. Sliding his hands under her dress, he lifted the heavy fabric up to her thighs, hands tracing over her skin.

She sucked in a breath, eyes lifting to his, and he let himself smile, despite the worries in his heart. Shelbie was like pure sunshine, banishing the darkness from the corners of his soul. Seeing her downtrodden was like a physical wound he couldn't bear.

"You try. You believe in yourself. You work harder and faster than anyone else. You do your very best, and you trust that you're not the only one in this battle. I've fought in more wars than I care to relive and so have most of the people in this city. And you have faith that your *dragon* is far more capable than you're giving him credit for. You're not alone, Shelbie. Not even close."

She nodded, a soft smile returning to her face, and Domari lost his breath. Whatever he'd done to make their Fates cross, he couldn't regret it, no matter how tortured his soul felt.

"I love you, Shelbie." Domari's hands slid higher up her thighs, settling on her waist underneath her dress. "I'll do anything I can to help you. You just need to lean on me. Trust me when you want to shut down and run away. No matter what, we're in this together, and nothing but death can pry me from your side."

"Don't say that." She leaned forward to cup his face. "Don't even think it. We're going to survive this and get Gunnar and Signe back. Save this city and make Draugr pay for everything he's ever done."

Domari leaned his face into her palm, closing his eyes. He wanted to believe it. Wanted to believe her. More than anything, he wanted a future with Shelbie. To grow old with her. To have a family or build a home. To live a life worth living.

She stroked her fingers over his face, fingers scraping against his beard. "I love you too, Domari. I see how tortured you are, and you have to let it go."

His breath hitched, feeling exposed the way he always

did with Shelbie, but rather than hide, he forced himself to open his eyes, basking in her presence rather than the darkness of his memories.

"None of this is your fault. You are doing everything in your power to protect us all, and no one is more capable than you. I believe in you, and I like to think I'm a pretty good judge of character, so I need you to believe in you, too."

Domari pushed out of the water, sliding a hand behind her neck as he pulled her into a kiss.

9

SHELBIE

The soft scrape of Domari's lips on mine was enough to snap me out of the dark tunnel my thoughts had been in since this morning. His hands tightened on my nape, and I groaned into his mouth, heat pooling low in my belly. Looping my fingers around his neck, I tugged him closer and opened my mouth, savoring the way his tongue laved across mine.

Here, in Domari's arms, the rest of my problems seemed far away. Nothing felt more right than this, together with him.

His hand slid back down my sides, slipping under my dress again, and I lifted my hips enough to move the fabric up. With soft touches, he pulled it up over my torso, his calloused hands leaving a trail of goosebumps across my exposed skin. I pulled away from our kiss only long enough for him to lift it over my head and toss it to the side with his clothes. Suddenly the thought of creatures lurking in the dark didn't matter as much. If I didn't have more of Domari right this minute, I'd probably die anyway, so what difference did it make?

"*Astin min,*" he whispered against my skin as his mouth drifted over my neck, kissing a path down. My head tipped back, eyes squeezed shut as I savored his touch. I'd missed this in the last few days, needing the anchoring presence his body always brought me. It was impossible to be in my head when he made me feel so very *alive.*

Together, we removed the last of my clothes and he pulled me into the water. A shocked gasp escaped me at the cold, my skin pebbling instantly. "Holy shit, it's cold."

"See if you can warm it up for us, then," Domari said, unaffected by the chill. He kissed across my collarbone as he dropped to sit on the shallow perch and pulled me into his lap. Sitting like this, the water reached the tops of my shoulders, my braid dipping into the water behind me. My arms squeezed around Domari's neck and my heart thundered, both from how desperate he made me feel and the adrenaline coursing through my body.

"I don't know how," I answered between chattering teeth.

Domari's hands slid over my chest, pinching and pulling just right, and my heart threatened to break my ribs, it slammed so hard. "Ask Hadriel."

I chuckled, imagining what he'd read in my mind right now. This seemed an awkward time to open the telepathic channel between my dragon and me. Instead, I tried to remember what it had felt like when Hadriel and I had used my powers during battle in the Eriksson village.

My hands tightened on Domari's shoulders while I

concentrated, closing my eyes as I recalled the feel of the magic passing over my skin, the heat wave that had washed from the tips of my toes to the top of my head. Last time, it had been like a roaring fire, blasting out of me all at once. This time, I needed it to be different. Slower. Intentional. Like sinking into a hot tub, the warmth gradually taking over.

Feeling the swell of magic that hummed in the pendant around my neck, I reached toward it, picturing a pool just like the one I sat in, glowing as green as Hadriel's eyes.

One toe at a time, I lowered myself into that magical pool, feeling the heat of it, willing it to spread to the water around me.

"Shelbie," Domari whispered, his mouth pulling away from my skin. The loss of touch was enough to have me opening my eyes, but I clung to that magical pool in my mind.

Instead of darkness, the cavern around us was bathed in green light, lit by the glowing onyx stone resting against my chest. Gone was the dark, endless pool around us. Instead, I could see the far side of the cavern, about thirty feet away. I lifted off Domari's lap, mouth hanging open, and slid through the water, inspecting the cave around me. "Holy shit, Domari."

He came up behind me, arms lacing around my waist, and kissed my shoulder, the water around my hips heating. It wasn't a hot spring, but the temperature was no longer unpleasant. "I knew you could do it."

I shook my head, disbelief warring in me. All of this was unreal. Days ago, I'd been in my very human world, living a very human life, and now I stood in a cave carved into the earth thousands of years ago, wielding magic gifted to me by a dragon. A delighted laugh bubbled out of me, a weight lifting off my chest as I turned back to Domari.

The proud look in his eyes was enough to make my eyes burn. I lifted my hands, framing his face, and kissed him deeply, dragging him into the water behind us. It was too deep to touch, but with the glowing pendant around my neck, I could see the bottom ten feet below. Thankfully, it was free of any lizard-dragon creatures.

Domari shook his head, a smirk playing on his lips. I laughed, tipping my head back in the water, letting my body float as I stared at the stalactites above me. He swam to my side, and I dropped my feet, grinning back at him.

"Told you there weren't any creatures waiting to snack on you."

I opened my mouth to retort, but Domari's arm lifted, pushing on my head as he shoved me underwater.

Gasping, I resurfaced, my mouth hanging open in shock. "Did you just *dunk* me?"

"Should have believed me the first time."

I shoved my arms through the water, splashing him, and Domari chuckled. God, I loved the sound of his laugh, so hard-earned. It meant more somehow, knowing how rarely he cracked, and I was the one he'd chosen to share it with.

He reached forward and I batted his arm away, but not soon enough. Down I went again, grabbing his arm as he pushed me under. I lifted with him, letting him drag me into his chest as I resurfaced.

"Also, it wasn't nice to tell you that you stink."

I shrieked, then put both hands on his shoulders as I pushed him under the water. "You asshole!"

Domari's arms laced around my waist underwater, then tugged me with him as he swam toward the shallow end. I cackled, the playful moment between us exactly what I needed to break me out of this funk.

He flung his head, water swirling in an arc off the tips of his long hair as he set us back in the shallow end with a broad smile. Water dripped down his beard and through the sinewy muscles of his chest, lit by the pendant around my neck. My breath caught as my hands laced around his neck, memorizing every line of his body.

This was why I was here, willing to do whatever I had to to protect these people.

I'd never loved anyone as much as I loved Domari, and I knew without a doubt, I never would again.

Tears welled in my eyes, but I didn't want to cry. Didn't want to feel this vulnerable. So I deflected, what I did best. Leaning down, I exaggeratedly sniffed Domari's body, which annoyingly smelled like pine and musk, the way he always did. Rather than tell him that, I fanned my hand in front of my nose, wrinkling it in distaste. "It's *you* that stinks."

Domari chuckled, kissing me gently before standing and walking back to the ledge he'd left the soap on. And hot *damn,* his ass. I whimpered in my head, admiring the muscles in his back, the shield tattoo painted over his side. From the mischievous look Domari cast over his shoulder, maybe it hadn't just been in my head.

He threw the bar of soap to me, the same pine and rosemary scent I'd become familiar with over my time spent here. I grabbed it from the water, pulling it over my body until Domari sat again, settling at my back. His fingers worked through my hair, undoing the braids, and I leaned into the touch, savoring each stroke of his hand against my scalp.

Wordlessly, he took the soap from me and worked it into a lather, then into my wet hair. Together, we bathed, feeling as intimate as anything I'd ever done, even if we did nothing more than kiss and touch.

"Don't you feel better?" he asked once my hair and body were clean.

I turned in his hold, resting my head on his chest as his arms came around my back. "Much."

He kissed my temple, then rested his chin on my head. I closed my eyes, dragging the moment out as long as I could. Just us, like this, I was untouchable. I could do anything.

Outside these walls was a whole world of problems, most of which I didn't have an answer for, but maybe I could try to use my magic the way I'd heated the water and shone light in the cave.

"I want to try to See Signe," I whispered.

Domari's hands tightened around my back, pulling me closer. For him, I wanted to do this. Wanted to find any tidbit of information I could to help him get Gunnar back. "Are you sure?"

I tilted my head up, resting my chin on his chest as I looked up at his face. "I've never tried to have a vision intentionally before, so I don't know if it'll work. But I'd rather try here, with you, than by myself or with someone else. You'll keep me grounded. Won't let me get lost to it."

Domari nodded but his brow creased. I lifted, enough to kiss him, then rested my forehead on his. "I need to try, Domari."

He nodded again, and I offered the barest hint of a smile I could muster, worry churning deep in my gut.

Afraid I couldn't do it.

Terrified I could, and I'd See some horrible Fate we'd left our friends to.

No matter how afraid I was, I had to try. I had to believe in myself, the way Domari believed in me.

With a slow breath, I inhaled and closed my eyes, looking for that same pool I'd found before.

This time, rather than dipping my toes into the pool thinking of warmth and light, I leaned over it, turning my mind to thoughts of Signe. Time slowed, my breaths deep while I waited for something to happen. Just as I was about to give up, the surface rippled, changing from gentle waves to an image.

Orange light washes over the trees in the setting sun, the last of the farmers returning to Torvik for the night. Soldiers mill about the open gates, waiting for the mother and daughter carrying a basket between them, full of the days' crops. Together they walk, the sound of their laughter carrying across the fields.

A wolf's howl pierces the serene setting, and the mother pauses, looking over her shoulder. Her eyes dart around the trees, wary apprehension creasing her brow.

Movement in the forest snags her attention, fading light catching on something silver hidden in the shadows. Her head snaps to the gates, then to her daughter, eyes wide. "Run." She rips the basket out of her daughter's hands, pushing the girl forward. "RUN!"

With a gasp, the daughter gathers her skirts, face scrunched. Her feet pound in the dirt, headed for the gates in the distance, not needing to be told twice.

Noticing her, the guards at the gate look from the women to the trees beyond. Birds scatter from the outstretched limbs, a flock of black dotting the crimson sky as the wolf howls again, then is answered by another.

"CLOSE THE GATES!" the mother yells, dropping the basket in the dirt and following her daughter, slowed by hobbled steps. The guards snap to attention, looking at the women as they frantically run for the wall, dozens of feet away. "CLOSE THE—"

An arrow soars through the air, piercing her throat. With wide eyes, she topples forward, hand reaching toward her daughter.

"Mama!" the girl cries, frozen in terror as she looks over her shoulder at her mother laying in the dirt. The bell above the gates begins to toll, one after the next, shaking her back to the present. Her eyes snap to the trees, and then she moves, running harder than before.

The howling grows louder, rippling through the air in an ominous tune. Shouts sound as guards emerge from inside, pulling the gates closed.

"Wait!" she cries, hand outstretched. Her skirt flares around her as she sprints the last few yards, but she isn't fast enough. Arrows rain down from behind, catching both her and the guards at the gate. Immediately, they drop, blood staining the dirt around them.

"We're under attack!" The guards on the wall bellow as the bell rings, sending those inside the city walls into motion. "Attack!"

Fire lights the sky, flaming arrows soaring toward the wooden walls, catching fire everywhere they land. With quick efficiency, the guards on the ramparts move, dumping water onto the flames, but no one is fast enough to keep up.

Out of the forest in the distance walks a raiding party, faces decorated in black paint and runes, covered in furs and leathers. That same howl pierces the air, and together, the warriors answer it.

All but the woman standing in the front line.

She stands with her chin tipped down, showcasing the black paint streaked in lines from her forehead to her cheeks. The coppery strands braided down her back shine in the dimming light, drawing attention to the severity of her posture. Unlike the other men around her, she seems at peace, not caught up in the frenzy building around them. Her fingers wrap around the wooden shaft of a spear taller than her, and a bow and arrow rest across her back over her dark tunic. Blades of all sizes hang from the belt around her waist, the woman a living arsenal.

A war drum pounds in the distance, and the men at her sides lift their weapons as they wait for the signal.

No one moves, waiting for her.

The drum pounds a rhythm, a heartbeat for the chaos around her. Eyes closed, she walks forward, free hand drifting across the tall grass separating the forest from the fortress. Her steps are steady, showing no fear as she walks blindly toward the wall, return fire beginning to rain down on the fields she crosses. An arrow sails towards her, aimed true, and blindly, her hand snaps up, catching it mid-flight inches from her chest.

It would have been a killing blow, but not for her.

After all, a Valkyrie can't die in battle.

With a controlled breath, her eyes snap open, the brightest emerald shining from within as she turns towards the wall. Lifting her chin, she shoves her spear into the air, a harrowing scream leaving her lips.

As one, the men behind her answer, moving towards the wall.

"Shelbie."

My body shook lightly, a grip firm on my arms as my heart raced in my chest.

"Shelbie, that's enough."

The grip tightened, and I frowned, trying to place the voice.

"*Shelbie,*" the voice said, desperation lacing his deep tone.

Pull back, Shelbie, a voice said in my head, and this one I recognized.

Listening to Hadriel's command, I gasped. My eyes snapped open, and my chest heaved, trying to pull in air.

Domari held me in his arms as my body shook, the temperature in the cave plummeting as the magic ebbed out of me, leaving us back in the dark lit only by the torch Domari had brought with him.

"You're freezing." His hands bracketed my face, and my teeth chattered in answer.

Quickly, he stood, pulling my clothes up from the ground and dressing me with efficiency. Even the warmth of my wool dress wasn't enough to chase away the bitter cold in my blood at what I'd seen.

"Signe," I whispered, trying to remember every detail.

It all clicked in place, and my hands shot out, gripping

Domari's arms as he pulled on his tunic. "Domari. An attack is coming. They're going to attack the wall, and no one is prepared."

Despair settled heavy on my shoulders as I thought of the mother and daughter, slain as they ran to the gates. "They're coming, and Signe is with them, leading the fight. But she wasn't," I stopped, unable to find the words to explain the difference I'd seen in my friend. Something wasn't right about her, aside from the fact I watched her catch an arrow with her damn eyes closed. I shook my head to clear my thoughts, trying to remember the important things, but felt more useless than I ever had. "I don't know how to stop this, Domari. My vision stopped before the battle began. I don't know what to do."

Panic seized my lungs, tightening its grip once more as I dug my fingers into Domari's skin. His hand reached out, grabbing my chin as he pulled my gaze up to his face. "You tell me everything you saw, and then you trust me to take it from here. That's what you do. Already, you've given us more than we could ever hope for, just with the small glimpse you saw."

I nodded, but nothing seemed like enough. Reaching for that well of magic in me again, now I was greeted by nothing but ice.

Did I mess it up? I asked Hadriel in my head, fingering the stone around my neck.

You used too much power at once, uncontrolled, he answered. *We're lucky Domari pulled you back when he did, or the ice would have killed you.*

I squeezed my eyes shut, searching for even a sliver of

calm to keep me from giving in to the panic tightening in my chest. *How do I fix it?*

Time, Hadriel answered. *You drained your well, but it will refill. Ask Yrsa to teach you control, and then we'll practice together.*

With a sigh, I slid my hand in Domari's and let him tug me back out of the cave.

10

DOMARI

"Let's go through it again." Asmund perched on the edge of the table in the center of his longhouse. "Tell us exactly what you saw. Do you recognize anyone here" — he waved his hand around the dimly lit room, indicating the soldiers normally stationed on the fortress walls — "from your vision?"

Shelbie's shoulders slumped, her brow creased as she studied the men. "I can't be sure."

Domari gritted his teeth, frustration warring in him each time Asmund asked her the same question in a different way, needling her for answers. Maybe this had been a mistake, coming here to Torvik. No matter how they needed these allies and how competent Asmund was, Domari itched to take charge.

An hour had passed since Domari had hurried her through town and into Asmund's longhouse, the dogs finding them along the way. They sat on either side of Shelbie's chair, Thor staring at Asmund, a look of pure focus on his dark face. Even Freki seemed alert, his body rigid where he laid his head across Shelbie's lap, her fingers tangling in his dark fur. The lamps in the center of the table burned low, flames licking just above the surface of the bowl. Firelight danced across Shelbie's face, the hollows beneath her eyes appearing that much deeper.

As Asmund asked Shelbie to recount every minor detail of her vision again, Domari shook his head. "Enough." Thor growled in answer. "She's told you plenty to craft a defensive plan."

Asmund's gaze swung to Domari, standing to his full height and staring him down. "Something to say, *Akolouthos?*"

Domari breathed, jaw working at the challenging tone. He'd overstepped, but Asmund would keep pushing Shelbie until she crumpled at his feet. "She's tired and has given you more than enough information. None of which you'd know if she wasn't here."

"Maybe we should consult our Seer before we take her word as gold," Hamund said from his position near the door. "Hear what the runes have to say about this. Besides catching a dragon's interest, how do we even know the woman is as powerful as they say? Our world hasn't seen a Promised in my lifetime."

Asmund held up a hand to stay Hamund's words, but not before Domari spun on the man, letting the anger boiling deep in his heart take over. "The woman has a name," he ground out, "and far more honor than you've ever had, Hamund. And the only interest a dragon could ever have in you would be to whet his appetite. Shelbie is

Promised to Hadriel, and she is the only thing standing between you and a cold and dark forever in Hel."

Hamund stepped forward, glancing around the room at the men gathered there. Domari noted every single one who showed even the slightest inclination to side with Hamund, memorizing their faces. "We wouldn't even *be* under attack if she wasn't here."

Domari's hand settled on the axe on his hip, fingering the blade as his blood roared in his ears. Freki stood, both dogs' hair standing on end as the tension in the room rose. "The last I heard, you couldn't see the future, but maybe I'm mistaken. If you're willing to bet the lives of those in your city on posting a white flag on the walls so Draugr knows you mean no harm, then be my guest. We'll take our leave tonight."

Hamund grinned, the look as smug as Domari had ever seen, and he itched to lunge across the room to put Hamund in his place. His focus zeroed in on every weak point in Hamund's body, calculating how to end him in a death far swifter than the man deserved.

"Domari." Shelbie slid her hand into his, pulling him back as he moved towards Hamund, done with this vile piece of shit passing for a trader. "He's not worth it."

Her hand squeezed, and his focus fractured, turning to look down at her. While he'd seen how exhausted she was, he hadn't seen until now the pained expression in her eyes. They were bloodshot, drooping as her energy ebbed, and that sight was enough to wipe everything else from his mind. She opened her mouth to say something else, but stopped, her brow furrowed before her body started to slump.

Moving quickly, he stooped, sliding a hand beneath her knees and around her back as he carried her towards the door.

"The attack will come at dusk, at the wall, when the farmers are done for the day. Close the gates an hour early every day. Douse the walls so they can't catch fire. Send scouts into the forest beyond the north fields. That's far more information than you'd ever have on your own. Prepare for battle, men." At the last minute, he swung his gaze back to Asmund, needing him to understand the importance of the details Shelbie didn't spell out as explicitly for the men here. He didn't want to paint a target on Signe's back. "A Valkyrie rides with Draugr, and she cannot be stopped. Flee now if you're too much of a coward to fight at my side but know the halls of Valhalla will be closed to you forever."

Asmund jerked at his words, but didn't argue, connecting the dots the way Domari had hoped he would. Voices broke out at the truth he'd just dropped at their feet, but Domari pushed out of the longhouse, long strides carrying them across the city towards their hut.

"Hold on." He pressed a kiss to Shelbie's temple, and her eyes closed. "Almost there."

"Thank you," Shelbie said, her voice far too quiet as she drifted off in his arms, the last of her energy gone.

Panic clawed at Domari's chest as her body sagged, feeling helpless to protect her from the Fate in front of her. Thor whined at his side, attuned to her like he always was.

This was the third time she'd collapsed from overextending herself — once in her own home that had triggered their frantic journey back in time, and again at the root of the Tree when they'd arrived. She'd never explained exactly what had happened that day, but whatever it was had scared her. The memory of her pendant changing from its usual green to red, burning her skin until he'd ripped it from her neck, was one of the many that played on repeat in his mind, haunting his every moment.

Even without understanding, the magnitude of her power was glaringly obvious. No one needed to spell it out for Domari — she'd kill herself if she went too far. No matter how much their future depended on her, he had to do everything in his power to make sure she didn't bear this burden alone.

"Magnus!" he bellowed as they neared.

His cousin came out of his house. His ever-present smile disappeared at the sight of Shelbie in Domari's arms, and he rushed forward, looking for enemies at Domari's back as he reached for his sword.

When Domari didn't break stride, Magnus rushed ahead, shoving aside the door to their hut. "What happened?"

Domari twisted, stepping sideways through the doorway, careful not to bump Shelbie's fragile form. The home was empty and quiet, Frida and the children not yet returned from working in the fields. Even the hearth had died down, leaving the space chilly and dark.

"She used her powers." He laid her gently on the pallet of furs they shared at the back of the one-room house, then pulled blankets over her still too-cold body. Both dogs hopped up onto the bed, settling in with their heads over her waist. Everything here seemed barren after months spent in her time, no electric heater to warm the room or hot shower to stave off the chill clinging to her skin.

Working with quick efficiency, he moved around the hut, stoking the hearth and bringing fresh water to her side. Thor's dark eyes followed him around the room, but his head never left her body. Freki huffed, nuzzling into her neck, before licking her cheek, as if even the dogs were worried about her. Domari brushed his hands through his hair, feeling useless as he stared down at her sleeping form, pendant dark where it laid on her chest.

Gone was the soft green glow from earlier today, and somehow that made her look so much more vulnerable. It was as if her inner light had been doused, the strength she radiated without even knowing it sucked dry.

The warrior in Domari pounded his chest in frustration, screaming against the thought of any harm coming to this woman who held his heart. He was charged and ready for battle, but against an enemy he couldn't fight.

Sliding down to the pallet, he lifted Shelbie enough to settle her head in his lap, his hands sifting through her curls as he tried to still his own racing heart.

"Is she okay?" Magnus's eyes darted between Shelbie and the door.

"I think so." Domari hoped it was true. She'd come to on her own the other times, but he had no way of knowing if this was the same as before. "Find Yrsa. Maybe she'll know."

Magnus nodded, then was out the door, moving quickly.

Domari stared at the flames in the hearth, looking for an answer to the questions running through his mind.

He hadn't meant to tell Asmund and his men he thought Signe was a Valkyrie, but the moment he'd said it aloud, he knew it was true. While he hoped her allegiance to the Erikssons and her children was enough to count on, he couldn't be sure. He'd never heard of a Valkyrie with a *family* before.

Legend said their duty was to the gods, not to the humans of Midgard. From what he knew, once a Valkyrie was on a battlefield, nothing mattered until the field was leveled and she was crowned the victor, choosing those she deemed ready for Valhalla.

But whose side was she fighting on?

From Shelbie's vision, it wasn't the Erikssons, and that was enough to dig a pit in the bottom of Domari's stomach. As much as Shelbie's vision was a gift, Domari couldn't help but think this was a curse no one deserved.

"Stay with me," Domari whispered as he kissed her forehead, holding her close as the minutes ticked by agonizingly slow, unwilling to think of what life would be like without her at his side. If that was what Fate demanded of her, then he'd fight it, defy it with his every breath.

She was worth fighting for.

She was worth everything.

"Stay with me, *astin min*."

11

SHELBIE

A steady *thump, thump, thump* pulled my mind from sleep, and I opened my eyes. The night sky stared back at me, painted with green and purple wisps and stars dotting the dark blanket laid over the world. Everything was hazy, just slightly out of focus.

The last I remembered, I was in Asmund's longhouse, smoke muting the colors of the dark space, leaving only the anxious and frustrated faces of the many men who doubted me. Then, Domari was carrying me home.

How I ended up outside, I had no idea.

Cool air blew around me, carrying a fresh pine scent, but a bitter tinge of smoke lingered in the air. Something about that seemed wrong, but mind-numbing pain split my head when I reached for my memories.

My hands curled at my sides, sifting through a rocky beach, and water lapped softly at my fingertips. Pain seared through my body as I shifted. A groan slipped free, the sound grating against my dry throat. A tree sat anchored on a small island in the center of a lake. Moonlight shone on the glassy surface, but it was utterly still, as if time had stopped.

I blinked, trying to clear my vision, but everything was still blurry, hidden behind a hazy fog. Everything, except the tree.

Pushing my hands into the sand, I tried to sit up, no matter the pain in my head.

"Domari?" I shifted to my knees, the world spinning around me as I waited for his answer, but none came. Not from him, or anyone.

Wherever I was, this wasn't Torvik.

My knees scraped in the rocky sand, the small sensation grounding me in the eerie quiet of the scene. Sitting back on my heels, I searched for anything I recognized, but the pounding in my head made it hard to focus anywhere but the tree.

At first glimpse, it looked like the Tree I'd time traveled through, branches reaching high into the sky and roots clawing their way towards the water like bony fingers desperate for a drink.

But this tree glowed with an otherworldly light, reaching higher into the clouds than I remembered. The beach around it was different too, barren of any sign of life. No moss grew on the exposed roots, no mushrooms bloomed in the dark corners, no birds nested in the branches, and not a single sign of new life sprouted on the tree.

Unease settled over me the longer I stared at the tree,

the few leaves clinging to the branches limp and brittle. It seemed wrong, an omen of sorts, but I couldn't make sense of it. I rubbed my eyes, willing the headache to dissipate.

Hadriel? I called out in my mind, hoping he answered. He was always quick to respond, but my mind stayed silent. Anxiety crept in as I tugged the pendant out from under my dress, staring down at the dark stone no longer shining green.

"He can't answer you here," a woman said from behind me.

I spun toward the voice, staring wide-eyed as the woman walked towards me. Long blonde hair, almost white in the moonlight, hung to her waist over her cloak as dark as the sky. She was so beautiful; it was almost difficult to look at her. But this close, I noticed her eyes were lined with a heaviness I was becoming all too familiar with. She moved with a silent stealth, leaving no footsteps in the sand, almost as if she hovered over the ground.

"You're Skuld, aren't you?" I asked, remembering the names of the other Norns. I'd seen her before — she appeared as a panhandler in Denver back when I drove home on my birthday, then again at Winter Nights with her sisters to send me home. She'd featured in several of my visions over the last few months, and the same unease radiated off her now as it had then.

Urd, the crone, was the keeper of the Past; Verandi, the matron, the holder of the Present; Skuld, maiden, the seer of the Future.

She nodded, and I glanced over my shoulder at the tree

in the distance. Was I somehow staring at *Yggdrasil?* Fog crept off the water, covering everything but the Tree of Life in a magical haze. My mind raced as I pieced together everything Magnus had told me about Norse mythology, trying to understand the implications of my presence here with Skuld. "Am I dead?"

"No." Skuld smiled, but her eyes were filled with a sadness I didn't like, as if what she meant to say was, *Not yet.*

Before I could ask more, she held her hand out to me, pale skin glowing in the moonlight. I placed my palm in hers and rose to my feet. Together we walked along the water's edge, the fog moving away from her as if repelled by the magic she carried.

The night was absent of all sound but the steady *thump thump thump* in the distance. I looked around the lake for the source of the sound, and noticed a hut on the far side, clear of the fog just like the Tree. Smoke curled from the chimney into the sky, blending in with the lights dancing overhead.

Unease clawed at me the closer we drew to the hut, the preternatural silence confirming my suspicion that this place — wherever I was — wasn't of this world.

No wind rustled the leaves in the Tree. No waves broke the surface of the lake. Nothing moved save the lights in the sky and the smoke in the chimney.

It was too quiet, too still to be real.

The *thump thump thump* grew louder as we neared the hut, light shining softly from the open door. A small porch wrapped around the front of the rough-cut wood building, a rocking chair pointed out towards the lake, but Skuld led me past it and inside.

Firelight flickered in the hearth, but no heat emanated from the flames, devoid of sensation the way everything else was. I couldn't focus on anything but the woman on a stool hunched over a loom, a tapestry of unimaginable colors stretching as far as I could see beyond her.

The woman's grey hair was braided, draped over her elbow as she worked tirelessly, not bothering to look up. Urd, I knew, without having to ask.

Skuld led us around the loom and to the side, my eyes struggling to comprehend the weave in front of me. Each strand wove together, forming pictures that moved within the fabric, shifting with each *thump* of the loom. Urd's fingers moved continuously, mesmerizing as she threaded the loom.

"What is this?" I asked.

"The Tapestry of time," Skuld said as she lifted the fabric, inspecting the images within. "The Fates of every mortal, woven together. Each life, a Thread, interwoven with those around it to craft a lifetime unique to them. Individually, each Thread is nothing, almost useless, but together—"

She traced a finger over a line of Thread, and the Tapestry shifted to show a young woman's face, so similar to Frida I leaned forward.

"—they create a beautiful and tragic story. Full of life—"

The girl in the Tapestry transformed into a child, running hand in hand with a dark-haired boy, two others trailing behind her.

"—and love—"

She aged, her face filling out as she became a teenager, her arms wrapped around the dark-haired boy's neck as they kissed.

"— and heartbreak."

This time, she hadn't aged much, but she lay lifeless, and the dark-haired boy sobbed over her body, his face morphing in rage as he turned to look at the other two boys with them.

My breath caught in my chest. Domari from ten years ago, no tattoos lacing his arms, the same knot tattoo I'd kissed so many times on his neck. His face painted with grief as he pulled Raud off Tove's fallen body, holding him back as he lunged for Gunnar who looked on with shock.

Her death had broken something in all three men, irreparable even now a decade later. A tear traced down my cheek as I reached forward, wishing I could take this pain from Domari, heal the grief that had driven him away from his family.

Before my fingers touched down on the fabric, it changed again, this time following Raud. He left the Erikssons' longhouse, headed for the forest beyond. His face twisted with hatred as he stood on the edge of a hill, looking back down over the valley.

My fingers itched to touch the scene, my breath coming quick, but I resisted and waited to see what happened next.

Raud climbed up a steep rock face, eyes bloodshot as he moved, then entered a cave. The moment I touched the fabric, Skuld's hand slid into my free one, and the breath was sucked out of my body.

❄

Water drips from the cave above him, sliding down Raud's face just as the tears had days ago. Like everything, the tears had left him. Nothing exists for him anymore, swallowed by the unending rage.

Darkness encases him as he slides to the floor, falling to his knees. Giving in to the exhaustion trailing him, his body folds forward, head resting on the rocks, breaths coming in pants as he pulls in the stale air. This was never what he wanted, to be alone again.

But unlike when he was a child, this time Raud isn't afraid. This time he's angry. Furious.

Fingers curled into fists, he slams his hands down, focusing on the pain lancing up his arms, the rocks digging into his skin. Channeling that pain, he screams, letting the agonizing throb in his chest break free.

The sound echoes off the cave walls, bellowing until his voice cracks, giving way to a desperate breath. He shudders, fingernails digging into his skin as silence settles in once more, like a heavy blanket.

Everything is too much without her. Or maybe it is too little.

His shoulders slump as he closes his eyes, wishing his life away.

As if in answer, a phantom wind rustles his hair, carrying the scent of death and decay from deep within the cave.

Raud's head snaps up, staring into the dark depths in front of him. Something red glows within, a pulsing light like a beacon calling him forward. He pushes to his feet, rage momentarily forgotten as curiosity takes over.

"Who's there?" His voice is hoarse with exhaustion, but no one answers, the red light flickering, then fading out, like the last embers of a fire.

Stooping, Raud picks up a rock and throws it into the darkness. It should clatter against more rock — either the walls or the floor — but instead, it lands with an odd, muffled thump.

Turning back to his pack he'd left at the entrance, Raud grabs a torch and slams his flint together, lighting it. Flames dance over the cavern tunneling deep into the mountain, light bouncing off the stalactites hanging down from the ceiling like a gaping maw. Wiping his face to clear the last of his emotions, he weaves his way through the wide passages.

Bones lay scattered around the cave, a mixture of sizes that should have given Raud pause, but he moves onward, unafraid of whatever predator once lived within these walls. If something is alive here, it would have already found him.

With a phantom breeze, his curiosity peaks, the flickering torch enough to show he wasn't imagining it. His dark eyes widen as the cave opens to a wide room, rising high above and triple the width of the passage behind him. Lifting the torch, he waves it in a slow circle, taking in the sight.

Here, the rocks are different, the color morphing to a grey that doesn't blend in with the stones around it. He steps forward, inspecting the strange sight, then jerks upright, nearly dropping the torch.

No matter what he imagined laying at the back of this cave, he never imagined what lay ahead.

There, in the back of the cave, lies a sleeping dragon. Raud's breath catches. Dragons are all but myth now. And not just any dragon — the white dragon. Nidhoggr, the beast of the end of days. His leathered skin has faded from bright white to a dull, almost lifeless grey. Even as Raud approaches, the dragon doesn't move, no breath leaving his chest, no life flickering behind his eyelids.

On quiet feet, Raud creeps closer, torch illuminating the nest of bones the dragon lay within, highlighting the beast's massive size. Even *curled in on himself, Raud's eyes are barely level with the spines trailing Nidhoggr's neck, the rest of his body arching up so far, it blends in with the dark cave.*

Waving the torch to the right, the dragon's broken wing is evident, lying at an odd angle, fractured in several places, signs of a battle fought evident in the scars on his body.

Fireside stories were told of the last battle between Hadriel and Nidhoggr, the former protecting the Tree against Nidhoggr's attack, but Raud had always dismissed it as fable.

Seeing the dragon here, all of it seems real, remembering the dragon's single-minded purpose of destroying the realms, renewing the world with a new birth.

Ragnarok.

A new world, where he might find Tove again.

Staring death in the face, Raud should be afraid, but any lingering emotions died with Tove three days ago. Anything but rage, he no longer had a use for.

Standing toe to toe with the dragon, he reaches out a hand. "Take me," he says, his palm touching down on the dragon's face between his eyes, feeling the leathery skin beneath him. "End me. Send me to Hel to find her."

But Nidhoggr didn't stir. Didn't swallow him whole.

Raud seethes, slamming his hand down on the dragon's body and crumpling to the ground. "You were supposed to destroy them all! Use me and end it."

Snapping echoes in the cave, but Raud is too numb to move, rage blackening his vision.

Even death denied him.

With a deep breath, he grabs the sword at his side, ready to hack the dead dragon to pieces in his agony but freezes at the sight of Nidhoggr's wing.

Another snap, and this time Raud stares at the wing, jerking into place. Watches as it begins to mend itself.

Pushing to his feet, he scans the dragon's broken body, confusion clouding his expression. Raud reaches forward again, placing his hand on the dragon's face as he did before, and this time, those grey scales shudder.

Between one heartbeat and the next, Nidhoggr opens his slitted red eyes.

I gasped, snapping back to the hut, and gaped at Skuld.

Her hand lifted mine from the fabric. "Now, do you understand?"

I shook my head, replaying everything I'd seen. Urd still worked at the loom, her eyes glossed over in her single-minded focus, just as before. "Did Raud craft a new bargain with Nidhoggr? Like Lovisa did for the first Promised?"

The smile she offered me was full of heartbreak, and dread settled in my core.

"He did, didn't he? He bargained with the dragon, the same as Lovisa had to find her lost love."

"He traded his own life for Nidhoggr's," Skuld whispered, her hand reaching out to touch the stone around my neck. "Unlike your connection with Hadriel, Raud's life force is fueling Nidhoggr. Lovisa bargained with a magical talisman — your pendant, a piece of that — creating the connection between sorceress and dragon.

"Nidhoggr did no such thing, pulling the power directly from Raud himself." Her breath shuddered, a hint of fear showing in her wide eyes. "He is very human, never meant for this kind of bargain, and Nidhoggr has overtaken his mind. This was never part of Raud's Fate, never to be a part of the Tapestry. Dragons exist outside of our Weave, a story all their own."

"So, what does that mean?"

She looked over her shoulder towards the door, framing the tree in the center of the lake like a portrait, then sighed. "In every vision I See of the future, this can only end with the two dragons. Only Hadriel can stop Nidhoggr from destroying the Tree, bringing Ragnarok down on us all. And only through *you* can he have enough power to do so."

"Why me?" I asked the same question I'd wondered a thousand times. "Why was I chosen as Hadriel's Promised?" Her words settled on me, crushing in their weight as my mind raced. "I'm not even *from* here. You had to find me in the future. None of this should be possible. I shouldn't be here." My breaths came faster, chest growing tight. "I can't do any of this, can't have the lives of *everyone* on my shoulders."

Her hand lifted to cup my face, and I sucked in a breath at her touch, a soothing calm spreading through me as the loom thumped behind me in a never ending rhythm.

"It was always you."

Her thumb caressed my cheek, leaving a trail of warmth that spread from my face down my neck and pooled in the pendant resting on my chest. Like a warm blanket, the gentle touch carried the feeling of *home*, the same as

Domari's fingers laced in mine, Hadriel's scales under my skin, Thor's nose bumping my knee.

"It was always meant to be you."

Her soft smile soothed the ragged edges of my fear well after her hand dropped back to her side. "When Nidhoggr last attacked the Tree, he altered the loom, and your Thread was lost, moved to a time it shouldn't have been."

I shook my head, trying to make sense of her words. "What do you mean?"

Her fingers drifted to the stone around my neck, touching it as the black lit to a soft green again. "You were never meant for the future, but we couldn't See it when we found you there. Your Thread was cut, split between two lives, two times, but they cannot coexist in the Tapestry. With each day you've spent here, as Fate intended, your Thread is mending, placing you where you were always meant to be."

Her words were confusing, but I understood the meaning, and I couldn't argue with her. From the moment I'd found the Erikssons, I'd felt… different. Felt accepted. Felt wanted. Felt *me*. Even while I was far out of my depth, everything here felt right.

"So what happens to my family? My friends? My life I've had for the last 31 years?"

Skuld moved, looking back to the Tapestry as she picked it up again. I followed her, peering over her shoulder as the images formed once more.

This time, it was my family, gathered around the fireplace in my parents' house, a Christmas tree lit in the background. My parents sat on the couch, appearing young as I remembered them from my childhood. My brother sat on the floor unwrapping presents alone, a red sled propped in the corner. I remembered that sled, that Christmas, nothing else looked the same as my memories. Gone was the stocking with my name on it, hanging above the fireplace.

"Why are you showing me this?" I asked, dread settling heavy in my stomach.

"The Tapestry is mending itself." She dropped the fabric, and, again, it morphed. "Once it's mended, you cannot go back. You will have been erased from your time forever, as if you'd never been. Each day you spend here, the more it mends, repairing itself to its rightful state."

"Erased?" My chest constricted with a soul-deep ache. Tears welled in my eyes as the words sank in, the image I'd seen replaying in my mind. They wouldn't even know I was gone — wouldn't know I'd ever existed.

"It had already begun to repair when you went back last time. There were signs everywhere."

"No," I argued, not willing to believe it. My legs shook as I moved away from her, sinking to the floor, clutching my head. "You're wrong. They didn't forget me. They knew who I was. I was still a part of my family. My friends knew me. Charlene knew me."

Skuld nodded. "You weren't here long, but their memories of you were already fading."

I snapped my head up, ready to argue more, but stopped. At first, I'd dismissed my family's distance once I'd returned home, thinking they were just giving me space. But what if it was more than that?

The longer I thought about it, the more things I'd glazed

over stood out. They'd commented on Thor's size, as if he'd grown, when he'd been the same size for years. My mother had even commented on my hair, noticing I was wearing it curly instead of how I'd straightened it as a teenager.

There had been a growing distance between myself and my family for the last several years, made worse after my trip, but I'd blamed it on my mental state. Were there more examples, more things I'd missed?

"So, what does this mean for me?"

She lowered herself to the floor, gripping my hands. "You never asked for this. I, more than anyone, know what lies ahead for you, and I cannot live with myself if I don't offer you one last chance to escape it."

Her eyes filled with sadness as I studied her, unable to look away. "You mean, leave?"

"Yes." She squeezed my hands. "If I send you back to the future now, we can stop the Tapestry from repairing itself. What's left of your Thread will remain there, and you can live your life as you did before, leaving dragons and Vikings and war behind."

I swallowed, my heart racing at her words, gut churning with indecision. The thought of leaving Domari, Signe, Magnus, *everyone* here, was like a dagger to the heart, but I didn't trust myself enough to believe that my presence here was the make-or-break point. "What happens here if I leave? Will Nidhoggr win, triggering Ragnarok?"

She shrugged, and that hurt more than anything she'd said so far. "I don't know."

I nodded, looking down at my hands as I breathed deeply. The thought of my whole life disappearing was crippling, the relationships I cherished dissolving into nothing, but so was the idea of letting everyone here down.

Stay with me, Domari's voice rang in my head, and a tear tracked down my cheek, my heart swelling at the desperation in his words.

I couldn't leave him, not now, not ever.

Stay with me, astin min.

So, I did.

DOMARI

The hearth crackled as Domari squatted in front of it, watching the flames dance in the breeze from the open doorway. He stoked the fire, trying to ease the restless energy coursing through him. Dusk would come soon, the air chilling with evening approaching, closing the second day he'd watched over Shelbie's sleeping form.

The second day of unending torture, worry for her eating him alive.

Yrsa dragged a cool towel over Shelbie's forehead and sang a haunting tune in hushed tones. It sounded far too much like a death hymn for Domari's liking. Björn sat on the far side of the hut polishing his blade, humming right along with his wife in perfect harmony.

Dusting his hands off on his trousers, Domari stood and resumed his watchful stance, leaning against the wall. Here, he could watch both the door and Shelbie.

If not for her even breathing, Domari would have ripped the hut down, frustration easier to deal with than the gut-wrenching fear he felt every time he looked at her still form.

"Go," Yrsa said, not turning to look at him. "Björn, get him out of here."

Björn set his blade aside and brushed his hand through his beard. "Come on, son."

Domari scoffed, refusing her command the way he had every time she'd suggested he leave. "No."

This time, she did turn. Yrsa's steady gaze bored right through him, the same as a weapon. "Your energy is poisoning her, the same as the magic she overused. Go find something more useful to do than hold up the wall."

Björn rested a hand on Domari's shoulder, and he shrugged out of the comforting touch. "I've sharpened every blade. Fed every horse. Met with the guards on the wall. Spoken to the scouts. Climbed the cliffs to get to Hadriel's perch, but I can't speak to the dragon, same as anyone else." Domari waved his hands towards the door, frustration making his voice drop into a growl. "He can't understand me, and his lingering presence tells me I have *every* reason to worry." Recrossing his arms, Domari clenched his jaw. "I'm not leaving her. Not until she wakes. So if you want me gone, *do something,* Yrsa."

His words were clipped, desperation leaking through, but Yrsa only shook her head at his dangerous tone. "I cannot call her back. She'll come back to us when she's ready."

Pushing off the wall, he moved across the small hut to

squat at Yrsa's side, brushing Shelbie's curls off her face. "She can't keep doing this," he whispered, willing the anger back. "We have to make this stop."

Yrsa's wrinkled hand laid over Domari's, and she ran a thumb over the back of his skin as warmth radiated from her touch. "I need to teach her to control her power, letting it out in a slow trickle rather than blasting it all out at once. My powers are only a fraction of hers, but the idea is the same."

Calming energy trickled into his skin from where Yrsa held his hand, taking the edge off his anger. His chin tipped down until he rested his forehead against Shelbie's, the tightness in his chest easing.

While that didn't sound good enough, it was more of a plan than they'd had before. Yrsa let go of his hand, tapping him lightly, then stood.

"We'll get through this together," Yrsa said, then moved to replenish the fresh water.

He hoped it was true. Hoped they'd all survive this journey.

Domari's fingers pushed through Shelbie's curls, counting every freckle that dotted her face, memorizing every line until she was tattooed on his soul. He'd known it before, but the last two days had confirmed that Domari would do anything to help her battle what lay ahead. Asmund's welcome had been less than what he'd hoped, and fear was a weight riding heavy on them all.

But Domari's was a different fear. Not of Draugr, or the dragons, or even the gods. None of it mattered if he lost her.

His fingers tightened in Shelbie's hair. He squeezed his eyes shut, ready to face his own demons and a past he thought he'd left behind if it could help her. With a shuddered breath, he kissed Shelbie's forehead the same way he had dozens of times over the last two days.

This time, she moved, shifting in her sleep.

"Domari," she whispered, but didn't open her eyes.

"I'm right here." His fingers slid down her arm until he found her hand and squeezed it.

For the first time in days, the pendant around her throat glowed bright green, bathing the room in neon light. Shelbie groaned. The sound spiked Domari's fear, and he frowned at the stone.

The evening bell tolled in the distance.

With a gasp, Shelbie opened her eyes, her back arching off the furs. Gone was the icy blue gaze Domari knew and loved, her eyes entirely white.

"Yrsa!" he cried, and the woman rushed back to his side as a vision held Shelbie in its grip, her body writhing with power. "Is she strong enough for this again?"

Yrsa grabbed Shelbie's other hand. Hadriel shrieked from somewhere outside, the sound shaking the walls. "We need to get her to Hadriel. He's the only one who can help her through this."

"Stay with me," Domari said, the same words he'd said so many times as he scooped her up, rushing past Bjorn and through the open door into the streets beyond. "Don't you dare leave me." His voice broke on the words. He hurried to the beach, searching the sky for the black dragon.

"Hadriel!" he shouted, feet sinking into the sand as he

pushed towards the water, looking to the cliffs where he'd last seen the creature.

"HADRIEL!" He dropped to his knees, Shelbie's trembling body cradled against his chest. Panic held him in its grasp as his fingers dug into her woolen dress, holding tight, afraid if he let go, so would she.

"Don't you dare fucking leave me," he bit out, his hands shaking. "I can't do this without you. I don't want to."

The pendant shone bright, the green light as ominous as the shriek piercing the sky again. Yrsa dropped to Domari's side, the sea breeze sending her auburn hair in a cyclone around her head.

Yrsa smoothed a hand over Shelbie's face. "Breathe."

Domari wasn't sure if she was talking to him or Shelbie, but the wind picked up, forcing him to take a deep breath of the briny air. He inhaled, focusing on the sound of wings flapping that merged with the waves crashing against the shore.

Yrsa's hand drifted to the pendant, clutching it in her palm, the green light shining between her fingers. "Breathe, my child."

All at once, the pendant winked out, and Shelbie's body sagged in his hold. Her eyes shifted from white back to their usual bright blue, and a strangled cry left Domari's lips.

She blinked, her chest heaving as she struggled for air.

The bell tolled again.

Domari's head snapped up when Hadriel shrieked for the third time. Instead of looking to the cliffs for the missing dragon, he looked to the wall, the scent of smoke seeping into the air.

One bell meant the gates were closing for the night. Two meant…

Shelbie's fingers wrapped in Domari's tunic, pulling his attention back down to find her eyes wide and panicked. "She's here."

13

SIGNE

"Move."

Signe stumbled as the hulking man wrenched her out of the tent, hand around her upper arm. Her feet slipped in the dirt, catching on an exposed root of a tree and her bound hands broke her fall. The copper braid holding her hair back fell forward, blocking her vision, but the bitter tang of her captor's fear was enough to break the surface of the drugs keeping her compliant.

A growl slipped free, and she bared her teeth, ready to rip his arm off. A flash of silver caught her eye, stilling her movements. With a quick jerk, the irons that had bound her wrists fell free. The metal clanged to the ground, and her captor backed away quickly, just short of running.

She licked her lips, savoring the taste of freedom almost as much as the fear pouring off the man who dared touch her. Her body hummed with energy, like the first breath of air after free diving to the bottom of the sea. Except she wasn't a treasure hunter scouring the sandy bottoms in search of shipwrecks. She was the monster waiting in the dark ready to bring ships to their doom.

The leaves rustled in the trees around her, and she rubbed her arms, smoothing over her chafed skin. With a deep breath, she tilted her head to the sky.

Pink tinged the clouds in the setting sun, lighting the world on fire. Despite the fog blocking most of her mind and hiding her memories, she could feel the magic in the air. Taste the tension brought on by blood lust. Smell the sweat beading the brows of those ready for war. Hear the fast heartbeats of the ones who would die tonight. They wove together, crafting a tune only she could hear.

Battle was coming, singing to her in a gruesome lullaby, and she was the melody.

The hair on her neck stood up, catching in the energy of the camp, the men around her growing more boisterous with every moment. Even with the chill in the evening air, sweat beaded her brow, adrenaline coursing through her veins. With a jerk, she wrenched the furs off her shoulders, leaving her in a thin tunic and pants, and a wide belt around her waist — the same as every man in this camp.

Leaning down, she swiped a water skin from a nearby pack and dumped it over her head. The cool drops slid down her face, her neck, the tips of her braid hanging down the center of her back, practically steaming off her.

"If you need another skin, love," a deep voice said from her left, "you can have mine."

She turned, trying to locate the speaker. Everything was blurry, hidden beneath a hazy sheen, until she focused on a brute missing his two front teeth standing just under a copse of trees.

He twirled a blade in his hand, then held the skin aloft, pushing it towards her. "All the easier to see your tits through that shirt."

Signe chuckled, swaying her hips from side to side while she glided towards him and took the proffered skin. "How generous of you."

He licked his lips, eyes roving her body with a heat she'd seen too many times in these camps. Fury built like a rising tide in her chest as she tipped it to her lips, tasting the first sip of cool water. Despite quenching her thirst, it did nothing to dull the fire in her veins.

The man flipped the blade in the air again, and she reached forward, grabbing it out of the air before he caught it. With one back-handed swipe, she slit his throat.

Blood spurted from the wound as he choked, dropping to his knees, and she licked her lips at the coppery scent. She chuckled again, her gaze swinging over his companions.

The men at his sides fell back, muttering curses the way they always had, and she took another sip.

A voice in the distance shouted, and all the men in camp stood. In quick movements, they strapped on weapons and shields, then moved towards the voice.

A hand grabbed her arm, and Signe spun, dripping dagger outstretched.

The hand dropped, and Signe blinked, staring at the wide-eyed boy, trembling against a tree. She didn't recognize the child, but something about his pale hair and blue eyes pulled at her memory, begging her to clear the fog shrouding her mind.

"Draugr wants you up front, Valkyrie."

Signe tilted her head, listening to the sound of men traipsing through the forest around her. "For battle?"

The boy swallowed, nodding. His eyes kept darting to the blood on her dagger, dripping to the ground as the slain Viking laid behind her, but he didn't move. Didn't run like the others had.

A smirk stole over her lips, and she stepped towards him. His breaths sawed in and out of him, clouded with fear, but he tilted his chin up, locking eyes with her. With slow movements, she dragged the flat side of the blade on the boy's trousers, smearing the blood across the fabric and marking him for the halls of Valhalla.

"Go," she whispered in his ear. Her breath rose the hairs on his neck. "I will follow."

He ran off, eager to get away from her, and she followed at a leisurely stroll. Her arms lifted beside her, moving to the beating war drums, even if they were only in her head.

The song of death called to her, and she would dance for it.

She wove between the trees, fingers brushing across the white bark of the trees as she moved through the crowd of warriors. Men twice her size cleared her a space as she walked among them towards the clearing up ahead.

The air was cooler, the wind carrying the scent of the sea with every step. Each breath brought her back to herself, most of her memories still gone, but her pounding heart clearing the haze that held the rest of her senses captive.

Her steps slowed. The energy in her veins hummed, magic pulling her towards a tall man standing just inside the cover of the trees. When she stopped at his side, his fingers tugged her chin and turned her to face him as he pried open her mouth. She spluttered against the drinking horn he tilted to her lips, then pulled away, clashing her teeth together, staring at a face so similar to her own.

Draugr the Demon. Her father.

His copper beard was a shade darker than her own hair, trimmed short under his helm. Instead of a simple helm like many of the men wore, the Demon's had curved horns protruding from the top, runes extending down the nose plate and around his eyes. The intricate metal curved down over his cheeks was purely ornamental, but the shadow his formidable form threw on the ground in the fading daylight painted him every bit the image of his title.

Signe lifted her arm to strike but he blocked her blow, her movements less controlled than they'd been a moment before.

"Are you ready?" He searched her eyes, but she jerked out of his grip and spat at his feet.

"Signe, don't do this," a pained voice rasped out. "Remember yourself, *astin min.*"

She tracked the sound to a golden-haired man on his knees. His face was nearly purple with bruises, cheek sunken under the bandage covering one of his eyes, his clothes were filthy and torn, and his hands were tied behind his back.

Frowning, she tried to place him, his face somehow familiar.

Between one blink and the next, she was tugged down

beneath the surface of her mind, whatever memories tried to surface drowning as surely as she was. He blurred in front of her; his voice faded out of her mind.

The only sounds left were the battle drums and the beat of her own heart. She closed her eyes, feeling the rhythm, giving in to the tide.

It was time.

Turning, Signe ignored whatever the Demon shouted at her and strode through the forest, following the lure of a fight she'd be able to sense anywhere.

She drifted through the trees, almost gliding, almost weightless, her mind racing but empty. Her skin burned across her brow and down her nose, magic tingling in her fingertips.

Somewhere in the back of her mind, she knew people marched behind her, but she lost awareness of them, relishing the call of battle. Time stretched out and twisted as she moved under the trees, the only marker the fading light behind her, until a wall appeared in the distance, a high wooden barrier. And at its base, gates.

Her magic tingled down her spine, anticipation building, but the battlefield before her was empty.

A bell tolled in the distance, then once more, calling her like a beacon. Her hands tingled as men gathered around her, drawing weapons from their sheaths, their words muffled in her single-minded focus.

"Mama!" a voice screeched, and her gaze zeroed in on the small shape in the distance, the child kicking into a run towards the gates.

"Mama!" they called again, and her gut lurched at the word.

"Come! Come quickly!" another screamed, beckoning the child, both of them running. "The gates! Quickly, the gates!"

Beside her, someone knocked an arrow. Pulled back the string. Fired.

Signe traced the perfect arc, the way the feathers glinted orange in the light, and her fingers twitched.

With a shriek, the child barreled into its mother. Together they tumbled to the ground and out of the arrow's range.

"Damn," the man who'd fired it chuckled, and Signe frowned, casting a glance his way. He shifted under her gaze and stepped back into the crowd of men behind her.

Finally, the others caught up, the Demon assuming his place beside her.

"To the wall!" the Demon shouted. Torchlight glinted off his metal helm. A wolf howled in the distance, and the men around her answered. Energy crackled in her veins, the same as the torchlight blazing its way through the fog in her mind.

As one, the men hoisted weapons and shields. They snapped together, creating an impenetrable barrier and moved out of the treeline and into the field separating them from the city walls ahead.

Feet pounded on the farmland between the forest and the wall, flaming arrows launching into the sky from behind her, glowing pinpricks lighting the dusk, and she grinned.

The adrenaline of the men around her roared in her mind as it unleashed a beast inside her.

But something was wrong.

Signe's focus stayed on the child, scrabbling back to its feet. To its mother, her face white as death already as she pulled the child along towards the swiftly closing gate.

Men ran by her, flooding the clearing as they attacked, but still, she didn't move, holding tight to the leash on the beast within her desperate to break free.

Arrows rained off the wall, thudding into shields and flesh alike, but her men charged forward, undeterred. These walls weren't tall enough, this gate not strong enough, to stop the Demon's men. To stop her.

Then a thunderous roar sounded, followed by the beat of giant wings.

A black form appeared over the cliffs in the distance, growing swiftly larger as it neared. Flaming arrows highlighted the gold woven between his scales, and Signe's temples pulsed, a memory trying to break free.

A flash of green lit on the wall, and an answering flash of green glowed through the twilit sky. With a deafening eruption, fire blasted from the dragon. Battle cries turned to desperate shrieks as flames ate flesh.

The dragon cut a line of flames in front of the wall, protecting its city. Wings extended, it roared as it passed, then tilted in the air to turn back for another pass. Heat washed across her skin, far hotter than a normal fire, and sweat dripped down her back.

The Demon's men retreated, pulling away from the fire,

but arrows rained down from the wall, stabbing through the backs of the men who'd charged forward moments before.

In the distance, another, fainter roar echoed across the valley, and the black dragon paused, hovering mid-air. Signe stepped out of the trees enough to look, too, her lip curled in disgust.

Another dragon, silhouetted against the setting sun far in the distance.

The black one continued his path back, raining down another stream of fire, blocking the city walls entirely.

Signe stared into the flames, then her gaze rose, meeting that of a figure on the wall. The space between them seemed to disappear. Her vision somehow sharpened until the figure appeared all but in front of her.

Curly blonde hair blew in the wind, blue eyes wide. Green medallion, glowing as bright as the flames between them. The woman gasped, as though she could see Signe just as clearly, too.

Signe didn't know how long they stared at each other, didn't know how they *knew* each other. She only knew they did.

A fist wrenching her hair pulled her back to reality, back to the charred and smoking field she stood upon. She kicked out blindly before she was thrown to the ground, landing hard on her knees.

"When I tell you to fight, you *fight*." The Demon's boot found her ribs, knocking her to the ground. "You are a blade." *Kick.* "A weapon." *Kick.* "Or you're nothing, and that *thing* you call your man is nothing."

This time, when he brought his foot back, she reached

out and grabbed his ankle. She twisted it with a satisfying crunch. His body crumpled, landing hard on the ground as Signe shot to her feet, standing over him, teeth bared. Her foot descended on his exposed throat, pinning him to the ground.

"Enough, Signe," someone said, and his voice cut through the blind rage in her mind. She looked up, that same green-eyed gaze she always seemed to remember, even when hidden beneath a bear's open maw crowning his head, fangs descending over his face.

In his grip was that same golden-haired man missing an eye who'd spoken to her earlier. Instead of the pleading sadness she'd seen there before amidst his bruised and broken body, there was shimmering pride.

And for some reason, that stilled her.

Signe pulled her foot back and turned into the forest, fire crackling at her back as she left the city behind.

14

SHELBIE

Splinters dug into the skin under my nails from where I gripped the battlement's wooden wall. I was afraid to let go, even as my fingers cramped. If I did, my body would crumple to the planks beneath me.

Scorching heat washed over my face, smoke rising from the trail Hadriel had carved between Draugr's army and the city. I blinked against the ashy burn, but couldn't tear my eyes away from Signe, frozen at the edge of the forest.

Standing here on the battlements was different than flying over the attack in the woods like I had weeks before. That had allowed a measure of detachment, like a movie playing out below me. But this — this was a violent assault on the senses — the scent of burning flesh, the screams of the wounded, the rush of bodies surging around me on the walls, all of it palpable, visceral.

An endless stream of men poured onto the battlefield shields locked together in strict battle formations I'd only ever seen on TV, but the blistering heat rising off the fire separating me was a reminder this was all too real. Thor and Freki sat on either side of me, their black fur both standing on end, fangs bared, as ready for battle as the men and women around me.

I tried to count the bodies huddled together behind their shields, weapons aimed at us. Even with Hadriel doing his best to deter them, the line of approaching soldiers stretched the entire length of the city walls.

There were far more in that field than had warred against Magnus and the clan weeks ago, or that I'd Seen in my vision. Draugr's numbers were staggering, especially in comparison to the meager forces here in Torvik. The Erikssons were traders or farmers, and Torvik was a trade city — neither clans were warriors like Draugr's men, nor had the numbers to battle against the force they presented.

I'd seen Magnus and the Erikssons use the same strategy, locking their shields together like this, but it wasn't the same. There was organization, and a blood craze driving anyone who hadn't fled the fires Hadriel left in his wake. It was a death mission, and yet they didn't turn back.

Each breath was shallower than the last, my chest aching from the smoke. But I couldn't walk away. Couldn't turn my back on the death surrounding me. With each pass Hadriel made, soldiers broke formation, fleeing back into the trees, but no orders to retreat came from the leaders standing at the edge of the forest.

Chaos reigned, and if not for Hadriel overhead, we wouldn't have stood a chance. He let out a deadly shriek, and I looked up in time to see another dragon, far in the distance, framed by the setting sun.

Nidhoggr, Hadriel said, his voice a deadly rumble as it echoed in my head. *He rises once more.*

I held my breath. The other dragon's wings beat as he rose into the sky. *Is he coming?*

Not today. He isn't strong enough to take me on yet.

I tried to find relief in that, but the destruction around me was enough all on its own. *But he will be eventually,* I thought, finishing his unspoken words.

Soon, yes.

Thor leaned against my leg, his weight the only thing grounding me from the panic clawing at my chest. Turning my focus back to Signe as she stood, frozen in place while men fled from Hadriel's flames, rushing past her back into the forest. She didn't move, her gaze focused on the woman and child slipping through the city's gates at the last second before they snapped shut.

A large man stood to her side wearing a Demon's helm, marking him for exactly who he was. He screamed in her face, pointing towards the battlefield, but she didn't move, didn't react to his voice or commands.

Wind kicked from Hadriel's beating wings, blowing my hair in all directions and threatening to bring me to my knees, but power thrummed in my veins, rooting me in place. Even from this distance, I could tell there was something wrong with Signe, just as I'd Seen in my vision of her.

Sweat dripped down her brow, but the black war paint arched across her brows and down the center of her nose didn't smear how it had on others around her. It stood out in sharp contrast against her pale features, like black wings mimicking her brows. Her tunic and trousers hung loose from her frame, but it wasn't just the change in her body I noticed.

Her focus was too intense, her posture too still. All the passion that drove my friend was leached from her, replaced with a vacant stare. The battle hadn't gone as I'd originally Seen it, but the blank look in her eyes was just the same, the intensity just as wild.

As if feeling my attention, her gaze lifted, locking on me instead of following the men into battle. I gasped, my heart breaking for my friend across the battlefield, hating the turn of events that had led us to stare each other down like this.

The pendant around my neck glowed almost as bright as the flames when Hadriel made another pass, swooping low over the retreating army, a loud cry rattling the walls beneath me. Our men cowered, ducking down behind the battlements as my dragon flew over us.

"Hadriel!" they cried, and my dragon answered with another bellow of fire that bathed the twilight in a deadly glow.

Watching him from the ground put into perspective just how terrifying my dragon really was. He soared above the flames, light cascading across his black and gold scales as he forged a ring of fire around the city a hundred yards from us, splitting the distance between the forest beyond and the walls we perched on. Freki barked, tail wagging as if he were desperate to charge into battle alongside the dragon. I gripped the fur at his neck before the puppy could do something stupid.

Arrows shot towards Hadriel, Draugr's men returning

fire, and the dragon banked. Arrows ricocheted off his scales into the flames below.

Draugr roared again from the treeline, but Signe didn't react, didn't move from where she stood, eyes still focused on me. The archers switched targets from Hadriel back to the wall, and a volley of arrows soared through the air towards us.

"Take cover!" Domari's commanding voice rang out, rumbling with thunder-like intensity, and the men around me ducked low behind the battlements.

But I couldn't look away from the scene in front of me. Couldn't break Signe's stare. Couldn't move from my perch as Hadriel soared overhead.

MOVE, Hadriel shouted in my mind, and it snapped my focus.

Before I had a chance to react, a band of steel wrapped around my middle a second before I was body-slammed to the ground, my breath leaving me in an audible *oomph*.

"What in Odin's name do you think you're doing?" Magnus yelled in my face, anger painting a vicious picture over his expression.

"I-I'm sorry." He rolled off me, and I sat up.

With a grunt, Magnus peered over the battlement. His jaw worked as he stood, grabbing the bow he'd dropped at my side, a deep frown marring his face. With a steady breath, he drew an arrow from the quiver on his back and pulled the string taut.

His arm raised, eyes locked on the battle below, but I focused on the intensity trailing off the male who had a joke ready for every occasion. With an exhale, he let the arrow loose, not hesitating as he immediately nocked the next, launching them in a slow and steady rhythm.

Domari's battle prowess, I understood. He'd fought as a mercenary for a decade with the Varangian Guard, but Magnus… Magnus hadn't left home. As far as I knew, he hadn't seen battle before my presence had drawn the attention of too many enemies. He had a pregnant wife, and was a trader and farmer, his life so far removed from this gruesome scene in front of us.

But no one here would come out unscathed.

My breath caught in my throat, a wave of nausea overcoming me. The Eriksson clan... They huddled in huts just inside these walls, counting on us to protect them.

Gathering my strength, I pushed to my feet, rising as Hadriel soared overhead, pushing the last of Draugr's men off the battlefield and back into the forest beyond.

Signe turned, spear held loose in her hands, and disappeared into the waiting trees. Draugr spat, stepping towards a warrior to his right, firelight glinting off the bear helm covering his head.

Not until that moment did I notice the other man held tightly in the warrior's grip. His body folded over as Draugr's fist wailed into his torso, fading sunlight highlighting the golden tones in his hair.

I felt the punch as if it was my own, my heart beating wildly at the sight before me. The injured man limped into the forest, held up by the other warrior.

"Gunnar," I whispered.

"What?" Magnus dropped his arm, and his gaze swung across the clearing, searching for his brother. The moment he spotted Gunnar, his face crumpled in grief before a wall of anger took over and he raised his bow again.

Quicker than I could comprehend, Magnus launched an arrow directly at the warrior dragging Gunnar back through the trees. It sank into the bark to their left. One after the next, he fired in rapid succession, landing where the men had been only moments before until they moved out of his reach, too far gone.

Magnus continued to launch arrows with his brow furrowed and a bloodcurdling scream erupted from his lips. Something in me shattered at the sound, feeling his desperation in my bones as I reached up for his arm, pulling it down.

"Magnus!" I screamed, voice hoarse from the smoke. "Stop!"

He reached over his back for another arrow, the movement jerking me back against the wall. His quiver was empty. Without a sideways glance, he tossed the bow to the side and ripped the axe from its sheath on his belt. He gripped the battlement and leaned his weight over the wall.

"Magnus, no!" I reached for him, but what could I do to stop this force of a man who was ready to chase the men back into the forest. Willing to do *anything* to free his brother.

"*STOP.*" Domari ripped him back from the wall and tossed him to the ground.

Magnus fell back, axe clattering to the side. He sneered up at Domari, viciousness like I'd never seen on his face. He leaped back to his feet, shoving past Domari, but Domari didn't give in. In a quick move, he grabbed Magnus by the shirt and spun, slamming the bigger man's back against the battlement wall.

"Listen to me," he growled in Magnus's face, pushing hard on his chest as he held him in place.

"They have Gunnar!" Magnus shouted back, teeth bared in anger. Domari slammed his back again.

"I saw it, just as clear as you did." Domari's fist tightened in Magnus's tunic, shaking his younger cousin. "I saw them both. This is far bigger than you and me, Magnus. This isn't something you can solve alone, unless you think your life means nothing. Flinging yourself from these walls and charging through dragon fire to bring them back won't work. Despite what you think, you're *not* invincible, and I can't lose you too. Astrid can't lose you."

The fight left Magnus as quickly as it came, his body shuddering. Domari shifted his hold, letting Magnus fall on him.

"They were right there," Magnus said, pain lacing his words as sure as an arrow to the heart.

"I know."

I sniffed back my own tears, looking back over the battlefield, now empty but the roaring flames. Hadriel soared overhead and returned to his perch atop the cliffs to the north, standing guard.

Are they gone? I asked, wishing I could do something to ease the never ending worry. The fight had been over almost before it began, and yet it left a heavy toll on everyone here.

For now. Hadriel sounded exhausted, adding another layer of worry to my mind.

If this was the extent of our power together, the most we

could do, then we had a lot of work in front of us to be ready for the day Nidhoggr was strong enough to enter battle.

At that thought, my vision doubled. Two scenes overlaid in my mind, replaying everything that had just happened, and everything that *would have* happened had I not woken up in time.

The gate wouldn't have held. Draugr's men would have scaled the low walls. Their archers would have shot flaming arrows towards the wall, incinerating the wooden supports beneath my feet, holding me aloft. They would have torn the city apart, raping and pillaging in the name of Ragnarok, just as vicious as Viking history.

My chest tightened, breathing becoming difficult as anxiety pulled me under. With shaking hands, I gripped the pendant around my neck, trying to take comfort in the warm stone.

I needed to know we would be okay. Needed to know Gunnar and Signe could both be saved. Needed to know I was capable of everything these people expected of me.

Domari's hands settled on my shoulders, gripping tight as my breaths came in heavy pants, magic humming under my skin. I couldn't focus on him or anything around me. Instead, I reached for that same well deep inside me, leaning over the lip as the liquid within settled, images forming beyond just like before.

"Shelbie." Domari's voice was a low warning, but I ignored him. I closed my eyes, tipping my chin to my chest, warmth spreading from my hands up into my ribcage. He shook me lightly, then pulled me into him, gripping me so tight I could hardly breathe. "Don't push yourself. Do not do this. Knowing what lies ahead is not more important than your life."

The longer I looked into the well, the more everything hurt. But I couldn't stop, couldn't step away, not when everyone needed me. Not when I was this close.

"Shelbie." Domari's hands bracketed my jaw, forcing my eyes up to his. His forehead tipped down to lean on mine, agony written across his face. *"Do. Not. Do. This.* Not right now. Not when I need you."

His voice cracked, and that was enough to grab my attention. My hands fell away from the well in my mind, and I stepped back from the visions that lay within.

"Okay." My voice was hoarse, exhaustion weighing me down. Magnus stood behind Domari, but rather than focusing on where Gunnar had disappeared into the forest, his worried gaze was on me.

"Not today," Domari muttered only for me when I lifted my hands to rest on his forearms. "We'll figure this out, help you understand your powers better, but not at the expense of your life."

I nodded, then drew a steady breath, pulling away from his hold. His hands fell to his sides before reaching forward and seizing my own. Together, we made our way to the stairs and off the battlement, ready to craft a new plan.

15

GUNNAR

Sparks flew into the air above the bonfire, crackling bright in the early morning light. Ominous storm clouds blocked out the rising sun. Petrichor permeated the air, thick with fog. The temperature had dropped, and a chill raced across Gunnar's skin, too far from the fire to feel its warmth. He sagged against the tree they'd bound him to, listening to the leaves rustle in the wind.

Everything hurt.

His face, hollowed and bruised from losing an eye.

His chest, stitched and healed from where Raud had stabbed him weeks ago, but still limiting the mobility of his left arm and now covered in fresh bruises.

His eye, a dull headache that never quite went away, even under the patch pressed tightly against his face.

His muscles, sore from too little food, too much travel, and repeated abuse.

His heart, trampled on each time he saw the vacant look on Signe's face.

His soul, feeling so helpless to protect his family from whatever Fate had in store.

A weary sigh escaped him, and Gunnar tipped his head back, waiting for sleep to claim him.

After their hasty retreat from Torvik, Draugr had led his men on a grueling journey through the night, putting distance between them and the dragon who'd sent them running. Knowing Hadriel stood between these men and Gunnar's family was a relief, a breath of air in an existence that continued to drown him, day after day.

"Storm's coming," a soldier said nearby, followed by a *thwack*.

Gunnar blinked, trying to focus on the men around him, setting up their tents to sleep through the worst of the incoming storm.

"What made you say that, you idiot?" another said, thumping the younger one on the back of the head with a tent pole again. "Was it the clouds as black as a raven's wing that gave it away?"

He yanked the cloth out of the soldier's hands, walking away with a shake of his head. The men around the bonfire chuckled, none of them paying attention to Gunnar.

In the month he and Signe had been with her father, Gunnar hadn't realized the extent of the men Draugr had gathered to fight with him. The Demon's numbers were terrifying, far larger than Domari and his men could handle. But none of it mattered, not when Gunnar had seen the raven show up on Signe's skin on the battlefield. Long, inky black wings stretched across her brow, a thin line running down the ridge of her nose. Even if you couldn't feel the power radiating off her or hadn't seen her fight, the symbol was clear as day.

A Valkyrie.

She really was a Valkyrie.

Hoofbeats sounded through the trees, and he leaned forward, looking for the commotion the same as most of the men around him. Whoever rode towards them was in a hurry, the horse whinnying in protest as they raced towards the clearing.

Everyone stopped what they were doing, hands resting on weapons and bows pulled taut, aimed at the woods. A black stallion broke through the treeline, foaming at the mouth and covered in sweat. Raud sat atop the horse, face alight with fury like he'd never seen before, eyes as bloodshot as the horse that collapsed the moment Raud dismounted.

"Useless beast," Gunnar's old friend spat out, pulling a dagger from his waistband. He stepped towards the horse, and Gunnar sucked in a breath, turning his head at the last minute to avoid watching what he knew came next.

His chest heaved, the loss of innocent life so casual and tragic. Even if Gunnar hadn't seen the lost look in Raud's eyes when Raud had stabbed him weeks ago, this disregard for life was enough to tell him whatever hope he'd held out that a remnant of his old friend was still in there was misplaced.

"The same can be said about your dragon," Draugr said behind Gunnar, his tone laced with bitter hatred. "Why didn't you come?"

"I *told you* he's not ready." Raud stomped across the clearing, throwing the bloody dagger to the side. "But you didn't listen. You charged into battle without Nidhoggr, and you *lost*, even with her at your side. It's you the gods laugh at tonight, Draugr."

The Demon's hand shot out, gripping Raud by the throat as he pulled him in close. "Without my men, without her, your dragon doesn't stand a chance. Make no mistake, Raud, it is *you* who needs *me*, not the other way around."

No one in the clearing moved, their weapons still at the ready. Gunnar's back straightened, searching the clearing for any sign of Signe, but she wasn't here.

"Loki was clear." Raud shoved his hands into Draugr's chest. "We do this together."

Draugr bared his teeth, ready to argue back, until a throat cleared to Gunnar's right.

"Let's discuss in the tent," Vermund said, hand held towards the largest canvas on the other side of the clearing from Gunnar's perch. A soldier held the tent flap aside, and Gunnar sucked in a breath, catching sight of Signe within.

Her copper hair was braided down the center of her back, same as on the battlefield, but any clarity he'd seen in her expression was gone. That same drugged haze holding her captive once more. Her forehead was pale again, the mark of the Valkyrie gone.

Together, Draugr and Raud ducked under the canvas, and whatever conversation they had was carried away on the wind. Even after the displays he'd seen, it was hard to reconcile this version of Raud with his childhood friend.

Ten years had passed since Tove's death, but his sister's loss was still a bone-deep ache for Gunnar. That day had changed all of them, altering their paths forward. Domari had run as far as he could, losing himself in his never ending quest to erase the memory of her broken body. Raud had snapped, leading him to the choices that brought everyone here. And Gunnar… Gunnar had stayed, vowing to be a man who would never let his family down again, chasing wisdom instead of glory as he did everything in his power to protect his family.

The fire crackled, and Gunnar blinked against the dreariness of the morning. Draugr's tent flap lifted, blowing in the wind as Vermund stepped out, dark hair pushed back from his forehead. Light flickered from the torch within, highlighting the cruel sneer on Raud's face where he loomed over Draugr, standing with his arms crossed and chin raised.

But none of it mattered, not with Signe stepping out of the tent, following her uncle. Gunnar's breaths became shallow, his good eye tracking her as she moved woodenly.

Vermund stopped at the fire long enough to grab a steaming bowl, and Signe passed him in favor of a tree stump on the far edge of the clearing. The moment she sat down, her gaze trained on the forest, unfocused as always. Gunnar tugged at his bindings, hoping for a way to get to her, but the ropes held tight.

The hair on the back of Gunnar's neck stood on end, thunder rumbling in the distance as fat rain drops began to fall. Vermund's green eyes flashed towards Gunnar, the light catching them just right to make them glow with an ethereal light. The warrior's steps were steady as he passed by the whispering men and over those sprawled on the ground under trees, already passed out drunk.

Vermund crouched in front of Signe, but her eyes never

left the forest. A loud croak, then a steady whoosh of wings drew Gunnar's attention, a dark raven taking flight from where she'd focused. Black wings were silhouetted against the stormy sky. Not until the bird was gone and out of sight did Signe look at Vermund, the bowl's steam rising in front of her face.

As always, the sight of her nearly took Gunnar's breath away. Gone was the happy smile she'd worn often over their last eight years together, and in its place, the severe intensity from that first day, when she'd arrived at Summer Nights ready for battle.

Then, she'd walked into their village, countless weapons strapped to her body as she approached the shore, not even offering her name. Gunnar had stood posed to leap, ready to win the race across the river, but stopped when he'd noticed her. That same intensity she wore now had radiated off her in waves, her focus as single-minded on the boats dotting the river as she plotted her way across. And, like today, he couldn't look away.

Vermund reached down to touch her hand, and Signe's gaze snapped to her uncle. Her plush lips were down-turned, her face a scowl while she stared at Vermund.

Her uncle held the bowl up to her face, tipping it toward her mouth until she sipped the broth. He didn't let go, tenderness in the way he held her chin, urging her to eat. Not until her shackled hands rose to take the bowl from him did he lean back.

"A Valkyrie," someone from Gunnar's left scoffed. "Isn't she supposed to *lead* us into battle, not stand in the trees, cowering like a fuckin' woman?"

"Best not let her hear you say that," another man answered, then hiccuped. "Did you see her cut out Thidrik's throat this morning for his water skin? She's brutal, I tell you. The Demon's Spawn, indeed."

Gunnar's jaw worked. He hated that name.

Signe *was* brutal. She *was* violent, and intense, deadly in both words and weapons. She was fierce and fearless, a Valkyrie, through and through. But she wasn't Draugr's *anything,* even if the man had sired her.

She wasn't vicious. She wasn't cruel. She wasn't cold, like Draugr.

Signe burned bright as the hottest flames and was just as temperamental. Like a fire, she was capable of both life-giving warmth and life-ending power. She was the truest friend, the most loyal companion, a steadfast partner, and the fierce mother of his children. She was made for him, just as she was made for battle, and he knew it to the depths of his soul.

Vermund stood, taking the empty bowl from Signe. Her eyes closed, shoulders sagging as her face cleared of all expression, as vacant as before. Whatever they were putting in her food and water had done its trick, pulling away her instincts to fight until Draugr was ready to wield her again.

It broke his heart, watching her be used like this, knowing how much she'd hate what she'd become in Draugr's hands. A deadly tool used for his amusement.

But Gunnar had seen her expression shift yesterday, her hand pause as she readied for battle, watching that mother and child run for their lives to escape Draugr's men. She hadn't charged into battle the way everyone expected her to.

Hadn't even left the cover of the trees, save to look behind her at the white dragon far in the distance.

She hadn't claimed a single life yesterday the way the Valkyries of lore did, so Gunnar wouldn't lose hope.

Signe was still in there.

No matter how far gone she might have been this morning, lost to the drugged haze these men trapped her in, Gunnar knew the woman he loved more than any other lay within, ready to strike.

He only had to find a way to reach her, to make her remember.

There was so much to live for. To fight for. To die for.

Liquid splashed out of the bowl as it was thrust into Gunnar's bound hands, a looming shadow of a man standing in front of him.

"Eat," Vermund said, the same green gaze as Gunnar's wife steady as he focused on him.

He eyed the bowl warily, wondering if it was laced with the same magic as Signe's, but his stomach grumbled, too desperate to refuse. As Gunnar sipped the warm broth, Vermund pulled a water skin from his side and sat with his back against the same tree as Gunnar, staring off into the forest. He couldn't help studying the man, his thoughts as stormy as the clouds overhead. Scars laced his arms—not uncommon for warriors—but these looked different. Claw marks extended from his elbows down to his hands, savage and deep, as if he'd shielded himself from a bear as fearsome as the helm he wore into battle.

When Signe had told Gunnar about her past, she'd spoken of her uncle as the one bright spot in her life, even if he was as brutal as the rest of the men here in Draugr's forces. Vermund Oathbreaker was a fearless warrior, the right-hand to Draugr in battle, and, if stories were to be believed, as savage as any Viking before him.

Maybe it was their matching eyes that made Gunnar think there was more to him, just as there was his wife. For some reason, this villainous man had sent innocent children to Gunnar for protection, choosing to risk their lives as they trekked across the land in the dead of winter, rather than leave them at the hands of Draugr. That alone told Gunnar that Vermund wasn't all he seemed.

"Why are you keeping me here?" Gunnar looked away from Vermund and drank the last of the warm broth, savoring the taste of the stewed meat and root vegetables. "Why drag me along when I'm of no use to you? Why feed me, heal me, when you could leave me to die?"

Vermund sipped at his skin, head tilted back against the tree. "You are nothing but a tool, wielded by the gods just like the rest of us. Who am I to betray those orders?"

Gunnar chewed on those words, his gaze drifting back to Signe, still sitting in a trance-like state.

"You said the gods, not the Demon," he murmured low enough for only Vermund to hear, unable to dismiss his wife's uncle's choice of words.

He hummed, pushing to his feet and dusting off his trousers. Leaves crunched underfoot as he walked across the clearing towards Signe, helped her to her feet, and then led her to the tent set up nearby. Together, they ducked beneath the fabric.

Gunnar couldn't look away, questions rolling in as fast as

the gathering storm. Vermund emerged minutes later, eying the sky as thunder rumbled in the distance.

Their gazes met again, and Gunnar tilted his head, trying to understand this man.

He answered to the gods, not to Draugr.

That changed everything.

16

SHELBIE

Wind rushes past my ears as I tip my face up to the night sky above. Everything is quiet this high in the air, only the soft and steady song of Hadriel's wings beating in a soothing lullaby. Lights twist around us, pinks and greens changing to purples and blues as they swirl against the starry sky. Hadriel soars between them, weaving in and out of the phantom ribbons.

I'm dreaming — I know that's what this is — but in this moment, riding on Hadriel's back, I've never been more at peace. Felt more right. In this alternate reality, my fear of falling, or even worse, failing, doesn't exist. Here, I can savor the feel of his smooth scales underneath my palms, soak in the warmth of his skin, let go of the crippling doubt that has held me in a chokehold lately.

Slowly, I pry my hands off the horns positioned in front of my legs like handholds, lifting them into the air as I grip Hadriel's back with my thighs. Stretching, I spread my arms like they're my own wings, mirroring Hadriel's beneath me, free from the confines of my body and mind left in another world.

Wind chaps my skin, feeling so real, but so does the calm this dream brings me. The lights dance, a bright contrast against the dark sky as we fly, power humming in my veins. I stare in awe at the constellations around us, marveling at the expanses of the universe, feeling so small in the grand scheme of things.

Growing up in the mountains, I'm used to seeing the stars with crystal clarity. I know these stars, unchanged even across a thousand years, and something about that is soothing.

Everything about my life here is different, but these stars are the same. I am the same.

Breathing deep, I find Ursa Major, the bear charging through the night sky. Above the bear sits Draco — the dragon — and I grin at the sight of the serpent circling overhead. This one was always my favorite to find in the night sky, just another sign I am right where I was always meant to be.

The stars twinkle, mesmerizing, and I smile at this respite, this sliver of time meant only to soothe.

Tracing my fingers through the sky, I draw the line of Draco's back, ending on his tail with a flourish of my hand. A carefree chuckle slips free, and then the last star of Draco's tail winks out — there one minute, gone the next.

I sit up straighter, hands falling back to Hadriel's horns, searching the sky.

Any calm I'd felt moments before dries up as I stare at the hole in the sky.

Why does this feel wrong? *I ask Hadriel, not sure if our mind connection will work here in this dream reality.*

Before he can answer, another star winks out, the hole in the night sky growing. I tighten my thighs around Hadriel's back, gently nudging him towards the spot, unease gathering in me quickly.

The Northern Lights around me pulse, turning as they move towards the dark spot in the sky, like a tether pulling me in.

Death, *Hadriel's raspy voice rings in my ears.*

An icy chill rakes across my skin, robbing me of any peace this moment had offered before.

Together, we fly as more stars wink out, the sky darkening by the minute. Dread pools in my belly. That same feeling of being small returns, except this time, I feel helpless to fight back against the coming night.

Somewhere below us, a war horn bellows. The sound echoes in the quiet night, and I crane my neck to look down, but we're too high for me to see the ground.

Hadriel, *I say hesitantly, afraid of what this means.*

I've waited a long time for this day, Promised, *a new voice scratches across my mind, cold and thin as a winter wind.* I'll enjoy watching you fall from your dragon as much as felling the Tree.

With each word, the stone around my neck heats until it's burning into my skin, power gathering in me. Hadriel's chest rumbles under my fingers, and he banks hard away from the darkness.

Wake up, Shelbie! *he cries, and I shriek as the stone at my neck turns from a steady heat to a searing fire.* GET OUT NOW.

A silent scream ripped from my throat as I jerked awake, clawing at the pendant around my neck. Quickly, I removed it, tossing it on the bed. My chest heaved. Panic still thrummed through my body.

The chain was hot to the touch, but nothing like it had

been in my dream. There, atop the woven fabric, it was a simple black stone, encased in a golden dragon, suspended on a matching chain. It was beautiful, but nothing about it screamed *magic* as it lay dark, the glow that connected me to Hadriel lost.

Thor grumbled where he lay at my feet, lifting his head to shoot me an annoyed look before resting his chin on my leg. The weight was a steady comfort as I pulled in a deep breath, hoping my heart would slow back to an even pace.

"Just a dream," I said aloud, but was that true anymore? Was *anything* just a dream? Even without Hadriel's command, something about that dream had been wrong, but I didn't know what it meant.

I closed my eyes, still exhausted from the battle, but was too afraid of that lingering darkness to fall back asleep.

A wet tongue dragged across my cheek, and I grimaced, pulling away from it. "Freki, *no.*"

I pushed the puppy away from my face. He wagged his tail, tongue hanging out as he hopped from foot to foot beside the bed, impatient for the day to begin. Mindlessly, I reached over, rubbing his head between his ears, to which he leaned in. He looked so much like Thor had as a puppy — jet black, a block head, shaggy fur, and dark eyes — but this little guy's personality was Thor's opposite. The longer I pet him, the more settled I felt, gaining distance from the panic the dream had instilled in me.

Thor stood on the bed, walking towards me, until he dropped down close enough for me to pet him too.

"Feeling jealous?" I ran my other hand across his nose, smiling at my big guy. He huffed, his eyes the same deadpan expression I'd seen so many times, and I couldn't help but chuckle. "You two are like your own grumpy-sunshine bromance, aren't you? The next Domari and Magnus duo."

Freki barked, which I took to mean he agreed with me. Thor's eyes shifted to the side to look at the miniature, chipper version of himself, but his tail didn't make a single thump.

Just like Domari and Magnus.

At the thought of the men, I looked around the empty hut. The hearth still glowed, casting the room in a soft light, but everyone was already gone for the day — I'd slept later than I'd intended. While I felt slightly guilty for being lazy, I couldn't help but savor the moment alone, just me and the dogs. In less than a year, I'd gone from living alone in my apartment in Denver, to living with Domari in Charlene's ranch house, to living with his extended family in a one-room hut. It was a jarring change, but so was everything about the Viking world.

Freki whined, and I sat up with a sigh, rubbing a hand across my face before sliding it down to the stone laying on the bed. *All good?* I asked Hadriel as I rubbed the smooth stone, uneasiness still gripping me tight.

Yes, he answered, but he sounded as tired as I felt. I slipped the chain back around my neck, restoring our connection, and immediately felt the change in him. Together, we were stronger, and I resolved to climb the cliffs to his perch today, wondering if proximity would make it even better.

Three days had passed since the attack on the wall, and everyone in Torvik was on edge, but life had to move on.

With warmer weather coming each day, trading season was about to begin, and an entire fleet was readying on the docks. It pained me to think of so many able-bodied men leaving these walls, putting us at an even greater disadvantage over Draugr's army, but trading was their livelihood — they couldn't stop, even knowing the risks.

Yrsa had asked me to stop by later today, so I planned on doing that, but in the meantime, I wanted to find Domari and tell him about my dream. Maybe he'd see some meaning in it I had yet to think of.

The dogs followed me as I dressed, donning a different version of the same tan and green dress I'd worn every day here. I babbled useless conversation at them, savoring the comfort the simple task brought while I readied for the day. Snagging a piece of warm bread from the table by the hearth, I pushed the door open, mind set on finding Domari. My first guess was the training yard in the courtyard by Asmund's longhouse.

The sun was high in the sky and I held a hand up to shield my eyes as they adjusted. Gulls called over the sea in the distance, the briny air refreshing after the spring storm. Usually, children played just outside the huts in the clearing to the west, but no one was here, the town eerily quiet for this late in the morning. I frowned, working my way through the streets, passing Yrsa's hut, and then Magnus's — also empty.

Where is everyone? I asked Hadriel, not knowing where exactly he was, but he favored a perch on the north cliff side overlooking the town, right above the Eriksson's compound.

He didn't answer, and I hurried my steps, the dogs at my

heels. As I turned the next corner towards Asmund's long-house, raised voices drifted out to reach me, an argument breaking out. I rushed forward, following the tug in my gut that pulled me right into the courtyard.

My feet froze on the edge of the square, and I rose on my tiptoes, searching for my family. Half the village was already up and here, but unlike the other gatherings, this crowd felt angry, primed for a fight. Thor growled, and several villagers turned to look my way, making a small space for me to step towards whatever everyone focused on.

Standing right outside Asmund's longhouse was Domari, Magnus at his side.

"If those fleets leave" — Domari gestured towards the docks, his face pinched with barely contained frustration — "we're all as good as dead."

"You were at that battle as much as I, Domari," Asmund said, his voice portraying a calm Domari seemed to have lost. "As I recall, we had a dragon defend us. Smoke is still rising off the scorched farmland between us and the forest, an ominous sign for any who dare to attack us again."

I stepped forward, my necklace glowing faintly as Hadriel listened in through my connection.

For now, he said. *But when Nidhoggr rises, I can't protect you all. I can't fight both wars at once.*

I know. My gut churned, remembering the silhouette of the other dragon in the distance and everything I'd found out about his and Raud's connection. *So does Domari.*

As if mirroring my thoughts, Domari pushed forward, crowding Asmund, but Magnus and Björn grabbed his arms, holding him back. "I never took you for an ignorant man, Asmund. But you cannot be that stupid. You saw Nidhoggr as well as I did. You know what's coming. You know what this means."

Asmund's jaw worked, his eyes squinting as Domari sized him up. "I also saw the land your dragon ruined, leaving my people all but helpless this season. My responsibility is to *them*, not you. Trading is the only way we can refill our stores, and life has to move on. You bought us time, but time doesn't fill empty bellies."

Domari shook his head, as angry as I'd ever seen him. Sweat trickled down his bare chest, muscles drawn taut with controlled rage. He shrugged out of Magnus and Björn's hold and moved towards the training yard, standing among the dozen men and women holding wooden practice weapons. "What about this do you not understand, Asmund? No one will live long enough to starve if we don't train your people as fast as we can. And even then, it's not enough. We're farmers and traders. Draugr's army is three times the size of ours, and we don't even know if that was all of them."

When Asmund didn't give him the reply he wanted, Domari spun to face those gathered in the town square. "Not only does Draugr have numbers on his side, but every one of his men wouldn't hesitate for a split second to murder anyone in their path — mothers, fathers, children, babies... all of you will die at their hands. All of you will be sacrificed on his path to greatness. Hadriel saved you this time, but the moment there is another dragon in the picture, that advantage is no longer ours."

The gathered villagers argued, voices rising as they picked sides, but my ears rang, anxiety creeping in.

A muffled grunt broke through my panic, and I turned, finding the twins and several of the smaller children. Viveka had baby Erik on her hip, harshly shushing the two children grappling on the ground, clearly affected by the contagious atmosphere. Brown braids whipped as a hand connected with a chin, and instantly I knew who was fighting. Stepping away from the crowd, I leaned down and grabbed the back of Revna's dress, pulling her off the local boy I didn't recognize.

"Hey," I whispered as she jerked, trying to break my hold. Dropping down to my heels, I gripped her shoulders lightly.

Frizzy brown hair encased Revna's head, her braids all but undone as blood smeared with the dirt on her face. Her blue eyes were daggers as she pointed at the boy. "He said we're better off dead."

I frowned, not dropping my hands from her shoulders as I turned to look over at the boy, wiping blood from his lip. "Where's your mother?"

Sensing trouble, he darted through the crowd, disappearing. I hesitated only a moment, glancing back at Domari in the center of the commotion, but he and Magnus could handle that, as much as it could be handled at all. Turning to the kids, I held a finger over my lips, forcing half a grin to intrigue them enough that when I jerked my head, they followed me away from the fighting.

Fortunately, the two dogs followed me, and we made our way to the beach. I bent and grabbed a piece of driftwood, throwing it out into the water, and Freki dove into the waves to fetch it. Thor sat at my feet, back turned to the shoreline as he watched the other children, on guard as always. When Freki dropped the stick at my feet, wagging his tail excitedly, I picked it up and handed the stick to Revna, urging her to throw it again. She did, and one by one, the children took turns playing with the dog. Thor never moved, but Viveka sat on the beach next to him, setting Erik in her lap.

"Thank you," Viveka said as she ran her fingers through Thor's thick fur while the other children sprinted through the shallow water, chasing after Freki.

"Of course." I smiled down at the young girl. Her black hair was as dark as Thor's coat, but the bright green of her eyes was the exact same as Signe's, something I couldn't seem to let go of.

"Domari isn't wrong." Viveka shifted Erik in her lap, placing the baby up on her shoulder until I held my hands out for him. "Vermund was the one sneaking children out of the villages Draugr raided, sending them Signe's way, knowing she'd protect them. She'd done it for me, and even eight years later, he knew she'd do it again."

"Your father, right? Vermund?" Erik nuzzled into my shoulder, letting out a happy coo as he settled in for a nap.

"That's what they say." She shrugged, her hands tugging on the seams of her woolen trousers. "I was left on his doorstep as an infant, so I've never met my mother. We have the same eyes, but so does Signe, and she's not Vermund's daughter."

I nodded, not sure what to say to the girl I knew next to nothing about. Astrid appeared on the far end of the beach closer to our huts with several more children in tow, and I waved to her as she waddled towards us. Birgita and Bo ran to join the twins in the shallows, peals of laughter a refreshing tune after the scene we'd witnessed in the town square.

Astrid walked towards where I stood, but I pointed towards the docks, urging her to sit down while I oversaw everyone. She offered a thankful wave, then did as I suggested, closing her eyes and letting her hand fall to her belly.

"I saw her," Viveka said after a moment of silence lapsed between us. I turned back to the girl, bouncing Erik as the baby dozed in my arms. "Signe."

I blinked, trying to think if I'd seen Viveka on the wall, but the entire battle was a blur in my memory — it was entirely possible she'd been there, and I hadn't seen her.

"She's a Valkyrie." Viveka's even tone held no surprise, but my mind stuttered on the words, a cold chill slipping down my spine. I'd heard Domari say the same but hearing it again after Seeing that vision of her on the battlefield was different. Even if it hadn't come to be, I understood what it meant. Understood just how deadly she was. Understood the power thrumming in her veins, meant to be wielded in battle.

"She's a Valkyrie," Viveka repeated. Her green gaze swung up to me, taking on a deadly flint so like Signe. A shadow passed over her face, like a bird in flight as it darkened her brow, there and gone in an instant. "And so am I."

17

DOMARI

"You're out of line," Asmund snapped. Anger coursed off him as he glared at Domari, Hamund standing at his back with a satisfied grin.

Domari's jaw worked, barely containing the rage that built with each passing second, not helped by Asmund grabbing a wooden sword at his side and tossing it into Domari's chest. It slapped against his skin, then fell to the ground, as useless as logic to these pig-headed men.

"Know your place, *Akolouthos*. Torvik is a democratic society. The people here choose their paths, and I cannot stop any who wish to pursue trade as they always have. Hamund's fleet leaves tomorrow at first light, and any who wish to join him can do so. Those who choose to stay are free to train with you, if that's what they want, or they can move elsewhere to safety."

Domari shook his head, tired of this confrontation. "We don't stand a chance, Asmund. I need every able-bodied person here ready to fight. Even then, we're outmatched and outnumbered."

Asmund leaned in, and the friendly demeanor Domari had always known from the man was gone. "Let's see this battle skill then, Domari. You're the one they speak of all the way to Miklagard, the famous leader of the Varangian Guard. From the stories I've heard, you don't even need an army at your back."

"Considering I led a *bandon* of three-hundred elite Guards, your stories are false." Domari's eyes flicked over the crowd, their anger from earlier morphing into fear with every passing second of this argument. And Domari couldn't blame them. For the last few minutes, he'd done nothing but shout about their imminent failure.

Frustrated, Domari dragged a hand through his dark hair, then dropped it to his side in defeat. "We need a miracle."

"Isn't that what your woman is for?" Hamund offered, and Domari's fists clenched.

"She is not a weapon," Domari growled, wanting to slam his fists into Hamund's smug face. "Shelbie and Hadriel can't be wielded as such. And I refuse to sacrifice her uselessly when we have no support to offer her. One warrior, no matter how powerful, cannot win a war. We need a plan. We need weapons. We need a fucking *army*."

Equally worn out, Asmund threw his hands in the air. "Then find me one, *Akolouthos*." Asmund turned towards Hamund, his body language as much of a dismissal as his words. "Your fleet leaves at first light. Spread the word at every outpost of our call for help. Gather any support you can."

Hamund nodded, pulling back through the crowd, and Asmund turned to the rest of his clan gathered in the square. "You heard the stakes. This may very well be a losing battle. Draugr's men are skilled warriors, and we have a fight ahead of us. Anyone who wishes to train with the Erikssons is welcome, but I won't force any of you."

His gaze swung over the crowd, settling on the group of women huddled together with their children. "If you wish to hide, I'll help find safe locations for your families, or you can barter passage with Hamund's fleet. Knowing what we face ahead, I cannot blame any who wish to leave, but I am a man of my word. Just as I've promised to protect all of you, I promised my allegiance to the Erikssons long ago, and I will honor it until Valhalla."

"Until Valhalla!" a feminine voice echoed him from behind Domari. Looking over his shoulder, he saw Asmund's daughter holding her wooden sword above her head, turning to those in the square as she repeated the chant.

Several picked up the call but more turned to leave the square.

"Fighting stances," Magnus barked from Domari's side, turning back to those in the training yard. He nudged Domari with his shoulder before walking by.

Defeat weighed heavily on Domari as he looked over those who remained in the courtyard — less than sixty men and women choosing to fight, most untrained. They clacked their wooden weapons together, the sound a dull thump as he watched, his mind spinning through every possible outcome for the coming battle.

Draugr had over four hundred trained warriors, a dragon, and a Valkyrie.

Domari had sixty farmers, a dragon, and an untrained Promised.

While he had immense faith in Shelbie's ability to overcome this hurdle and figure out her powers, he also wasn't a fool. They needed a miracle, and the only idea left to him was one he didn't want to consider. Even if he could make it happen, the risks were too high, and there were too many unknowns.

Magnus shouted instructions, doing a surprisingly good job leading the training exercises. He fixed postures, adjusted grips, applauded those who were executing moves correctly, and encouraged those who still needed work. Trusting him to oversee this, Domari touched his shoulder, then left the courtyard, needing to speak with Shelbie before he made any decisions.

He wove his way through the town, passing the armory as the steady beat of the hammer pounded against the anvil. Racks of swords, axes, and spears stood against the side of the lean-to, open to the air to let the heat from the forge out. Asmund stood inside inspecting a helm while he spoke with the stout blacksmith, Brokkr, but neither man looked his way. As hard as it was to trust anyone to lead anything to do with battle, Domari had stepped on enough toes today.

The Eriksson's compound was oddly quiet, Frida and a few of the older women laundering clothes. Before Domari could ask where everyone was, Frida pointed towards the sea. "Astrid and Shelbie have them down on the beach."

He thanked her, then turned on his heel, headed back that way. Freki splashed in the waves, chasing children in and out of the surf while Kára oversaw them, painting a peaceful picture he wished would last. Shelbie sat slightly removed from the children but watched attentively where she perched with Thor and Viveka. The two were deep in conversation, and a frown marred Shelbie's face, a sight Domari always hated.

"Everything alright?" Domari asked as he approached, and Shelbie's startled gaze snapped up to him.

"I should ask you the same."

It was Domari's turn to frown, but the look was much less unexpected on his own face.

Shelbie pushed to her feet, brushing off her skirts and handing the baby to Viveka as she stared down at Thor. "Stay here and watch the kids." Whether she was talking to the dog or the girl, he wasn't sure, but both Viveka and Thor turned their attention to the water, doing as she said.

"Come on." Shelbie slipped her hand into Domari's, pulling him up the beach away from the crowd, and he followed. "We need to chat."

Momentarily surprised she'd read him that easily, Domari nodded. With each step forward, his heart sank, knowing what he needed to do.

Waves crashed against the rocks as they neared the cliffs on the north side of town, just below Hadriel's perch at the top of the rocky outcrop. The black dragon circled high in the sky, contrasting against the cloudy afternoon, and

Shelbie tipped up her face, the pendant around her neck glowing green. He'd seen this happen enough lately to understand it meant she was using her magic, probably communicating with Hadriel mind-to-mind.

She smiled as she opened her eyes, blue shining as bright as the sea, and Domari hated himself. He was about to steal that smile. His heart thundered, cracking in two as he slid his hands to her neck, thumb trailing across her jaw.

"I love you, Shelbie," he said.

Her smile wavered, eyes tracking over the deep lines marring Domari's face. "I know you do. But the look on your face makes me feel like you're giving up."

Domari shook his head, leaning down to kiss her tenderly. "For you, I'll fight until my last breath. No matter the odds, I'm yours forever."

"Well, it's a good thing we can even the odds a little, then, right?"

Domari's eyes snapped up and searched her expression. She gripped his forearms, resting over the ten bands tattooed there, a hopeful expression on her face. How she'd guessed his plan, he didn't understand, but that she knew and could smile in the face of this next challenge had hope returning.

"Viveka is a Valkyrie," she said.

At the same time, Domari said, "I leave with the fleet at first light."

18

SHELBIE

"What?" I stuttered, eyes wide as I stared up at Domari, trying to comprehend what he'd just said.

He blinked, equally as surprised at my words as I was at his. "Viveka?"

"You're leaving?"

"Yes, but let's go back." Domari frowned, his thumbs rubbing across my jaw. "What do you mean, Viveka is a Valkyrie?"

"I don't know." I shrugged. "She just dropped that bomb on me a few minutes ago. I don't entirely understand the implications of what that means, but you keep talking about Signe as a Valkyrie, as if this gives Draugr's army some sort of silver bullet. I saw her in my vision — I can connect the dots to put together a picture of what you're afraid of with her. But if Viveka is *also* a Valkyrie, that's a good thing, right?"

Domari looked over my shoulder towards where Viveka

sat further down the beach with the children, his hands drifting down to rest on my shoulders. "Yes, I would think so. She's young though, and I don't know enough about Valkyries to know if that makes a difference."

"We'll have to ask her for more information," I agreed, then slapped his chest. "But what the hell do you mean, *you're leaving?*"

He turned his attention back to me, his frown even deeper. "I'm in the way here, Shelbie. Asmund doesn't want me taking charge. And I don't know if I'm capable of backing off, knowing what's at stake." He brushed his hands through his dark hair, the move flexing the tight muscles in his bare chest. "We need more warriors. Hamund is leaving with his trade fleet in the morning, headed to Miklagard. Asmund asked Hamund to put out our call for help, but I know him."

Domari dropped his arms, his brown eyes full of defeat. "He doesn't care about anyone here. He'll take his family and flee, framing it as his trade mission. He has no intention to return until after the war. If I go, I can get off at Staraya Ladoga, the outpost I left my Guards at, gathering as many as will leave with me."

"Okay." My brow furrowed, trying to think through this. "So, we'll go and convince them, and just hope we're back in time."

The look on Domari's face turned pained, his hands coming back to my jaw. "You need to stay here. Train with Yrsa and figure out your magic. I can't have you risking your life every time you wield it. I can't lose you, Shelbie."

I shook my head, fighting back tears. "I can't lose you

either, Domari. What am I going to do without you here? I don't know how to do any of this. What if they attack while you're gone? Then even you won't be here?"

Domari stepped back into my space, his hands settling on my hips as his head dropped to mine, our foreheads resting together as my heart broke.

Tell him about the dream, Hadriel's tired voice said in my head.

"What?" I said aloud, not thinking clearly as tears slid down my cheeks.

Domari pulled back, studying me while my pendant glowed green.

Tell him about the dream.

"What's he saying to you?" Domari touched the pendant with one finger. The stone warmed, then glowed brighter, casting shadows on his face.

"I had a dream last night." I tried to think through it again. "Or, this morning, I guess. Hadriel and I were flying, weaving through the Northern Lights. And then there was a horn, and I think Nidhoggr spoke to me."

Domari's head snapped up. "How do you know it was Nidhoggr?"

A shiver ran down my spine at the memory, and I wished I could forget it. Forget how invasive, how *wrong* it felt. "He spoke in my head the way Hadriel does. And it was the same voice I've heard before, when we came through the Tree, and when I dreamed of the cave."

Domari's expression hardened with every word I spoke. "What did he say?"

I blew out my cheeks, knowing how well this would go

over. "It wasn't good. Talked about wanting to see me fall, just like the Tree."

Domari cursed and dropped his hands away from my face. He turned to look out over the water, thunder rumbling in the dark clouds on the horizon. "We can't win a war against them if Nidhoggr is at full strength. He didn't even attempt to engage when they attacked the walls, so I'm assuming that means he's not strong enough yet. But we have no idea how long that will take."

I sighed, my eyes burning with frustrated tears. "Why can't my dreams ever be *useful?* Why can't it be me pointing at a calendar, saying 'This day looks like the best day to end the world, don't you think?' But *no.* I just admire the stars like I'm back home on my back porch on any old Thursday."

Domari froze, turning back towards me. "Which stars?"

I wiped the tears away, studying him. "I don't know. I was looking at the constellations. Ursa Major, the bear, was the one I noticed first. You probably don't call it that, though. Why?"

Domari stepped away from me, grabbed a stick from the sand, and put it in my hand. "Can you draw the constellations you saw for me? Show me where they were on the horizon?"

"Why does it matter?" I asked, still not following.

"Maybe you saw the time of year." He touched the stick in my hand, urging me forward. "Just show me."

I dropped down to my knees in the sand and dragged the stick through it as I tried to picture Ursa Major and

Draco, pointing out their positions in the sky above the horizon.

"*Wain*," he whispered excitedly. "Do you know which direction you were flying?"

I glared up at him. "You're joking, right? I don't know my directions when I'm on *land*, let alone the sky."

North, Hadriel supplied, and I huffed as I told Domari.

"And you saw the lights," he said, his body language downright giddy as he stood back up, pacing down the beach and back. "You saw the lights, right?"

"Yes, I saw the lights. I actually flew right through them." I brushed the sand off my dress as I stood, understanding the utilitarian nature of these earth-tone dresses the women wore. "Care to explain now?"

"Shelbie." Domari's hands slid to my neck again, a wide grin taking over his face. "You saw Winter Nights."

"What?" I shook my head, resting my hand on the shield tattoo covering his left side. "How do you know that?"

"We navigate by the stars when we sail," Domari answered, his grin never faltering. "I've mapped the stars since I was a child. I'd recognize those anywhere. You saw Winter Nights."

"And you think it means that's when they're going to attack?"

"Was the vision ominous? Did you see anything that led you to believe it might be then?"

The memory of the sky slowly darkening, stars winking out one by one, came back. The sound of the war horn in the distance. A nervous chuckle slipped free, my timing shit as always. "It wasn't good, that's for sure."

"Then let's choose to trust it." Domari nodded. He wasn't the most optimistic man, so seeing him this ready to buy into my vision was odd. I wasn't sure *I* even bought into it. "I can be back in plenty of time."

I jerked back. "That's" —my heart plummeted as I realized what he'd just said— "that's in the fall. You'll be gone all summer? How far do you need to sail to find them?" I pointed to the storm inching closer on the horizon, my heart rate accelerating with each passing second. "What if there are storms? What if your ship capsizes?"

"Trust me, *astin min.*" Domari leaned forward and kissed my forehead. "I will pray to the gods for a swift journey and will be back in your arms as soon as I can, with an army in tow."

I wanted to trust his words, and I knew he'd made the journey before, but sea travel was so risky in this era. I might not have been a historian, but I knew that much. So much could happen, so many unknowns, and we'd have no way to contact each other.

When we were together, it was almost easy to forget the convenience of cell phones, but if we split up? If anything happened to him out there, would I ever even find out? Or would I just be here, facing a battle I was woefully unprepared for, without him? Suddenly, the deal Lovisa had struck with the dragons that had created the Promised and this whole mess made a lot of sense.

"I hate the idea of being apart from you for that long," I managed to get out, boiling it all down to the heart of my concerns. "Of not knowing if you're safe, or if you've found them, or —"

"It won't be easy for me either," Domari admitted. "But this is our best chance to get more help. I've made the journey before, and it should only be a few days at sea each way. I'll find my men and be back before you know it."

Light rain began to fall as I tried to pull myself together, but that was easier said than done. "I don't want to do this alone, Domari."

He gripped my face, and tears mixed with the rain as they slid down my cheeks. "You're not alone, even when I'm gone." His hand slid down my neck, resting just to the left of my pendant, over my beating heart. "I'm here with you, always. You'll have Yrsa to train you, Hadriel to protect you, Magnus to entertain you. By the time I'm back, my family will love you more than me, I'm sure of it."

My fingers gripped his arms, and I pulled him down to me. His mouth touched down on mine, heat shimmering like a wave between everywhere we touched. My hands traced over his bare chest, memorizing each dip, each scar, each curve. I wished I could suffuse the kiss with some spell of protection, to keep him safe when he was apart from me. He must have felt my desperation, deepening the kiss as if we were both too afraid to say it might be our last.

Thunder cracked above us, and Domari broke away from the kiss, staring up at the sky. Sliding his hand into mine, he dragged me forward, our feet sinking in the wet sand as we ran past the turn for our huts.

"Where are we going?" I yelled over the rain, coming down harder now. Stray curls plastered to my face, thunder rumbling above us.

Domari didn't answer, urging me faster as we neared the

paddocks where he kept his horse, Mjölnir. A barn stood to the side, doors open, and Domari ducked as he rushed us inside. The moment we were out of the rain, he spun, and his mouth crashed down on mine.

His hands landed on my waist, pushing me back towards the wall until he pinned me in place. Kicking my feet a step apart, his thigh landed between my legs, his weight pressing into me. I gasped as his head dipped, lips trailing across my neck. "When I come back, I'm finding a hut for just the two of us, even if I must build it myself. I'm tired of sharing you with my whole family. Tired of having to sneak off to our cave for a moment alone with you."

I grinned, tilting my head to give him better access while my fingers trailed over his hot skin. "Barns aren't good enough for you anymore, cowboy? Is this how we always say goodbye?"

"This isn't goodbye." His teeth dragged across my shoulder as his hands lifted the skirt of my dress up over my hips. "I found my way back to you then, and I will again. You should know by now, not even Fate can keep us apart."

Tears pricked my eyes at the thought of him leaving in a few hours, but he was still here, and I chose to live in the moment.

Domari shared in my urgency, and we quickly stripped, wet clothes puddling on the floor beneath us. Rain pounded on the thatched roof as I gripped his shoulders while he lifted my leg, settling it high on his hip. Our kisses became a race against time, as wild as the storm raging outside. Nothing else mattered. He pushed his hips forward, sliding across me in a tantalizing brush, but not enough.

My heart raced in a breakneck speed as he teased, a battle between fear of the future and an insane need to cling to him forever warring in me. "Domari," I moaned, the sound barely encompassing how desperate I felt as his tongue laved over my peaked nipple.

He sucked hard on the bud in answer and my hands slid up his back, feeling the corded muscles there. My fingers dug in, needing to feel him everywhere until his face lifted to mine. Our tongues danced, singing a tune of passion, urgency, and a fear neither one of us wanted to speak aloud.

Our days were numbered.

We both knew it.

I broke away from his kiss, reaching down between us to guide him in. "I need you."

His lips trailed across my jaw while he pushed into me from below. My fingers tightened on his shoulders, head tilting back to the wooden walls behind me.

"*Astin min,*" Domari groaned, hands tight on my ass as he moved inside me. "I can't get enough of you."

I mumbled some incoherent babble, but whatever I said made Domari laugh. And why was that so much hotter?

I clawed at his skin, needing more. Like always, Domari read me like a book, pushing me further back into the wall. He lifted my other leg and pinned me into place as his hips drove in harder than before.

Gripping his face, I pulled him back to me in a searing kiss, needing this to last for an eternity. Thunder shook the walls behind me as my body tightened. My breaths were uneven as I soared the way I always did in his arms.

"That's it," Domari groaned, his head dropping to my

shoulder. I held him to me, our bodies flush, even an inch of distance feeling too much. "Leave me feral to be back in your arms. Make me think about this every day. Come with my name on your lips."

Even if I wanted to prolong this, I couldn't, not when he hit me just right. I moaned his name as my body spasmed, and he pounded into me harder, chasing his own release.

Sweat dripped off my body, and I clung to him until Domari finally set my feet on the ground. His chest heaved, eyes closed while he tipped his head forward, resting it on mine. "Two weeks. Three, maybe. Then I'll be back."

I nodded, unable to speak around the lump in my throat. My fingers traced over the knot tattooed on his neck — his connection to Gunnar, Tove, and Raud. I knew Domari was loyal to the depths of his soul. I knew he loved me. I knew he wouldn't leave if he thought he had another option. I also knew he had a level of faith in my ability I couldn't help but doubt.

But I had two weeks to prove him right. Two weeks to practice, two weeks to train and figure out my magic. Two weeks to have *something* to show him when he returned.

"You'll be back," I echoed, leaning my head on his chest, soaking in his warmth.

"I promise." He kissed the top of my head and brushed my damp hair off my forehead. "Until Valhalla, I'm yours."

19

DOMARI

Pink light streamed through the narrow streets of Torvik while Domari walked towards the dock the next morning. Shelbie met his strides, hand firmly in his as she looked around the sleepy town, just beginning to rise for the day.

Domari squeezed her hand, silently reassuring her this was right, the way he had all night. They'd waited out the storm in the barn, crafting a plan. Sensing her unease, he talked not only of the battle, but after.

A house, just for the two of them. Horses, dogs, maybe a goat. Farmland they could work together. Children they'd raise together. Everything Domari had never let himself dream of before her.

He only hoped he could make those dreams come true.

"Domari." Asmund's brows rose as they neared the dock. The chieftain's eyes lingered on the small pack in Domari's hand, as well as the weapons strapped to his person. "Come to see the fleet off?"

"I've come to join it," Domari said, and Shelbie squeezed his hand.

Hamund laughed, stepped up to Asmund's side, and clapped his hands together. "What a surprise. The great *Akolouthos* is running scared. That's what you called leaving, right? My, how far the mighty have fallen. But this is what you do best — abandon your people in their time of need. Your family, your Emperor, your Guard, your woman. I should have seen this coming."

Domari's jaw tightened, but Shelbie tugged on his arm, pulling his attention back to her. "Don't engage. Gather the Guard and get back to me as soon as you can."

Asmund sucked in a breath. "The Guard? You mean to bring them home?"

But Domari didn't answer to Asmund, and neither did the Guard. He turned his back on the men, tipping Shelbie's chin up. "I'll come back. You owe me a forever."

"Gladly," Shelbie said, her smile doing nothing to hide the fear he saw within. "And you better."

Domari smirked, then dropped a kiss to her lips. Then another, her fingers tightening in his tunic. "Until Valhalla, *astin min.*"

She nodded, then loosened her grip and stepped back. Already, he felt her loss.

With a deep breath, Domari steeled himself for this journey and stepped down the dock. The boats bobbed in the shallow waves, and he climbed onto the nearest one taking a seat along the starboard side near the center mast. An oar rested across the bench, and he hooked his shield onto the side, stowing his belongings under the seat.

Refusing to look back, Domari stared out over the open water, already counting the moments until his return.

Nervous energy hummed in his veins, thinking through every possible scenario that might await him in Staraya Ladoga. He hadn't wanted to worry Shelbie further, and she didn't know this world well enough to understand the title Asmund and Hamund kept throwing around like a weapon.

Akolouthos.

Over the last ten years, Domari had risen in the Varangian Guard's ranks, taking over the premier position. When he'd left Constantinople a year ago, he'd worked in the Great Palace, serving as the personal bodyguard and advisor to the Emperor. All six-thousand Guard members reported to him, scattered as they were around the world.

And he'd walked away from it all without ever looking back.

He'd left the city in the night after Skuld had appeared to him, telling him he was needed at home.

Hamund had said it right — he'd left when the empire was beginning to fall, leaving his post in the Emperor's time of need just like he'd left his clan so many years ago.

The punishment for deserting the *Hetaireia* was death, and yet he was willingly headed back to the continent with the risk his very presence posed.

Quickly, the rest of the seats filled, and the boat untied from the dock, pushing away from the shore. A drum beat from the stern, setting the rhythm. In time with the men around him, he dipped his oar into the water. Together, they pulled, the lightweight ship cutting through the waves as if it were nothing. Stroke after stroke he moved, thinking only of the future and the promises it held.

"Dragon!" someone cried, and Domari's gaze snapped up, spotting Hadriel leaving his perch above the city. He spread his dark wings wide, then launched himself into the sky. With a screech, he flew low over the water, parallel to the ship. Men missed their beats, their rhythm stuttering until the captain bellowed orders, and everyone resumed rowing with the drum.

Hadriel flew with them for a while, then rose above the water. His wings beat as he hovered in place while the men raised the center mast, and the sail snapped open. Domari looked up, finding Hadriel's steady green gaze trained on him, just as he knew it would be.

"Take care of her for me, Hadriel," Domari said, his voice drowned out by the beating drums and churning wind as the boat picked up speed. Somehow, he knew the dragon would hear him. "Teach her everything you can, and I'll bring you an army. I swear it."

Hadriel roared, his head tipped to the rising sun, then turned and flew back to Torvik.

20

SHELBIE

I stayed on the beach long enough to watch the ships crest the horizon, Hadriel flying overhead. As tempted as I was to ask Hadriel to follow them all the way to Staraya Ladoga, I couldn't. It was too far for him to fly, and I needed to train with him here if I ever wanted to understand how to wield the powers of a Promised.

A hand slipped into mine, squeezing tight, and I finally pried my eyes away from the dots on the horizon to Yrsa at my side. Her auburn hair held more grey than I remembered seeing lately, but these last few months had been trying for all of us.

"Are you ready, child?" Yrsa asked as Hadriel flew back to his perch up on the cliffs. The steady beat of his wings matched my heart, tying us together at our core.

I forced a nod, unease churning in my gut. "I'm nervous."

Yrsa squeezed my hand again and we walked down the beach away from the docks. The dogs trailed behind me as they so often did, my shadows in animal form. "I don't blame you. You haven't had the easiest time with your powers so far, and much of it is still untried."

"You were a Promised, right?" I asked, trying to remember our conversation a few weeks ago.

"Yes." She smiled, but the look didn't match the sadness in her eyes, glancing back to the cliffs above. "Vyara was to be my dragon, but she perished before we could be matched. Traditionally, a ceremony is held on the shores near the Tree, the pendant is bestowed upon the next Promised, and you are paired with your dragon for the first time. From there, you'd begin your training with the other Promised and their dragons, learning how to use your powers without draining you or your dragon."

"What powers are we talking about here?" I asked, wondering if I was about to breathe fire like Hadriel. While that might come in handy in battle, I'd be much more likely to singe off my own eyebrows than do any damage. "More than just Sight, like I've had so far?"

Yrsa pursed her lips, studying me. "It's different for each Promised, but healing, foresight, and an ability to speak to the gods are the most common."

My feet stopped, waves lapping against my boots as I stood near the water's edge. "Hold up." I gripped my skirt, holding it out of the water, trying to work my way through what she'd just said. "You expect me to *speak to the gods?* Is that even a thing? And are we talking like, Odin? I'm supposed to find a giant raven and have a conversation with it?"

She chuckled, glancing over her shoulder at the dogs for

a beat. I looked down at them, Thor looking pissed as ever and Freki holding a stick longer than my arm. Leaning down, Yrsa took the stick and tossed it into the surf. Freki bound into the waves after it, tongue out.

"He takes on more forms than just the raven, but essentially, yes." Yrsa began walking again, turning us towards the cliffs. "If that is to be one of your powers, they'll present themselves to you in whatever form they wish — sometimes in their animal counterparts, sometimes just as themselves, sometimes speaking through humans as a vessel they've deemed worthy. You never know exactly what you'll get with the gods."

I stared at her, trying to detect sarcasm, because she couldn't be serious, right? She stared back, a hint of a smile hidden behind her otherwise stony expression. My mouth opened and closed as I tried to figure out what the fuck you even said to something like that.

When she didn't elaborate further, I waved my hand through the air as if I could swat the completely outrageous idea away like a bothersome fly. "We're just gonna shelve all of *that* for now and talk about the other things you mentioned. Foresight. Is that just the visions I've had? Or is there more?"

"Yes." Yrsa stopped to inspect small stones, dropping some in her pocket and others back to the beach with no apparent reason. "We should be able to get you to a point where you can guide your visions like leading a horse to water, although you cannot force it to drink. The magic is still much broader than us — it's difficult to pinpoint an exact person or thing you'd like to See, but I can teach you to aim it in a general direction."

"I did that last time when I tried to find Signe," I said, thinking back on the vision I'd had of her attacking the wall. Thor leaned into my leg, his warmth anchoring me here rather than getting lost in the anxiety I felt anytime I relived the battle in my mind. "Which, I guess it worked. I Saw her."

"You did." Her smile carried a hint of pride, the sea breeze blowing loose strands of hair around her face. "But we need to work on your control to make sure you understand when you're overextending yourself."

She dusted the sand off her hands, turning back towards the cliffs, a hand over her eyes to block the morning sun. "So far, you've been lucky with your attempts, visions pushing themselves to the forefront of your consciousness whether you were ready for them or not. But, with time, we can make it so it's more of a door you can open and close, at will. Urgent visions may still filter through, but the rest should subside, keeping you in control."

"Well, that sounds preferable. Can you teach me not to pass out after each vision?"

"Yes," Yrsa laughed, stopping at the edge of the rocky outcrop leading up to the cliffs. "Your stamina and understanding your limits will be our first priority. But before we even get there, you need to learn to draw your powers forward quickly, and at will." She spun back towards me, brows high. "Are you ready to begin?"

I held my arms up, pointing at the absolute nothing around us. "Not a lot going on at the moment."

"Then come with me, child."

Yrsa ducked down and tied her skirts up around her thighs, freeing her legs for easier movement. Glancing back up, she nodded, then began working her way up the uneven rock face, finding hand and footholds to help her over the boulders making up this stretch. I watched from the shore for a minute as the woman nearly twice my age climbed up the boulders I was hesitant about, but shit, if she could do it, I could, too.

Famous last words.

"Stay," I told the dogs, and Freki sat down hard with a *thump*, dropping his stick to the ground. Thor growled low in his throat, but sat as I asked. "Good boys. I'll be back."

With quick movements, I hiked up my skirts the same way Yrsa had, then did my best to follow the path she'd taken over the rocks. The stone dug into my hands, slippery with sea spray, challenging me every step of the way. The wind felt stronger with each foot of altitude we gained above the beach, but Yrsa kept going, so I did too.

"Odin's beard," I wheezed between breaths, bent over at the waist with my hands on my knees when we made it to a plateau a few dozen feet above the water. I stood too close to the edge, but the thought of moving even another inch was too much. "Fuck, everything here is humbling in the *worst* way. I've got a stitch in my side so big it could sew the realms together."

Yrsa chuckled, not showing any of the wear and tear I felt. She tilted her face towards the sun, light gleaming off her long auburn braid as Hadriel circled overhead. I stood, hand clutching my side, trying to breathe in through my nose and out through my mouth, taking in the view.

The Baltic Sea stretched for as far as I could see, white-caps dotting the deep blue water. Gulls floated in the sky just above the water, diving towards the surface and back up again. The wind whistled as it blew through the rocks around us, and my skirt came untied, the fabric rustling in the wind. "Beautiful."

Yrsa hummed and lifted her hands out the side. The sun seemed to find her, the clouds clearing until hazy light shone directly on her face as if called to her. It was ethereal, as so many moments here had been. So far removed from my life until now, I couldn't help but feel the immensity of all that had happened to me in the last year.

The wind moved around us in a cyclone, sand spinning around her legs with each passing second, the power in the air palpable. I was mesmerized by how at peace she looked here, how *right*. Even without a pendant or a dragon of her own, the serene expression on Yrsa's face made me believe everything she'd said the Promised were capable of. She was a healer, and from what I already knew of her, her intuition was off the charts. Hell, maybe she was communing with the gods right now.

"Ready for your first lesson?" she said, still bathing in the sunlight with her eyes closed.

"Why the hell not." I dropped my arms, unsure what to do next.

Her chin tipped down, eyes open and focused on me with blazing intensity. "What are you most afraid of?"

My brows met my hairline. "Right now?"

"Yes, right now." She lowered her arms, turning towards me.

I glanced over my shoulder at the fifty-foot drop down to the sea. "I mean, it would probably be wise to move away from the cliff. Kinda afraid of that."

"Don't deflect," she chided, and I looked back at her. While she still wore the same caring expression as always, there was an edge to Yrsa I'd never seen before. "Are you, or are you not, afraid of falling off the cliff?"

I moved to step away from the cliff towards her, but before I could, she rushed towards me, hands landing in the center of my chest and *shoved*.

Air sucked out of my lungs as my eyes blew wide, my arms flailing in a windmill around me as I plummeted to my death. Every thought, every emotion except blinding fear disappeared, leaving me flayed open and exposed in my final moments.

Maybe this was for the best — maybe I was never meant to be some great and powerful thing. Maybe every moment had come to this — too trusting, too out of shape, too naïve, too freaking *blind* to ever make a difference in this world or any other.

My hair whipped at my face, the biting wind drawing tears out as I studied the sky, unable to see the rocks below, knowing this was the end.

I'm sorry, I sent to Hadriel, the words woefully inadequate for the raging grief in my soul. He needed me, and I'd failed him before we even stood a chance.

An ear-splitting roar rent the air before my world went black.

21

DOMARI

Water lapped on the hull as they sailed through the night, a crew awake and navigating while others slept, stretched out wherever they could. Domari lay on the floorboards of the ship under two seats, his hands folded behind his head as he stared up at the sky. The night was clear, stars twinkling against the dark blanket of night, the same as they'd been eleven years ago when he'd first made this journey. But everything was different now. *He* was different, changed by life and grief and love until he'd morphed into a version of himself he hardly recognized.

The first time he'd made this journey, he'd been running to escape heartbreak, needing space and time to heal the wounds Tove's death had carved. Now, his heart broke with each oar stroke putting distance between him and Shelbie.

"Domari, right?" a young man said from his perch on the bench to Domari's left, pulling him from his dark thoughts. "I've heard about you."

Domari grunted, not bothering to look away from the starlit sky, but his lack of attention didn't deter the sailor, who moved to the bench closest to Domari. He sat nearly over Domari's head, making it almost impossible to avoid the excited and curious look on the boy's face. His blond hair was pulled back in a knot on the top of his head, similar to how Magnus wore his, but it was the excited look in his eyes that reminded him of his cousin.

"You were in the Guard? They called you the *Akolouthos*. That's the leader of the Guard, isn't it?"

Again, Domari didn't answer, but the kid must have taken his silence for an agreement.

He grinned, then kicked his feet up on the bench across from him, the toe of his boots resting on the wooden edge. "I think I'm going to join. Several of our men left from Torvik a few years ago and I've heard of the riches they've earned in Miklagard, working for the Emperor. They've sailed all across the world, seeing more than I can imagine."

Domari said nothing as the adolescent prattled on, his leg bouncing with excitement as he talked of battle in a glamorized way that said he'd never seen one before.

"When Hamund returns, I'm going to stay back and join."

Sensing the opportunity to sleep was lost to him, Domari sat up on the bench. "If they'll have you."

He jerked back, confusion clouding his eyes. "What do you mean? I thought the Emperor accepted all Northmen who applied."

A dark chuckle rolled through Domari's chest. "And you think your pale hair is enough to buy your entrance, yes?"

He shook his head, pulling a dagger from the belt around his waist. "What's your name, *knut*?"

"Edgar." His eyes trailed over the blade in Domari's hand. He dropped his feet to the floorboards, the water splashing as he knocked an oar loose. It slapped against the water, but Edgar moved quickly, grabbing the handle and righting it again. "Edgar Sighaddsson."

"And how old are you, Edgar Sighaddsson?"

"Seventeen." Edgar's chin tipped up defiantly, his eyes staying focused on Domari even as Domari pulled the blade across a whetstone, moonlight catching the metal and reflecting out into the dark night.

Only two years younger than when Domari had joined the Guard, but there was an excitement to this boy that told him his life had been far easier than Domari's.

"Have you ever killed a man, Edgar Sighaddsson?" Domari leaned forward to rest his elbows on his knees, holding the dagger out in front of him. He rested the pad of his thumb on the tip of the blade, blood welling instantly at the small prick. "Stood so close, you watched the life leave his eyes? Knowing he took his last breath because of you?"

Edgar didn't blink, but the boy's shoulders inched up. "I know how to fight."

Domari sat up, already tired of this conversation. Every Northman who showed up to join the Guard was the same — seeking glory and riches with their blades but more died in battle their first year than survived to craft a legacy for themselves. That, somehow, was never talked about at home. "I'm sure you do, Edgar Sighaddsson."

"Why do you keep saying my name like that?"

"Because" —Domari flipped the blade in his hand, then stabbed it into the wooden bench just outside Edgar's thigh, slicing a hole in his trousers— "a Guard has no name, *Edgar Sighaddsson*. The Guards are tools, weapons wielded by a greedy Emperor to protect himself against the many who want him dead. We fight battles for people we don't even know, not sure if they're the enemy or we are. It is bloody, and gruesome, and a stain on your soul you can never remove. You, Edgar Sighaddsson, are not a Guard."

Edgar's excited expression shuttered. He clenched his jaw and sat back, looking over the open sea. A tinge of guilt crept over Domari, but he couldn't find it in him to regret his harsh words and discouragement. The Guard wasn't a glamorous goal to strive for. It was a bloody and brutal means to an end, and an end that didn't matter.

"Return with me," Domari said, and Edgar's gaze swung back towards him. Domari wasn't sure who was more surprised by his words. "If you want to fight, then at least choose something worth fighting for."

"I heard you in the square." Edgar lifted his chin, his blue eyes the same color as the foam lapping against the edge of the boat. "You doomed us all. Told everyone there this was a losing battle, and we stood no chance. Why would I choose that?"

Domari's brow quirked, a low laugh rumbling in his chest. "Maybe. I certainly shouldn't be in charge of morale, but I can lead an army."

"Do you have one?" Edgar said, his head tilted to the side. "Why are you here" —he waved his hands out over the open sea— "if you're supposed to be leading an army?

Doesn't seem as if you're much use here, days away from your forces."

"Because." Domari stood, taking a deep breath of the night air as he looked in the distance. When he spoke next, it was loud enough to draw the eyes of other sailors among them. "I've come to bring my army home."

"You're —" Edgar looked around at those now focused on their conversation. "You're calling the Guard home?"

"Yes." Domari still studied the horizon, looking for any hint of land. "And any of you who I can convince to return with me."

"You said it yourself," someone called from behind him. "There's no chance."

"Maybe not." Domari turned towards the man, a stout trader draped in furs and gold, wearing his status like a shield. "But can't you feel it? Can't you feel the work of the gods in this? Can't you see that this is about far more than you and me?"

He held his arm out, pointing back towards Torvik. "Dragons have surfaced in our world once more, right as the way of the Vikings will be changed forever. You and I both know that these trade routes are more profitable than the raids of old — there is no going back from here."

Domari dropped his arm, gesturing towards the piles of goods weighing their boats down. "This is the way of the future, not that. Draugr hopes to start anew, restoring the ways of the Vikings of old, raiding and pillaging the way his father and grandfather did. But I want more than that. I've seen more battles than all of you combined, and I can tell you, a battle to protect my family is the only one I plan to engage in ever again."

Waves lapped against the hull, the wind whipping through the sail the only sounds as the crew stared at Domari, waiting for more. And fuck, this was what he hated most about being in charge. How could he convince anyone to willingly go to their death?

"We adapt, we survive, we fight for our families, for our people, for our land. No matter how tempting it might be to go back to the ways of old, we cannot succumb to the darkness, not even on the darkest night."

His gaze caught on Edgar's eager expression, so like Magnus's it gave him pause.

"Besides," Domari said, channeling his younger cousin, "even if we die, we'll have the best seats in Valhalla. Who else can say they fought alongside *and against* a dragon? Maybe you'll even slay one for me on your way out."

Men chuckled, but no one called out against Domari or argued back. He took his seat again, trying to find solace in the fact that he'd at least tried to convince them to join him.

Days bled together as they sailed. The journey was uneventful if slow in the mild early summer weather. Domari's knife cut into the wood chunk in his palm, the small figure finally beginning to resemble Thor's hammer, Mjölnir, as he'd intended. The legendary weapon had always been a symbol of strength for Vikings, only capable of being wielded by Thor, the god of the people and protector of Midgard.

A gull cried in the distance, and Domari's head snapped up, looking ahead as he set the toy on the bench next to him.

"Land!" someone called, and the excitement spread quickly along the ship. It had been a year since the last time Domari had seen the pale stone walls and red roofs of Staraya Ladoga, but the fortress looked the same, perched at the mouth of the river beyond.

The crew lowered the sail, and the drum beat resumed. Domari and the sailors took their places, oars dipping into the water. The wood dug into Domari's hands as his mind focused on the walls in the distance, hoping Grim and his men were still stationed here.

Breathing in time with the drum, Domari's muscles burned, steely resolve settling into his bones at the sight of dozens of boats moored outside the town.

He had one week to fill those boats with as many men as he could find. One week to convince them to fight a battle they very well may lose. One week to bring hope back to his people. One week to make a difference and give Shelbie the army she needed.

The boat bobbed in the shallow water, boots splashing as he climbed over and made his way ashore. Several men watched him as he took off through the familiar streets, but only Edgar followed.

A mixture of stone and wooden buildings rose high above his head, signs of the bustling trade route everywhere.

Dozens of inns and taverns lined the dirt-packed roads, horses and wagons mixed with signs of sea-farers. Tents dotted the horizon, the beginning of the trade season leaving hundreds of travelers ready to make their way to the markets in Constantinople. While not as developed as the markets in Miklagard, the port city was far busier than Torvik.

Domari tightened the belt around his waist, and the axes on his hips clattered together. Wary glances followed him everywhere he went, standing taller than most like many Vikings did. He ignored the trailing stares with no time to waste.

Luckily, his soldiers were relatively lazy creatures of habit, and by the third tavern, he saw the telltale signs of their presence — shields stacked outside, leaning up against the hitching posts and garden wall.

Raucous laughter boomed from within as a man stumbled drunkenly through the door and onto the streets, spitting curses. He teetered on his feet, angry gaze swinging from the tavern to the shields haphazardly left outside, the Varangian Guard eagle symbol enough to deter anyone who might think to steal one.

"Northmen." The drunk spat at Domari and Edgar's feet, then wiped at the blood on his face, streaming from his broken nose. "Savages, all of you. Even your women are beasts."

Edgar's hand slid to the knife on his belt, but Domari grabbed the back of his tunic, holding him back. "If you intend on fighting every person who spits our name, you'll be dead before the night is over."

It was enough to still the boy's hand, and the drunk pushed past them, weaving down the street.

"Are there women in the Guard?" Edgar asked as Domari released his tunic and stepped towards the tavern doors.

"No." He walked into the dim interior as shouting rang out from within, the sounds of fists hitting flesh unmistakable. Memories of nights spent drinking and fighting with his men flooded him. He didn't miss the hangovers and bruises, but these men had been his family for ten years. They'd lived and died together, as brutal and proud as they came. "They'd never last."

Before his eyes adjusted to the dark space, a fist sailed through the air, whipping Domari's face to the side, sending him into the wall. He slid down it, ears ringing at the impact. In the mere moments before darkness consumed him, Domari swore he heard a woman's voice.

"If I had a coin for every time I heard that, I could buy all my shield maidens brand new daggers to gut you with, plated in gold."

22

DOMARI

"When I said 'guard the door,' I didn't mean to level anyone who walked through it," a voice boomed from across the room, moving towards where Domari still slumped against the wall, trying to get his bearings. His ears rang, bringing the noise in the room to a deafening roar.

Gods, it had been ages since he'd been bested in a fight, but a one-sided blow could hardly be called such.

Edgar stooped in front of him, a wide grin on his youthful face as he looked between whoever loomed over Domari and back. The boy held out a hand, pulling him upright. "Looks like times have changed, Domari."

The noise in the room went quiet, his name whispered between the patrons. Tugging on his tunic, he fought down the urge to touch his temple. He cleared his throat and scanned the room looking for familiar faces.

"Saints, it really is you," that same voice said.

Domari turned slowly, blinking to clear his vision. In the

center of the room stood Grimbold, his brown hair and beard contrasted against his suntanned skin. His dark tunic and trousers were the same as most of the men in the room, except for the eagle stitched onto his chest, the same as the shields outside. Gone were any signs of youth he'd once had when he fought alongside Domari years ago, leaving behind a battle-hardened *Komes*, the leader to the 300 Guards stationed here in Staraya Ladoga. Grimbold's hand rested on the blade at his side, but he didn't pull it free, his gaze raking over Domari.

"I see you've let lawlessness take over in my absence, Grim." Domari stepped forward, willing the last signs of the blow to dissipate. He held out a hand to his old friend in greeting, hoping he hadn't misjudged this entire mission.

Grim's dark eyes flitted from Domari's face to his hand and back, the moments ticking by agonizingly slow. He didn't lower his hand or look away, lifting his chin to hide the worst of his fears.

If this didn't go well, a punch to the temple would be the least of his worries. Knowing the Emperor, there was probably a price on Domari's head, a sum that would tempt every mercenary in this room.

Domari swallowed, and a broad grin took over Grim's face. He gripped Domari's arm, then pulled him into a hug, slapping him on the back. "Welcome back, asshole. I hardly believed the rumors you'd left your post, but you stink of fish and seawater, not those sweet perfumes the Emperor favored."

He chuckled, shoving Grim away. "And you smell like

piss and stale ale. All these years and you still haven't learned soap works on more than your dick."

A booming laugh burst out of Grim. "Where's the fun in that?"

With a shake of his head, Grim spun back towards the room, arms held high. "Tonight calls for a celebration! Domari, the most legendary warrior and Guard of our time, has returned!"

Shouts echoed around the room, ale spilling out of cups held aloft. Domari followed Grim back to his chair in the far corner of the room, the setup here almost a throne. Candle wax dripped off the sconces on the wall, leaving puddles on the floor underneath them. The dim, flickering light disguised most of the filth, but his boots stuck to the sticky floors.

Grim dropped down onto the thick furs draped over the chair and threw a knee over the armrest. He leaned back and held out a tattooed hand, waiting until a barmaid handed him a fresh ale. His fingers trailed over the woman's hip, and she blushed, a small smile tugging on her lips. When she leaned her weight into his touch, he pulled her down onto his knee.

"Nothing has changed for you, I see." Domari took the ale the woman held in her other hand. "Still boozing and fucking through your time off."

"Is there any better way, my friend?" Grim kissed along the barmaid's neck, free hand resting on her thigh.

Domari took a sip of the ale, his eyes scanning the drunken men in the tavern. Most of them wore the eagle emblem, the same as Grim, and were in the same level of disarray. "Clearly, your new *Akolouthos* hasn't left you enough responsibility if you've grown this comfortable."

"Clearly, our new *Akolouthos* has forgotten we even exist here in Staraya Ladoga," Grim drawled, his expression shifting to bored disinterest. "We've had no word from the Emperor in three moons. My men are restless and ready for battle. So much so, they've started fighting each other, and apparently anyone who walks into the tavern."

"Who else is still here?" Domari looked back out at the crowded room. At least two dozen men were scattered around the small space, but this was barely a tenth of the men he'd stationed here with Grim before he'd left his post. The hope he'd clung to for the last several days of his journey dwindled as he looked around at the men — drunk, disorderly, and nothing like the Guard he'd left behind.

"The usuals." Grim gulped his ale, patting the barmaid's bottom until she moved off his lap and returned to the kitchens. "More are back at camp for the night." He clapped Domari on the shoulder, squeezing quickly before he nodded his head forward. "But come with me. Meet your assailant, and get your payback, as is fair."

Domari followed Grim to the bar counter across the room where warriors leaned against it, chatting and gambling over dice and board games.

"You haven't had orders in three moons?" Domari asked, studying the drunken men who looked far from the battle-ready squadron he'd sent to Staraya Ladoga last year. While Grim was strict enough to keep his men in shape, to see so many of them in their cups at once was enough to tell him standards had slipped.

"Nothing," Grim said, his dark eyes betraying his bitterness over this turn of events. "And our last payment is due. I cannot keep mercenaries in line with no coin. That's why we're here, after all."

Domari nodded, an uneasy feeling settling in his stomach. How far had the empire fallen if a squadron 300-strong was forgotten? Did they consider Staraya Ladoga, what had always been the entrance to the empire from the north, now useless? And if so, what would happen to these men here? Was it his fault Grim and his squadron were forgotten assets?

Grim leaned against the bar next to a small figure, hood pulled over their head. While there was nothing special about the brown rough-spun cloak, that its wearer wore the hood up *inside* a dark tavern spoke of secrets.

Grim and Domari both towered over the patron, whose shoulders and hands were slight in comparison to the warriors in this room. Their posture was relaxed as they sipped their ale, unfazed by the commotion around them.

Noticing Domari's focus, Grim smiled, his elbows leaning back against the bar next to the stranger. "Do you have any idea who you took out this time?"

The hooded figure set their drink down, slowly turning in Grim's direction.

The stranger's face was obscured by the thick fabric and the dark room, but Domari felt eyes focus on him, flaying him open to inspect his every thought and emotion. He held his breath, unable to look away, feeling something *more*.

"I know exactly who he is," a blunt but unmistakably feminine voice said, surprising Domari. Her slim hands raised to her hood as she dropped it back, revealing brown hair braided in neat rows with pale skin, marked with black war paint. Most prominently was a design Domari recognized immediately — two black raven wings formed a half-moon between her brows, drawn into long lines running down the center of her nose. Even if her eyes hadn't been the same vivid emerald green as Signe and Viveka's, the mark alone would have told Domari exactly who this woman was. *What* she was.

"A Valkyrie," Domari whispered, awed by this woman's presence, and what it might mean to find a Valkyrie this far from the North.

Those piercing green eyes flashed in recognition as she turned to face him. "A shield maiden," she amended, downplaying what Domari already knew.

"And a downright fearsome one at that." Grim took her discarded ale and chugged the remaining contents. "I've never seen her lose a fight. But that's easy to do when you hit first, ask questions later."

Grim laughed at his own joke, but Domari couldn't look away from the calculating expression on the woman's face.

"Have we met?" He tried to place what about her was so familiar aside from those green eyes.

She shook her head, then stepped closer to Domari, laying a hand on his arm, finger tracing the bands tattooed there. "No, we haven't."

"Why'd you hit him then?" Grim burped, then pounded a fist against his chest. "I figured this was some scorned lover bullshit from years ago."

Her lips tipped up in a smirk, but her eyes betrayed her

— the Valkyrie before him found nothing funny about this situation. "I've traveled the world chasing you, Warrior. You're a hard man to pin down, Domari Njalsson."

His brows dipped. "Why? What do you want of me?"

This time, her emerald eyes crinkled with true amusement. "To help you fulfill your true calling. Your destiny. I hold the key to the very Fate you wish to defy."

Her fingers trailed over his skin as she dropped her hand and moved to the door, leaving him with far more questions than answers.

Grim slapped his back, moving to follow her. "Come. Let's head back to camp. I'm sure the others will be glad to see you."

"Who was that?" Domari asked as they wove through the crowded tavern and out into the night.

"She showed up sometime last summer. Must have been about the time you left your post, I suppose."

"Alone?"

Grim shook his head, grabbed a shield from the pile, strapped it to his back, and strode down the street towards camp. "No. There are six other shield maidens who travel with her."

He missed a step as he fought to breathe normally.

Seven. *Seven* Valkyries.

Mentally recounting every legend he'd ever heard, Domari's mind raced. Odin was said to have *nine* sacred Valkyries. If seven were here, that left Viveka and Signe.

Every battle strategy he'd imagined went up in flames as he recalculated the odds with this new information. To have all nine Valkyries on a battlefield at once was unprecedented, a sure sign of Ragnarok. They didn't just even the scales — they demolished them.

"You all right?" Grim asked when Domari didn't move, frozen just outside the tavern. "Shit, maybe Hilda hit you harder than I realized. Come, let's get you some food."

Domari nodded, heart racing as he thought through his course of action, knowing now, more than ever, he had to convince everyone here to follow him home.

This was the end, the battle to end all battles.

And he refused to lose.

23

SHELBIE

Istared at the sky, every piece of my body feeling broken and battered since Yrsa threw me off a cliff several days ago. Landing on Hadriel's back was preferable to crashing to the rocks below, but only slightly. His focus had been more on saving my life than softening my landing, and my body still bore the bruises to prove it.

"We're not done yet," Magnus barked from my right where he led others through drills on the beach each morning. "You've only gone through the warmups, Shelbie. Reyna can do more than you."

I held up my middle finger in answer and earned a swift rap from a training staff to the knuckles in response. "I've never hated you as much as I do right now."

"Yeah? This is only day *three*. Just you wait."

I glared over at him, red-faced from exertion and beaming, and only felt marginally better at how sweaty my relentless drill sergeant was himself. Unlike me, the 20-something

Viking was in fantastic shape, built for this lifestyle. Every inch of his exposed skin — which was currently all on display aside from the brown pants and boots — was covered in dark tattoos, runes and symbols lacing the wide expanse of his chest and arms, up his neck to the neatly trimmed beard. His blond hair was tied up in a knot on the top of his head, a light sheen of sweat glistening on his skin.

"Do I need to get your dragon over here nipping at your heels? I bet he'd take my side."

I peered over the tops of my feet to where said dragon was curled on the beach, sunning himself and definitely *not* here to hang out. It just so happened this was a good sun spot, or so he'd insisted when he'd appeared shortly after we started training for the day.

"Go ahead," I yelled back to Magnus. "See if Hadriel lets you within arm's reach of him. I've always wondered if he needed to chew before he swallows a human, or if one bite was enough."

Don't tempt me. Hadriel yawned wide enough to show every tooth in his very large mouth, a lazy trail of smoke escaping as well.

As tough as Magnus was, I saw the flicker of fear in his eyes. He shook his head and moved back down the beach towards the rest of his trainees, leaving me be.

Thanks, big guy. I waved my hand in Hadriel's direction, still unable to move. Damn, I wished Yrsa had taught me how to heal myself first instead of her whole, *if you're a bird, I'm a bird,* lesson.

You do need to train though, Hadriel added. *Even for a human, you're woefully unprepared for battle.*

For the second time in as many minutes, I held up my middle finger. *Bite me.*

You would have hardly any nutritional value. I require muscle.

Okay, I answered, groaning as I pulled myself to a sitting position, *that was rude.*

I could feel Hadriel's grumbled answer, even if his words were unintelligible. He was always surly, but ever since he'd plucked me from the sky, something between us had changed. Neither the dogs nor the dragon were willing to put too much distance between us. Fine. By. Me.

I'd even taken to sleeping with Hadriel in his cave above the town, finding comfort in the rough-hewn home and the built-in space heater in the shape of a dragon. The moment when we both thought I'd drawn my last breath was a reality check for us — I was much more fragile than him, and we needed each other for whatever lay ahead.

Crawling across the beach towards him, I slumped onto his side, soaking in the warmth from his dark scales heated by the morning sun. *Gonna close my eyes for a minute,* I told him, breathing in the fresh sea air, throwing my arm over my face. Thor brushed against my side, spinning once before settling between my knees. *Keep the beasties away. And by beasties, I mean Magnus.*

Up, Hadriel said, and I jerked awake, blinking rapidly to clear the sleep from my eyes. *High tide will be here soon, and we need to move.*

I sat up, then groaned as I held my abs, sorer than I'd

been in years after three freaking days of training with Magnus and the fall from the cliff before that.

If you went back for more training with Yrsa, she could teach you to heal yourself.

I turned a stink-eye on my dragon, not bothering to voice my thoughts on the matter. That psycho woman I thought had been a mentor and a friend had shoved me off a cliff, and I wasn't thrilled at the prospect of whatever other *lessons* she had planned.

Did she know I had a dragon ready to snatch me from the sky? Yes. But she could have *warned* me that was her intention.

You humans whine a lot, Hadriel said.

I rolled my eyes, then shoved off him to get to my feet. *Someday, you'll understand what it means to be injured and weak. Let's hope someone is there to give you shit for it, every step of the way.*

A smoke ring left Hadriel's nostrils, and he rose to his feet, stretching like a cat. His wings extended out on either side, shaking the sand off the dark leathery muscles in what I could have sworn was the dragon equivalent of flexing his biceps. *Not likely.*

Males. I shook my head, brushing my skirt clean. *You are all the exact same.*

Hadriel lifted into the sky, flying just overhead as I skirted around town, avoiding the street the Erikssons resided on. Time ticked by faster than I cared for, but even three days later, I couldn't bring myself to face Yrsa again. Did that make me a chickenshit? Probably. Was I fully aware that I had nothing but battles ahead of me and was ducking out at the first sign of hardship? Yep. Could I bring myself to do better? Big fat nope.

As if the two giant dogs trailing me weren't enough to garner attention, Hadriel's increased presence as he hovered over me drew the eyes of everyone in town. If they hadn't known I was his Promised before, they most certainly did now. Since we always left our telepathic connection open, the onyx stone around my neck glowed constantly, and I couldn't find it in me to hide it.

Nearing the docks, the sounds of the gentle waves and the gulls overhead gave way to children's laughter. I stopped to watch them run into the incoming surf, splashing and playing in the afternoon sun. Hadriel flew overhead and they all stopped and pointed, awed as everyone in town seemed to be.

It was hard to wrap my head around how rare dragons were in this world since I'd met Hadriel within days of arriving here. He was as much a part of this version of history I was living as the boats tied on the docks, bobbing in the waves.

Hadriel swooped low, dragging his talons through the water and sending a spray towards the children, all shrieking in delight at the playful move.

I should have known you're a big softie.

With a backward glance my way, Hadriel lifted into the sky, letting go a plume of fire I felt all the way to my bones even with it pointed to the sun.

Now you're just showing off.

He flapped hard, rising higher, and I looked back down

at the villagers gathered on the beach, startled to see faces I recognized among them. Namely, an auburn-haired woman I'd been avoiding for days.

"Ah, shit," I muttered, and Thor's chest rumbled. "I know, right?"

Freki barked, and Yrsa turned towards me. His tail wagged, and I frowned down at the puppy. "Bad dog."

With a glance over my shoulder, I looked for an exit. "Stay," I commanded both dogs. Thor shot me a deadpan expression before dropping down into the sand, as sassy as the dragon in the sky.

Earning my chickenshit title, I grabbed my skirts and hurried towards the open air market on the edge of the beach, hoping I could duck behind one of the buildings and hide.

You are an embarrassment.

I stuck my hand in the sky, flipping off Hadriel for the second time today, and hurried through the crowded stalls.

Going incognito when there was a giant glowing green stone hanging from your neck was more difficult than I'd planned. Vendors stopped and stared, whispering when I hurried past, but my heart pounded from both sheer exhaustion and anxiety.

Furs, fruits, fish, jewelry, and carved wooden dishes and toys were a blur as I raced past them, the smells and sounds lost on me as I focused on getting *away*. I glanced over my shoulder looking for any sign of Yrsa following me, but didn't see her in the crowd.

I slowed, face screwed up in pain as I held my side. Limping into the next row of stalls, I leaned against a tent pole. Two canvas flaps were tied to the poles along the front of the building, held open during the fair weather, but I assumed could be closed if the weather turned. I glanced down at the table, taking in the variety of breads and… was that cheese?

As if my senses were all coming back to me, I inhaled, savoring the scents that were as close to home as I'd felt in ages. "Oh, my God. This smells heavenly."

The woman in the stall had her back to me, bright red hair tied in a dizzying array of braids hanging past her shoulders over her simple dress and apron. She glanced over her shoulder momentarily, but didn't look away from her task at hand. "Bread fresh from the hearth is always best."

"What are you making it from?" I asked, studying her worktable set up near a hearth at the back of the hut. Flour dusted most of the table as she kneaded dough, leaning her whole body into the motion. I couldn't help but step closer, trying to peer over her shoulder to find out what was different about this bread than the ones I'd had so far. It smelled sweeter, almost honeyed, and my mouth damn near watered.

"My husband brews the best mead in Torvik." She lifted the dough into a wooden bowl and covered it with a piece of fabric, then clapped her hands together, flour scattering in a cloud. She turned towards me as she wiped her hands clean on her apron, a bright smile lighting up her freckled face. "You should try so—"

Her eyes dropped to the pendant around my neck. Just as quickly as she'd offered it, the smile was gone, her gaze bouncing between the stone and my face, a mixture of awe and hesitancy playing out.

"It's you," she whispered, her eyes finally settling on my face again as she stepped closer. "You're the woman they speak of. The reason the dragon is here. The savior of our people. Our Promised."

Well, fuck me.

The most awkward laugh I'd ever heard came out of my mouth as I lifted my hand and waved, taking this situation from weird to downright painful. My cheeks heated, a whole gamut of emotions flooding me, but none more so than shame.

I'd done *nothing* to earn this woman's awe, nothing to deserve this title thrust on me, nothing to give these people hope for a victory I wasn't confident in myself. Sure, I wanted to believe there was a way out of everything coming our way, but they thought *I* was capable of being the force to turn tides.

I could barely even get on a damn horse, crippled by my own fear after that one had sent me careening ass-backward down a cliff and straight into this whole predicament in the first place. In a terrible full circle moment, I stared all my inadequacies in the face, finding myself wanting.

"Gertrud." The woman bowed low in front of me. "It's truly an honor to meet you."

"Please." My voice sounded choked, holding the damn over the emotions threatening to spill free. "You don't need to bow."

"I'm sorry." She wiped her hands on her apron nervously. "The legends of the Promised have been spoken of for so long. Seeing you here before me... I don't have words."

Forcing a smile, I glanced to the side, trying to find an easy exit once again, but she reached forward, gripping my hand, holding me in place.

"Your timing when we need you most speaks of the gods' involvement. This is Fate, that the dragons rise again when battle nears. We've seen the world changing around us, especially here in Torvik as trade routes expand. The people speak of Ragnarok, the end of our world, but then you arrive, our last hope."

Tears shimmered in her eyes, and something inside me broke. I was going to fail so many people here, unable to rise to the challenge.

Dammit, I needed Domari, needed Charlene, needed my family — someone to hold me up when it felt like everything was too much to bear.

I pulled my hands free, nodding stiffly as I backed away from her. Before I could leave, Gertrud turned and grabbed three loaves of bread from her table and shoved them into my hands. Then, she grabbed two wineskins from a bowl below the table, balancing them on top of the bread in my arms.

"You don't have to do this," I said, feeling guilty and unworthy of anything, especially her gifts. "Please, I don't need this."

"Nonsense." She waved me off, studying my overflowing hands as if she could figure out how to give me more when I struggled to hold everything she'd already given me. "This is the least I can do, face to face with as close to the gods as I may ever come in Midgard."

I managed to stammer out a thank you before I turned and fled, afraid she'd find some way to gift me more things I was unworthy of. Weaving my way through the streets, I hurried towards the cliffs, needing to get away from everyone.

Feeling my distress, Hadriel soared overhead, leading the way back to our cave, and I broke into a run, not caring how badly my body hurt. I couldn't break down here in front of everyone, couldn't let them see how hopeless I felt.

Stares followed me as I raced through town and down to the beach, feet sinking into the sand. I lost my balance, falling to my knees and sending the bread and wineskins scattering. A choked sob escaped when I grabbed them, dusted everything off, and got to my feet. My knee revolted with each step, the fall bringing the extent of my injuries to the forefront of my brain, but I limped forward, bread and wine clutched to my chest.

Hadriel landed on the beach in front of me, his green gaze steady while he watched me rush forward. *Climb on.*

I shook my head, unable to even telepathically communicate how low I felt. I didn't deserve to have an easy way out of this. I didn't deserve his kindness, his friendship, his help. I wasn't worthy of any of it, hadn't earned even one ounce of this.

Hadriel didn't say anything else, but I could feel his pity through our bond, making me feel that much worse. He pushed off the beach, rising into the sky and circling overhead, watching me.

At the base of the cliffs, I looked up, studying the rocky path ahead. While the path was somewhat manageable, it was far from a clear hiking trail, full of boulders I had to climb over, needing both of my hands free. I rearranged the bread and wine, tucking things into my belt and the top of my dress. I looked like an idiot, but the thought of throwing Gertrud's hard work to the birds felt like a slap to the woman's face. I should have given everything back, but it was way too late for that.

Hands somewhat free, I stepped onto the first rock, pushing off my good leg. Everything in my body screamed, the pain a harrowing reminder of just how fragile and weak I was. My back seized, pulling the air from my lungs. I fought to put one foot in front of the other, clutching anything I could get my hands on. The dogs barked at the base of the cliff, annoyed to be left behind, but I knew they were safe with the Erikssons, and I didn't deserve even their comfort.

Tears streamed down my face freely with each passing second, everything I'd tried to hold at bay slipping free. I made achingly slow progress, the wind whipping off the water below sending my hair into a wild disarray around my face, making my watery vision that much worse.

I stopped at the base of a boulder I'd struggled with the last few days, scrambling over on my hands and knees every time I'd gone this way so far, but the first foothold was on the left — the knee I'd just twisted on the beach. Raising my leg, I tested the hold, then pushed down, trying to leverage myself off the ground. Rather than rising high enough to grab the first handhold, my entire body folded in half, my mouth falling open in a silent scream. I collapsed to the ground in pain.

Curling into myself, I let my head drop to the rocks below and sobbed. For the man who'd sailed away from me and might never return. For Signe and Gunnar. For the orphans in Frida and Astrid's care. For the lives of the people in Torvik who wouldn't make it through this final battle.

But mostly, I cried for myself. For the life I gave up to be here, for the family and friends I'd left behind, for my battered and bruised body and soul, unwilling and unable to face everything that was coming. I was so fucking lonely, and sad, and afraid. *So* afraid.

My body shook as the tears poured freely in this epic pity party, party of one. Every fear, every emotion I'd buried deep came to the surface, showing the ugly insides I hid from everyone.

I couldn't do this. Couldn't learn how to wield magic, couldn't get over how desperately I wanted to go home and forget it all. I wanted to hug my parents, to fall into Charlene's open arms, to play with my nieces, to laugh with Sabrina. Without Domari here reminding me of why I'd chosen to stay, everything seemed desolate.

Frustrated with myself, I screamed, the sound ripping through me. Clutching the pendant around my neck, I ripped it free, tossing it to the side.

"*FUCK!*" I shouted, the word echoing against the rocks, sounding so much larger than little old me. But that was the crux of it all, wasn't it?

This wasn't about me.

This was about the Fate of the whole fucking world, and I played a minor, but crucial part in saving it.

I wiped at my face, pulled myself to sit with my back against the boulder that had bested me, and pulled the wineskin free of the belt around my waist. Taking a long pull, I let the honeyed mead wash over my tongue, barely tasting the sweet wine as I drowned my melancholy thoughts.

24

SHELBIE

I laid on the rocks, bemoaning my Fate and overall existence as one does, when a shadow darkened my vision shortly before something soft pelted me in the face.

"Ow! What the —" I rubbed my nose, blinking at the loaf that rolled off my face and onto my stomach. Propping myself up on my elbows, I looked for my attacker.

"No bread left behind," Magnus chastised, easily lumbering over the boulders to join me on my perch.

"How'd you find me?" I still hadn't made it any farther up the cliff, having parked my butt halfway and called it a day. It was as good a place as any to drink myself into a stupor.

"Two black dogs barking constantly at the base of the cliffs was a good starting place." Magnus plucked the loaf off my stomach, dusted off the sand, and took a bite.

I wrinkled my nose. "Really?"

He shrugged, then sat down next to me. "Little dirt never hurt anyone."

"In a couple hundred years" — I tilted my head, and the world spun with it — "or thousand, I'm not sure, science is going to have a lot to say about that."

He hummed, his squinty eyes studying me with too much astuteness for my usually jovial friend. The weight of his gaze left me to look out over the ocean, the sunset streaking pink across the sky.

"You've looked better."

My mouth hung open. "Wow. You sure do know how to cheer a woman up."

Taking another bite of the bread, he draped his hands over his knees, eyes crinkling with humor. "Who said I was here to cheer you up? It looks like a bird landed in your hair and decided to roost."

I shoved his shoulder, but my aim was off, sliding right past his arm until my hand rested on his pectorals. Which were naked, of course. "Do you have a personal vendetta against shirts?"

He dropped his eyes to look at where my hand still rested on his chest. "How else would women randomly fondle me?"

Yanking my hand back, I shook my head and took another long drag of the wineskin. "I do not know how Astrid puts up with you."

Magnus chuckled, then grabbed the mead from my hands, draining the last of it.

"Hey!" I cried, reaching for the empty wineskin before he tossed it to the side. "That was mine!"

"Not anymore, it's not."

I crossed my arms over my chest, then glanced down at the weird lump under the fabric, noticing the loaf of bread I'd stored in there earlier. "Backup," I muttered to myself, tugging it, and the second wineskin, free.

Magnus leaned forward, peering down the front of my dress with an awed expression. "What else do you have in there?"

"A billowing bosom," I replied coolly, uncorking the skin.

He barked a laugh, head tipped back as I quoted him. "I suppose this is you embracing your inner Northman. Drowning your sorrows in mead. We'll have you spouting poetry before the night ends."

"Not sorrows," I snapped. Sorrows didn't feel quite right. "Pressure. Pressure is closer to how I'm feeling."

Magnus nodded. "Ah, I see. You're afraid."

While I could admit that to myself, admitting it to anyone had my hackles rising.

"No," I scoffed. "It's just — I wasn't meant to be here, and yet I was, and here I am. And I left everything behind — my friends, my family, my life — and yes, I *chose* to do that, but it's still a lot. It's still a huge adjustment, only I never got a second to adjust, because oops, we're on the brink of Ragnarok. And somehow, it's on me to learn how to fly a dragon and fight and use magic, mostly on my own, because who else has a dragon? No one. And if I fail — which, let's face it, why wouldn't I fail? — then all these people that I've come to know and love will die, and it will be my fault. *And* on top of all that, Domari up and leaves me. And I *know*" — I held up a hand when Magnus opened his mouth — "I *know* he had to go, and try to get backup, and he'll be back and it's for the best. But it doesn't mean it doesn't suck, too. It doesn't mean it doesn't also make it harder for me."

I let out a heavy sigh, my shoulders sagging as I took a huge bite out of the loaf of bread in my hands, tasting the honey mixed in with the dough. "Fuck, that's good."

"All right." Magnus leaned back on his hands, staring out at the horizon. "Tonight, embrace your despair. Tomorrow, it's done, because there's too much to do."

Had he not been listening? How the hell was I supposed to just turn it all off? "But I can't —"

"You might always be afraid," he cut me off. "That's fine. I'm afraid every time I enter a fight. I'm afraid for the children in my care, because who the fuck decided I was trustworthy enough to raise kids? I'm afraid I'll lose Astrid in childbirth or lose the baby I haven't even met yet. I'm afraid that my brother is dead, that Signe is hurt, that Domari is lost at sea. That we'll lose everything my father worked for."

"Shit." I picked up the wineskin and handed it to him. "Maybe you need this too."

He took a much smaller sip than last time, then handed it back. "Drink isn't going to make me any less afraid of any of those things."

I squinted at the horizon, watching the pink and blues merge together at dusk, and took another drink. "I mean, it *might* help. What else am I supposed to do?"

"You just do it." He shrugged. "You do it afraid."

"That easy, huh?"

"Easy?" He raised a blond brow, looking my way. "No, I

never said easy. Simple, though. Who else will do it, if not us?"

I blinked at him, the fuzziness in my brain making it hard to match the man beside me with the joking one I'd first met. "When did you get all wisdomous?"

His eyes twinkled as he fought to hide a smirk, pointing at his head. "This isn't just for growing this beautiful mane, you know."

"Well, you had me fooled."

"That's it." Magnus stood and dusted his hands off. "Time for a cooldown for you."

Before I knew what was happening, he'd wrapped his arms around me, plucking me off the boulder like I weighed no more than the very loaves I'd consumed, and carried me the short distance to the cliff above the water. I shrieked, true terror coming over me again as I clawed at his skin. I cursed my own stupidity, staring at where my onyx stone was laying across the rocks from me. *"Magnus, no!"*

"Hey." Magnus's brow furrowed as he stepped away from the rocks and stared down at me. My heart beat frantically in my chest, sobering me instantly until my feet touched down. Because my body hated me, my knee buckled, leaving me gripping Magnus's arms to hold myself up. Between the pain and my terror, I choked on a sob, hating myself all over again.

"Shit," he said, all humor leaving his tone when he looked over my body. "You know I'd never actually throw you over."

I shook my head, taken right back to the moment three days ago where Yrsa had pushed me so far past my limits, I broke. "Pendant." The word came out hoarse, but I pointed, and Magnus left me long enough to grab it.

The moment the cool chain touched my hands, I breathed a sigh of relief, wrapping it around my neck once more. The stone settled on my chest and immediately glowed green.

Don't do that, Hadriel growled instantly.

Never taking it off again. I nodded, not needing to be told twice.

I know you're afraid, but we have to do this together.

"Are you okay?" Magnus rested his hands on my shoulders, squeezing lightly. "What's got you so scared?"

My fingers circled the pendant, clutching it like a lifeline. I forced my breaths to even, my heart to slow. "Yrsa threw me off the cliff three days ago as my first 'lesson' in being a Promised."

He jerked back, his face a mixture of disbelief and rage. "She *what?*"

She needed you to understand our bond, Hadriel said, and I frowned. *She needed us both to understand that we are a team. You need me, and I need you. Our connection is tied to our very souls. We have to rely on each other, from here on out. I can't hide away in the cliffs like I have for years, and you can't carry on as if you're a mere human. Our Fate demands more from us, and we have to answer the call of the Norns together.*

I relayed Hadriel's message to Magnus, who let go of me, pulling up the sleeves of my dress to see the bruises littering my body.

"For fuck's sake," Magnus groaned. "Why have you let

me train you for the last three days when you're already this injured? Why haven't you asked Yrsa to heal you?"

"She threw me off a fucking cliff, Magnus. I'm not exactly racing back to her for more help. Who knows what her next lesson will be? Throwing daggers at an apple on my head?"

"Fine." Magnus threw up his hands. "Then I'll go with you."

"I'm —" I went back over his words again. "Wait, what?"

He shrugged. "You don't go to lessons without me. You don't go *anywhere* without me. Understood?"

"Magnus, no." I shook my head. "You have way too much on your plate already. I don't need a babysitter."

"If the positions were reversed, I'm positive Domari would do the same for Astrid."

I wanted to balk at him, list all the reasons this wouldn't work, but Magnus scooped me up, depositing me as far away from the cliffs as we could get on my little perch. Once I was seated just as I'd been before, he picked up the wine-skin and put it back in my hands and slid to the ground next to me.

I raised a brow. "What about lessons and training and doing things afraid? About drinking not making our problems go away?"

"That's tomorrow's problem." He nudged me with a shoulder, the last of the setting sun making his golden hair glow. "Tonight, we drink."

I took a long swig of mead, then passed him the wineskin, resting my head on his shoulder when he began to hum a tune.

"Thank you."

Magnus nodded, his hand squeezing my knee, and I closed my eyes. "Until Valhalla, Shelbie."

Cotton candy sky hovers above the mountains, painting the world in pinks and blues as the sun dips behind the mountains. I tilt my head back, closing my eyes and breathe in the clear mountain air, fingers roving over my mare's black coat. Spring rains have left the valley the deepest green for now, but soon summer sun will dry and wilt the grass.

"Doubting yourself, are you?" Charlene's blunt appraisal gives me a start, and she chuckles from her horse beside me.

"Why do you say that?"

"You wouldn't be showing up here, seeking me out, if you weren't."

I blink, her words shocking me even if this is a dream. "Is this real?"

Charlene gestures to the spring-filled valley around us, her caramel brown hair piled high on her head, barely moving in the wind. "Well, it sure isn't a memory."

Unable to wrap my head around this, I reach across my horse. The saddle tips to the side when I grip her arm and pinch.

She pulls back, humor lighting her hazel eyes. "Convinced?"

"Not in the least."

"Fair enough." She grins, grabbing her reins and steering her horse to the left. Instinctively, my mare follows, and we weave our way through the trees.

"How is this possible?" I ask, thinking back over my other memo-

ries and visions I've had. Aside from speaking with the Norns, I've never been corporeal, or spoken to anyone.

"There's a lot to my story I haven't told you," she answers, the setting sun catching on the rhinestones on her back pockets, temporarily blinding me. Yep, this is the Charlene I remember.

"I thought you weren't supposed to remember me. No one was."

She glances over her shoulder, her dark eyeliner making her hazel eyes almost glow a golden hue. "Magic doesn't work the same on me as it does other humans."

I pause, even more confused than I was a minute ago. "What does that mean?"

"There is so much of this world we don't yet understand," she begins, looking at the trees ahead of us. "Like why I have a knack for choosing the worst men. Except Nash."

"Obviously." I nodded at the mention of her third, must beloved husband, no idea where this is going.

"Life has taken me down avenues I never could have predicted, and somewhere along the way, I got myself into a spot of trouble that left me just a little different."

I frown. Tilt my head. "Are you human?"

She tosses her head back in a laugh, but a tinge of sadness creeps across her features I've never seen there before. "Sure as shit, I am. But magic and me go way back."

My mouth opens and closes, words lost to me. When Charlene doesn't elaborate past that, I shake my head, trying to clear the confusion. "Explain to me what this means for me."

"Time traveling is magic. Until you mentioned it, I didn't know it was possible."

"Okay."

She shrugs. "I don't understand it either, but my best guess is that *the remnants of magic I've touched remain in my soul, making what-ever your magic is work differently on me."*

"So —" I swallow, all this feeling too good to be true. "So, you won't forget me?"

"I hope not. I haven't yet."

Tears well in my eyes, but I blink them back. Even if I lose the rest of my past, maybe I can hang on to this one piece, this one person.

"Don't cry, darlin'." Charlene pulls her horse to a stop until my mare steps to her side. Charlene reaches across, squeezing my hand. "All of this was meant to be, even if it's all messed up right now."

"Charlene," I choke out, blinking rapidly as I stare up at the sky. "They think I'm some hero. That I'm the key to saving their entire world from imploding into an apocalypse."

She raises her brows, letting out a long whistle. "That's a lot."

"So much."

Movement over Charlene's shoulder catches my eye, and I lean in my saddle to stare into the forest. One by one, ghostly figures appear in the shadow of the trees, and I suck in a breath, realizing who stands there.

My mom, smiling at me.

My dad, blowing me a kiss.

My brother, waving goodbye.

Sabrina, her hand clutched over her chest.

"I love you all," I whisper, the words carrying across the clearing as a tear slips free, unable to be contained.

"They know," Charlene says, and I look back at her. "So, what are you going to do?"

I slump in the saddle, my shoulders dropping. "I don't think I have much choice in the matter."

"Well." She tugs on her reins, pushing her heels into her horse's

side. He lurches forward, ready to run through the clearing ahead. "Sometimes the only way out is through. Good thing they picked a bad bitch like yourself. Zippers up, Shelbie."

A laugh stutters out of me as Charlene leans forward, taking off across the clearing into the setting sun. My mare stomps her feet, shuffling side to side, but I hold the reins, keeping her in place.

As quickly as the dream came, it fades, the scent of the forest gone, replaced by the familiar salty air. I keep my eyes squeezed shut, holding on to my friends and family for just a moment longer.

"Zippers up, Charlene."

25

GUNNAR

Acrid smoke overwhelmed Gunnar's senses, blurring his vision and burning his lungs with each step. His hands were tied together in front of him, a rope leading from his shackles to Vermund's saddle, holding him hostage as he had been for days.

Peering around the dark woods, he looked for any sign of where they were, but the smoke made it hard to see much of anything aside from Vermund's back, rising and falling with each step of his horse. Tired of the eerie silence and unknowns, Gunnar hurried his steps and closed the distance.

"Do you believe in the gods?" Gunnar asked, his throat burning. Since their last conversation, his mind had replayed it on a loop, dissecting it.

Vermund turned in his saddle, green eyes near glowing in the haze. "As much as the next man. Why do you ask?"

Biting the inside of his cheek, Gunnar thought how to phrase his words. Like Domari, Vermund didn't speak much, but they'd come to a sort of silent truce in the weeks since he'd become Gunnar's jailer. For all the bloody rumors he'd heard of Vermund Oathbreaker, he had yet to see the brutality that had earned his reputation. Even on the raid yesterday, he'd held back, staying out of the fight as he watched from the hill with Gunnar.

"This feels *more*." Gunnar looked through the smoke again for any sign of life aside from their party, but whatever caused the smoke had likely scared off any wildlife too. "Valkyries. Dragons. A Promised. It's all enough to give even a non-believer pause."

"And are you?" Vermund pulled back on the reins. "A non-believer?"

Gunnar tilted his chin up, meeting his gaze. Losing an eye had altered his vision, but Gunnar didn't need to see clearly to hear the intensity in Vermund's words. "I don't know what to believe anymore."

Vermund nodded. A flash of disappointment passed over his expression before he squeezed his legs into his horse's side and motioned him forward once more.

Silently cursing himself for his answer, Gunnar hurried forward. "I believe in Signe. Even without the rumors swirling of her being a Valkyrie, I think I knew. I've known since the day she showed up in my village."

"And what of it?" Vermund didn't bother to look down at Gunnar this time.

"It changes nothing." And Gunnar meant it to his very core. "I love her. I always have."

"Even if she's lost to the battle magic, called to a grue-some destiny? Even if she destroys your family, you'll love her then? Even if she's the catalyst for Ragnarok, the end of days, you'll follow her?"

Gunnar tripped over an exposed root, hidden in the ashy haze. He shook his head, refusing to acknowledge his words. "No."

Vermund turned to look at him, and Gunnar hurried to clarify.

"I don't believe any of that. Signe is stronger than you give her credit for. She isn't lost. She won't hurt those she loves. She's not the catalyst, but yes, I would follow her anywhere, to whatever end."

Vermund sighed and stared ahead, urging his horse on. "I've known Signe since the day she was born, Gunnar. I watched her grow into the woman she is. I trained her with every weapon she wields. I've fought at her side and at her back in battles you'd be appalled to hear the details of. You do not understand what her childhood was like." His jaw worked, head shaking. "She's been crafted to be the exact weapon she is. You do not truly understand what it means to be a Valkyrie, no matter how well you think you know your wife."

"You're wrong." Frustration burned Gunnar's throat almost as much as the smoke. "I know her better than anyone. I *see* her. I've never been blind to the icy rage that lies beneath the surface. I watched her yesterday during the raid, the same as you did. We both know why they call her the Demon Spawn."

Vermund hummed in agreement, likely remembering yesterday's bloodbath. Draugr had led a raid on a nearby village along their path, killing their way through the entire town. They burned crops, murdered innocents, and stole whatever riches could be found.

Gunnar had hoped to see that same crack in Signe's mental fog he'd seen in Torvik, but whatever had given her pause before was gone. She was a killing machine, slicing through men as if her body had been born for battle. He'd seen first-hand how Signe had earned her title — like her father, she showed no mercy, left no prisoners, and shed no tears.

The haze turned red as they worked their way towards a clearing, the sounds of a roaring fire merging with that of the men in the forest around him, but he had to finish this conversation before Vermund shut down again.

"I may not understand what it means to be a Valkyrie, but I do know my wife," Gunnar bit out. "You may have seen Signe fight more bloody battles than I have, but I watched her grieve for her stillborn baby, the loss hitting her so hard it was difficult to breathe. I held her hand as she brought my children into the world, fighting *for* them from the moment they were born. I stood back as she led my people, giving them hope in our darkest hour. I saw her love *your* daughter as her own. And I know you did, too."

Vermund's green gaze flicked to Gunnar, then went back to scanning the men around them.

But Gunnar wasn't done. "I wish I could say I helped her become the woman she is today, but the truth is, I'm nothing without her. She's everything good in me, my reason to breathe."

A horse whinnied behind him, the panicked sound enough to have Gunnar shifting closer to Vermund, away from the horse in case its rider lost control. He looked over his shoulder and drew in a sharp breath, descending into a coughing fit.

As if summoned from the depths of Hel, a black warhorse stepped through the smoke. Gunnar stared at the beast, trying to rationalize what he was seeing.

Signe sat atop the stallion, her pale copper hair flowing freely down her back, rising in the faint wind. Black leather clung to her chest, matching vanguards on her wrists. She was otherworldly, as always, but Gunnar couldn't look away from the horse. The beast's eyes glowed, nearly shining green in the dark light.

"Raud killed that horse," Gunnar said, not meaning for the words to slip out. "I saw it die."

Vermund hummed, slowing to watch his niece approach. "And yet, Death rides with her."

Signe seemed unbothered by the stallion's wild footsteps, holding control over the animal when it tossed its thick mane, its front two hooves leaving the ground. Her unblinking gaze set ahead towards the clearing when the horse slammed back down, the ground shaking around them.

Gunnar stopped. The sight of her squeezed his heart the way it always did. But the cold, unresponsive woman sitting atop the wild horse wasn't his wife, wasn't the woman he'd proclaimed his undying love to.

This was the cage Draugr locked her in, the drugged foods he fed her keeping her compliant and unresponsive until he decided otherwise.

Black war paint still streaked her face, smudged by

sweat, giving her a fearsome look that only seemed to emphasize her beauty. Everything about her was cold, and yet, Gunnar refused to give up hope. His Signe still lay under that icy exterior, no matter how bloody her hands were.

"Signe," Gunnar whispered as the warhorse passed to his left, his feet rooted in place. "*Elskin min.*"

She pulled back on the reins, the horse threw his head and stomped its feet, its whinny piercing the night around them. Signe rode out the stallion's anger, her green gaze swinging to Gunnar.

His heart stopped, breath caught in his throat as he stared at her, hoping to see something, *anything*, to show she recognized him, she remembered.

"*Elskin min,*" he said again. "You're more than this. More than his weapon. You're everything. Come back to me."

She blinked, but her emerald eyes still held that faraway haze, his words failing to draw forth any reaction.

Her horse reared again, lashing against her hold. Its dark hooves kicked at the smoke before landing hard and charging forward. Signe held tight. Her head swiveled back away from Gunnar as she lowered herself to the horse's neck and rode out his frantic charge.

"You think it's the power of the gods she wields," Gunnar whispered, still focused on the sight of her fleeing horse, "but Signe is a power all her own."

A sharp tug on the rope jerked Gunnar forward, Vermund's scowl in place. "Hurry up."

Crimson light glowed, the blaze causing the smoke just

ahead where the trees thinned. Heat washed over Gunnar, and he held his hands up to block it.

Vermund stopped near the edge of the forest, tying his horse to a nearby tree, then pulled Gunnar along toward the roaring fire. Loamy earth gave way to sand; his feet sank with each step.

Logs were stacked several feet high, the flames licking into the night sky on the beach. A war drum sounded in the distance. It drew everyone here towards the blaze, a beacon in the dark night. Men moved in a circle around the fire and tossed the remnants of their last raid into the flames, shouting and drinking in turn. This was a sacrifice, a plea to the gods, but for what purpose?

The hair stood up on the back of Gunnar's neck as he tried to take in his surroundings, the flames illuminating the area much clearer than the moon, hidden behind the clouds.

Firelight flickered across the lake on the far side of the beach, the water gently lapping on the shore a direct contrast to the frenzy happening in front of him. In the distance stood an island at the center of the lake, a tree standing tall, the branches clawing at the clouds overhead. Gunnar had never been to the Tree before, but he knew its lore as well as any Viking — this was the root of all magic in Midgard, the mirror image of Yggdrasil in the other realms.

Bile rose in his throat as he studied the white form wrapped around the Tree's trunk, the dragon he'd caught glimpses of during their march.

Nidhoggr, the cursed dragon, the sign of Ragnarok.

While he'd seen Nidhoggr in the distance, hovering

above the trees, this was the first time Gunnar had seen the white dragon outside of the cave the day they'd been captured. Whatever Raud was doing to heal him had worked well enough to repair Nidhoggr's wings, but the overheard arguments between Raud and Draugr told Gunnar that Nidhoggr was still too weak to bring into battle.

A familiar voice sang out over the crackling fire, haunting against the steady drum beat Gunnar felt in his bones. Despite the heat the blaze emitted, a chill raked its nails over his skin.

Vermund tugged him towards Draugr, firelight glinting off the sharp horns of his demon helm. Beside him stood Raud, his head tipped back towards the sky, eyes closed as he chanted an eerie tune.

Gunnar's chest tightened with each word, his former friend losing himself to the magic threading through the air, as thick as the smoke filling his lungs. The flames danced to the beat of the drum, drawn higher as Raud lifted his left hand. Tendrils of fire stretched and danced around his fingers, practically twining around him as he continued to chant.

No matter their past, or Raud's continued poor choices, Gunnar couldn't help his flinch, his urge to break free and drag his old friend back, to find some way to save him and restore him to the boy he'd grown up with.

Chanting sounded over the crackling fire. Men wore animal skins over their heads and formed a circle around the blaze. They shouted and howled in a savage tune, moving in time with the drum until a gap opened in their circle.

Two men led a giant stag, the beast's eyes bloodshot and frantic. It limped forward, thrashing its antlers to break free, a dried trail of blood from its chest showing how it was caught. Raud stepped toward the animal, drawing his dagger. Gunnar's stomach lurched. He pulled on his binds, wanting to stop this.

"This is blood magic," Gunnar said only loud enough for Vermund to hear, the words tasting like ash in his mouth. "He can't do this. Not here, not on the shores of the Tree. The gods will strike him down for the offense. They'll strike us *all* down."

Vermund didn't react, and Gunnar's gaze swung to Signe. Next to her father, she looked small, but her body was rigid, eyes trained on the fire. Like a honed weapon, she stood at the ready.

His breaths came in ragged gulps as the stag stilled when Raud placed his fire-warmed hand on its face, right between its eyes. Without missing a beat, Raud sliced a clean line through its throat.

Grief clawed at Gunnar's throat, not only for the stag but for the friend he'd lost. This wasn't Raud—not even close.

Until Valhalla, they'd promised each other, but every action Raud took doomed him to an eternity far from the hall of the warriors.

Raud stepped back as the stag crumpled to the ground, the animal's blood coating his hands and arms. He held his dagger up, the metal still dripping, and the men increased their chant at the sight.

A boy came forward with a wooden bowl, kneeling

beside the fallen stag, and placed it under its wound. After a moment, he held the bowl out to Raud, who took it without acknowledging him, then hurried back into the crowd.

Raud raised the bowl over his head to shouts and stomping feet in encouragement. "Tonight, we bargain. Ragnarok is near, brought by the flames of Nidhoggr's soul and the Draugr's blade."

The men cheered, wolf howls echoing through the night.

"I offer the blood of *Eikthyrnir*, the Sacred Stag, as a sign of our loyalty to Loki. May he hear our plea, raising the giants in Jotunheim to fight at our side."

Draugr shouted, his sword raised high. Several men stepped forward, dragging the stag into the flames, the fire crackling at the new offering. Raud tilted up his chin and poured the blood over himself. Crimson streaked over his tattooed skin, the sickening sight enough to turn Gunnar's stomach. His head dropped back down, red eyes staring right at Gunnar.

"And I offer myself as a bargain to heal Nidhoggr," Raud said, a sinister grin tugging at one side of his face. "May the air in my lungs lift his wings. May the marrow in my bones heal his wounds. May the life left in me be his. May our souls become one. May chaos rein in the hands of Loki."

Gunnar flinched, unable to believe what he witnessed, and glared at Vermund. "He's going to kill himself. We have to stop this."

Vermund barely flicked his eyes to Gunnar. "Odin's Chosen will not die tonight."

Raud turned towards the fire, his back streaked with blood. Panic clawed at Gunnar's chest, his breaths coming rapidly, searching for another way out of this. When he found Signe, she had turned slightly towards him, but didn't seem bothered by the display, as still as ever.

Desperation finally broke through the tentative hold Gunnar had held over himself for the last few weeks, and he rushed forward. "Raud, my brother," he pleaded, his voice a croak from the smoke in the air. "Don't do this."

"Soon you'll see this is all as the gods intended," Raud shouted over his shoulder, the words carrying over the cries of the men around them.

"No." Gunnar lurched forward, the ropes around his hands biting into this skin, but the pain hardly registered. "I don't believe that, and neither do you. I promised you I'd fight for you and with you until Valhalla. I can't let you curse yourself like this. Turn back now, before it's too late. Stop this madness, Raud. Don't kill yourself for them."

"You will not taint the ritual," Draugr hissed, grabbing the back of Gunnar's shirt and dragging him out of Raud's reach. He hurled him with enough force, Gunnar fell to his knees. "I didn't bring you this far to ruin everything." Draugr followed up with a kick to his gut that had Gunnar falling onto his hands, the wind knocked out of him. "That ends today."

The chanting stopped as the men watched this interruption, but Gunnar paid them no mind. He struggled to plant one foot, intending to rush Raud again, whatever it took to stop this madness.

Fingers gripped his hair, wrenching his head back. He

reached up, but Vermund yanked on the rope binding his hands, pulling them back down.

"Signe," Gunnar said, his eyes watering from the fierce grip she held on his hair. Her expression showed no softness, no recognition, that piercing green gaze as sharp as the dagger in her hand.

His nostrils flared, staring at the weapon. Signe wouldn't hurt him, but this wasn't really Signe anymore. No matter his argument earlier, that glimpse he thought he'd seen from time to time was gone. Only the bloodthirsty Valkyrie stood in her place.

She sank onto a knee in front of him, tossed him back when she released his hair, then pressed the dagger into his throat.

"I love you, Signe," Gunnar whispered. The blade cut into his skin, wetness trailing down his throat. "I always have, and I always will."

She leaned forward, her lips ghosting over his cheek. "Until Valhalla."

He gasped. Hope soared through him—

Signe wrenched her arm back and plunged the dagger into his side.

White-hot fire erupted inside him, and he collapsed. No matter his agony, he swallowed the scream in his throat. He wouldn't give Draugr the satisfaction. Panting through the pain, Gunnar blinked away smoke and tears.

Signe stood without a backward glance and returned to Draugr's side, the bastard sporting a smug grin at his daughter's actions.

Darkness swirled at the corners of his vision, his body

urging him to unconsciousness to handle the pain, but Gunnar stubbornly forced his eyes open. His hands gripped his wound, warm blood seeping between his fingers.

With a final nod to Draugr, Raud stepped forward, disappearing into the bonfire itself, flames engulfing him completely.

A deep voice started up a chant again, drumbeats accompanying the plea to the gods for power and healing. But the fire, aside from the crackle of the logs, was eerily silent. No screams or cries of pain at all. If Gunnar hadn't witnessed it himself, he wouldn't even know a man had stepped inside.

Gunnar could hardly breathe. He fought the agony, needing to stay awake to see what happened next. To see if Raud could truly come out the other side of the fire unscathed.

The chant rose to a spine-tingling crescendo, then cut off completely, the drums also falling silent.

No one even dared whisper.

The fire snapped, a rush of sparks shooting into the air, followed by a billowing gust of smoke despite the air's stillness.

Then, a shadow formed within the flames, and as it stepped from the fire, the light revealed Raud's face.

Gone was the blood that had marred his skin. Gone were the tattoos inked into him that told his story. Gone were all signs of his humanity, any sign of his past. Raud emerged from the fire naked, as pale and clean as the day he was born. His eyes were closed as he stepped away from the flames, approaching Draugr.

An ear-splitting cry sounded in the distance, drawing Gunnar's gaze away from the man he no longer recognized to the dragon rising in the distance. Flames licked in the sky from Nidhoggr's open maw. Every leaf on the Tree was singed, smoking as they floated away from the burning Tree and fell to the ground below.

Gunnar's breaths came in uneven pants. He struggled to stay conscious, his good eye looking back to the crowd around him, searching for her the way he always did.

Signe stood with her hands relaxed at her side, gaze focused on the Tree in the distance. As if feeling his attention, he could have sworn her eyes flicked to where he lay for the briefest of moments before she turned her back to the roaring flames, walking into the forest towards her horse.

"Bow to me," a low, smoky voice boomed over the clearing, coming from Raud's mouth but sounding nothing like the man Gunnar once knew. As one, everyone in the clearing dropped to their knees, laying their weapons before them in offering.

Draugr stepped towards Raud, dipping his head the barest amount in respect. "My army is yours, Nidhoggr. May Loki's will be done."

Raud's lips lifted on one side as he opened eyes, the once pale blue of Gunnar's old friend glowing a steady, pulsing red.

Gunnar closed his eye, giving in to the pain until a shadow passed between him and the flames. Drawing in a ragged breath, Gunnar blinked, opening his eye one last time.

Vermund squatted over him with his spear draped across

his knees, green eyes glowing almost as bright as the fire. His right hand dropped, fingers pushing into Gunnar's wound. Pain exploded, dotting his vision as Gunnar screamed, the sound as broken as his heart.

"Goodbye, Gunnar. May the ravens lead you to Valhalla."

26

SHELBIE

"Shelbie," a deep voice said, but I could hardly hear him over my roaring pulse. "Hey. Wake up."

My eyes flew open, chest heaving as I fought to pull in air, panic seizing my whole body. "Not again."

"Yeah." Magnus twisted his neck to the side with a grimace. "Let's not drink ourselves to sleep on a cliff face again. That was a terrible plan."

I blinked and tried to remember the last of my dream. "No." I shook my head. My heart raced, and I exhaled to slow it. "I mean, yes. This was a terrible plan. But I think I just Saw Gunnar."

"What?" Magnus said, all traces of discomfort and sleepiness gone at the mention of his brother's name. "Was he okay?"

I scrambled to my feet and winced when my knee threatened to buckle under me again. My ass hurt from sitting on the rocks for so long, and my back was screaming, but none of that mattered right now.

Hadriel! I called out through our mind connection.

Already on my way, he answered just as the sound of his wings carried to me over the night. *I can't land where you are. You're going to have to jump and trust me.*

"Oh fuck," I whined, my heart galloping even faster.

Hands tightened around my arms as I leaned over the cliff face, looking down at the waves crashing on the rocks below.

"What the hell are you doing?" Magnus growled and pulled me back. "Tell me what's happening."

I turned to look up at him, the green light of my pendant casting shadows across his features. His usual grin was gone, replaced with a serious scowl and a worried crease between his brows. "I think he's hurt."

Magnus snapped up, his arms dropping from me. Every muscle in his body tensed, posed to charge into battle. "How are we getting to him?"

Hadriel's cry carried over the sound of the waves just as he broke through the cloud cover, flying directly towards us.

I'll tell you when, Hadriel said, and I let out a panicked whimper.

"Hadriel is going to fly me to him."

"Good. Let's go, then."

My head snapped up at his words. "You can't go."

"Like Hel I can't," Magnus bit out. "Where you go, I go. Especially if my brother's life is at risk."

I shook my head, but didn't have time to continue this argument.

Get ready.

My hand shot out to the side, wrapping around

Magnus's much larger one and I squeezed. Sensing my terror, Magnus squeezed back, staring at Hadriel soaring towards us at a startling speed.

"We have to jump, don't we?"

I mumbled an assent, bile rising in my throat at the idea of leaping off the cliff, *willingly* this time.

He squeezed my hand again, his weight tipping forward when Hadriel soared closer.

Now!

I echoed his words for Magnus, who dropped my hand, grabbed my waist, and tossed me off the cliff. A scream ripped out of my throat as my body fell, but I refused to close my eyes. Tears streamed across my cheeks as adrenaline coursed through my body. Between one breath and the next, Hadriel was under me, banking hard to skim the edge of the cliffs.

I slammed down onto his back and my fingers scrambled for any purchase when I slid across his smooth scales.

"Shit shit shit!" I screamed, the waves crashing below us, the water spraying up into my face.

Before I could scream again, Magnus landed next to me, far more graceful than myself. Hadriel veered back over the water, leveling out. I pressed my cheek into his warm scales, panic seizing every muscle in my body.

"I've got you." Magnus crawled across Hadriel's back towards me, his heavy weight pressing me into Hadriel.

You need to move forward, between my wings, Hadriel said, and I groaned at the thought of moving at all. Every beat of his wings shifted the muscles of his back and altered the wind rushing around us.

"I won't let you fall," Magnus and Hadriel said in unison. The dragon's head turned, his green slitted pupil taking us in. I could have sworn there was a hint of approval in that gaze, his head bobbing in a nod.

With Magnus's help, I moved into position, his body settling in behind me. I gripped the spines along Hadriel's neck like I'd done on our previous flights, my fingers tight around the warm horns.

"I'm good," I said aloud for Magnus's benefit, but the words were meant for Hadriel. I wasn't *good* by a long shot, but I'd already been too late to save Gunnar once. I couldn't let my own fear stop me from saving him again. "To the Tree, Hadriel."

With a roar, Hadriel's wings beat, carrying us higher into the sky. Wind chapped my cheeks as I closed my eyes, trying to remember everything I'd Seen.

"Tell me what you Saw," Magnus said, his mouth close to my ear. His hands gripped my waist, hanging on as we rushed to his brother's rescue.

"A fire." My throat hurt at the memory, as if I'd been there when Raud stepped into the flames, emerging unscathed. "I think it was a ritual on the shore by the Tree."

"What were they doing that made you think so?"

"Raud sacrificed a stag, doused himself in the blood of the slain animal, and then walked into the flames."

"Fuck." Magnus's hands tightened around me. "A blood ritual, then."

"I think so," I answered, remembering Nidhoggr's white wings spreading wide as he flew into the sky, lighting the Tree on fire. "I'm pretty sure it was to heal Nidhoggr."

"That's not good," Magnus said, and Hadriel grumbled his agreement. "What happened with Gunnar?"

"Signe…" I frowned, trying to rewind my mind to replay what I'd Seen again. Something felt off, but I couldn't figure out *what* was wrong with the image.

"Is she alive?" Magnus asked, and I nodded.

"Yes, she seemed physically okay." I thought back over the vision and what I'd Seen of her when they attacked Torvik, trying to figure out how to best explain Signe's state. "I think they're drugging her. She seemed off when we saw her on the battlefield, and then the few visions I've had of her, it's like she's there, but not."

Magnus hummed, giving me time to collect my thoughts, but as always, he never argued with me, never doubted a word I said. His open acceptance was something I'd never take for granted.

Not until that moment had I let myself think about what we might find when we arrived. If my vision had already passed and we were too late, I'd brought Magnus this far only to find his brother dead. And if it was the future, we were about to drop into the center of a ritual with an entire army training their sites on us.

I dismissed the worry — it was far too late to do any sort of planning, and I'd never forgive myself if my hesitation cost us Gunnar's life.

How are they controlling Signe? I asked Hadriel, focusing on her in my mind. *That's what's happening, right? She'd never hurt Gunnar.*

It takes a powerful spell to keep a Valkyrie in thrall.

How powerful? I didn't know enough about magic or

Vikings or Valkyries to make any sort of educated guess on my own.

The only spell I know requires wolfsbane from Jotunheim, the realm of the Giants.

"How would one go about getting to Jotunheim?" I asked, and Magnus barked a laugh.

"*No one* can go to Jotunheim, Shelbie. Jotunheim is the frost realm of the Giants, inhabited by gods and giants alone. A human can't travel there."

"What about a Promised? I'm not exactly human, right? Could I go to Jotunheim?"

His hands tightened on my waist, and I looked over my shoulder in time to see the wave of concern wash over his features. "Don't even joke about such a thing."

I placed my hand over his, squeezing it in reassurance. "Relax. I'm not trying to go. I'm just trying to figure out how Draugr and Raud could come by wolfsbane from Jotunheim. That's what Hadriel says they'd need to keep Signe in thrall."

Magnus jerked back, his eyebrows climbing into his hairline.

"I'm guessing this" — I waved a hand to indicate his facial expression — "means that's pretty unlikely."

Magnus's deep blue eyes flicked between mine and then down to my dragon. "Hadriel. Does this mean what I think it does?"

Hadriel lifted his face, a fierce cry released as he pulled his wings in tight to his body, beginning a rapid descent. *The gods are involved, Shelbie. Only they could get wolfsbane out of Jotunheim and to Draugr.*

A nervous laugh escaped me, and I leaned down into Hadriel, lowering myself to become as aerodynamic as I could with the increased speed Hadriel put on.

Magnus's hands slid from my waist to lay over top of mine on Hadriel's spine. "Loki is on their side. That's the only answer. He's preparing for Ragnarok."

I didn't have time to think through what the fuck that meant. We broke through the clouds, smoke lingering in the air. Early morning sun cast a golden glow on the hazy scene, and I fought back the nerves at the sight below us.

"He was on the beach when I saw him last," I said, and Hadriel banked to his right. I shifted my weight, riding out the turn with Magnus's steady grip on my hands anchoring me in place.

The smoke made it hard to see much of anything, but I searched the sky for white wings, regardless. We dropped to just over the treetops, and Magnus's hands tightened on mine, his body going rigid as we approached.

The beach was empty save the dying fire, smoke billowing off the charred wood. The Tree rose from the island in the center of the lake, now barren of leaves. Nidhoggr was gone, and a mixture of relief and dread coursed through me at what that meant. Hadriel lowered to the shore, landing smoothly.

Instantly, Magnus's hands released me, and he slid to the ground, taking off across the beach. "Gunnar!"

I followed him, my skin tingling with the lingering magic in the air. Magnus shouted his brother's name on repeat, each call more desperate than the last. My heart broke as I stared at the beach, remembering everything from my dream.

Signs of Draugr's forces were everywhere: boot prints scattered across the beach, the blood marring the sand where they'd slain the stag, forgotten and discarded drinking horns littering the forest floor. But no Gunnar. No Signe.

"We're too late."

Frustration welled in me, my eyes pricking with tears at my own uselessness. I couldn't help but bemoan my own stubbornness. If I had learned more about my powers, would I have been able to discern more from my visions and dreams? Could I understand them better, giving me more information as to whether something had already happened or not?

Magnus ran back towards me, his mouth set in a hard line. "He's not here, but I think I can track him. There are traces of blood leading away from the beach into the forest."

I nodded, forcing back any tears for his benefit. "How can I help?"

Magnus pointed at Hadriel. "You two get back in the air and fly low over the trees. Chances are he hasn't gone far. Maybe we can catch up with him. If he sees Hadriel, he'll know we're looking for him. Meanwhile, I'll set out on foot, trying to follow any signs of him."

"You can really do that?" I looked back at the many boot prints scattered around the area. "How can you track him when it's all such a mess?"

"I have to try."

His words were laced with a desperation I shared, so I did as he said. Climbing back onto Hadriel's back from the beach was much preferable to the jump-and-trust method, and we were airborne again in seconds.

We circled the lake while Magnus took off into the woods, his body hunched as he inspected everything around him.

Hadriel banked, then came back over top of Magnus, flying as low as we could over the trees, then circled back, over and over.

Anything? I asked when we made our fourth pass, following Magnus's lead from the ground.

Magnus stilled as we flew overhead. His head snapped to the left. I followed his gaze, looking for something, and then I heard it.

"*Knut!*" a voice shouted in the distance.

Two birds took off from their perches, rising into the sky around us. Ravens as black as Hadriel's scales circled above the treeline, and Hadriel turned in their direction, Magnus taking off at a sprint below us.

Place your hand flat against my scales.

I did as Hadriel asked, confused for only a moment as my vision doubled. A gasp ripped free from me, staring at the world through Hadriel's eyes. Everything was mostly grey, but far clearer than my vision had ever been. Inter-mixed among the grey were glowing reds and yellows, which I quickly realized were heat signatures, animals scurrying away from the predator overhead. All, except one.

I turned in my seat, looking for Magnus trailing us through the woods, and his little red dot moved towards us at an almost inhuman speed.

Hang on tight, Shelbie, Hadriel said.

I lifted my hand from his neck, letting go of the double vision as I tightened my grip on his spines, squeezing with my thighs just in time. Hadriel lifted his head into the sky, his body floating almost vertical as he marked Gunnar's location for Magnus below. His front legs clawed at the sky as fire erupted from his mouth, heat washing back over me.

My legs started to slip, all my weight hanging on by my hands. Sweat dripped down my spine, panic surfacing again. My fingers dug in for purchase against his spines, but not enough to hold me in place. With a scream, my grip broke, and I tumbled down Hadriel's long body.

In a flash, his tail whipped out, curling around my torso before I could drop off his back. His grip was an iron vice, squeezing the air from my lungs as my vision started to black out.

I've got you, Hadriel said. *I've always got you.*

He lowered himself above the trees, dropping as close to the ground as he could. His tail unfurled, and I fell the six feet between me and the dirt.

If I hadn't already been injured, maybe it would have been easier. But the moment my body hit the ground, I collapsed in on myself. Pain lanced through my body like a hot poker. Bile rose in my throat as I bit back the scream, needing to focus.

"Shelbie!" Magnus yelled as he ran through the forest towards me. *"SHELBIE!"*

"I'm here." I breathed in shallow breaths, trying to push myself to a sitting position.

Magnus was on me the next instant, pausing his mad dash through the woods. "I saw you fall."

"I'm okay." I waved a hand dismissively. "He's just up on the left, I think. Hadriel needed to go find some place to land."

Magnus's eyes darted over my body, then to the woods to my left, chest heaving with the exertion it had taken to get here this fast.

"Go," I urged him. "I'll be right behind you."

With a sharp nod, Magnus took off again, headed in the direction I pointed.

Hadriel. I tried to stand. My vision almost blacked out when I tried to put weight on my left leg, my knee screaming in pain. *How do I heal myself? Can you teach me, or do I need Yrsa for that?*

I can heal you, Hadriel answered. *But I do not think we have enough power to heal both you and Gunnar at the same time. For that, you need to drink from the well for more power, and that's something you need to practice first.*

"Fuck," I groaned, then grabbed the nearest tree and began limping forward, putting as little weight on my injured leg as I could.

I'm about a mile ahead. There's a stream to your right — follow it, and I'm waiting for you.

A tear slid free at the thought of walking a mile like this, but I had to. I had no other choice.

My hand itched to grab my pendant, to see if I could wield the magic to heal myself on my own, but if there was a possibility that my magic could save Gunnar if he needed it, then I couldn't use it.

Time was lost to me as I worked my way forward, grabbing tree after tree. I wasn't sure exactly how he knew where

I was, but Hadriel guided me telepathically every time I got off-course. Male voices spoke ahead of me, and I tried my best to hurry toward the brothers.

Gunnar slumped back against a tree. He gripped his side, a dark red spot soaking the tunic under his palm, his face drained of color. I fought to hide my shock at the changed man before me, his cheekbones cutting through his gaunt, ashen face. His once trimmed and clean golden blond hair was longer, dirty, and in desperate need of a trim. His beard hung down to his collarbone, streaks of white shooting through the darker colors. But nothing was as jarring as the black patch over his eye, reminding me just how much this man had suffered these last few months.

I limped forward, and Gunnar's good eye opened, that frosty blue settling on me. "Shelbie."

Magnus jumped up to help me forward, his brow drawn down as he stared at my knee. "Why didn't you tell me how bad it was?"

I slid to the ground next to Gunnar, keeping my leg straight. "Are you hurt? I thought I Saw Signe—" I swallowed, not able to say the rest of the sentence, but Gunnar's quick nod was enough to tell me I'd Seen true.

He lifted his hand from his side, showing the hole burned through the fabric. The skin beneath was angry and red, a blackened, jagged scar showing beneath, but it was sealed shut.

My eyes snapped back to his face. "What? How? When did this happen?"

"Last night." Gunnar's hand fell to his side, gripping a wooden spear. "She stabbed me before Draugr could do worse, and then Vermund cauterized the wound. They left me for dead on the beach when they retreated."

"I don't understand." Magnus frowned. "*Signe* stabbed you?"

Gunnar never looked away from me, his focus almost unnerving. "She saved me. She's not lost. And Vermund is not who we think he is."

"Then who is he?" Magnus said, a hint of frustration bleeding into his tone.

"I don't know, but he speaks of the gods often."

"Shit." A heavy exhale left Magnus I couldn't help but mirror. "First Loki, and now this."

Gunnar's gaze finally snapped to his brother. "Loki?"

"Yeah." He scrubbed a hand through his pale hair, pulling at the strands before dropping his hand to his side. "Hadriel thinks they're controlling Signe with wolfsbane from Jotunheim. The only way that Draugr could get his hands on wolfsbane is through a god, and only Loki would be this deeply involved in Ragnarok."

Gunnar put his hands behind him, ready to push off the tree to stand, but groaned before he moved an inch. I scooted towards him, reaching out to place a hand on his torso. His heart raced against my palm, beating wildly as he breathed in ragged gulps against the pain.

Tell me how to do this, Hadriel.

Hold your pendant and find that pool of power in you.

I closed my eyes, my free hand tightening on the warm stone around my neck. Instantly, I stood on the edge of the pool of my power, soft ripples cascading over the surface. Hadriel continued to walk me through the steps as I dipped my hand into the well, feeling the cool water wash over my skin. Relief washed over me, the pain sucked from my body as it healed me instantly.

No! I tried to pull my hand free from the well, but power continued to pour through me, healing every bruise and scrape I bore, every wrinkle, every grey hair. For a split second, I was pain free, feeling better than I had in a decade. *I don't want it!*

Push it from yourself, Hadriel said. *Will it into your hands and pass it on to Gunnar.*

I tried to do as he said, picturing my blood circulating to carry the magic away from myself and into Gunnar, feeling heat gather under my palm.

"It's working!" Magnus gasped.

The heat became almost unbearable, pain closing in on me like a vice as the circle of magic passed through me, into Gunnar, and then came back to me again. Somehow, I was absorbing all of Gunnar's injuries into myself. The pain was blinding, leaving me more battered and bruised than I'd ever been before, but I couldn't pull away, not when Gunnar needed this.

STOP! Hadriel roared, and I pulled my hand free, my body collapsing to the ground as the world faded out around me.

GUNNAR

"Shelbie!" Gunnar lurched forward, but Magnus was quicker, spinning and catching Shelbie when her eyes rolled back in her head.

"Shit." Magnus tried to prop her up to standing, but she was out.

"Her side." Gunnar pointed, a dark stain spreading on Shelbie's ribs, a mirror of where his injury had just been. He raised his own tunic, but the blackened and burnt skin was gone, healed by whatever magic she possessed. "We have to get her back to Yrsa."

Magnus nodded and leveraged Shelbie enough to swing her up into his arms. Her head rested on his chest, and his hands settled behind her back and under her knees. "Can you stand, brother?"

To his surprise, Gunnar could. In fact, he felt better than he had in days, in months — really, since Draugr had taken him. Pushing off the ground, he steadied himself on the tree at his back, shaking his limbs to test this wasn't too good to be true, but his pain was gone. Magnus watched him carefully for any sign of distress, but one look at Shelbie slumped in Magnus's arms was enough to bring him back to the moment.

"I take it we're riding the dragon back?" Gunnar tried to suffuse his voice with nonchalance, but the thought terrified him.

Magnus smirked, amusement glittering in his eyes. "Don't worry, he doesn't bite that often, and it only hurts a little. But you're weaker than me, so maybe I'm wrong."

Magnus turned, leading the way out of the trees, and Gunnar huffed a laugh, hurrying to follow. "Weaker, my ass."

Even with the pain gone, Gunnar still clung to Vermund's battle spear, leaning on it for support. Magnus damn near sprinted, and Gunnar did his best to keep up, exhaustion still nipping at his heels. A low rumble of thunder sounded ahead of them as they stepped past the tree line into a clearing, and Gunnar nearly ran into Magnus's back.

"Easy there," Magnus murmured. His voice was low like he might use with a spooked horse. Gunnar looked around Magnus to see the black dragon in front of them, his body lowered to the ground, green eyes staring directly at them.

Not thunder, then.

The giant, rather angry-looking dragon had sparks and smoke shooting out of his nostrils, his vibrant green eyes flicking between the crumpled body of his Promised and the two men he likely deemed responsible for her state.

"Can she mind-speak with him?" Gunnar spine snapped

straight as he eyed the deadly beast far more alive and threatening than Nidhoggr had been the last time he was this close to a dragon. "Does he know what happened?"

Magnus nodded briefly, never breaking Hadriel's intense stare. "She healed Gunnar, but something went wrong." Magnus eased towards Hadriel slowly with Shelbie in his arms. "We have to get her back to Yrsa."

Hadriel's lip peeled back, revealing teeth the size of longswords, and snapped at him. Smoke billowed from his nostrils and Gunnar's fist clenched around his spear, the dragon as terrifying as every story ever told about him.

"I know you probably want to leave us here for dead, but she can't ride on her own." Magnus took steady steps forward, slow enough to not be threatening, but confident enough to tell the dragon he had no intention of turning back.

Gunnar stared at his little brother, a mixture of gut-wrenching fear and disbelief sending his heart into a thundering beat. While Magnus had always been cocksure and almost foolhardy, Gunnar had never seen him *this* brazen. The last three months had forced Gunnar to shed all remnants of his former self, and for the first time, he considered how these long weeks might have changed everyone else in his life.

"We need to take her back." Magnus stopped near Hadriel's right eye, Shelbie slumped in his arms. The pendant around her neck pulsed with green light, her limp hand almost touching the dragon's black scales. "You can't fly with her alone. I promise to protect her, if you get us home."

A long, tense stare-off followed, and Gunnar stayed where he was, afraid to anger the dragon further. Finally, Hadriel turned away with a loud huff and lowered one shoulder enough to make it easier for them to climb on.

"I see you've made a friend," Gunnar commented under his breath when he stepped up to Magnus's side.

Magnus let out a breath, his same smug grin shining bright. "Depends on the day."

Together, they approached, and Magnus handed Shelbie off to Gunnar so he could climb on first. Once Magnus was situated, they traded, and Gunnar passed Shelbie up to him as gently as he could.

Gunnar had never been this close to Hadriel before, the dragon's black and gold scales glittering in the morning light. His back, even while laying on the ground, stood high above Gunnar's head, lined with sharp spikes. Magnus sat in the gap between the spikes near the dragon's shoulder blades, the position smooth as if it were meant for a rider. Horns protruded around his neck joint, feathering out in a circle around his head, but two sat directly in front of Magnus, as if they were handholds.

A chill raced down Gunnar's spine, realization dawning on him that this Fate was truly inescapable. This dragon was always meant for a rider, always meant for battle, always meant for the girl draped over Magnus's lap.

He sucked in a breath, then tossed his spear to Magnus. His brother caught it in midair, and Gunnar placed a palm on the dragon's body. It was cooler than he'd anticipated for a fire-breathing creature, smooth like a stone tumbled in the sea.

"Just like riding a horse," Gunnar muttered to himself, adjusting his grip on the closest spike. Maybe Hadriel sensed his hesitation, because the moment Gunnar's foot touched down on the dragon's foreleg, it rose into the air, damn near tossing the man onto his back.

Hadriel snorted, the sound derisive even to Gunnar's ears.

"If that horse was the size of a ship, had no saddle or anything to hold on to, and banked at steep enough angles to slide you right off, then yes" — Magnus nodded — "almost exactly like a horse."

Clumsily fitting himself behind his brother, Gunnar glanced for a handhold, finding none. He tried to grip with his thighs how he would a horse, but Hadriel's ribs were too broad for him to find purchase.

"Death by dragon seems a good way to go, don't you think?" Magnus chuckled at his own terrible joke.

"Don't even think it," Gunnar mumbled, then snapped his mouth shut when Hadriel's wings unfurled. With a powerful push, the dragon launched from the ground.

They rose at a steep angle, and Magnus slipped back, shoving Gunnar further back down the dragon's spine. All the blood left Gunnar's head, bile rising in his throat. He fought for purchase on Magnus's waist, then found a spike to lean his foot against, like a stirrup holding him in place.

Magnus let out a loud whoop when they passed the tree-line, then higher, until Gunnar could just make out the beach where the ritual had taken place, and in the distance, the island with the Tree. Wind circled around them threatening to unseat him with every breeze as Hadriel shot forward, his speed increasing with every beat.

"What's happened since I left?" Gunnar asked, desperate for a distraction from their current situation, dizzyingly high off the ground, and the memories of the night before.

Magnus made it look easy to keep hold of both an unconscious woman and an ever-moving dragon, only half-turning his head to recount what his people had endured since Gunnar's capture. Hearing the details of his clan's harrowing journey to Torvik, then their less than warm welcome, had unease settling like a weight in Gunnar's stomach.

"We've been getting ready for battle ever since," Magnus finished. "I've been doing my best to train those who stayed behind so we're ready when Draugr attacks again. Is that where they're headed now?"

"I assume so, not that they openly shared plans with their prisoner." Gunnar swallowed heavily before asking, "And the children?"

Magnus met his eye. "Safe."

Gunnar's shoulders dropped, all the worries he'd held on to shedding their weight. "I knew I could count on you."

"Don't know what you were thinking." Magnus chuckled. "With any luck, I can go back to counting on *you* soon. I don't know how you handle being in charge, brother. I keep having to be serious and make *decisions*." Magnus gave an exaggerated shudder. "I haven't had a pie in a month. Horrible."

The corner of Gunnar's mouth twitched up. Though

perfectly capable of it, Magnus had never wanted the yoke of responsibility. Then, once his words sank in, Gunnar frowned. "What about Domari?"

Magnus groaned. "Don't get me started on Domari."

Gunnar's heart clenched. "Is he —"

"He's fine, probably," Magnus assured him, somewhat indignantly. "But he decided the best course of action was to haul off to gods know where to track down the Guard."

Gunnar blinked, sure he had misheard. "He *left*?"

"We do need the men." Magnus shrugged, but Gunnar saw the way his jaw clenched tight, glancing down at Domari's woman in his lap. "Draugr's failed attempt to attack Torvik showed us how woefully unprepared we are, and Domari did what he thought he needed to. What he thought was best for her."

Gunnar's mind raced, working to set the scene for battle in his mind, counting Draugr's men against how many of their own remained, according to Magnus. From what he'd seen in their camps, Draugr had hundreds of men, and more joined with each raid he led, choosing to believe in his cause rather than parish at his hands.

The runes were oppressively stacked against them, barring a miracle. A miracle like an outside army falling on their doorstep.

"When will he return?"

Magnus sighed. "Hopefully, before."

Before the battle. *Before* it was too late.

Hopefully, indeed.

❄

Gunnar's limbs ached, his hands cramped from clutching the spines, his thighs sore from trying to hold his seat. If he'd thought flying was bad, descending was worse.

He pressed his eyes shut as Hadriel tilted forward over the sea. Waves crashed against the rocks surrounding Torvik. The wind around them doubled, the sea breeze making his already smooth scales slick with moisture, and nearly impossible to hold on to.

Over and over, he counted down from ten to pass the agonizing seconds, his torso pressed into Magnus's back. The dragon seemed to have no cares about if he lost his passengers along the way, and Gunnar was painfully aware of how easy it would be to die if he crashed down to the rocks below.

Finally, with a sand-blowing *thump*, movement mercilessly ceased.

"Viveka!" Magnus called as he slid off Hadriel's back, Shelbie clutched in his arms. "Fetch Yrsa!"

Gunnar's knees hit the sand when he climbed off, his body still fatigued from his travel and lack of food, and the toil his injuries had taken even if the worst of them were healed. His stomach turned, bile rising in his throat as he fought to breathe evenly, then used his spear to push himself to his feet.

Hadriel dogged Magnus's steps as he carried Shelbie towards the village, the ground shaking with every step the beast took. Planting the butt of the spear in the sand, Gunnar followed.

Torvik was the same as always. Busy streets faced the water crowded with people, a mixture of farmers and merchants wandering through the rows of small huts. Magnus moved with confidence and hurried down the beach with a familiarity that stung Gunnar. Each turn his brother made was a painful reminder that this was now home for his people, not the village his father had built and Draugr had burned to the ground.

Everyone stopped to watch as they hurried down the beach towards the cliffs, lingering stares following in their wake. Hadriel lifted into the air, flying out over the water with a bone-rattling screech before he landed again at the far side of the beach ahead of them. Magnus hurried forward, shouting Yrsa's name, and Gunnar tried his best to keep up, no matter how his body screamed to rest.

Yrsa ran out to meet them, her deep auburn hair tugging free of the tight braid in the breeze. With an urgent wave of her hand, she ushered Magnus to set Shelbie down in the sand. She dropped to her knees at Shelbie's side while Hadriel hovered over her until Yrsa batted him back.

"You're obstructing my light, dragon," she chided, then gasped when her eyes shifted to Gunnar.

"Can you heal her?" Gunnar indicated Shelbie with a nod, needing Yrsa to refocus. Shelbie was more important now. "We think she somehow absorbed my wounds."

Yrsa's gaze flicked over Gunnar's body, eyes stopping on his torn tunic and the smooth, pale skin underneath. Her breath stuttered, and she returned her focus to Shelbie. In quick movements, she pulled a knife from her boot to cut away Shelbie's dress, exposing the wound on her torso, blackened and burned into her side.

His wound.

"I need my kit." Her fingers danced over Shelbie's skin. "Viveka, you know where it is? The brown satchel in my hut?"

The girl nodded.

"And water. Hot water."

Viveka shot off back into the village, and Yrsa went back to inspecting Shelbie.

"Any other injuries? You said she absorbed yours, Gunnar. Where were you injured before?"

"My eye. She may have broken ribs. My wrists were chafed and bleeding regularly," Gunnar answered, trying to think of everything that had hurt only hours before. Magnus's eyes flicked up to his brother, anguish written across his features.

"And what of her own injuries?" Yrsa said. "She never came to me after our first lesson, so it's possible she's still battered and bruised on her own."

"Her knee was the worst of it, I think." Magnus cleared his throat and returned his focus to Shelbie. "I'm not sure if her magic healed that for her or not."

Yrsa shifted down, her hands gently pressing into Shelbie's legs from thigh to calf, feeling the bones, comparing the two against each other. When she reached her left knee, her leg jerked.

"Probably twisted," she muttered. "We'll deal with that one later."

Waving her hand in the air, she called, "Hadriel?" Instantly, the dragon shifted closer, his tail sending a cascade of sand into the air. "I'll try to help you tap into your connection, though I'm not sure this will work."

The dragon lowered his head to right above Yrsa's shoulders, his breath blowing the hair off Shelbie's face. He didn't blink, his green gaze intent on Shelbie.

Yrsa guided Shelbie's hand to her pendant, closing her fingers around it and wrapping her own hand around Shelbie's, holding it in place. When she closed her eyes, the stone began to glow a faint green.

"Does that mean it's working?" Gunnar whispered to Magnus, gaze darting from the woman who'd saved his life to the dragon looming over them, a low rumble emanating from his chest.

Magnus crossed his arms, frowning. "It's usually brighter than that when their magic connects."

Please, Gunnar sent up a prayer to the gods, his grip tightening on the spear until the wood creaked in his hand. *Spare her. My life is not a worthy trade for hers.*

The ground shook when Hadriel's tail thumped in the sand, two black dogs streaking down the beach towards them. Sunlight glimmered around the dogs as if they too glowed. Gunnar closed his eye, exhaustion playing tricks on his mind.

A wet nose pressed into his cheek, sniffing at the bandage, and Gunnar reached up to pet the puppy hovering nearby.

Magnus nudged him, and Gunnar's eye flew open in time to the gash in Shelbie's side began to knit together, her skin returning to the pink of health.

Sweat beaded on Yrsa's brow, her arms shaking and flexed while she held Shelbie's hand. The stone around her neck glowed brighter than before, light leaking between their clasped hands. Then it flickered and banked entirely.

Gasping, Yrsa's eyes opened, and she leaned over Shelbie. "Did it work? Was it enough? My power gave out —" Her fingers traced over Shelbie's side, the wound faded to a dull purpling bruise, but the skin closed.

Shelbie's eyes fluttered open, and all three of them let out a breath.

"Gunnar?" she croaked, her eyes scanning those hovering near her. Gunnar lowered to the sand beside her, gripping her hand.

"Here, thanks to you and that dragon of yours." He pressed a kiss to her knuckles. "You saved me."

"Try not to need saving again soon. I don't think I did it right." Shelbie attempted a chuckle, then winced.

"Here, Yrsa!" Viveka ran down the beach towards them, a leather tote flapping at her side and a jug of steaming water in her hands that looked far too big for a girl her size.

"Oh, good," Yrsa breathed. "Let's get that knee wrapped, Shelbie, and then both of you are going to sit here until you finish the teas I make you."

Gunnar reached for his spear, ready to stand again. "Both?"

Yrsa raised an imperious brow. He sank to the ground beside Shelbie, sitting on his heels.

Movement along the edge of the beach snagged his attention, and a sob clutched in his throat at the dark-haired child watching them.

"Papa?" Revna's eyes were wide as she stepped towards him tentatively, her bare feet sinking in the sand.

He dropped the spear and it landed in the sand with a soft *thunk*. Tears welled in his eyes, and he rose up on his knees, holding his arms for his daughter. "Little bird."

Her gaze flicked to Magnus, then back to Gunnar, and her hesitation was more painful than losing his eye. But he could hardly blame her — nothing about Gunnar was the same as it was when she'd left for Torvik with Frida. Not his looks, not his personality, not his life.

Just as he was about to lower his hands, Revna took off across the beach, running straight into his open hold. He jerked back at the impact and her arms flew around his neck, squeezing tight. He wrapped himself around her, his body shaking as the sob ripped free.

"I'm here, little bird." He brushed a hand over her dark braids, hands trembling with each pass. Burying her head in his shoulder, he let all the emotions he'd held back flow free, knowing how close he'd come to losing everything. "I'm home."

DOMARI

"Ready to stop avoiding her?" Grim clapped Domari on the shoulder, squeezing tight. He raised his dark brows, the jovial smile his friend wore at odds with the churning in Domari's stomach.

Over the last two weeks, they'd met with almost every soldier in the *banda* stationed here, posing his argument as to why they should join Domari for this final battle back home. All except Hilda and her Valkyries.

"How did they come to join you here?" The question had been plaguing Domari for days. Valkyries were tied to the gods in the North, and they were far from home here in Staraya Ladoga.

Grim let go of Domari, adjusting the thick leather belt over his tunic. Sheaths held two axes like many of the Northmen here, even though Grim was a Saxon. "We ran into them on our way here from Miklagard almost a year ago. I'm not sure what they were doing there, or why they stayed with us for so long, but they're good company. Have you met them yet?"

Domari shook his head, staring out over the camp. Tent flaps blew in the gentle breeze off the sea, their camp in a cove surrounded by trees and water. While the men had grown lazy in their time off with no instructions from the Emperor, Domari was pleased to see the strict code of conduct and cleanliness held in the camp the same as always. Grim's tent was set up on a small rise, giving him a view of the neat rows of tents below, filled with 300 of the fiercest warriors to walk the earth.

Each day that ticked by ate away at Domari's patience, his unease growing with every sunrise. "How much longer until you think you can have your *banda* ready to move?"

"Within the week," Grim said. "I've been bartering passage with the local ships here, trying to pinpoint how we can move all of us at once. We need ten ships, and as of yesterday, seven are ready to be outfitted. I have a meeting this morning with another merchant from the North who thus far has refused to budge on his asking price."

"I'll repay you," Domari said, thinking over how he could access the wealth needed to pay these mercenaries for their time. Spending a decade in the Varangian Guard had helped him amass wealth, but most of it he'd left behind when he fled Miklagard a year ago.

Grim waved him off. "Everyone here is restless and ready to move. Besides" — his gaze swung to Domari, a mischievous glint in his eyes as he raised his brows — "my men are eager to see you in battle. They've only heard me talk of your glory days, never seen the speed with which you move." He slapped Domari on the back. "Don't let me down, my brother. Don't make a liar of me in front of my men."

Domari clenched his jaw, then strode away from the tent, headed towards the row on the far side of camp. Grim shouted orders behind him, and men hopped to follow their *komes'* command.

Despite his earlier words, it wasn't only Domari these men were ready to follow into battle. Grim was a fierce leader, thoughtful and intentional with every interaction he had. The last two weeks in his presence had proven how deeply his men loved him, and Domari was thrilled to have him for an ally.

They'd stayed up late into the night every evening, going over every possible battle strategy to be ready the moment they touched land. Grim had been a talented soldier when they'd fought together before, but the warrior striding off from his tent was worthy of far more than his post as *Komes*.

Between the two of them, everything was ready, save the ships to carry them home and the uncertainty swirling in Domari over the presence of the women across camp.

Wind lapped at the flag atop the tents as Domari strode down the rise and into camp. The Valkyries' setup stood apart from the rest, formed into a small circle around a fire all their own. Unlike the other sun-bleached canvases, their tents were made from a cloth that almost camouflaged them to their surroundings, dark against the trees at their back. Light seemed to hit them different, reflecting to hide their presence, a reminder to everyone how very different these women were. From what Domari had seen over the last two weeks, they mostly kept to themselves, which made their presence here in camp for nearly a year that much stranger.

The morning sun streaked between the trees, adding a hazy glow to the hustle and bustle of the camp. Smoke rose from several fires, the smell of roasting meat lingering in the air. Men moved with the quick efficiency of battle-hardened and trained soldiers, stopping only to watch as Domari strode past. He paused long enough to greet those he could remember by name, thanking them for their service, and did his best not to flinch when hero-worship was thrown at his feet like rose petals for a passing royal.

"Domari!" Edgar called from where he stood around a fire with Atsurr and Torfi, two fellow Northmen who had fought with Domari and Grim against the Normans. Domari tilted up his chin in recognition, and the boy jogged to his side with a smile. "I haven't seen you in a few days."

"I thought you were headed to Miklagard with Hamund," Domari said, never taking his eyes off the forest in the distance. The Valkyries' canvases were dark this morning, dots against the deep greens of the pines surrounding them.

"I've been thinking about what you said on the boats, and what you warned us about in Torvik. You really believe this is Ragnarok?"

Domari grunted, not bothering to look at the young boy. He was tired of explaining himself. The thought of Edgar willingly going into battle soured his stomach, no matter how much he needed every willing and able soldier at his disposal.

As on the ship, his silence didn't deter the boy, still

trailing his steps when they neared the circle of tents on the outskirts of camp.

"They're Valkyries, aren't they?" Edgar whispered, moving closer to Domari. "That's what the symbol on their brows is, right? Raven wings. The mark of Odin."

A chill raked down Domari's spine at the open admission, but he offered a brief nod. He'd only gotten passing glimpses of the other women in Hilda's camp. They were varying heights, skin tones ranging from the palest white to the darkest brown, but they each wore the same mark on their brow.

Edgar's questions stopped as they neared the small circle, approaching the four women around the fire. A cauldron hung over the flame, two nearly identical copper-haired women peering into the pot.

To their left sat another woman with her legs crossed and eyes closed, her face tipped up to the rising sun. Light danced across her dark skin, her hair braided in long ropes down her back. She hummed a low tune, ignoring everyone else here. Even wearing the same molded leather armor as the others, everything about this woman was ethereal.

On the other side of her sat her opposite, this woman's pale hair and features almost white as snow. Her green eyes flicked up when Domari and Edgar approached, her lips turned down into a scowl meant to scare off a lesser man. A longsword lay across her lap, sun glinting off the metal blade, highlighting the runes carved into the deadly weapon. A stone as bright green as her eyes decorated the pommel, a wolf's open maw holding the gem in place. Her long, pointed nails were a weapon in their own right, painted as black as the mark on her brow.

Her focus turned to Domari as he entered the circle, long nails tapping against the metal blade. He swallowed, words lost to him as he came face to face with the women legends spoke of.

Edgar took a step closer, his arm brushing against Domari's, probably regretting his curiosity.

No one said anything, and the silence was almost as eerie as their deadly stares, like ravens perched in the trees above your passage. A pale hand pushed aside the tent flap across from him, and Hilda stepped out into the morning sun. The light seemed to find her, spotlighting her passage towards the fire where they all congregated.

Like the others, she wore fitted battle leathers, hugging her curves. Most had belts around their waist for sheathing weapons, but the leather around Hilda's hips was different. It was etched in runes with a metallic sheen to them, glittering in the light. Domari couldn't tell exactly how old the woman was, or any of them really, but something in Hilda's emerald gaze spoke of years of pain and suffering.

"I've been waiting for you for a very long time."

Domari straightened his shoulders, standing just inside the circle. Edgar shifted his weight from foot to foot, resting his hand on the dagger tucked into his belt.

Hilda's gaze flicked from Domari to Edgar, a small smile tugging at the corner of her lips, a predator acknowledging their prey. "So young. So foolish."

Domari put his hand out to the side, placing himself between Hilda and the boy. "He's not a part of this."

The women chuckled, and Hilda's emerald eyes focused back on him. "We all are, Domari."

Two more women stepped from the tents, hands resting on weapons when they took up their place behind Hilda. Domari sucked in a breath, counting silently.

All seven Valkyries stood before him.

His heart raced under their inspection, different and yet the same as the idolizing view of the men in the camp. Hilda stepped forward, crossing to stand in front of Domari. He towered over the woman, but her green eyes stared up at him with a satisfied gleam.

"Why are you here?" Domari cut straight to the point. "Why now?"

"I've waited 28 years for you, Domari," Hilda answered, then looked over her shoulder at the women behind her. On a silent command, each one tilted their face towards the sky, the sun peeking through the clouds to shine down on their brows, the ravens' wings marking each of them as gods' touched and Odin's Chosen.

Despite his racing heart, his breaths evened, that same calm he felt on the eve of battle. When Hilda turned back to Domari, her bright eyes glowed with an otherworldly sheen, magic shimmering around her body. Unlike the green light Shelbie emanated when using her magic, this was white, as bright as the clouds above.

Hilda's hands were the brightest, near blinding when she splayed her fingers at her side. The runes etched into her belt shimmered, seeming to move with each twitch of her hand, magic coating every inch.

"Twenty-eight years ago, the gods foresaw the end of

days at the hand of a Demon. As is told in every story, Loki will betray his family, working with creatures and humans alike to bring about Asgard's demise."

The symbols pulsed with light when she twisted her palm face-up, the magic glowing around her absorbing back into the belt.

"But this time, Odin thought to play a trick on the Trickster himself. He sent me to charm the Demon, to give him a child. A Valkyrie born of the Demon's own blood, unmarked by Odin until he calls upon her."

Domari's breath caught in his throat, understanding dawning on him. "Signe. You're Signe's mother."

Hilda nodded, a hint of sadness in her otherwise expressionless face. "*Victory*, Draugr named her. Irony in its truest form. If she wins this coming battle, the world will perish as we know it. If she loses…"

Hilda cut off, her eyes flicking to the ground as her shoulders dropped the smallest amount. Her voice took on a steely quality, hardened like the warrior she was.

"Odin has far too much faith in his own wisdom, and too little in Loki's cunning. He might have thought to create an ally behind enemy lines, but I disobeyed a direct order to leave the girl alone. She is my *daughter,*" Hilda bit out, her eyes coming back up to Domari's face, full of the same fire he'd seen in Signe on the battlefield outside Torvik, "and I will not leave her to the Fate the gods have decreed."

"What did you do?" Domari asked, his eyes casting to the women around him. All of them wore the same fearsome expression, and a buzz raked over Domari's skin, alight with the magic in the air.

"I sought out the only ally I could trust to see my side, to understand the Fate of Midgard is just as important as that of Asgard."

Thunder rumbled in the sunny sky, and Domari looked at the belt around her waist again, recognizing it for what it was.

Megingjord, Thor's magic belt.

Before he could confirm, magic shimmered around her once more, her right hand a blur as power coursed over her body. Between one breath and the next, a hammer appeared in her hand, the leather-wrapped handle worn with use. Metal almost as dark as the tents behind them shimmered, a knot the same as the one tattooed on Domari's neck etched into the side.

"'*Find the warrior,*' Thor said so many years ago, and so I set off in search of the one most worthy. Along the way, I found every other Valkyrie I could, gathering them to the cause."

The weight of the weapon seemed almost unbearable, the corded muscles in her arms rippling with the effort to hold it.

"'*Find the warrior.*'" Hilda dropped to her knee. As one, the Valkyries behind her followed suit, laying their weapons at their feet and bowing their heads in respect. "'*You can't change the will of the Fates, but whoever is strong enough to wield Mjölnir is your only hope to defy them.*'"

She set the hammer on the ground to unclasp *Megingjord* from her waist. Power shimmered off the magical belt when she held it up for Domari, her mouth tugged down in a firm line.

His hands shook as he reached towards it. A shock of electricity ran through him when his fingers skimmed the leather, warm to the touch, but he didn't pull away, caught in thrall by this moment.

A phantom wind picked up, lifting the belt from her hands and settling it around his waist, the buckle engaging. Thunder rumbled in the distance again; the trees around them shook with the sound. Domari's chest heaved as he looked down at his hands. Heat gathered in his right palm. He flexed his fingers, and the hammer lifted off the ground, flying into his grip.

"Find the warrior," Hilda said again, the hint of awe in her voice cutting through Domari's shock. He looked up to find her gazed locked with his, green eyes glowing with power. "And so, I have."

SHELBIE

"Can you feel it?" Yrsa said, her breath tickling against the side of my neck.

I breathed deep, my back resting against Hadriel's warm side. Everything magical was easier when my dragon and I were touching, like I needed another reason to not leave his side.

"Yes." I trailed my fingers over the surface of that magical well inside me. Over the last two weeks, Yrsa had worked with me daily, teaching me how to find this place of power, how to draw from it in small amounts, and how to use myself as a conduit for the magic within.

Here at the magical well in my mind, my physical surroundings disappeared: the sandy beach under me, the rocks to my right, the waves crashing against the shore, the dogs sleeping nearby. Instead, I was in this space between, where nothing existed except Hadriel, me, the well of magic, and the night sky above. Stars twinkled on the surface of the water, dancing with the ripples I caused, as serene as anything I'd ever experienced.

Under Yrsa's instruction, I'd healed scrapes and cuts on residents, checked on Astrid's baby due any day, and strengthened my bond with Hadriel, always alerting me to his presence. And I'd learned to heal myself.

Gone was the twinge in my knee, the bruises dotting my skin, and the muscle fatigue that had kept me from the daily training sessions with Magnus.

Flying became easier with each trip we took, finding my rhythm and seat the same as I had on horseback as the magic moved freely between us, two rivers flowing in the same direction towards the sea.

"Good." Yrsa's voice sounded far away even though I knew she sat within touching distance from me on the beach outside Torvik. "Gather some of it to you, cup your hands, and lift up just a small amount."

I did as she said, dipping my hands into the cool well, feeling the liquid wash over my skin. Magic buzzed through my veins, but I withdrew them, holding only the smallest amount in my palms. "What now?"

"Think of what power you'd like to manifest, then lift your hands to your mouth, and drink."

My hands stuttered as I held them in front of me. *This seems like an epically bad idea. I shouldn't do this, right?*

Aside from tossing you from a cliff, Hadriel answered, his side rumbling behind my back, *she has yet to steer you wrong. And even then, her intentions were good, although her execution could have been better.*

I grumbled, hating the reminder of that first session, and stared down at the liquid in my palms.

"Drink it, Shelbie," Yrsa said again, her tone as patient as ever. "Tell me what you See."

I clenched my teeth at her words, fearing yet another vision I wouldn't understand. Instead, I focused on what it had felt like to see through Hadriel's eyes.

My hands trembled when I lifted them to my lips, taking a tiny sip of the liquid as sweet as honeyed mead. Aside from the slight buzz of magic in my veins, nothing catastrophic happened, so I drank the rest.

My throat warmed as I swallowed, and then my vision changed, back to that same doubled vision I'd shared with Hadriel on our flight to rescue Gunnar. Hadriel blinked, his head lifting as he looked out over the waves.

"I'm looking through Hadriel's eyes," I said for Yrsa's sake, and felt her hand squeeze mine in encouragement.

"Was that the power you sought?"

I nodded, staring out at the sea as I so often did, hoping to see boats crest the waves headed home, but no sails dotted the horizon.

"Good. That's very good, Shelbie. What else can Hadriel show you?"

Hearing her question, Hadriel moved his attention back to the beach, down the shore to where Magnus led training sessions.

Shades of red and orange blurred together where the pairs fought, but one stood off to the side, glowing a brighter shade. The warrior moved with quick efficiency, swinging a spear in rapid movements. The weapon spun wildly as whoever wielded it went on the attack, pushing back a circle of people hovering around them. The spear glowed, which was strange. I looked around the space, seeking out any other glowing weapons, but no sword or axe held the same greenish tint to it.

Who is that? I asked, and Hadriel blinked, his reptilian eyelids shuttering. Gone were the colors, leaving a crystal-clear image of the fight taking place on the shore hundreds of yards away.

Gunnar stood in the center; the same battle spear he'd used to help him walk the first few days here gripped in his hand. His chest heaved as he waved forward the next group of opponents. Magnus stepped up this time, a broad grin on his face as he twirled his own staff.

"Ready brother?" Magnus cracked his neck to the side. His voice was faint, but I was doubly surprised Hadriel could hear anything at all from this far away and that his shared senses extended not just to sight but sound as well.

Four men stood behind Magnus, but none followed him when he moved forward, ready for a fight. Sweat already glistened on his bare chest, twice as wide as Gunnar's, but there was something *more* about Gunnar since he'd returned. Something angrier. Something fiercer. Something harder.

In a blur of movement, Magnus attacked, and Gunnar sidestepped the first blow. They circled each other, weapons rapping hard. Magnus yelled taunts that Gunnar never answered, but Hadriel didn't pick up the words, focusing instead on his expression as hard as the wood in his hands.

Hadriel's vision shuttered once more, that same heat

register coming back. The colors blurred together as the two moved around each other so fast I could hardly keep up.

"Gunnar's spear is glowing," I said, my intonation relaying my confusion.

Yrsa's gleeful laugh had me breaking the spell. I pulled out of the magic effortlessly, blinking back into my body. The faint sounds of the fight blended in with the waves, but the figures were so small in the distance, I couldn't make out any details with my own eyes. "Why is it glowing?"

Yrsa pushed to her feet with a grin, shaking the sand from her skirt. "Isn't that an excellent question. Why don't we go ask him?"

I followed her as she walked down the beach, excitement evident in her hurried steps.

Do you understand what the hell is happening?

Hadriel grunted, but didn't answer.

Rolling my eyes, I hurried to catch Yrsa, matching her long strides. "So, the glowing spear thing is important? Is that what you wanted me to look for?"

"You channeled Hadriel's powers by ingesting it, something that can only be done in small doses. It alters the bond between you, tipping the scales in your favor to allow you a dose of his magic. For instance, if you were gravely injured and Hadriel was not, you could drink from the pool to borrow his healing magic. But if you drank freely from the pool, it could sever your connection, draining the magic from one of you into the other." Her hazel gaze swung in my direction, mouth in a serious line. "Don't ever do that."

I nodded. "Don't eat yellow snow, and don't guzzle from the well."

Yrsa chuckled, but her gaze focused back on the men in front of us.

Gunnar and Magnus were both covered in sweat and breathing heavily. Together, they lowered their weapons, turning to watch us approach.

"Done already?" Magnus asked, that same broad grin I loved so much splayed on his face even though his skin was dotted with red welts from his brother's weapon. "You can join my next group."

"Gunnar," Yrsa said, and he turned towards us. He'd trimmed his blond hair and beard to look more like his former self, but his cheeks were still hollow, the skin of his chest stretched tight over the corded muscles beneath. The same black patch covered his missing eye, cutting his face in a harsh line. "Your spear. Where did you get it?"

Gunnar looked at the weapon in his hands. "It was Vermund Oathbreaker's."

"I see." Yrsa bit back a grin. "And he just *gave* it to you? He didn't say anything?"

The smile dropped off Magnus's face as he looked between Yrsa and Gunnar, a cloud of confusion I couldn't help but share.

"It was after—" He looked over the gathered troops, his attention snagging on his mother sitting to the side, his children around her feet. Revna stood with a piece of driftwood she'd whittled into a battle staff of her own, held at the ready to fight off Viveka. "After I was injured. I can't remember exactly what he said. But when I woke up, the spear was there. Why?"

"Did he happen to say anything about Odin?" My head

whipped toward Yrsa, whose sole focus was on Gunnar's face. "The one-eyed god."

Gunnar looked down, his fingers tightening on the weapon. I followed his gaze. The faint glow of magic skittered along its surface, carved into the runes covering the weapon. His voice was so low, I barely heard him whisper, "May the ravens lead you to Valhalla."

Yrsa grinned, pointing at the spear in Gunnar's hand. "That is no mere spear." Her voice lifted, glee coating every word. "That is *Gungnir,* Odin's spear. You have been chosen by the gods, Gunnar Eriksson. He's calling you to battle, aiding you the only way he can. They cannot interfere, but they've chosen a side. *Our* side."

I was dumbstruck, not understanding the true significance of such a thing, but the mixture of awe and disbelief warring on the faces around me told me how monumental this was. Hell, even if it was a placebo effect Yrsa played on those around us, the excited chattering said it was working. Everyone around Gunnar moved closer, many pointing at him.

If I hadn't seen the magical glow with Hadriel's vision, maybe I wouldn't have believed it, but that Gunnar still stood in front of us after everything he'd been through… Hell, maybe he really was protected by the gods.

Magnus looked at the weapon then up to his brother. "Well, now I demand a rematch for every fight you've won this week."

Gunnar chuckled, resting the butt of the spear in the sand, and raised a brow. "Any more surprises for me, Yrsa?"

She pursed her lips, completely dismissing the sarcasm

lacing his tone, and waved at the young girl sitting next to Frida. "Viveka!"

Viveka looked around the gathered army hesitantly, then moved through the crowd. Everyone parted to clear a way forward for her, her black hair tied back in braids against her scalp. Dirt smudged her face, making her green eyes glow that much brighter. Unlike most of the women in Torvik, she wore pants and a tunic, a small belt tied around her waist holding an array of daggers and two small axes perfectly sized for her small hands.

She stopped a few feet from us, her expression as fierce as any I'd ever seen, making her seem much older than twelve.

Yrsa smiled and clasped her hands in front of her, stepping back out of the battle arena. "Excellent. Gunnar, why don't you fight Viveka next?"

Gunnar shot Yrsa a baffled look, then opened his mouth to argue when Magnus held up a hand.

"You've yet to see her fight, Gunnar." Magnus's eyes glittered with pride when he put a hand on Viveka's shoulder and dragged her forward. "Give it a go. Maybe she can teach you a thing or two in your old age."

Gunnar's fingers tightened on the spear as he stared at the young girl. I held my breath, glancing around at the wary villagers around us. As far as I knew, he didn't know Viveka's secret yet, and I was dying to see what happened next.

Viveka pulled her axes free, her knees bending to lower her center of gravity. She held them loosely in each hand, sliding her grip up and down the shaft until she seemed satisfied with her grip. Her lips turned down in a scowl as she shuffled to the side and circled Gunnar's much larger form.

He stood in the center of the circle, eyeing her, but didn't make a move. "This isn't a fair fight."

"You're right," Viveka said, her teeth bared in a savage sneer.

Before he could say more, she launched herself into the air, flying towards him with her left axe raised high. Gunnar jerked into motion, bringing the spear up to block it with the shaft. The metal slid down the wood until Gunnar flicked the butt of the spear out, pushing her back.

Quicker than I could track, she reacted and was on him again. With each blow she screamed and snarled, her voice as much of an intimidation factor as her quick movements. She kicked her feet out, swinging wide and slicing at his ankles, then rose, chopping down again.

Gunnar batted her away with the spear, using his size to his advantage as he threw her back, staying on the defense. What should have sent her careening to the ground only knocked her aside, landing lightly on her feet each time.

Magic hummed in the air, as thick as I'd ever felt it, and I reached for my pendant, letting myself drift back to the well within me. Without Hadriel close enough to touch, it was like walking through mud, but I was too curious to let that stop me. I cupped my hands like Yrsa had instructed, dipping it into the water, then took the smallest sip, letting my vision take over as Hadriel's.

Once again, my vision doubled, and magic danced across Gunnar's spear, much easier to see at this distance. It practically vibrated in his hands the power was so potent, but it paled in comparison to the white glow Viveka cast, as bright as the sunlit sky.

Unlike Gunnar, it wasn't only her weapons that shimmered — it was *all* of her.

She was the weapon sent from the gods.

Her axe caught in the wooden shaft of Gunnar's spear, wrenching it out of her grip and sending her backward into the sand. Time seemed to slow as she lay prone, but then her expression changed from fierce focus to a deadly calm. Tossing her remaining axe to the side, she tipped her chin down, her eyes mere slits.

Gunnar took a step back, grabbing the axe to pry it free, and Viveka's hands shot out to her sides. She splayed her fingers out wide, and the wind picked up off the sea behind her. My breath caught in my throat as I watched the magic flow freely around her, an orb of white light in Hadriel's vision. It shimmered like heat waves over hot concrete, dismissing any doubts I'd ever had about Valkyries and gods.

"Viveka," Gunnar warned, but his hand stilled on the handle of her weapon.

She shoved her left hand towards him, and that white-hot power shot forward, arching through the air and wrapping around Gunnar's weapon. Hadriel's vision flickered, and I switched back to my own in time to see the axe wiggle free of Gunnar's spear and fly back across the clearing into her outstretched hand.

While everyone else gasped over this revelation, I couldn't look away from the dirt smudged on her forehead, dark black against the glowing white power washing over her skin. Two wings formed a semi-circle on her brow, thin lines trailing down her nose.

With a kick of her feet, her body arched off the ground and landed in a crouch, ready to strike. She charged towards Gunnar again, a blur of motion, and with each second she fought, the mark grew darker.

I blinked between Hadriel's vision and my own, trying to decide if the mark was there only in my magical sight or evident for all to see.

"A Valkyrie." Magnus laughed, his hands resting on his hips. "She's a fucking Valkyrie."

Gunnar stopped; his focus glued on the mark on Viveka's brow. "Does Signe know?"

Viveka shook her head, barely even breathing hard in comparison to Gunnar's heaving chest. "No. He didn't tell me until after she left."

"He?" Magnus asked, but Gunnar cut in.

"Is Vermund really your father?"

She shook her head again. "No, he's Odin's man, sent to train us."

Magnus laughed again, his hands brushing through his long blond hair. "Oathbreaker. We should have known. His name isn't a title he earned, it's a fucking *warning*."

"Are there more of you?" Gunnar looked between Viveka and Yrsa, the older woman standing next to me with a delighted smile.

"Odin has nine Valkyries." She looked out over the water, and I followed her gaze. "I haven't seen them in years. It was too dangerous for them to be near Draugr, but Vermund had his orders to stay with him."

Magnus clapped his hands together, then spun back to the army around him. "Show's over. Back to work! We have a Valkyrie among us, so stop acting like this battle is a lost cause, you sad little fuckers."

I couldn't help but take in the excited expressions of those around me, everyone's movements faster, sharper, more intentional than before with this new hope.

I only hoped it was enough.

SIGNE

Signe plunged her hands in the icy stream again and again, scooping sand into her palm to scrub the blood from her skin. Gunnar's blood.

Even after two weeks, her thoughts spun constantly. Was he dead? Had she really killed him? She couldn't decide which was worse — if he was still alive and suffering. Or if he was dead…

Everything was a blur over the last few months, lost to the hallucinations she'd been held under. But something had changed that night. When Vermund had said Odin's Chosen wouldn't die tonight, the haze snapped. She understood.

Before Draugr could make a move to kill Gunnar himself, she stepped forward, serving a hopefully non-fatal blow. If Draugr had done it himself, there was no chance Gunnar was still alive.

They'd left the beach shortly after Nidhoggr took flight,

and Signe hadn't been able to turn back to stare at Gunnar's crumpled form.

That night, she'd battled the last of the drugged fog, dreaming of Hadriel flying in to save Gunnar. Now that her mind was clear, that possibility seemed less and less likely.

That was two weeks ago, and still she felt his blood on her fingers, no matter how much she cleaned them. Despite how many men's blood she'd had there before, Signe knew this time it was a stain she'd never be free of.

"I think you got it all," came a low, steady voice behind her.

"Worried about me now?" she sniped back with a bitter laugh, her copper braid hanging down just above her rippling reflection in the water. "How kind of you, Uncle."

Vermund propped a boot on a boulder beside her, casting a glance around the camp. Men moved around them, but as they were often together, she and Vermund garnered no more attention than usual.

"Draugr wants you in the tent." He pulled a skin from his belt, one Signe recognized all too well, then tugged on his trousers before bending at the knee. Once lowered next to her, he pulled the stopper free and tilted a sickly-looking black liquid into the stream.

The water rushed over the rocks here, gurgling loud enough to block the sound of his low voice. "You'll need to be clear-headed soon, Signe. But no one can know."

She stared at his reflection in the water, not daring to lift her chin and acknowledge his words. Those same green eyes she saw in her own face stared back, then nodded once.

Pushing back to his feet, he pulled her up alongside him and shoved the skin into her arms.

"Drink," he ordered, his tone back to normal volume. Like always, he grabbed her chin and squeezed, pulling her mouth open. The water sluiced across her tongue, cool and crisp from the nearby mountains, and she swallowed.

Only the barest hint of the bitter herbs still tainted the water, so she drooped her eyelids, feigning the same foggy haze she'd lived in these past few months. She tricked her brain into believing her limbs were heavy, then weightless, then followed Vermund to her father's tent.

Draugr barely glanced at them as they entered, deep in discussion with Raud and three other men. It wasn't the first time Signe had been allowed inside, but she remembered nothing of the temporary headquarters. An open perusal of the space would be out of character for her drugged stupor, so she forced herself to keep her face neutral, her eyes downcast. Even still, she took in everything she could without giving herself away.

Raud's glowing red eyes made her skin slither — all traces of the human she barely knew gone. Now, he was a mouthpiece for the white dragon outside, his skin as pale and clear of tattoos as the beast's scales.

On a low table in the center of the tent lay a map. She wasn't close enough to read it, but the cliffs to the north and the sea to the east made it an easy guess this was Torvik. Stones were piled in various spots on the map — white, presumably, for Draugr and his men, for their white dragon. Black, clustered in the middle — the others, who would be in the town.

"Their village would be nothing for me to decimate." Raud's voice far deeper than she remembered with a smoky tone that sent a chill raking down her spine.

"No." Draugr cut a hand through the air. "The village is meaningless, as are their men. Their dragon is your concern, and has to be taken out first, then their leaders."

Raud tilted his head, considering that, while Draugr turned to Signe.

"You will lead the first charge." Her father indicated the open space between stones — presumably, the field in front of the village where their first skirmish took place. "Show the men what a Valkyrie can do."

Signe stepped forward and trailed her fingertips over the stones, plucking up a handful of black ones. She crushed them in her palm, a flare of her Valkyrie magic rendering them nothing more than sand in a flash. As she let the sand pour out of her palm, she met Draugr's cold gaze and grinned.

"An honor," she murmured.

"What if we cannot kill their dragon?" Vermund cut in, and Signe didn't miss the irritation that flared in Draugr's eyes. "Do we have a backup plan?"

Draugr's gaze flicked to Raud's briefly, and his lips tilted up in a mockery of a smile.

"I have every faith in Nidhoggr," the Demon replied, and Raud's eyes glowed a little more red. "But, in the event they are unable to complete their task, I do have a plan."

Signe stepped back, as much to keep the men in the tent in her line of sight as to evade her father's notice any further. Vermund clenched a hand into a fist at his side, doubt written in every line of his face.

"Have faith, old friend. When have I ever let you down?" Draugr squeezed Vermund's shoulder, then shook him lightly. "We have a Valkyrie on our side, the fiercest dragon in the North, and *me*." His smile was all teeth, and Signe's heart rate ticked up in her chest. "Their dragon will not see another dawn."

31

SHELBIE

The melodic tune of a lyre blended with the drums in the distance, contrasting the crashing waves behind me. After yesterday's revelation about Gunnar's spear and Viveka's demonstration of her powers, everyone was feeling lively. Aside from Gunnar's return, this was the best news we'd had all summer.

The chill bite to the air was an unnecessary reminder that summer was almost over, and we were running out of time. I pulled the cloak over my shoulders, fingers tightening on the cool stone around my neck. It buzzed with power, Hadriel in the nearby cliffs, but I let him rest.

My green dress swished between my legs while I walked behind Magnus and Astrid towards the town square, both dogs flanking me. Voices mixed with the music as we neared the celebration quickly forming in the streets. Laughter floated through the air with the scents of roasting meat and fresh bread. The children ran ahead but stayed within sight of us.

Magnus had his arm draped over his wife's shoulder, holding her to his chest as if even an inch of space between them was too much. They spoke in hushed words I couldn't make out, but the smile she gave him when she tipped her face up to his was precious, adoration written in every glance.

I rubbed a hand over my sternum, trying to ease the pain at the sight, wanting to turn around for a glimpse of the sea. Missing Domari was a bone-deep ache, as relentless as the tides. I was all too aware of the passing time, each hour an hour Domari was late.

Glancing over my shoulder, I spied the faint blues of the sea beyond, birds flying just over the docks. Domari should have been back over a week ago according to his original estimate, and each sunset he didn't see with me was another wound carved into my soul.

Thor grumbled, then shoved at the back of my knee, urging me on.

"Okay, okay." I flicked my cloak out and hid his black fur until he shook the fabric free. His dark eyes stared up at me, unamused, and I couldn't help but smile. Squatting down, I pushed my hands through his fur, taking another glance out to the water over his shoulder. Freki nudged at my arm until I made room for him too, his wet tongue bringing a laugh to the surface.

The sound of the waves crashing against the docks was drowned out by the noise behind me. Dropping my head to Thor's, I let myself feel the pain just for this moment. My eyes burned with unshed tears, and I scrunched my nose to keep them that way. Both dogs leaned in, and I clung to them, losing myself in their steady comfort. Breathing the salty air in, I searched for a sense of calm to carry me through another worry-filled night.

My fingers trailed over the warm stone on my chest, wishing Hadriel were here with me. *Anything yet?*

Still nothing, Hadriel answered. Unease radiated down my connection to the dragon, sharing the same sense of foreboding from these new omens. Part of me was tempted to try for another vision, but I was afraid of what I'd See.

"Magnus!" someone called up ahead.

I stood, brushing the dog hair off my skirts. By the time I turned around, Magnus stared at me, one brow raised.

"You coming?" he asked, holding Astrid at his side.

Her belly had dropped over the last few days, the baby riding lower as her body prepared for birth. Magnus had hovered constantly today, canceling training after Yrsa had said the baby would be here within the next few days. Excitement radiated off him, and young Astrid wore a tight smile, her eyes telling me how tired she was of carrying this child.

He kissed her pale blonde hair, rubbing a hand over her belly. "I need to feed my family, and I smell honeyed apples."

I waved him forward, plastering on a smile. "Who am I to turn down such a delectable item?"

Magnus winked. "I knew I could convince you."

We wandered through the crowd, everyone giving us a wide berth, but eyes followed us everywhere. I wasn't sure whether it was Magnus's size, towering above almost everyone here, the two black dogs walking at my side, or the glowing green pendant I didn't bother to hide anymore, but no one dared approach our party.

Even after months in Torvik, I wasn't used to the awed expressions on every face. They stared at me the same way they had at Gunnar's spear and Viveka's Valkyrie mark, like I was some magical *other*. With Yrsa's training, I felt slightly more confident in my Promised powers, but nothing that deserved the level of attention thrown my way.

"For your dragon." A young boy held out a ruby red apple, his head bowed. His whole body shook as he stared at his feet.

I looked up at Magnus, grinning broadly, then back to the boy, taking the apple from his hands. "Thank you. I'll make sure he gets it. What's your name?"

"Gilli." The boy's chin tipped up enough to show me the bright blue of his eyes, filled with reverence. "My favorite stories were always of Hadriel, the great black dragon. To see him fly is a dream."

Magnus chuckled, and I couldn't help but smile, brushing a hand across Gilli's cheek. "He'll be delighted to hear that."

Grumbling came through our mind link, and my grin became genuine. *What? Not a fan of apples?*

That child would make a better snack than an apple.

"He says thank you, and that he loves apples, especially before a battle."

That is not *what I said,* Hadriel sniped and Magnus boomed a laugh. Gilli's jaw hung loose, his bright eyes wide as he stared at my pendant, then took off running back through the streets.

"What did Hadriel *really* say?" Magnus threw the arm not holding Astrid across my shoulders, pinning me to his side.

I shook my head. "That dragon is an asshole, through and through."

Magnus looked down at Thor pacing at my side, one blond brow raised. "Dark and broody is certainly your favorite. You collect those males like you're making your own hoard."

I forced a smile, refusing to look towards the sea again. "I do have a type."

Magnus's hands tightened on my shoulder, turning me towards the same vendor I'd gotten the bread from weeks ago.

"Gertrud," I said, proud that I'd remembered her name. Her face lit with excitement, glancing between the three of us standing at her booth. "Thank you again for the bread. It was the best I've had in ages."

She blushed, then turned and grabbed three more loaves, handing one to each of us. "Take it! Take it! The Erikssons are a blessing to us all. The gods' chosen ones."

I tried to hand mine back, but Magnus plucked it out my hand, taking a large bite out of the side. "*You* are the blessing, Gertrud. A goddess among women for creating something so heavenly. My child will be born with the taste of your honeyed bread on her tongue and will never be able to settle for anything less than this divine flavor. You *must* teach me how it's made after we win this battle."

Her dark eyelashes fluttered as she blinked away the compliment, and I bit my cheeks not to laugh. Magnus was a sweet talker, winning over loyalties with his words and actions everywhere we went, but the confidence with which he talked of victory had bile rising in my throat.

I wanted to believe him. Wanted to believe we had a chance. Wanted to believe Domari would be back in time and this all was worth it, but everything seemed so impossible. There were too many ways for things to go wrong still.

Astrid gasped and grabbed her stomach as her face contorted in pain. I rushed forward, my hand flying to my pendant and the other to her belly the same way Yrsa had taught me. Astrid brushed me aside, pushing my hand away with a shake of her head.

"I'm fine," she said, but the jovial grin on Magnus's face was gone. He thrust the bread into my hands, then bent and scooped up Astrid, carrying her down the street.

"That baby will be here tomorrow," Gertrud said, and I hummed in agreement.

Leaning a hip against the table behind me, I stared out over the crowd with Gertrud. A band played in the center, Björn singing a tune of strength and bravery while he plucked the chords.

Asmund stood on the far side of the street, laughing with several men I'd met at training practices with Magnus. His eyes met mine and he lifted his ale with a bob of his head, then sipped.

I'd been avoiding him since Domari left, not sure what to say to smooth over the disagreements the two had had, but he'd kept his word. Those who didn't intend on going into battle had long since left Torvik either by boat or on foot, and those here he'd help outfit with weapons and armor, preparing the best way we could.

Ripping at the bread Magnus had already bitten into, I ate my feelings. Worry. Doubt. Fear. So much fear.

"Here." Gertrud pulled a pitcher from behind the table, removing the cloth over the top. I turned my back to Asmund as she poured some of it into a wooden cup and passed it to me. "You look like you could use this."

I chuckled, but took the mead she offered, needing the liquid courage to get through these next few days.

"Is your husband a fighter?" I asked, remembering she said he was the one who brewed the mead.

Her head tilted to the side as she eyed me. "It's easy to forget the rumors you're not from here until you say something like that."

My brow scrunched, trying to think through what exactly I'd said.

"We *all* are, Shelbie." Gertrud reached across the table and patted my hand. "My husband, my sons, my daughter and I… We will all be there to fight at your side. This is a battle foretold in every legend, every story, every song. We would not miss it. The stakes are far too high to sit back and not offer aid."

I ducked my head, my eyes burning again. I needed to be strong for Gertrud, for these people. They were counting on me, and I'd do the best I could by them, but *my best* might not be good enough.

"Thank you." My voice was more of a croak, but I looked up at her once the tingling in my face subsided. "Thank you for your loyalty."

Her smile was soft, her eyes gentle, and it was hard to imagine her picking up a weapon and charging into battle. But then again, Magnus was perhaps the biggest softie I'd ever met and also one of the most ruthless warriors I'd ever seen. These people were a conundrum, a living contradiction, and I loved them for it.

I set the two untouched loaves back down on her table but drained the mead and took the loaf I'd eaten my way through. "Your generosity and support will not be forgotten, Gertrud."

"It is always better to fight bravely and lose than to not fight at all and give up hope." She reached across the table and squeezed my hand again. "Don't lose hope, Shelbie."

I nodded, then moved away from the table, the dogs trailing me. If I didn't believe we had a chance in this coming fight, how could I expect anyone else to either? Everything in my stomach soured, a heavy weight settling on my shoulders.

How am I supposed to do this, Hadriel? How am I supposed to lead these people when I've already lost hope?

You lean on me, Hadriel said.

I closed my eyes, leaning against the side of a building, a lump forming in my throat.

You trust me, Hadriel said again. *You trust yourself. We can do this. I battled his men away from the wall once, and I will do it again.*

I scoffed, panic now mixed with guilt. Pushing off the building, I turned away from the party and headed back to the beach, needing to be alone. *They have a dragon this time though, Hadriel. You won't have time to take out both Nidhoggr and all Draugr's men. A fight is coming, whether we want it or not.*

You're right, Hadriel answered. *But these people are warriors, each one of them.*

Bonfires were scattered along the beach, revelers soaking up the late summer night. I stopped to watch the Erikssons, gathered around one of the fires near the dock. Gunnar's blond hair shone in the firelight where he sat with Frida and several children. Erik perched on his shoulder, Gunnar's large hand patting the baby's back. He laughed at something Ulf said between his crossed legs, reaching forward to ruffle the boy's hair. Revna stood to the side with that same piece of driftwood she carried around lately, batting it against Viveka and Kára's weapons. The other children played with small wooden toys I knew Domari had carved, and my heart lurched.

Everyone had so much to lose, and they needed me to stop it.

Get me out of here, Hadriel.

The sound of his heavy wings reached me before I saw him, his dark scales blending in with the coming twilight. Chatter stopped as he soared over the waves, heading our direction. Gunnar sought me out, but I didn't stop to talk to him, wading into the surf towards my dragon.

Water soaked into my dress and boots, weighing me down as much as my poisonous thoughts. I reached up, unclasping the cloak, desperate to be free of these burdens. It floated behind me in the waves, carried back onto the shore. I dove into an oncoming wave, the icy water stealing my breath and the world faded away. Bubbles swirled around me, the green glow of my pendant casting light over the creatures scurrying across the seabed.

I surfaced as the wave passed, throwing my head back to clear the curls from my face. By the time my vision cleared, Hadriel swooped low, his talons closing around my upper body in a tight squeeze. Even though I knew it was coming, the moment he tossed me into the air, my stomach bottomed out.

Biting back a scream, I tumbled through the air, trying to right myself while he banked to the left. My teeth cracked as my body slammed against his spine, landing right between his shoulder blades. An ungraceful *oomph* left me, but I scrambled into place along his shoulders, hanging on when he banked a turn and headed out over the water.

His warm scales felt divine against my hand, and I reached for that magical well, drinking the smallest amount to heal my aching wounds and dry my clothes, then another to take over Hadriel's sight.

Everything came in crystal-clear, a sharpness I'd never experienced in my own eyesight. I glanced behind me, checking on the dogs still standing in the surf, Gunnar standing between them. Knowing they'd wait for me, I scanned the horizon, feeling as desperate as Lovisa, the sorceress who'd made the original bargain for a dragon's Promised power to find her lost lover.

"Where are you, Domari?" The wind snatched the words away as quickly as I muttered them, my wet hair flowing behind me. "Come back to me."

We flew for what felt like hours until Gertrud's words came back to me. *Don't lose hope,* she'd said, and I clung to that last sliver of hope inside me.

Leaning down to rest my head on Hadriel, I let my

hands slide down his neck, hugging him tightly. Just as I was about to close my eyes and tell him to turn around, something blocked out the pink of the setting sun on the horizon.

I jerked upright, blinking to make sure I wasn't imagining it.

You see that too, Hadriel?

He didn't answer, but his wings tucked in tighter, his speed increasing. We soared directly to it, and my breaths came in short bursts.

A ship crested the waves on the horizon, and that hope inside me grew. Tears welled in my eyes, and I was hopeless to hold them back. One by one, more appeared, at least a dozen sailing in a staggered line as they headed for us.

A choked sob escaped me as Hadriel flew us closer, and I saw the shields lining the sides of the narrow boats. I could hardly breathe, my vision flickering to Hadriel's again and scanning the boats for a familiar face.

At the back of the first ship stood a man, towering above those around him. His dark hair was longer than it had been weeks ago, but I'd know him anywhere. He shouted something to the men on the boat, then stepped onto the side and dove into the water.

"Domari!" I screamed as he swam through the rising waves, headed towards me.

I've got him, Hadriel said. I gripped his horns moments before he dove, skimming just above the water. His talons dragged in the water, sending a spray up behind us, until he pulled Domari from the waves.

I leaned as far to my right as I could, staring down at the

man held tightly in my dragon's grip. Domari smiled up at me, and a weird sob-laugh burst free from me.

We rose into the sky, and I braced myself as Hadriel jerked to the left. Domari flew. Hadriel tucked his wings and fell then straightened out, making me realize just how choreographed this move was. Domari somersaulted much more gracefully than I ever had, landing on his feet on Hadriel's back.

I turned in my seat, and this time I did laugh, wiping at the tears streaming down my chin. Arms outstretched, Domari walked across Hadriel's spine as if it were nothing.

He dropped to sit behind me, and I turned all the way around in his hold. My arms and legs circled him, trusting him to hold me while sobs racked me. His hands ran up and down my back and I breathed in his earthy scent, in disbelief that this was real.

"I'm here." Domari kissed my temple and squeezed me to his chest. "I told you I'd be back."

Lifting my head from the crook of his neck, I wiped away the tears, then slapped his chest. "What the hell took you so long?"

Domari chuckled, his fingers tangling in my hair. His lips found mine, far too gentle for the adrenaline coursing through my body.

"I found some unexpected allies," Domari said, his grin as broad as I'd ever seen it. My brows hit my hairline, and his fingers tightened around my nape, pulling me back in for another kiss.

Shelbie, Hadriel said, and I looked over my shoulder at him, hating the unease in that one word. My doubled vision was still in place as I righted myself, my back resting against Domari's chest.

What is it?

Hello, Promised, another voice answered in my head, this one deeper, smokier, and sending a chill down my spine. The stone around my neck burned against my skin, flashing from green to red, and I sucked in a breath.

Lifting the chain away from my chest, I stared down at it, then snapped my gaze back up in time to see the silhouette of a dragon rising against the moon in the distance.

Your Fate is mine.

32

DOMARI

Shelbie's spine stiffened as they rode back towards Torvik, and he tightened his arms around her, inhaling her clean scent tinged with sea water and rosemary soap. The heat of her body was a steady comfort, a reminder he'd made it back to her.

"Domari." Her voice wavered, and her fingers tightened on his forearm. "They're here."

He looked at the shore in front of them, trying to see anything that would indicate her words were true. Everything was still, framed by the late summer sunset hanging on just a little longer. Thunder rumbled behind them, and his palm tingled where the hammer had disappeared. It sucked back into whatever magic hid it when not in use, but a wash of power flowed over him as he thought of the coming battle, raising the hairs on his arms like an electric current.

"It's too early still." Domari stared up at the sky, not yet the same as the vision she'd seen with the constellations and lights dancing overhead. "I thought we had time."

She shook her head, a ragged inhale betraying her fear. "Something's changed."

"Have you Seen it?"

"No, but I *heard* him."

"Who?"

She turned enough so Domari could see her pale blue eyes, her pupils blown wide. "Nidhoggr."

Dread settled in Domari's gut, the name like a sinking stone. While there was a lot he didn't understand, he also knew better than to doubt Shelbie. He looked over his shoulder at the boats behind them, trying to adjust all his plans. "Fill me in on what's happened since I left."

So, Shelbie told him of Magnus's training sessions with anyone interested, the reinforcements Asmund had made to the wall, the powers she'd practiced with Yrsa to prepare herself.

"One more thing is different," Shelbie said as they neared the beach, Hadriel swooping low over the waves. Seafoam sprayed up over them, the cold bite of the water inconsequential compared to the anxiety in Shelbie's voice. She didn't say anything further, so Domari scanned the town, looking for what else had changed.

Children ran down the beach toward them, several adults walking behind, including a tall man with blond hair hanging down to his shoulders, a patch over one eye.

"Gunnar," Domari croaked, emotions clogging his throat. "How?"

Shelbie laced her fingers through his, squeezing his arm to her chest. "Hadriel, Magnus, and I went on a bit of a rescue mission."

Domari's attention snapped back to Shelbie; his mouth turned down. "You *what?*"

"It's a long story and doesn't matter now. He's back, and he's okay."

"Where's Signe?"

Shelbie shook her head as Hadriel landed in the sand, then slid off his back to the ground. Domari followed her, the ground shifting unsteadily after days spent on the water. But nothing mattered more than the man coming towards him.

His steps were uneven as he rushed forward, straight into Gunnar's outstretched arms. The two men clung to each other, their grip almost crushing, belying the emotions both held deep down.

"You're not leaving me out of a group hug this time." Magnus threw his arms around both Gunnar and Domari, squeezing tight.

Domari shrugged out of their hold, shoving Magnus's chest playfully. He scrubbed a hand over his thick beard hiding his smile and stared at Gunnar, afraid to believe this was real. "I thought I'd lost you, too."

"I'm not that easy to get rid of," Gunnar said, the smile he offered not quite meeting his eye. "Ready to get my wife back?"

Domari pulled back and squeezed his cousin's shoulder. "More than you know."

He slid his fingers through Shelbie's and they all moved towards the docks, watching the boats row the last few hundred yards to shore.

"How many?" Magnus asked.

"Just shy of 300 returned with me. Guards, locals, and a few extras."

"Extras?" Magnus's brows climbed into his hairline, and he looked back over the boats.

Gunnar gasped, spying the boat at the front holding seven women covered in armor with a raven painted on their brow. He turned towards Domari, mouth hanging slightly ajar.

"Valkyries," they said at the same time, and Domari grinned. "You brought us Valkyries."

"I brought us Valkyries." Domari nodded, then held his hand out to the side. Magic thrummed in his veins as thunder cracked in the distance, a lightning bolt splitting the sky when *Mjölnir* appeared in his hand.

"And none for Magnus." Magnus rolled his eyes. "I'm fearsome enough on my own that even the gods don't think I *need* a special weapon."

Shelbie snorted, but Domari's brow dipped, wondering what he'd missed.

Gunnar looked between the hammer and Domari's face, staring at the tattoo on his neck — the one they both had. "Until Valhalla, we promised, and it seems the gods intend to have us see that through."

He turned the spear in his hand, the runes carved into the wooden shaft glowing with magic, but none more so than the knot beneath his palm. It was the same as their tattoos, and the same as the one on the side of the hammer.

Magnus let out a huff. "See, maybe if you'd let me get the tattoo, I'd also get a fancy magical weapon."

Gunnar gave his brother a playful cuff to the back of his head. "You were but a suckling babe."

"I was *eleven.*"

"And still followed Mother everywhere, hm?"

Domari chuckled at his cousins' bickering, but stared out at the boats coming closer to the shore. Catching Grim's eye as he disembarked his boat, he waved him over, Hilda striding along beside him.

"Gunnar." Hilda said his name not in question, but a statement, like she knew exactly who this man was. Gunnar straightened, and Hilda tipped up her chin, staring directly at his eyepatch. "A man strong enough to withstand that might just have what it takes to be with a Valkyrie."

Magnus barked a laugh, but Gunnar didn't share the sentiment, staring right back at the woman.

"We've heard so much about you." Grim stepped forward to grasp Gunnar's forearm below his elbow, squeezing tight. "I feel I know you already."

Gunnar's gaze flicked between Grim and Domari, a smirk tugging at his mouth. "Is that so?"

Grim managed to keep a straight face for only a moment before he broke, grinning. "Fuck no. Getting Domari to talk is nearly as deadly as sparring with the Valkyries. Be pleasantly surprised I even know your name."

Domari chuckled, leaning into Shelbie's hold when she slid a hand around his waist. He kissed her temple, holding her tight.

"And you." Hilda turned towards Shelbie, the rest of her Valkyries coming up behind her. "We've waited a long time for you."

Domari tightened his hold on her shoulders, making it clear to everyone here who *Mjölnir* would be wielded to protect.

Shelbie opened her mouth to respond, but footsteps down the dock drew their attention. Asmund hurried towards them, eyes wide as he scanned the boats docking. Hundreds of men disembarked, the eagle of the Varangian Guard stamped across their tunics and shields.

Fate was a strange thing, woven into the Tapestry without their knowledge, and yet everything in Domari's life seemed to have led to this moment.

"Just when I think the surprises are done." Asmund rubbed his hand over his beard, covering his mouth, but not before Domari saw his jaw drop at the sight of Hilda and her Valkyries. He turned wide-eyed back to Domari with a gentle shake of his head. "I told you to find me an army, and so you did."

Grim threw his arm around Domari's shoulders, slapping him on the chest. "He sure as fuck did."

Hadriel lifted off from the beach, launching into the sky with a shriek, the sound shaking the dock beneath their feet. Everyone turned to watch, and then stilled as an answering call rang out over the valley.

"I've always wanted to slay a dragon," Grim said with a wide grin.

"I'll race you to it," Magnus chuckled. "Magnus Dragonslayer has a nice ring to it, don't you think?"

❄

Sun peeked over the village walls at his back the next morning, the tinge of pink slowly creeping into the dark blue of night. Stars still twinkled overhead when Domari looked up, breathing in the night air for what could be the last time.

He stood on the fortress walls, battle armor covering his chest and thighs. Dark paint covered his exposed skin, protection runes painted to prepare him for battle. No matter how many times he'd stared out over what would soon become a battlefield, it never got easier. Phantom screams replayed in his mind, past battles bleeding into his thoughts. He listened to the banners flapping nearby, focusing on the briny air, and the smooth wooden walls under his hands, anchoring himself to the present.

Footsteps sounded on the stairs behind him, and Domari looked over his shoulder to find Gunnar approaching. He wore leather armor similar to Domari's, his blond hair tied up off his neck. Runes decorated his exposed arms, but his face was bare save the black patch covering one eye.

"Thought you might need this." Gunnar nudged Domari's shoulder, facing the scorched fields in front of them.

Domari looked down at the shield in Gunnar's hands, inspecting the wooden weapon. The Varangian eagle still decorated the center, but now a pattern of runes covered the rest, matching the shield tattooed onto his hip.

"Between this and *Mjölnir*" — Gunnar lifted the shield — "leave no doubt how you became the *Akolouthos*. Show our people how you became the most legendary warrior in the Guard."

Domari looked back out over the fields and clenched his jaw. He was used to battle but never had he had so much to fight for.

Maybe he should have been worried, but anger took its place. Fury that anyone would threaten his family. Rage that their Fates had come to this. Wrath, that so many innocent lives would be lost today.

The wooden walls creaked under his grip, and he let go. Warmth radiated from his hand, a current buzzing from his palm up his arm until the hammer appeared. Thunder rumbled in the distance, the wind changing direction and sending the banners askew.

Sensing Gunnar's attention, he looked over at his cousin, seeing the fierce determination in his gaze as he studied the weapon. Domari had only summoned it a handful of times since Hilda gifted it to him, afraid of the power within. This, as well as the spear in Gunnar's grip, was a sign that the gods were on their side.

"Take it." Gunnar held the shield out towards Domari again. "Wear your history with pride instead of shame. Everything led us to this moment, and we fight together until the very end."

With a small nod, Domari slipped his hand into the straps, feeling the weight of the shield disappear the same way the hammer did. His weapons were weightless, an extension of his body, and as deadly as they'd ever been. His fingers flexed, feeling the leather bands around *Mjölnir's* grip give, ready to be wielded.

"Do we even stand a chance?" Gunnar asked, the words barely above a whisper dancing in the wind.

Domari refused to look at the boats on the shore behind him. The boats that could take them away from here, away from their home, away from this danger. He wasn't a fool — they both understood if they didn't win this battle today, life as they knew it would be over.

The hammer buzzed in his grip, and Domari looked down at the knot decorating the scarred metal. He cast a sideways glance at his cousin, the knot glowing with magic where it was carved into Odin's own spear too, then looked out to the scorched battlefield in front of them.

If these gifts were to be believed, then Odin had chosen Gunnar, the wise leader. Thor had chosen Domari, the fearsome protector. And Loki had chosen Raud, the cunning betrayer. He clenched his jaw, unwilling to think through what other secrets might still be in store for them. "With you at my side, anything is possible, my brother."

Gunnar jerked a nod, gripping his spear tighter.

Domari hoped these gifts truly meant the gods intended to battle with them, for it was their only chance of surviving the day.

That, and a girl who held his whole heart, ready to defy Fate on a dragon's back.

33

SHELBIE

Thunder rumbled in the distance behind us, something I was beginning to think was a magical side effect of Thor's interest in Domari.

I sat in the dark hut that had been our home for the last several weeks, trying to breathe easy despite the panic gripping me tight. Yrsa braided my hair in tight rows against my scalp while I tried to absorb as much power from the well as I could. Her voice was soothing as she talked me through how to store the power, having it at the ready when I needed it most.

Frida stood in front of me, painting my face the same as the others headed into battle — dark streaks descending my nose, painted runes for strength and protection along my neck and brow — and a shiver skittered down my spine at the implication. At what we were about to face.

Since Domari, Grim, and the others had arrived last night, the town had been a flurry of activity, preparing for battle. I wished I could have spent more of those precious moments with Domari, but he and the others had been busy getting everyone ready and strategizing.

His reinforcements changed everything, but the glint in his eye when we crossed paths ignited a spark of hope in my chest. He wouldn't think we could win on blind faith — if he believed it, then it truly was possible. And as much as it terrified me, I had to admit I was starting to believe it, too.

"Almost ready." Yrsa kissed the top of my head. "Magnus dropped a gift off for you before he left this morning and asked me to get it to you."

I turned to watch her move across the small room to the bed Astrid lay in, sweat beading her brow. Frida moved to sit with her, holding her daughter-in-law's hand.

"To be born during a battle is a sign of the strength of the babe you carry," Yrsa brushed a hand across Astrid's brow, then laid her hand on her rounded belly.

Astrid smiled weakly, her face flushed. "As long as she has her father's courage more than his sweet tooth."

Tears pricked my eyes, but I brushed them away before they could fall, refusing to think of everything this could mean for their little family. We were going to come out of this and celebrate together — that was the only option.

Yrsa returned to my side, carrying molded leathers that shimmered in the firelight. They were the darkest black with hints of gold thread, almost the same as Hadriel's scales.

My hands shook as I took them from her, feeling the smooth texture. "This is beautiful."

"Turn around," Yrsa said.

I did as she said, pulling my braids over my shoulders, and she buckled the chest plate over my tunic. My pendant sat over it, shining as bright as Hadriel's eyes against the dark material, and I drew in a ragged breath. I traded my trousers for the leather ones made to match, then fastened my boots over them, feeling as badass as I ever had. The gloves fit as well as everything else, and I glanced down, in awe of my own appearance.

"Promised." Yrsa clasped her hands in front of her chest, a watery smile full of pride pulling me towards her. I wrapped my arms around her in a tight hug and kissed the top of her head.

"You bring that baby into the world, kicking and screaming," I said against her temple and her hands tightened on my waist. "I'll bring the party back to meet him or her later."

Yrsa nodded, then let go, pushing me towards the door. "Go. Store your power like we've planned, accessing it a little at a time. And Shelbie," Yrsa said, stilling my movement, "you were born for this. I believe in you."

I nodded, my heart beating fast as I went through the door and ran for the beach where Hadriel was waiting.

Black, Hadriel said as he eyed me, smoke curling out of his nostrils and into the cool dawn air. *I like it.*

I grinned, lifting myself off the ground to mount him. Last night Domari and Magnus had worked with Hadriel to create a sort of harness around his shoulders to give me a better handhold, and I looped my hands through the ropes like a bull rider, shifting to get my seat.

He lifted into the air, and I opened myself to the well of magic inside me. With that first sip, my vision shifted to Hadriel's. Everything was crisp even in the morning light,

Hadriel and I nearly blending in with the sky as we soared above the scene below.

The walls were already armed with Björn in charge, archers at the ready, as well as buckets of oil heating over bonfires, waiting to stop any who got near enough to the walls to breach them.

Lines of warriors stood in formation near the scorch marks Hadriel had left during our last battle here, cutting the farmland in half. Immediately, I found Domari, atop his horse, aptly named Mjölnir far before he'd ever been blessed with the weapon. Asmund and Gunnar flanked him on either side, the three speaking until we flew overhead. As one, they lifted their heads in my direction. Even from here, I could see the pride radiating off Domari as he watched me.

I grinned, feeling the warmth of his adoration as sure as the dragon beneath me. Raising my head, I looked into the distance, searching out the rest of our men, still hidden from sight. Not until Hadriel's eyelids shuttered to show heat registers did I see the Guard, hidden in the cliffs above the battlefield. Magnus was with them, and I swallowed my nerves, running my free hand across Hadriel's neck.

Ready? Hadriel said, and I tightened my grip, then squeezed my thighs in confirmation. With an ear-splitting shriek, Hadriel took off, darting into the dark clouds overhead, hidden from view.

34

The first light of day flickered through the trees, and Signe ducked her chin, staring at her fore-arms. Every hair stood on end, the air charged with energy like she'd never felt before. The promise of battle had always left her feeling ready to move, but this was different. Familiar. *More*.

Her senses faded, the sight and sound of the men moving around her lost. But unlike the drugged haze Draugr had kept her in for weeks, she wasn't lost to nothing. Instead, the sound of wings made her peer through the trees towards the battlefield.

"*Signe*," a voice whispered in her left ear, high and airy. Her brow burned, and she fought a wince, trying to keep her bored disinterest in place.

"*Signe*," another voice said to her right, different and yet decidedly feminine. She tightened the grip on her weapons, but didn't move towards the sound, somehow knowing it was only in her head.

"Signe," more voices joined in, one after the next, calling her forward. Her breaths came quicker, the sound of wings growing louder until a large black raven croaked from the trees in front of her.

She looked up, studying the bird, watching the morning light shimmer around it. Its beady black eyes stared at her, head tilted to the side. Wings rustled again, and another raven settled nearby, then another, until eight of them sat in the trees staring down at her.

Her brow tingled again, a wash of heat crossing above her eyes and down her nose.

"Valhalla is calling, and the Nine shall lead them home."

Her hand tightened on the axes hanging at her sides, her body nearly vibrating with the need to move. One by one, the ravens disappeared, blurring into the dark trees, and her senses returned to her.

"Today, we begin Ragnarok!" Draugr shouted from atop a boulder, holding his sword up to a frenzy of battle cries and stomping feet. Nidhoggr roared behind them, then launched into the air. Everyone's gaze tipped up, watching the white dragon crest the treetops, but Signe couldn't look away from Raud and the manic adoration in his glowing red eyes.

"Signe!" Draugr's sharp tone pulled her attention, and he pointed his weapon towards the town. "Lead the way."

She didn't bother answering, wearing that same bored disinterest her father thought he still controlled. Vermund stepped up beside her, his bear helm catching a ray of sun, glowing white. Clenching her jaw, she stepped into the forest, chin held high.

Vermund kept pace as the men thundered behind them, the energy in the air palpable as their blood ran high with battle fever. No matter how many times she and Vermund had gone over the plan, she couldn't help but recount the many ways this could go wrong. Everything had to be timed perfectly for them to get away with this.

Once Draugr joined them at the front, chaos would ensue.

Until the confusion and chaos of battle fully descended, they had over 300 men around them, eager to draw blood. She had to play the part of a vicious killer, something that was far easier for Signe to do knowing her family was on the other side of this battlefield, waiting for her.

Clearing the trees, Signe eyed the fortress walls and the dozens of men and women standing before it. At the center stood three men on horseback, one whose golden hair shone just right in the light.

"Do not react," Vermund said, his quiet voice at her shoulder. "I see him too."

Rage clouded her vision, her breaths coming faster the longer she stared. Her father had put her in this position, threatening her family and everything she loved. Signe licked her lips, the phantom taste of copper already on them as she imagined her father's death.

Energy flowed through her veins, forcing its way out her mouth in a savage howl. The sound set off the battle cries of the rest of the men, answering her cry.

Like last time, they locked their shields together, the wood clicking in place like a rippling wave. But somewhere down the line, a man broke rank, darting across the fields towards the fortress walls.

"Hold!" Vermund shouted, and the shields snapped back in place to cover the hole the man had left, an arrow flying from the ramparts towards the charging, screaming man. Signe flicked her finger to the side and the arrow's trajectory shifted just enough for it to strike true, sending the soldier to his knees.

Draugr's men inched forward, the sound of their shields dragging in the dirt scraping against her brain, and her hand flinched again.

"And wait for the dragon again?" someone screamed back. Another three men broke rank, following their friend into the clearing. One by one, they were shot down.

"HOLD, gods dammit!" Vermund shouted again, pushing his shoulder into the shields right alongside Draugr's men. Snarls picked up on her side of the battlefield, and she grinned, feeling their frustration.

This time, she didn't even have to urge men forward, encouraging their battle frenzy. The ranks broke, and men flooded the fields in a chaotic rush. They charged across the field, and the opposing fighters rushed towards them.

Domari led the charge from atop his horse, face painted with runes the same as the men around him. Signe's breath caught as she noticed the hammer in his hand, glowing bright when Domari swung it into the first man to reach him.

Weapons clashed in a clamor of noise, barely discernible over the cries of the men around her. Signe lost sight of her family as the battle began. With a hard push, she leaped over a warrior, whacking him hard on the back of the head. He slumped to his knees, falling face first in the dirt and Signe rushed towards the next in line. He'd have a good lump, but with any luck would be passed over for dead by the rest of Draugr's men. Again and again, she worked through them, incapacitating the Eriksson's allies without injuring as much as possible, at least for now.

Vermund stayed beside her, watching her back and following her lead. The field filled with battle cries and shrieks of pain, metal striking metal, and the gut-wrenching sound of tearing flesh.

A shadow passed overhead, and she looked up to see Nidhoggr circling above, darting in and out of battle the same as Hadriel had weeks before.

"Signe!" Vermund called, and she pushed the man off her with a hard shove and turned.

Draugr worked his way towards them, his eyes on fire with battle lust, his face and arms covered in blood.

"Can you feel the change in the air, daughter?" Draugr barked, swinging his sword toward a boy's side without a second look. "Victory, I named you before I knew how apt it was."

Signe raised her axe to block Draugr's sword, the shock of impact reverberating up her arm as she stepped in front of the boy.

His eyes widened a second before he snarled, "You try to keep me from my kill?"

She shoved the boy aside, pushing him back from the fight before she jumped, leaping over Draugr. Her feet touched down and she swung a leg out before he could turn to face her, landing a solid kick to his back. The force of the impact knocked him to his knees, but not for long. With a roar, he launched back to his feet and dropped his sword. In swift movements, he pulled two axes free and charged her.

With a grin, Signe ducked his first attack, distracting him long enough to feel the magic in the air, the current changing as another Valkyrie neared. Her eyes darted to the side as she circled her father, drawing him towards the fight. On his next swing, Vermund appeared at her side, shoving Draugr back, directly into the arms of the Valkyrie standing behind him.

"I've been waiting for this day," she snarled as she held a dagger to his throat, her eyes shining the same bright green as Vermund and Signe's. "Thank you, brother, for saving him for me."

Signe looked between Vermund and the Valkyrie as chaos ensued around them, but for her, time slowed almost to a stop.

"I'm tempted to beat you, leaving you inches from death as you've done to so many. Let you suffer for the rest of your days as you mourn the many mistakes you've made. Maybe you'll be trampled by your own army in a fitting end for such a man as you."

"A pretty thought, Hilda, but I need to see the life leave his eyes," Vermund spat, his glare intent on Draugr beneath the bear helm he wore. "The only question is who gets the honor."

"This will stop nothing," Draugr hissed, blood trickling from the dagger pressed into his throat. "Whether I feast with the gods tonight or not, Ragnarok will begin and it is my name they will remember."

Nidhoggr soared overhead, drawing their eyes up to the belly of the white dragon flying towards Torvik. Draugr wore an ugly sneer as he looked back at the trio around him.

With a shove, Hilda pushed Draugr away from her. He stumbled to regain his footing, the horns on his helm pointed towards the Valkyrie.

"Draw your weapons," Hilda sneered.

Power rippled through the air as Signe flipped her axes, waiting to see who Draugr charged first. Between one breath and the next, a bellow sounded from much closer than the dragon. Light shimmered to her left, and Signe turned to see Vermund drop to all fours, his body shifting from human to that of a bear, brown fur rippling over his body as he stood on his back legs and roared.

Signe blinked through her shock, but then, she'd seen stranger things than a Berserker of late.

Draugr tipped his head back in a laugh, his face pulled in a sneer. "I see you've been keeping secrets."

Vermund crashed back to all fours and charged Draugr. The Demon raised his weapons, aiming to hack Vermund's back, but the bear was faster. Vermund swiped a giant paw at his knees, throwing Draugr to the ground with his leather pants slashed, blood gushing from the fabric.

The bear's head swung their way, his green eyes glowing before he took off at a run, taking out as much as Draugr's army as he could.

Screams sounded behind them as Hilda and Signe approached Draugr, who lay panting on the ground. With a snarl, he shoved to his feet, his movements shakier than before.

Wordlessly, Hilda and Signe circled and parried Draugr, keeping him spinning to fend them off, tiring him out. Hilda landed a sharp cut to his bicep, and Signe got a solid whack at his ribs.

"I've dreamed of the day I'd get to fight at your side," Hilda said, her focus on Draugr. "My daughter, the Valkyrie Fated to bring down the human who thought he could start Ragnarok."

The words should have been shocking, but truth rang in every one, her brow tingling with power.

Draugr's attention swung to Signe, realization dawning on him that this battle was far outside his control. She dropped her weapons, a grin taking over her face when she shoved her hands forward.

White light shot from her fingertips, her brow burning with the power flowing through her veins. Draugr's body lifted off the ground, his toes hovering above the dirt. She stepped towards him and his head tilted up, veins protruding as he fought for air against her invisible grip.

"You took my family from me," she bit out, bringing her fingers closer together and Draugr gasped.

"You beat my husband." She lifted him higher, and Draugr clawed at the invisible hold on him, desperate for a way to break free from the magic.

"You taught me every fucking thing I know about mercy," she growled, unleashing every ounce of magic in her to rip out his heart.

His scream was stolen in a gasp as he dropped to the ground, blood pouring from the hole in his chest.

Signe held the bloody organ in her hand, then squeezed, the same magic that had killed her father turning it to dust. "No mercy, not ever."

Hilda kicked off his helm, then crushed her heel into his face. "May you be barred from the halls of Valhalla forever, Draugr Helvigsson." Hilda bent to retrieve his fallen axes and grinned up at Signe. "I always knew we'd make an excellent team."

Signe spread her fingers, the last remnants of her father's heart drifting to the ground, and her attention returned to the pandemonium around them. "Our work is far from done."

Hilda nodded, wiping sweat from her brow with the back of her arm. "After you, Demonkiller."

35

DOMARI

Domari's horse reared, legs kicking at the air as he leaped into battle. They charged forward and the men behind him followed him into the fray. Asmund took off to the left while Gunnar moved to the right, leading their party into forming a semi-circle around Draugr's oncoming front line.

A killing calm washed over Domari's skin as he sank into the same focus he always felt in battle. His breaths were even as he leaned down to his left, swinging the hammer in his hands in a circle before smashing it into the shield of the warrior aiming for him. A sickening crunch sounded when the hammer went clean through the wooden shield, knocking the man to his back. Domari's horse stomped on the man, then moved forward.

Blow after blow landed, thunder rumbling with every move he made. He lost sight of Gunnar quickly, but everything was going according to plan. Just as they closed around Draugr's forces, Magnus led the charge down from the cliffs, battle axe high.

All 300 Guard followed his lead, descending on the battle in the valley. Heads whipped in their direction, and Domari grinned. Pride radiated off him as Magnus cut into his first opponent, Grim at his side.

With renewed fervor, Domari worked his way through the crowd, looking for Raud. Despite the battle frenzy, it was easy to find his old friend, fighting at the back of the field. His chest was bare of battle armor and painted in blood.

The air rippled and Domari leaned down into his horse's back, the wave of magic washing over the valley like a weight pinning them down. A black dragon crested the cliffs, the heat of his fire aimed at the men who'd gotten past Domari's forces and moved towards Torvik's walls.

Arrows rained down, picking off any within range, but they bounced off the air around Hadriel and his rider, Shelbie's blonde braids flowing freely in the wind as she ducked low to the dragon's back.

Domari's army took up a new battle cry and moved forward, cutting down any that threatened to breach the walls, throwing them into Hadriel's path of fire.

As Hadriel lifted back into the sky, Nidhoggr turned his attention to the dragon. Domari kicked his feet into his horse's side, and they took off at a gallop. His hammer swung wildly as he took down any in his path between him and Raud, launching from his grip and returning just like legends had foretold.

If Raud and Nidhoggr's power worked similarly to Shelbie and Hadriel's, then Raud's death would significantly decrease the dragon's power. No matter the guilt that warred in Domari's stomach over ending his friend, he'd do anything to protect the girl in the sky and the family that fought beside him.

Raud's red eyes found him as he charged through their forces, a bear following his lead.

"I should have seen the signs." Raud chuckled, but his voice had changed, far older and holding a bitterness Domari didn't recognize. "Though it has been an age since I've seen a true Berserker, Vermund."

The bear roared, baring every long and bloody tooth. Domari took the distraction to leap from his horse, swinging his hammer. Raud spun around and slashed out at the bear, whose long claws swiped at Raud's axe and yanked it from his hold with ease. It flipped through the air, far out of reach. Baring his teeth, Raud flipped his second axe to his dominant hand, crouching low to reassess his opponent while keeping Domari in sight as well. He pulled his shield off his back, sliding his arm through the straps to pull it in place.

Domari circled to move behind Raud, but they'd trained together for years. Raud backed up to keep both him and the bear in front of him, the way Domari had taught his friend to battle multiple opponents when they were children. With a growl, the bear reared, and when Raud's attention caught there for a moment, Domari lunged.

His hammer met Raud's shield and crushed the wood on impact. Raud tossed it aside, snapped his arm back, and threw his axe at the bear, hitting it in the hip joint.

"Oathbreaker, your days are done." Raud ran towards

the bear, who limped back, blood flowing freely from the wound as the axe came free. The bear swiped at Raud when he stooped to grab the weapon.

Domari's hand tingled with power, *Mjölnir* vibrating as he lifted his hand and threw.

It slammed into Raud's low back, snapping his spine, and Raud crumbled to the ground, axe dropping from his grip. The hammer flew back to Domari who caught it easily, and he rushed forward to stand over Raud.

Domari toed him with his boot, rolling Raud onto his back as he screamed in pain, his red eyes lost to the dragon's magic. Distantly, a dragon somewhere above echoed the scream.

"Until Valhalla." Domari stared down at his long-lost friend, looking for any sign that the man he once knew was still in there. No remorse, no fear shone from Raud's eyes even as the red faded from them, slitted in anger.

He spat at Domari's feet. "You broke that promise the day you left, leading me to the path that ended here. Valhalla waits for none of us, Domari. There is only Ragnarok, a rebirth for all of us, even Tove once Nidhoggr kills your precious little Promised and her dragon."

Domari shook his head, the words all the confirmation he needed that his friend was long gone.

Magic hummed around him as the bear transformed into a man, his green eyes glowing bright. He limped forward and picked up Raud's axe. With a growl as savage as the bear on his helm, he brought it down on Raud's throat, severing his head.

Vermund fell to the ground, chest heaving. His eyes

dimmed from the bright glow back to normal, pain written in every line on his face. Slashes littered his back and chest, cutting through the armor and leaving a bloody trail as he touched his gloved fingers to the deep wound on his hip.

"Draugr had something else planned." Vermund closed his eyes for a second, then opened them again, his body slumping to the side. "Something to end your dragon."

Domari's head snapped to the woods behind him, dread coursing through his veins as lightning struck a tree a hundred yards away, the rumble of thunder almost deafening.

"It's been an honor," Vermund said, drawing Domari's eyes back to the dying man in front of him. "Hilda told me she intended to make a plea to Thor to protect Midgard, to protect me and Signe and all the humans living here but I only hoped to see the day a human was blessed with *Mjölnir*. To have *Mjölnir* and *Gungnir* on the same battlefield..."

He chuckled; his face tipped up to Domari's with a sad smile as blood trickled from his mouth.

"Go. Make all this worth it. End that dragon, and Draugr's army will flee. This will all be over."

36

GUNNAR

Gunnar ducked as a spear sailed over him, then lunged for the man who'd thrown it. Ripping into his side just under his arm, Gunnar yanked backward. He fell to the ground with a scream, but Gunnar was already moving to the next man, the dogs close at his heels.

All around him, the Valkyries fought like they'd been born to it, and he supposed they had. He'd never seen fighting like it, the way they effortlessly danced through their victims and cut them down with a mixture of unmatched fighting prowess and magical power gifted from the gods. Their piercing battle cry striking fear into the men before they even lifted their weapons.

Fuck, he needed to see Signe like that. Blood-spattered and victorious.

She was out here somewhere, he knew it. Could feel her near.

Geira, one of the Valkyries, caught up to his side.

"Take Odin's wolves and find your wife." She nodded towards the fray. "They will watch your back."

Odin's wolves. Gunnar's chest heaved, staring down at the black creatures on either side of him. The dogs had grown exceptionally large over the time he'd been gone, even Shelbie's dog Thor who had been fully grown when he arrived. Now, he and Freki both stood to his waist, larger and more powerful than wolves, and protected by the gods. Not one weapon touched them, and the enemy skirted around them as though they sensed their power, not daring to approach.

They had no such similar fear though, as evidenced by the blood dripping down Freki's lips.

With a parting nod to Geira, Gunnar whistled for the dogs to follow him, charging out into the field, trusting his gut to lead him to his wife.

The sharp tang of copper coated the air, along with the even less pleasant scents of urine and bowels, not to mention the smoke from the dragons scorching men and trees from above. Gunnar ignored it all, fighting his way through the madness.

A battle cry pierced the air, a voice he would recognize anywhere.

"We're close," Gunnar muttered to the dogs, though whether the gods had blessed them with understanding as well, he couldn't say. Still, they picked up their pace alongside him, Thor leaping to tear out a man's throat before he could swing at Gunnar.

The moment he saw her his heart soared, especially at the clarity in her eyes. Even more when he realized Hilda was beside her, tearing through Draugr's men together.

She was back. *His* Signe.

She whirled, gutting a man, then caught sight of the dogs first, then him.

Her lips broke into a fierce grin, blood and black war paint streaking her face, but it only made her green eyes all the brighter.

"About time you arrived," she teased, striding up to him. "Nearly all the good fights are over."

He was tempted to drop his weapons and wrap her in his arms. To say fuck the battle and tear out of there with her. Instead, she pressed her forehead to his, and Hilda and the dogs covered them to breathe together for a moment.

"You're back."

Her lips tipped up. "I see I didn't kill you."

He huffed a laugh. "Not yet, woman, but the day is young."

"Back to work, children," Hilda yelled, two men rushing her, but she cut them down easily, white power emanating from her skin.

Signe spun, and Gunnar followed her lead, their backs to each other as they rejoined the battle.

"Signe?" Hilda's voice was uncertain this time, and they both looked over their shoulder to see what was wrong.

Hilda's gaze focused on the tree line, where a huddle of Draugr's men wheeled forward a large structure. When they cleared the shadow, Gunnar swore.

Atop the structure was a giant crossbow, large enough to take down a dragon.

"Where is he?" Hilda called, and Gunnar's eyes scanned the sky for the black dragon.

A blade came out of nowhere, slamming into his shoulder and sending him careening to the side. He hit the ground, and a man leaped on top of him, but Gunnar threw up his spear just in time to block his axe. From his position on the ground, he tracked Hadriel's flight across the field.

Panting, Gunnar held off his attacker as the man snarled down at him, until an axe caught his opponent under his ribs, and he was thrown off like he weighed nothing.

Signe smirked, offering a hand to pull him up.

At the crossbow, four men loaded the largest arrow he'd ever seen into place, the arrow easily as tall as any of them.

"We have to stop that crossbow."

Signe nodded when a blond giant caught his eye, somehow sprinting through the bedlam faster than should be possible.

And alone.

"Fucking *Knut*." Gunnar cursed his brother's brash stupidity, then charged towards him. "Cover him!"

"We won't reach him in time," Signe called, a few paces behind him. "We should make a diversion."

"Do it!" Gunnar screamed, but he didn't stop. The dogs charged with him, helping to clear the path, but Magnus was so far ahead, having been at the back of the battle with the Guards.

Gunnar's heart was in his throat as he watched every axe, every sword that swung Magnus's way. His fingers tightened on *Gungnir*'s wooden shaft, but he only had one throw in it. He scanned the fray for Domari, but he was too far off to be of assistance.

He pushed through bodies, not slowing long enough to

kill his opponents as he tore across the field. Dozens of Draugr's men stood around the crossbow, arming it and protecting it. There was no way Magnus would be able to get there, disable the device, and get back without —

Gunnar stumbled, barely catching himself in time as realization crashed down on him. As rash as Magnus was, he wasn't stupid.

"MAGNUS!" he screamed, the name ripped from his throat. His feet pounded faster, his arms pumping as he poured every ounce of energy he had into running.

Fifty paces away, Gunnar hardly blinked as he lifted his spear, ready to launch it at the most opportune moment.

With a roar, Magnus launched himself up onto the crossbow, tearing down one of the men setting up the shot. Another came up behind him, and Gunnar screamed his brother's name helplessly when a dagger found Magnus's shoulder.

Magnus kicked off the man, blood streaming freely from his shoulder when he wrenched the dagger free, and climbed around the crossbow, eyeing the mechanics.

Gunnar sprinted forwards, watching Magnus fight men off left and right, keeping them away from the crossbow, but he wouldn't be able to keep them away forever. Already, more men were turning back towards it, seeing the problem.

Back in the trees, a blaze started, the rest of the giant arrows going up in flames, followed by the triumphant shrieks of Valkyries.

Slowly, between blows to attackers, Magnus started to turn the crossbow, shooting glances up to the sky any chance he got between fighting men off.

With a violent sweep of his axe, Magnus knocked two more back, their bodies falling in a heap that crumpled the men halfway up the device.

He had seconds before they regrouped.

Gunnar stopped breathing.

37

SHELBIE

ang on. Hadriel circled the battlefield, headed straight for where Nidhoggr picked off the Guard one by one where they emerged from the forests behind enemy lines. My fingers tightened in the harness, and we picked up speed.

A wash of heat exploded out of Hadriel's mouth as he raked his talons across Nidhoggr's wing, ripping at the thin muscle when we flew overhead.

Shield! Hadriel screamed, but I beat him to it, waving my hand in an arc around me. A bubble of magic formed around us, sealing us inside. Flames licked across the surface of magic but didn't touch us, just how I hoped it would work.

Hadriel's satisfaction rumbled through our bond, and he peeled away from Nidhoggr towards the cliffs above, the white dragon giving chase. We raced across the rocks, then veered hard as fire exploded out of Nidhoggr again.

My dragon barrel rolled, and a shriek left my lungs as I

was pried from my seat, dangling upside down. As quick as he'd flipped, Hadriel leveled out over the trees, moving with a speed I'd never gone before, and I found my seat again.

He darted in and out of the sky, using the rumbling clouds to our advantage as we lured Nidhoggr from the fight below, giving the Guard time to make it into battle, the surprise attack we'd been counting on. I craned my neck to look behind me, seeing his glowing red eyes as he readied his next attack.

Dive! I yelled, and Hadriel did, the flames missing us completely while we spiraled back towards the ground.

Ready to try your hand at your magic?

Nerves fluttered in my belly as I moved my legs, positioning myself backward until I looked over Hadriel's dark tail, cutting through the air. I gripped the harness again, my braids slapping against my cheeks, and pulled a larger dose of my power.

Thinking of the hammer Domari wielded below, I lifted my hand, imagining the weapon in my palm. I could almost feel the phantom handle as I reached over my shoulder and flung it forward.

The air rippled around us, my power exploding out of my hand aimed at Nidhoggr behind us. The invisible weapon slammed into Nidhoggr, knocking him backward as if he'd run into an invisible wall. He let a fierce cry go and flapped his white wings, trying to keep himself from plummeting to the ground.

I let out a loud whoop, then spun back around in my seat.

Promised, Hadriel said, the single word containing so

much pride. He dipped, soaring above the trees, and we raced back towards the battlefield.

Movement at the edge of the forest caught my attention, and my blood chilled at the sight of the siege tower. *What is that?*

Domari raced across the field towards it, his horse galloping with a dangerous speed. His hammer slammed into men left and right as his face tipped up to the sky, panic written across his face.

I looked back to the structure as we neared it, noticing the barbed tips on the end of a massive arrow pointed towards the sky.

HADRIEL! I screamed, and his attention snapped to the crossbow just in time to veer sharply to the left. My body was tossed aside, barely hanging on as I scrambled back onto his back. The crossbow moved slowly, tracking us through the sky.

SHIELD! Hadriel yelled back, but the last blast of magic I'd used had depleted me significantly. I tried to pull forth the power like I'd done before, but none came.

I can't!

Hadriel banked, which unfortunately gave Nidhoggr time to catch up, fire exploding from his mouth. I screamed as heat washed over me, but Hadriel tipped to his side, taking the worst of it with his belly instead of letting it hit me. He cried out in pain, but kept moving, putting as much space as he could between us and Nidhoggr.

From this vantage point I saw who stood atop the structure, aiming the crossbow. His blond hair was tied up in a knot, those tattooed hands I knew so well holding an axe high. Magnus waited for his moment, ready to release the mechanism when he had his shot.

"Hadriel," I breathed. "Head right towards it."

A chuckle in my head told me he understood my plan, and we banked around, heading for the crossbow head-on. With Hadriel's vision still in place, I didn't miss the grin on Magnus's face, understanding what I was about to do. Time ticked by slowly as we neared, my breaths coming unevenly.

With a scream, Magnus dropped his axe, hacking through the ropes holding the arrow taut. It launched into the air, and Hadriel pulled up sharply.

The ear-piercing shriek a moment later said our trap had been successful, Nidhoggr so busy tailing us, he hadn't seen the arrow coming straight at him.

I looked over my shoulder, watching blood spray from Nidhoggr's chest as he plummeted towards the ground, his wings beating too weakly to hold him up. Momentum carried him forward, and I looked back down at the field, realizing my mistake.

"MAGNUS!" I screamed, but there was nothing I could do from here.

On the crossbow, Magnus raised his axe, the giant dragon headed straight for him.

He leaped to meet the dying white dragon in the air, then the dragon's body crashed into the structure, crumpling it and Magnus, beneath him.

A cry was ripped from my throat as Hadriel lowered himself to the ground, wings spread wide to slow our speed.

I threw myself from his back the moment I wasn't afraid of the drop. My feet scrambled as I ran towards Magnus, tears streaming down my cheeks.

"NO!" Gunnar cried as he tried to move the dragon aside, pushing and pulling against the dead weight of the giant. *"NO!"*

My hands trembled as I reached his side, frantically trying to access the well of power within me for anything I had left.

"Do something!" Gunnar screamed when Domari reached us. He slammed the hammer into the dead dragon, but Nidhoggr didn't move.

"DO SOMETHING!" Gunnar screamed again. His face twisted in agony as he looked at me.

My whole body shook as I frantically searched for that magical well inside me. Except this time, the well was empty.

"I can't!" I sobbed, my heart shattering into a million pieces.

Gunnar wailed on the dragon's dead body, screams ripping from his throat as everyone around him tried to move the dead weight. I scrambled forward, my vision blurry from tears, pushing my whole bodyweight into the dragon, watching the smoking remains of everything around me.

What felt like hours later, Domari wrapped his arms around Gunnar's shoulders and pulled him away from the dragon.

"He's gone, brother," Domari said to Gunnar, and I slid to the ground, my body broken and battered. But nothing hurt as much as the desperate look on Gunnar's face while Domari held him back. "He's gone."

We can't bring him back, Hadriel said, *but we can take the rest down.*

Fire lit inside me at his words, and he was right. We had a lot we could still do. There would be time for grief later. I took off back towards Hadriel, climbing his back easily as I set my jaw. "Let's go, then."

Hadriel didn't wait, pushing back into the air.

Images flashed in front of me as we soared over the battlefield.

Magnus filling his shirt with berries.

We darted down, blasting a line of fire at a cluster of men trying to beat a retreat from shrieking Valkyries and Guards.

Magnus singing to Astrid's belly.

Hadriel circled back, catching a man in his mouth and throwing the body into another group of fighters.

Magnus clutching at a broken Gunnar in the forest.

I choked back tears as Hadriel and I tore through the battle, blasting and biting and destroying everything we could. Draugr's men had started retreating when they saw Nidhoggr go down, but we couldn't let them get away with this.

They all needed to suffer.

I lost all sense of time as we chased them down, both of us running on fumes but refusing to give up, refusing to stop until every one of them was dead.

If we stopped, then it was over.

If we stopped, we'd have to face what was next.

Eventually, we circled back to the field, unable to find any more of Draugr's men. My vision blurred, I was hardly able to control the line between Hadriel and myself, both of us spent.

Hadriel landed with far less grace than usual on the field, somehow managing to find a spot clear of bodies. My entire body shook as I slid off his back, my face streaked with tears. Leaning on him for support, I made my way to his face, pressing a hand to his forehead.

It is honorable to die in battle for those you love, he offered, but I felt his despair down to my bones all the same. He'd never admit it, but I knew he'd grown fond of Magnus too.

"Who gives a fuck about honor if it means your friend, your brother, your husband is gone," I choked out in response.

He made no reply to that, and the next thing I knew, arms were spinning me around and wrapping me in a hug.

"Thank the gods." Domari breathed in my hair. "It's been hours, where were you?"

Hadriel licked the blood from his lips in answer to that, and Domari grunted in acknowledgment.

"Tell me it's not real." I clutched at Domari's leather armor. "Tell me we were all wrong."

I raised my eyes to Domari's face, and he swallowed heavily. Though he didn't answer, the pain in his eyes told me enough.

"He ended the battle," Domari said instead. "We owe him our victory."

Dizziness overtook me, and I nearly stumbled. I glanced

down at myself, but I hadn't been injured — maybe just exhaustion, then?

When Hadriel's voice reached me, it was fainter than usual. *Remind me to name my firstborn after him.*

I dropped to my knees as Hadriel's eyes rolled back in his head, his body crashing to the ground.

38

SHELBIE

Everything hurt, but nothing more than my heart. I squeezed my eyes shut against the pounding headache holding me hostage, holding off the pain any way I could.

Magnus was gone.

He'd died saving me, a sacrifice I'd never ask of anyone. But like with everything, he offered his whole self, holding nothing back.

A warm breath skated over my skin, and I pried my eyes open, glancing up at a starlit sky.

Like before, everything was eerily quiet, the sounds of the crackling fire and moans of the injured gone. I wasn't on the battlefield anymore, but back on the beach in front of the Tree, the Norns' hut on the far side of the beach.

Shelbie, Hadriel said in my mind, and I forced myself to sit, looking for him. My pendant glowed, casting its light across the water in a mirror image of the dancing lights in the sky above. They blurred in the rippling water, but I gasped at the familiar scene.

This was what I'd Seen in my vision, not the battle from before.

This moment in time, the same as the night I'd arrived in this world a year ago.

Darkness gathered in the sky, the stars blinking out one by one as I looked down at the Tree in front of me. Leaves drifted to the ground, the Tree dying with every passing second.

"No." I scrambled to my feet and hurried across the beach towards the Norns' hut. "We stopped him! Nidhoggr is dead! I did everything you asked of me!"

Verandi stepped out of the hut, the loom working behind her thumping with each move Urd made. She reached forward, cupping my face. "You did wonderfully, child."

I pulled out of her embrace, fury lighting in me as I waved a hand back towards the Tree. "This was supposed to *stop* Ragnarok. They didn't win. *We* did."

Tears flooded me for the losses we'd taken to get here, and it still wasn't enough.

"The dragons have protected the Tree for as long as they've roamed the earth." Verandi walked back the way I came. I had no choice but to follow, needing to understand.

"With the last dragon, the Tree will also fall."

"What?" My brow furrowed, confused as to why no one had mentioned that until now. "But Nidhoggr wasn't the last."

Her steps slowed, and I looked around her. Hadriel lay

sprawled on the beach, the same way he'd lain prone on the battlefield. His chest moved in shallow breaths, and I rushed forward.

"No," I cried as I fell to my knees. "Not you too. I can't lose you."

His eyes opened, that green slitted pupil trained on me. *You were everything I ever hoped you'd be.*

I shook my head, my shaking hands resting on his face. "Tell me how to stop this, Verandi. Tell me how to heal him."

"Your power is all but drained." Verandi offered me a sad smile that made me want to scream. "There is no more you can do."

"I *refuse* to believe that." My fingers tangled in the chain around my neck, holding the stone towards her. "You gave me this, called me here, made me this Promised, and yet you tell me I'm not enough. I've already lost one friend today, I *will not* lose another."

Her eyes danced between the pendant and the lake to my left. Except, it wasn't a lake, was it? It was the well, the same one I'd always seen in my mind.

On instinct, I ripped the pendant from my neck and threw it in the water. It glowed even as it sank beneath the surface, the water around it lighting up the same green as Hadriel's eyes. I threw myself down on the beach and shoved my face in the pool, drinking down great gulps of it between gasping breaths.

"Shelbie!" Verandi screamed, her hands pulling on my shoulders as I felt the magic well in me more than it ever had before. "Don't do this! You don't know what you're doing."

But I did know. I knew *exactly* what I was doing.

When I drank as much as I could, I dragged myself in front of Hadriel. Draping my body over his head, I wrapped my arms around him.

More magic than I'd ever felt flowed through me, my skin near bursting as it pooled in my hands, my face, my lips. I kissed his head, the cool scales slippery with the water dripping off me.

"Take it all." Tears streamed down my cheeks and landed on his leathery skin. "Take it all, Hadriel. Heal yourself."

He groaned as the magic moved from me to him, channeling the way we'd done so many times before. Except this time it wasn't him letting me borrow his powers. I was giving *him* everything I had.

My body heated like I was being burned alive, and my mouth hung open in a silent scream while he absorbed everything he could. No matter the pain lancing my body, I refused to move. Refused to let him go, too.

Promised, that smoky rasp said in my head, and I gritted my teeth, forcing myself to hold on long enough.

"It's not enough," Verandi said.

"*Fuck. You,*" I growled, not caring who I spoke to as I forced myself to look at her. "*Make* it enough."

She hesitated, looking back over her shoulder before closing the distance between us.

"Your magic isn't enough to heal a dragon. He's too large," she said in a hushed whisper, her hand resting on the side of Hadriel's face. "There is something we can try, but I must warn you. It will change both of you, forever."

"If it means he lives, I don't care. Just do it."

She raised a brow. "*He* might care."

"Will he be alive?" I spat back, and she nodded. "Great. Then he can suck it up and deal with it."

Her eyes glanced back and forth between us, and then she closed them. She began chanting words I didn't understand, and the air around us shimmered in answer.

My hands skirted across Hadriel's neck, and the pendant rose from the watery depths of the source of all magic. It hovered above the surface before it flew into Verandi's outstretched hand. She held it above her head, fire dancing across her fingertips as the stone split in two.

The last of the power in me left in a rush and I curled in on myself, unable to breathe against the pain. My body fell to the side, seized by the power.

The Northern Lights above curled out of the sky in ribbons, descending on us as Verandi pulled them down. Greens, blues, purples of every shade wrapped around Hadriel's body, lifting the dragon from the ground.

I tilted my head to the side, tears streaming down my cheeks when his majestic body shuddered, but Verandi still chanted.

Slowly, so slowly I hardly believed it was happening, his body disappeared little by little.

"No!" I scrambled to my feet to stop Verandi, not caring that my body felt broken beyond measure.

But then he was gone, the lights drifting back to the ground as they faded, pulling into a tighter form. The light was near blinding, but I refused to look away, feeling the magic at work.

All at once, they winked out.

Where my dragon had lain only minutes before lay a man. Colors danced under his pale skin as they formed into runes, decorating his arms and legs and turning inky black when they settled in place.

My heart thundered, looking between Verandi and what was once Hadriel, trying to make sense of what just happened.

His chest moved with even breaths and my hands shook as I reached towards him.

A vice-like grip caught my wrist, tattooed knuckles pulling me down level with him. I raised my eyes to meet his bright green ones, alight with fury. His pupils flicking between human-round and dragon-slitted.

"Where the *fuck* are my wings?"

39

SIGNE

Smoke wafted off the battlefield as bodies littered the ground, the cries of the dying and injured a haunting tune Signe would not soon forget. She looked around the carnage for Gunnar, axe hanging loose in her hand. Fifty Guards stood around him, each pushing on the white dragon as they attempted to roll the beast.

"Together!" his voice cracked, having yelled it a dozen times already. Signe's heart broke for her husband, his grief a tangible thing as they finally moved the dragon enough to pry Magnus's body out from underneath.

She ran the last few feet to him, watching as Gunnar dropped to his knees and pulled Magnus into his lap. His body curled over his brother, rocking him back and forth and mumbling incoherently.

She threw her arms around Gunnar, holding him while he shook with tears. "I'm so sorry," she whispered, kissing his shoulder, his cheek, anything she could reach as tears streamed down her face. "I'm so sorry."

A dozen similar scenes took place around them including Hilda and the Valkyries, kneeling by a fallen Vermund. His loss hurt worse than she had anticipated. Despite his flaws, Vermund had been her confidant, her protector, her teacher long before she understood the meaning of his actions.

Now, having seen the Berserker powers he had, understanding just how much of his life he'd given up for the Valkyries on this battlefield... it hurt.

It all hurt.

She closed her eyes, hugging Gunnar tightly and wishing for a way to take this pain from him. He had already suffered enough at the hands of Signe's family.

The ground beneath them shook, screams sounding from within the city walls. She sat upright, her attention jerking towards Torvik.

The gates burst open, people running from within the safety of its walls as they fled out into the battlefield.

"Gunnar," Signe said, her voice filled with ice. "Gunnar. The children."

His head snapped up, that one beautiful blue eye glistening with tears as he followed her gaze to the shrieking citizens choosing a battlefield over the city walls.

The ground rumbled again as Domari's voice carried over the field. "NO!" he screamed, thunder rumbling in time with a lightning strike out over the sea. "*Shelbie, no!*"

With one last glance down at Magnus, Gunnar crossed his brother's arms over his chest and set him aside. Together they ran to where Domari sat with Shelbie in his arms, her eyes as white as snow, her mouth open in a scream, and her back arched off the ground.

The ground rumbled again, nearly knocking them to the ground, sending rocks tumbling from the cliffs down into the valley directly to where Domari lay with Hadriel and Shelbie.

"DOMARI!" Gunnar screamed, and his cousin looked up in time to see the oncoming rockslide. He stood, hand out to the side as *Mjölnir* appeared there, then slammed it into the ground.

The earth split, a wide crack opening enough for the rocks to fall into it, swallowing the bodies of the dead. It spread, crackling louder than the thunder in the distance, creating a jagged line through the dirt and headed straight for Domari, growing wider until she realized who lay in its path.

Signe dropped Gunnar's hand and sprinted, grabbing Shelbie's prone form right as the split in the earth devoured Hadriel, the same as everything else. The dragon's body sank beneath the surface, a cloud of dust thrown into the sky, blocking out the view of everything around her.

She held her friend to her chest when Shelbie began to thrash, then let out a cry of pain Signe felt down to her bones.

Domari raced the chasm, dove across at the narrowest point, and sprinted back to their side. Just as he took Shelbie back from Signe, her body began to shake with tears. Domari sat on the ground, rocking her back and forth, staring at where Hadriel had disappeared.

"If he dies, does she go with him?" Signe asked, afraid of the answer.

"I don't know." Domari's forehead dropped to Shelbie's, and an anguished scream ripped from her lips again.

"The sea!" someone yelled behind them. "The sea is rising! It's going to wash away the city!"

Signe's head snapped to the gates, and she and Gunnar took off at a sprint, the ground shaking violently beneath them again.

"It's too late," Gunnar said, his voice panicked. "This is Ragnarok."

Signe shook her head, then felt the presence of those around her.

Hilda was at her side, sprinting forward with the other Valkyries, young Viveka among them. Her breath caught at the sight of her would-be daughter, understanding dawning.

Together, they sprinted through the streets of the town, looking for Frida and the children. Gunnar and Viveka guided them down narrow roads as waves crashed against the shore. The water rushed up into the streets, and villagers ran from the oncoming flood.

Yrsa stepped out of the hut in the distance, her head tipped up towards the sky. She lifted her hands, her auburn hair tumbling down her back. As she stepped towards the water's edge, Signe's children came out of the hut behind her, eyes wide with fright.

"Revna!" Signe screamed, and the little girl's head flicked her way. Kára stood behind her, holding a baby with bright red hair, new since the last time she'd seen him. A choked sob slipped from her, her hand flying over her mouth.

"Mama!" Ulf was the first one to run to Signe, throwing his arms around her waist. Revna followed, then the others until Kára reached over their heads, handing Erik to her too.

The ground trembled again, several of the huts around them beginning to crumble, and a scream sounded from inside the hut, and water crashed over their shoes, rising to her knees.

"Be ready to get them out of here!" Signe thrust Erik back into Kára's hands, and the girl shoved the children behind their parents.

"Yrsa, no!" Gunnar cried, but the woman ignored him, walking into the incoming tide. She chanted, holding her hands cupped above her head.

"Life is given and taken away," she called, her words muffled against the crashing waves. They tossed her to the side with each pass, but she held steady. "As the Fates have foretold, Ragnarok is upon us, but only the Promised can stop it."

Green light glowed from her hands, lifting into the sky, and the waves began to pull back into the sea. Hilda pushed past Signe towards the beach, and the six Valkyries she'd traveled with followed. They linked hands and circled Yrsa, joining in her chant, the waves crashing against their legs.

The light grew brighter, the sky darker with each passing moment. Viveka pushed past Signe and joined the Valkyries. Her green eyes meeting Signe's before she began chanting along with the others, looking right at home.

Power rippled in the air around them as the waves began to recede.

Black winged marks glowed on each of their brows, labeling them as extensions of Odin. Signe's own brow burned with the phantom touch, and she looked over at Gunnar, wondering if he'd see the same symbol painted on her. Wondering what this meant for them.

His gaze was trained on her face, flicking once to her brow before he slid a hand behind her neck and kissed her. *"Elskin min,"* he said against her lips. "My forever."

Her hands tightened on his forearms, afraid to let go. Afraid that she found her way back to him too late.

But then the world went quiet. The ground went still.

She opened her eyes to find night had descended early, stars twinkling overhead. The green lights from Yrsa's hands now wove above them in the night sky. Signe held her breath, hoping it was over, but too afraid to believe it.

A long, guttural scream sounded from within the hut, then a baby's answering cry. Yrsa's hands dropped, her once auburn hair now completely white.

"She did it." Yrsa smiled, then walked back towards the hut, water trailing off her sodden skirts.

Steps sounded behind them, and Gunnar looked over his shoulder, then did a double take that had Signe turning as well.

Domari walked through the streets towards them, Shelbie carried in his arms, but her eyes were open, her chest moving with each breath. A tattooed man she'd never seen before walked behind them.

Hilda laughed, the sound so familiar and yet foreign to

Signe as she studied the trio, trying to figure out who this newcomer was.

"A rebirth." Hilda shook her head. "Welcome back, Hadriel. Or do you need a new name now, Odinsson?"

Her breath caught, staring at the broad man, trying to understand what Hilda meant. Sensing her attention, Odinsson's gaze met hers, that bright green shifting from human to slitted so fast she almost didn't believe it.

"I always liked the name Ryker," Shelbie said, voice weak as she smiled, eyes closed. "Ryker Odinsson sounds pretty badass for a dragon shifter."

DOMARI

Everything after battle was a blur. Funeral pyres were set up in the fields for the fallen, smoke casting a haze over everything in Torvik. The Valkyries had carried Vermund's body home, performing a ritual of their own that Gunnar and Signe had attended. Grieving families wept everywhere, but this was the price of battle.

Everything had changed that day, the world ending and beginning again in a different way than the stories told, but nothing was the same anymore.

Shelbie spent long hours talking to Hadriel, now Ryker, acquainting him with life as a human-dragon shifter, something they were just finding out was possible. No one was sure if there were more of his kind, but that she'd been able to save him when they'd lost so many others was a balm to his soul.

"What next?" Domari joined Grim on the beach, looking out over the dark water. The setting sun cast a glow across the surface, as bright as the torches held by those gathering for the ceremony.

Grim tipped his head to the side, then focused on the docks further down the beach. "The ships leave at first light."

Domari nodded, the thought of saying goodbye to his friend another bruise to his heart.

"I don't know though." Grim waved his hand around the beach, the cliffs split down the rocky edge, and the town still damaged from the rising waters. "All of this made the life of a mercenary feel small. Maybe it's time for a change. Think you can teach me to farm? Find me a wife?"

Domari shook his head. "The farming, yes. The wife… You're asking the wrong man."

Grim looked back over his shoulder. "I don't know. Doesn't seem like you did too bad on your own. Or maybe I should talk to Gunnar and find out how he landed himself a fucking Valkyrie."

Shelbie linked her arm through Domari's, leaning on him. "It's a good story," she said, her blue eyes red-rimmed from the many tears she'd cried this week. "As long as your ego can take a woman beating you at literally everything, you might stand a chance."

Grim puffed his chest, a wide grin spreading that reminded Domari of why they gathered here today. "I think I'll stay then, if you'll have me."

Shelbie carried the conversation, making plans for Grim's future endeavors, lightening the mood the way she always did. The two laughed, and the sound was as jarring as it was blissful.

"Ready?" Grim drew Domari's attention back to the present. With a solemn nod, the two moved to the small boat on the edge of the water. Grim took a torch from Frida, holding it in his right hand, his left settling on the lip of the boat.

Domari stood across from him, his breath catching as he stared down at his cousin and friend. Magnus's body was dressed in new battle leathers, arms crossed over his waist. His expression was serene, betraying none of the pain he'd experienced in his last moments. Someone had trimmed his beard and combed his hair neat the way he loved it, frozen in a moment in time.

Gunnar stepped up behind Domari gripping his shoulder, and Domari sniffed back the tears threatening to fall. Ryker joined Grim wearing only a pair of black trousers, his tattooed chest on display, but somehow that seemed fitting for Magnus's final goodbye.

Together, the four of them lifted the boat, carrying it down the beach and into the surf. Astrid walked beside them with Magnus's son in her arms, the baby already the spitting image of his father. Her long blonde hair was braided into a crown, her cheeks flushed with emotion they all felt.

Waves lapped against the hull as the boat floated in the shallow waters, and Domari forced himself to let go.

"Odin called us forth to lead the most noble to their final resting place." Hilda stepped into the waves, her Valkyries following her. "Magnus Eriksson, no one is more worthy of the halls of Valhalla. Your sacrifice saved this world, giving the Promised time to stop Ragnarok. May your name be spoken reverently, your loyalty a new standard, your courage never forgotten. It is our honor to guide you home."

Power tingled along his spine as *Mjölnir* appeared in Domari's hand for the last time, and he set it in the boat next to Magnus. He reached down to his waist, sliding *Megingjord* free, and laid the magical belt across Magnus's chest. Gunnar followed suit, placing *Gungnir* in his brother's hand, closing his tattooed fingers around the legendary spear. While the gods may have gifted the weapons to Domari and Gunnar, no one was more worthy than Magnus to hold them until they were gifted to the next chosen ones.

Astrid leaned over, brushing his blond hair from his face. "No one could love you more than I," she said, and Domari ducked his chin, unable to stand looking at the pain in the young widow's face. "Every moment spent with you was a gift from the gods, and no one was as blessed as me to be loved by you. This isn't goodbye, *elskin min*. Your legacy lives on in our memories, in the beating heart of your son. In this life and the next, I am forever yours."

She leaned into Gunnar's side, her face tipping down to kiss the top of her baby's head. Gunnar wrapped an arm around her and guided her back toward the beach and to his mother. Frida laced her arm around Astrid's waist, tears streaming down both women's cheeks.

Domari took the torch Grim held out for him, dipping it into the oils in the hull. Fire ringed Magnus's body as all nine Valkyries circled the boat, Signe taking her place at the rear.

Walking back to the beach, Domari went straight into

Shelbie's arms. Ryker and Grim came last, watching as the Valkyries accompanied the boat into the tide, fire licking high into the sky.

"This isn't goodbye," Shelbie repeated Astrid's words, her fingers digging into Domari's tunic. He pulled her tighter into his chest, kissing the top of her head.

"Until Valhalla," Domari said.

"Until Valhalla," Gunnar echoed louder, the chant picking up as those gathered on the beach repeated the vow.

Magic shimmered around the Valkyries, as bright as sunlight. Signe stopped, glancing over her shoulder to her family on the beach, then back to the others.

"Are you coming?" Hilda looked between Viveka and Signe.

"My life is here," Signe said, her eyes on Gunnar and her children. "A life Magnus sacrificed himself for."

Hilda nodded, wearing a proud smile. She ran a thumb across Signe's brow, and the mark of the Valkyrie disappeared.

"Goodbye, my child," she said. "You were worth it all."

Signe held her hand out for Viveka, but the dark-haired girl looked between Hilda and Signe, chewing her lip. Sensing her uncertainty, Signe pulled the girl into a hug, the waves lapping around their chests.

"Your Fate awaits, my girl." She kissed her brow, covering the mark the others wore, then let go, walking through the surf back to those watching from the beach.

The Valkyries closed the circle around Magnus once more, the white magic enclosing them. Thunder rumbled right before lightning split the sky in a blinding light. Domari put his hand up to block his eyes, and by the time he lowered it, the ship and the Valkyries were gone.

SHELBIE

The steady *thump* of a hammer sounded in the distance, comforting in its familiarity. After Magnus's funeral, Domari and Gunnar had taken their family and any who wanted to join us up the coast, in search of a new homestead.

We'd walked for days, but the journey had soothed something in all of us, putting distance between everything that had happened and the new life we intended to forge for ourselves.

Like Torvik, our new home was along the beach, cliffs rising in the distance. Deep green forests covered the horizon, and the men worked tirelessly to clear enough space for farmland in the spring.

"Are you ready?" Frida called as she gathered the dozen children around her, my dogs standing guard. Signe stood by me with Erik strapped to her chest, Astrid on her other side in much the same position. Revna and Ulf were among the other orphans the Erikssons had taken in, never hesitating to do the right thing by any who needed them.

Ulf held his hand high, his grin wide. "I am!"

I smiled, leaning down to ruffle the boy's hair. "Do you remember the trick we talked about?"

His bright blue eyes looked up at me, and he nodded with excitement. "Take my shirt off, and use it as a basket, just like Uncle Magnus."

"That's right." I leaned down and kissed his cheek. "Make him proud."

Ulf's face took on a serious glint as he glanced sideways at his sister. She wore an equally as fierce expression, but that wasn't uncommon for feisty Revna.

"Go!" Frida called, and the children ran off into the woods with excited shrieks, racing to find the most berries for the Winter Nights feast tomorrow. Freki barked and chased after them, the massive dog just as exuberant as the children. I'd heard the Valkyries refer to my dogs as Odin's wolves, but chose to avoid thinking too hard on that topic — hopefully the god's interest in us was done.

Signe leaned her head on my shoulder, staring at where her children had disappeared. "Want to spy on the men? I'm not pregnant this time, so I can drink as much as I want with you tonight. You can tell me how much you love me and then yell at Domari, just like last year."

I snorted, wrapping an arm around her shoulders, then led her away from the forest and towards the sounds of the hammering in the distance. "You coming, Astrid?"

She glanced between the woods and us until Frida urged

her on, Yrsa and her standing arm in arm while they waited for the children's return.

Together, Astrid, Signe, and I walked through the rows of small huts the men had built since we arrived, rough timber forming cabins with grass roofs and blessings carved above the door. Each one was decorated with a black dragon and an M, and I smiled each time I saw it.

Thor trailed us towards the back of the small circle of homes. A large barn stood there, one we would all share this winter, enough to house the horses and livestock we'd brought with us from Torvik through the worst of the snow.

Gunnar worked inside, framing off stalls. Grim and Björn were pounding fence posts into the ground for a small paddock, and Ryker worked over a forge they'd created for him, melting down whatever weapons we'd taken from the battlefield into nails and usable items for our village.

Seeing him in human form was still jarring, but his personality hadn't changed. The surly dragon I'd befriended was alive and well, living inside a surly man who refused to wear a shirt whenever possible.

Magnus would have loved him.

I held a hand over my eyes, squinting as Signe let out a long whistle, catcalling the men. Domari stood up from the roof, sweat glistening on his chest in the fading sunlight. With a grin, he hopped down and worked his way towards us.

As he stepped up to our side, he looked out over the building. "It's a nice-looking building, sure," he paused, his eyes alight with mischief. I rolled my eyes, knowing what came next. "But not worthy of the drool escaping your mouth, just there."

He pointed at my face, and I swatted his hand away with a laugh. Domari pulled me into his chest, laced his hands around my low back, and dipped down to kiss me. His lips moved across mine in a slow sweep, savoring it, leaving me breathless when he pulled away.

"You need new jokes." I smiled up at him. "I've heard that one before."

"Couldn't resist." He winked and Signe shoved him in the back.

"Thank the gods you two built your own hut."

Domari slung his arm around my shoulder, turning us slightly. "I'm tired of sharing Shelbie with you. And I've heard enough moans from you for a lifetime. Gunnar is insatiable."

"I'm not the problem here," Gunnar said as he joined them, pulling Erik from the binds on Signe's chest, kissing the baby on the head. "How long before you're a big brother, Erik?"

Signe shook her head, then leaned into Gunnar's embrace.

Grim joined us, casting a glance in Astrid's direction but leaving distance between them. We'd all seen the way he'd stepped up to help care for the young widow and her son. Someday, I wouldn't be surprised to see the two of them end up together, but I respected him more for giving her time to grieve.

Magnus's loss was a blow for all of us, leaving a gaping hole in my heart, but I couldn't help but think how much he'd hate us to cry for him. He lived on in every laugh, every joke, every smile.

Björn walked towards us carrying enough drinking horns for everyone here, passing them out as Ryker joined the group.

"Until Valhalla," he said, raising his drinking horn, and we all did the same.

"Until Valhalla."

ACKNOWLEDGMENTS

I'm not crying, you're crying.

Four years ago, I started writing *Fates Illuminated* with a scrap of an outline that pretty much said, *SURPRISE! A dragon*, zero knowledge of Viking history and culture, and shaky confidence in my abilities. Sure, I had a degree in Journalism and had worked my butt off in the field for over a decade, but writing a *book* was different.

If you've been here for a while, maybe you've already heard this story, but I started writing *Fates Illuminated* in one of the darkest and loneliest times in my life. My husband, Chris, took a job across the country when the whole world was shutting down due to COVID, and we were apart for a year. He was living in a hotel, and I was at home with a first grader and a toddler.

Honestly, that year is kind of like a black hole in my memory. I was losing a battle to terrible anxiety and more tired than I knew was possible.

I'd always been an avid reader, but that year changed things for me. Books became not just a hobby but a lifeline. I started following a few Bookstagram accounts, and suddenly the whole world of Indie Authors was in front of me.

On one of Chris's and my late-night FaceTime dates, I

explained it to him, or at least what I understood of the process. He flew home the next weekend and burst through the door with a grin on his face. (If you know Chris, I promise I'm not lying. He really can smile.) I can still see the moment he grabbed my face and pulled me into his chest, saying, "I had a dream you wrote a book and it became a best seller. I can't stop thinking about it. Maybe you should try."

In the moment, I laughed at him. But as he likes to say, it was The Seed. He flew back across the country, and every single day he asked me if I had any ideas yet. I said no and waved him off, but then one day that changed. I finally admitted that maybe I did.

Enter Shelbie.

Suddenly, she was a real person, a friend going through a difficult time who needed to find her way, but it wasn't that simple. Heck, when is life *ever* simple?

So I started writing, and I couldn't stop. It got me out of bed early every morning to sneak some writing in before my girls woke up, and I sat in the rocking chair in the dark writing on my phone far after bedtime too. This book got me through, and for that, I'll be forever grateful.

Fast forward four years, and we're finally here at the finale. This is about two years later than I'd planned. When I started writing this series, I'd just lost my soul dog, Brodie, and wrote him in as Thor, an angry hates-everyone-but-you puppy, and it was so cathartic for me. Then I added Freki, my sweet, goofy Obi, into book two, and had no idea I'd tragically lose him within the year. His loss happened while I was drafting this book, and I couldn't bring myself to pick it up again for far longer than I'd planned. Now, with enough distance, I love that they both live on in this series, and I hope I did the two most loyal boys there ever were justice.

Beyond struggling with grief, this series was so hard for me to finish because boy, have I changed since I wrote *Fates Illuminated*, both in my personal life and in how I write. If you've been with me since book 1, then maybe you can see it, but I've spent the last four years learning everything I can about writing, marketing, all the things to make this successful, and no one is more aware than me of how much this series has evolved. Hopefully, it was a fun experience to watch me grow and improve, and I cannot thank you enough for bearing with me through these learning lessons.

But we're here. I did it. It's done, and I love that I finally got to bring this world to the ending I envisioned all along. I never imagined how much I'd love these characters and this world, and believe me, no one cried harder at this ending than me. I still do every time I think about it, and yet, if I could have a one-on-one conversation with each character about how they felt about their ending, I think every single one of them would agree it ended exactly as they would have wanted. And Hadriel… gosh, that has been a hard secret to keep!

Chris said I'd be a best seller someday, but that was never my goal (still isn't, but wouldn't that be neat?) All I ever wanted was to have fun doing this, to find an outlet that brought me immense joy, and to hopefully maybe find someone who needed these stories like I did. Never did I imagine so many of you would find me along the way.

❄

None of this would have been possible without so many of you:

To my editor, Brit: I just got back from spending the weekend with you, and we told the story of how we met so many times. But gosh, it hits me every single time that finding you was truly an act of fate. Thank you for your endless patience with me while editing, our late nights on speakerphone with kids yelling in the background, and every single mundane moment in between. Yes, I love knowing what you ate for lunch and what color you painted your nails. Yes, I'm going to tell you how much it cost to fill up my tank of gas. And yes, I adore being the first one you call when life throws you a curveball and you need a friend. This has been the most fun journey with you at my side every step of the way. I love you, I love you, I love you.

To my sometimes co-author and always friend, B: Talk about the first reader—*you* take the prize. It has been so fun to build this little hobby into a career with you. Here's to years of more writing nights in our future.

To my personal assistant, Britt: Bringing you on board was supposed to make my life easier, and it absolutely did. But it also made my life so much *fuller,* in the best possible way. Thank you for rolling with the punches, pushing me to challenge myself, and always being ready with the best ideas.

To my beta readers, Ashley, Lex, Riley, Sarah, and Vanessa: thank you for your excitement — it truly makes all of this work worth it!

To my street team: your unwavering support is still

astounding to me, and I absolutely could not do this without you.

To my dogs, Brodie and Obi: I miss you both so much it hurts, but I know, just like Thor and Freki, you'll be waiting to follow me around once more when the day comes. Obi's tongue will loll out to the side in a goofy grin and Brodie's scowl will be set in place, immovable for anyone but me.

To my puppy, Magnus: True to your namesake, you are a light in the dark, and I am so grateful your big brothers chose you just for me. You were the gift I needed, exactly when I needed you. Thank you for keeping my feet warm every time I write.

To my girls: No one cheers for me as loud as you do, and I am the absolute luckiest to be your mom.

And to Chris, Mr. Aimee Vance Books, the Bookmark Guy: You tripped in the parking lot on our first date, but I've been falling ever since. I love you forever.

THANK YOU!

ABOUT THE AUTHOR

Fueled by peach tea and chaos, Aimee Vance writes heartwarming and laugh-out-loud romance stories. She holds a B.S. in Public Relations from Texas Christian University and has always been an avid fantasy reader.

Residing in Texas with her husband, two young daughters, and Labrador Retriever, Aimee loves to transport readers to worlds hidden between the pages where magic and love intertwine. She prefers sassy heroines, grumpy heroes, and enough humor to keep you chuckling with every page.

facebook.com/aimeevancebooks

instagram.com/aimeevancebooks

goodreads.com/aimeevancebooks

amazon.com/author/aimeevancebooks

bookbub.com/authors/aimee-vance

ALSO BY AIMEE VANCE

Call of the Norns

Fates Illuminated

Fates Promised

Fates Defied

Deadlights Cove

Smoke Show

Deja Brew

A Very Merry Christmoose (Novella)

Wing and a Miss

Pier Pressure

Karma is a Witch

Foxing Day (Novella)

Timber Creek

Wild Wild Wolf

Love Bites

www.ingramcontent.com/pod-product-compliance
Lightning Source LLC
Chambersburg PA
CBHW020328010826
48973CB00005B/1173